Books by Jill Barnett

Imagine
Bewitching
Dreaming
The Heart's Haven
Just a Kiss Away
Surrender a Dream

Published by POCKET BOOKS

JILL BARNETT

IMAGINE

POCKET BOOKS

New York   London   Toronto   Sydney   Tokyo   Singapore

This book is a work of fiction. Names, characters, places and incidents are products of the author's imagination or are used fictitiously. Any resemblance to actual events or locales or persons, living or dead, is entirely coincidental.

An *Original* Publication of POCKET BOOKS

 POCKET BOOKS, a division of Simon & Schuster Inc. 1230 Avenue of the Americas, New York, NY 10020

ISBN: 0-671-52143-8

First Pocket Books printing September 1995

10 9 8 7 6 5 4 3 2 1

POCKET and colophon are registered trademarks of Simon & Schuster Inc.

Cover art by Mario Beaudoin

Printed in the U.S.A.

To Joe Corn and His Five Cobs;
to lullabies played on a muted trumpet.
To Saturdays at the lumberyard
and silly steps danced to the songs you played.
To Dodgers' baseball games and John Wayne movies;
to your gift of laughter
and your gift of life.
To the man who stomped around the roof,
pretending to be Santa's reindeer;
the same man of quiet strength
who had to tell a ten-year-old girl that her mother died
when part of him must have died with her.
To fathers who teach their daughters that
they can be anything
and who know when to let go.
To the man in my life who has always been there for me,
to my dad.

Acknowledgments

With sincerest gratitude I thank Jude Deveraux and Judith McNaught for graciously sharing their readers in *A Holiday of Love.* These talented and phenomenally successful ladies gave me the best Christmas gift a writer could imagine.

A special thanks to Susan Elizabeth Phillips, my very favorite writer, who kindly offered to read this book in a crunch and whose insight helped make it better.

And in my life, there are some very special people who are as much a part of each book I write as the words themselves: My family, who try to understand my passion for writing and the utter chaos of deadlines. My kindred spirits, Elaine Coffman, Penny Williamson, and Kristin Hannah—the real Smitty—who all are there at any hour and whose honesty and advice I treasure. Maureen Walters, my agent, who listens and understands when things get crazy. And my editor, Linda Marrow, who gives me guidance and opportunity, who greets each book with enthusiasm and never says, "Jill . . . you can't write that."

Thank you all.

To know is nothing at all;
to imagine is everything.
　　　　　—Anatole France

Imagine . . .

The bottle was as old as time.

It floated on the sea, bobbing along as if it were flotsam instead of intricately carved silver. The ornate stopper caught flashes of bright sunlight, which, to the gulls that soared overhead, made the shimmering bottle look like a plump silver herring—a prize for the plucking. Many a sea bird swooped down, only to quickly dart like reflections back into the sky when their bills hit not the soft flesh of glimmering fish scales, but instead hard metal.

It was a sad fact that there were no precious jewels on a bottle so old. A few gull pecks, a small scratch here and there, but no jewels. For gemstones, like an angel's wings, had to be earned.

A blood red ruby would have added a dash of character to the bottle. A diamond would have given it stunning richness. But a pearl was like a hero's medal of valor, a prize for a task so difficult that only the most unique of stones would do.

Ah, yes, a pearl was the ultimate adornment on a genie's bottle.

Yes . . . a genie. One, Muhdula Ali, purple genie of Persia, otherwise known as Muddy.

Since the beginning of time, men have argued that genies do not exist. Yet those same men believed in miracles and in the existence of angels. How many angels could dance on a pin? they had argued. (The answer is none. A pin is too small for angels. Only fairies can fit on pinheads.)

But those men were not dreamers. They were pragmatists and scholars, men with little time to dream.

Muddy wanted more than anything to be mastered by one of those innocents of heart who believed in that which they had never seen or known, people of faith who needed no debate to be able to imagine.

The knowledge that those people existed out there somewhere in the human race gave him hope, hope that had lived for some two thousand-odd years. He needed to find one of those believers. A lucky innocent. Someone whom fate didn't have it in for.

You see, Muddy had a problem. He needed all the luck he could get. His history was witness to the fact that his bottle was still embarrassingly naked. Not one single gemstone.

His first master had been none other than Paris, prince of Troy, and when it came to intelligence, Paris was . . . well, he was a few coins short of a drachma.

Indeed, for Paris had kidnapped lovely Helen, blithely ignoring the fact that she was another man's wife. The resulting war had lasted ten years. He went on to fell his father's kingdom when he decided that a giant wooden horse was, in truth, a Greek gift.

The basic problem for Muddy was that a genie was only as good as his master. And for some two thousand years, he had been mastered by some of humanity's most unfortunate and unlucky souls.

There had been Nero, a man so self-absorbed that he couldn't smell smoke. More recently, Benedict Arnold, who wanted desperately to be remembered throughout history. And there was that poor Chicago woman, Mrs. O'Leary. Her last wish had been for a milk cow. Those had been just a few of his unlucky masters.

Muddy sighed and lay back against the plump silk pillows that circled his small and confined world—

the world of his unadorned bottle. He slipped his hands behind his head and let the lazy current rock him to sleep.

But just before he closed his eyes he wondered how long it would be before someone found him. Would it be months? It could be years.

With his own wish and a helpless shrug, he fell asleep, never knowing that it would only be a matter of weeks.

❧ 1 ❧

San Francisco, October 1896

Margaret Huntington Smith looked as if she had everything. She carried herself with confidence, and her height reinforced that image. She was tall, blond, beautiful, and wealthy. And she was an attorney—at that moment, one very happy attorney.

She wore a cat-in-the-cream kind of smile as she moved down the limestone steps of the courthouse and stepped into a shiny black brougham. She tossed a calfskin portfolio on the plush velvet seat, sat down, and gave a sly wink to the older distinguished-looking gentleman who sat across from her.

Harlan Smith laughed at his daughter's expression. "Oh, Margaret, my girl, it's a blasted good thing that you can hide your emotions in the courtroom or you'd never win a case."

She tugged off her gloves and grinned at him. "I just won this one."

"Yes, you did, and soundly, too."

"A great compliment coming from my father, the judge." She laughed, the hearty clear sound of a woman at ease with her laughter. "It did go rather well, didn't it?"

"I remember when you tied your hair up in ribbons." He shook his head, then gave a wry laugh. "Now you cut the opposing attorney into ribbons."

"And you taught me everything I know."

"Yes, I suppose I did." There was a deep sense of pride in his look. And that one look from her dad made all those eternal months of work—the research,

5

the planning, the long hours of preparing for a case—worth every exhausting hour.

They sat in silence while the carriage rolled up and over the steep hills of the city. The horses' hooves clattered over the trolley rails while newspaper boys hawked the afternoon edition. A cool gust of October wind rode in from the Pacific and rattled the etched glass windows of the elegant carriage. In the distance, fog bells belched long and loud, and a trolley bell rang as it crossed an intersection where traffic came to an abrupt halt.

She could feel her father's look, and she turned.

"I wish your mother could see you now," he said. The pride was still in his eyes, along with the misty look of a distant memory.

She reached out and touched his hand. "I know, Dad. I wish she were here, too."

He looked away for just a second, one of those quiet imagined moments of "what if" experienced by those the dead have left behind. She released his hand, and when he turned back, his expression wasn't as wistful. He fumbled in his coat pocket and handed her an envelope.

"What's this?"

His face gave nothing away. "Open it and find out."

She tore open the seal and looked inside. She took out a set of tickets, turned the top one so she could read it, then looked up. "This is a first-class ticket on an ocean liner."

He nodded.

"Going where?" she thought aloud as she thumbed through the other tickets, then unfolded the itinerary. She whipped her head up. "The South Seas?"

"And vouchers for transportation between islands." He smiled. "French Oceania—Tahiti, the Cook Islands, and more. A little taste of paradise for a daughter who works too hard."

"Oh, Dad . . ." She leaned over and planted a kiss

on his white-whiskered cheek. She looked down at the tickets. "Thank you."

"Are you pleased?"

She gave him an easy smile and grabbed his hand. "Of course."

"Good." He began to talk about the islands, about how the South Seas still held a bit of paradise that the modern world hadn't ruined.

She listened as she stared out the window at the bay and the misty wall of fog sitting just off shore, at the tall narrow rows of candy-colored houses huddled so close together that after traveling past them for a few streets they almost melted together like the colors of a rainbow.

This trip was her father's dream. Not hers. But then she hadn't had much time in the last few years to have any dreams.

She looked at the envelope and knew she'd go. Because he had always wanted to go. She frowned for a second, then slid open the envelope again and shuffled through the contents. "Dad? There's only one ticket here. Where's yours?"

He cleared his throat, then said, "I can't get away right now."

"I'm going alone? But—"

He held up a hand and cut her off in the same efficient way he handled his gavel. "The state supreme court docket is full. We have to hear the Mallard case."

"So soon?"

He nodded. "It's due to start the day after tomorrow."

She closed the flap on the ticket envelope. "Then I'll wait until you can get away."

"Oh, no, you don't. By that time you'll be into another case and won't want to get away."

"But—"

"Don't even try to argue this, Margaret. You won't win with me. I'm the one who taught you how to argue a point. And I'm telling you that you will not have another case until after you take some time away."

"You're just throwing your weight around."

"Yes, I am. Shamelessly."

"Coercion," she muttered.

"I'm also your father, and for the last five years, I have watched you work endlessly and not take any time for yourself."

"I'm happy when I'm working."

"You just have a compulsion to make the world fair and equal."

"The world will be a better place if it's fair and equal."

"I know that, but you can't single-handedly change the world."

"I can try."

"Not to the exclusion of everything else. Margaret, for the past few years you have been an attorney and my daughter. What have you done for yourself?"

"Won my cases."

He pinned her with one of his direct looks. "Life is passing you by."

"You make it sound as if I've got one foot in the grave."

He laughed. "You're thirty-two, and not getting any younger."

"Thanks."

"Go. Just go." He paused. "For me."

She sat there, torn, because she didn't want to go on this trip. She'd rather work. There was comfort and safety in the law. It was something she knew well.

But she looked at her dad and knew she was going to lose this argument. She'd go. Because he wanted her to.

Her mother had died when she was barely seven. And that left just the two of them. She did have her maternal uncles, all attorneys and partners in her law firm. They had been there for holidays, there whenever her father thought he needed help parenting, and there when Margaret began to study law.

But in truth, her family was her father. And he was right. She'd go on this trip for him, because he was the single most important person in her life.

So a week later when she walked up the boarding ramp on a large Pacific liner, she did so with resigned acceptance. A number of male heads turned and followed her with their eyes. Something she had also learned to accept.

She understood that men found her attractive, but she felt her looks were a curse. She wanted, needed, to be taken seriously. Her father had always treated her respectfully, as had her uncles. But to others, once the pretty little girl with ribbons in her hair had grown up, she hadn't become a person, she was a shell, something to ogle.

To the world, there was nothing on the inside of Margaret Smith. There couldn't be, because she was pretty. She had to earn respect, because most of the world thought a woman who was beautiful had little else to offer.

She couldn't be intelligent, because she was pretty. She couldn't have any depth, because she had lovely blond hair. She couldn't think, because she had money. She couldn't have a heart, a soul, because she wasn't like them.

To them, she couldn't hurt.

She remembered how a college classmate, another woman, had looked at her once and said with vitriol, "How could you know anything about being hurt? You grew up with a silver spoon in your mouth."

And that was what too many people thought. That Margaret Huntington Smith had everything. No one knew that although she had a loving father and kind, caring uncles, wealth, and beauty, much of the time, deep down inside she felt alone and scared.

She hid her loneliness, her fears, along with those

instincts that were female—motherhood, sisterhood, even the occasional urge to cry for no reason. All things that her father couldn't explain.

With only men as role models, she strived to be strong and independent, capable and focused. She grew up thinking she had to be as perfect as she appeared to the world and, more important, to one person in her life who mattered, her father. Because she was all he had left.

Maybe that's why she worked so hard to try to make the world fair and equal. Because for Margaret, it never had been.

Two months later, Leper's Gate Penal Colony, Dolphin Island

Hank Wyatt believed in nothing. Because he'd never had anything. Well, much of anything. He'd had a mother once.

When he was five, she took him to a foundling home. "Smile, Henry James, and be a good boy," she had said. "Someone will want you."

Then she'd turned and walked out the door. As if he didn't exist.

But he did exist, and he spent the next thirty-five years making sure that everyone knew it. And no one forgot it.

No one at Leper's Gate forgot Henry James Wyatt existed.

He was an American, a product of the Pittsburgh slums. He was trouble, but he was a survivor. A fast learner. He had to be. Life hadn't dealt him aces. It dealt him deuces.

But he had aces up his sleeve and the instincts to know when to slip those cards into play. He knew when to cheat, when to lie, and when to run like hell.

He learned his lessons the hard way, learned early

that a code of ethics wasn't for him. No turning the other cheek. None of that do-unto-others crap. He did unto others before they damn well did unto him.

He was wrongly condemned to Leper's Gate. A mistake. And he'd fought like hell when they'd locked him away. He spent the end of his first week confined in solitary: a three-foot-by-six-and-half-foot wooden box buried in the dirt. In the tropical sun. They gave him water once a day. No food. Food wasn't for prisoners like Hank. They needed to be broken.

For the next four years they tried to break him. They were still trying.

He'd been standing in the sun for two days, his hands and feet tied to two log stakes that had been hammered into the ground. His hair stuck to his head in black sweaty clumps that had whips of silver gray tangled through it, its once-dark color worn like the leather straps of an overworked cat-o'-nine-tails.

The corners of his eyes were creased with wrinkles—nature's scars for every hard year of the forty he had survived. Hank Wyatt had resolute, determined eyes. They were gray, a carbonic iron color. Like a wall of steel those eyes reflected only the light that shone at them, giving no clue as to what went on behind them, but he was thinking. He had to think to survive.

His skin was brown, fried by a sun so hot it would blister the skin off the new prisoners. His jaw was ruthlessly square, stubborn, and covered with a dark shadow of a beard that was uneven from trying to shave with a piece of metal scavenged from the dark corner of a stone cell block.

He was tall, solid but lean. He had powerful, athletic arms made stronger from years of slinging a sledgehammer at the prison quarry. His legs were long and just as muscular. The weight of a chain gang either made men stronger or broke them.

But now, Hank's legs were stiff from standing. He refused to bend them. His bound hands were numb. His mind was not. His breath was shallow—a trick he'd mastered to fool the guards into thinking he was closer to passing out than he was.

To stay alert, he concentrated with the sharpened ears of one who was desperate. He listened to the hone of tropical flies. They buzzed around him as if he were garbage. He heard the defeated cry of another prisoner's punishment. He vowed no one would hear that sound from his throat.

He listened to the rattle of chains and ankle cuffs, the constant, monotonous ringing of prisoners' hammers smashing against rock in the quarry compounds. That sound could drive the mind from a weaker man.

In the distance he could hear the haunting call of the sea—the waves pounding away at the island. And every so often, the caw of a seagull flying free.

Sounds as far away as another lifetime. As close as madness.

He'd been staked before. But this time he'd laid the groundwork so he would never be staked again. He listened to everything. To anything. Hell, to survive Hank would listen to himself sweat.

It took two more days for them to think he was dead, or think him close enough to it. They cut the rope that kept his hands and feet tied to the stakes, dragged him to the center of the compound, then dropped him.

No sound came from his lips. No movement. Nothing. They hit him with bucket after bucket of water. Fresh water. Drinking water. No staked prisoner had ever been able to resist licking at it or finally cracking and gulping the water after being so long without it.

Only the dead lay unflinching. And Hank.

"He's dead."

Silence ticked by as it had for the past few days in minutes that seemed to take longer than a life sentence.

"Kick him just to make certain."

Hank heard the shuffle of the guard's boots. Near his head. He steeled himself for the blow.

"Not there!" came a sharp command. "Here!"

The bastard kicked him in the crotch.

He awoke to the jar of a wagon stopping. There was a dull ache between his legs that told him he wasn't dead. A reminder of his last conscious moment and the pain. He hadn't doubled over. He hadn't screamed. He had passed out.

He lay on the bottom of the wagon, the weight of weaker prisoners, now dead men, alongside of him. He took a shallow breath and almost gagged. He didn't know if the cause was the pain from his bruised groin or the stench of death surrounding him.

He knew the routine. One priest and one guard buried the prisoners outside the compound walls. In a pit in the jungle.

He waited, listening.

Just his luck. No one spoke. The wagon seat creaked. Boots hit the ground with a thud. Birds screeched in the distance. Tropical insects droned and whistled and buzzed. The chains on the wagon tailgate rattled.

Finally, a priest began to chant last rites in Latin. Slowly, one by one, the wagon was unloaded.

He couldn't screw this up, not now. Not when he'd come this far. But that dull ache burned through his groin again.

Escape? He didn't even know if he could stand. He thought of the last four years. Hell, he'd stand if it killed him.

Someone gripped his ankles and yanked.

The priest chanted and touched his forehead.

Hank opened his eyes and shot upright, his fist raised. He knocked out the guard with a right cross, then stumbled to his feet.

He scanned the area. There was no one but the stunned priest, who just stood there. Hank took a step toward him.

The prayer book fell from the priest's shaking hands.

"Keep praying for me, Father." Hank picked up the book and handed it to him. "I need all the help I can get."

The priest blinked once, then stared at him for a moment.

Hank grinned. The priest took the prayer book. Then Hank punched him.

❧ 2 ❧

Two days later, Port Helene, the north side of Dolphin Island

Hank walked down the crowded cobbled street that separated the town of Port Helene from its busy wharf. Pulled low over his sharp eyes was the wide-brimmed black hat he'd stolen from the priest. His hands were shoved in the deep pockets of the man's black tunic, and his fingers worried the rosary inside.

To his left, brightly painted houses with deep verandas looked like a row of smiling colored teeth next to the narrow gray clapboard customs house and tall coconut palms that reigned over the west end of the wharf. Nearer the street, dockside fruit sellers stood at makeshift palm stands and hawked bananas and papayas, breadfruit and mangoes.

Cotton-clad native women bought baskets of tropical fruit and fresh fish from peddlers who sold everything from food and machetes to tapa cloth and bamboo windpipes. Hank strolled through the crowds and managed to swipe three bananas and a harmonica.

Lined up like prisoners during roll call were wooden pallet crates, keg barrels, and stacks of thick island hemp. At the far eastern end of the dock was a wall of green lumber and three wagons of quarry rock for export to another island. He stared at the rock for a moment—a black memory of the last four years. Then he took a deep breath of fresh air and moved away.

A small local band played lively island music with bamboo pipes and hip-high pod drums while native girls and boys sold sugar cane and seashells from woven palm baskets slung on their small brown backs. Someone shouted to a fishing boat coming into dock, and the fishermen chattered back about the fat profits they'd make from a full net of tuna.

Nuns in their broad headdresses trotted along in twos, and other priests, their dark hats bobbing through the crowd, blessed the fish for Friday's meal, the goats, donkeys, even the pets of small children. Milling about the customs house were island plantation owners dressed in stark white. They haggled with rich merchants in dark tweed suits, sporting derbys and fat wallets as ripe for picking as the bright pink island mangoes.

All around him were the sounds of life and freedom, things that for too many long, hot days had seemed as unreal as a distant memory. While he peeled a banana and ate it, he stood there and watched for the briefest of moments—the sights, the sounds, the taste of freedom.

When he had been inside his cell, staked, or locked in a box, his mind had focused on seeing and living these things again. That had been part of what drove him to survive in a place where the chances of survival had the same odds as getting a home run on a bunt.

But as he stood there, watching island life go on without him, he remembered something else he'd forgotten. He had never fit in. Anywhere. And he still didn't. The trappings were there. He was wearing a black tunic, like the Catholic priests on the island, but he wasn't a man of God anymore than he was part of this life outside the prison.

He was an outsider. Always had been. For a reason. There was safety in being alone. He did things the way he wanted. And carried no one else's taint, only his own. Survival was easier alone. He'd learned early that even if he played by the rules, most people assumed he didn't.

In prison, he'd forgotten his solitary place in life. Now, as he stood there free, in the middle of where he had craved to be, he remembered where he actually was, where he always had been—outside, on the fringes of the life most people lived.

He tossed the banana peel away as easily as he had accepted the isolation fate dealt him, and he walked on.

He used the camouflage of the crowd so he could safely scan the dock.

There were five ships.

And no dogs. He'd only heard the hounds twice: once when he'd been running only for half a day and again that morning before he'd crossed the steep rocky gorge that separated the north and south sides of the island.

The first time the dogs had trailed him he'd used river mud to muck up his scent. The last time he'd used a tin of pepper he'd stolen from a small traders' outpost. He'd known he had one weakness: he'd never been able to run worth a damn. But he figured by crossing that gorge he had about two hours on them. Two hours to get away.

At dockside, two of the ships were ready to depart. One was a sleek wooden clipper, *L'Amelie*. The other was a squat ocean steamer with a steel hull that rose up to the main deck. It was small, one-tenth the size of a large ocean liner, the kind of double-stack steamship that served as both a packet and freighter between the larger islands of the South Seas. The ship's name was obscured by a group of pallet boxes and a wooden cage filled with a few braying goats.

After four years in a French hellhole like Leper's Gate, there was no decision. Hank finished the banana and moved toward the island steamer. He walked with slow purpose toward the boarding ramp, eyeing the crewman who handled the loading of the ship.

Sneaking on board was one option. He examined the ramp, then the winches that lifted the pallets and crates, weighing his chances of making it on board unseen.

It wasn't a cinch.

He rubbed the stubble on his jaw that had turned into a week's worth of itchy beard, then he weighed his options with what another prisoner once called his knack for mother wit.

He had liked that. Mother wit.

He could use some of that wit now. He supposed he could bluff his way aboard, then stow somewhere. He spent a moment listening and trying to gauge the attention and manner of the crewman on the dock.

The crowd suddenly shifted. There was a commotion nearby.

He froze, not looking and half waiting to feel the cold barrel of a French rifle pressed against his unlucky neck.

"Let me pass, please! That's my ship!" It was the sweet voice of a woman. Better yet, an American woman.

He turned, and the crowd shifted again, shoving

and pushing. There was a little shriek of surprise, then like manna from heaven, a tall blonde fell into his arms.

Oooo-wee. My lucky day.

She grabbed his priest's tunic to catch her balance. He steadied her, holding her waist with both hands.

She was so tall that her nose came up to his chin and the feathers on her brown hat brushed his face. He caught a whiff of that distinctive scent of a female. Something he hadn't smelled in years. He savored it for just a brief second.

She released her death grip on his black tunic and glanced up at him from a face too damned gorgeous to be real.

"Sweet Jesus Christ," he muttered, then caught himself with a cough and added, ". . . will bless you, my dear."

She straightened swiftly, her face flushed. "I'm so terribly sorry, Father."

He wasn't the least bit sorry. Hell, she was the damn best-looking woman he'd ever seen. And she was a woman, not some green eighteen-year-old fresh from her daddy. She looked to be . . . thirty. And all ripe female.

She jammed her cockeyed hat back on a thick wad of blond hair, giving him a direct look from an unusual pair of golden yellow eyes. She reached out and touched his chest, brushing the wrinkles from the front of his tunic.

Mating howls went off in his head.

"Please forgive me. I'm late." She removed her hand and waved a finger at the ramp, her voice rushed. "My ship is leaving."

He glanced at the crates still waiting to be loaded, then at the dark spout of coal smoke burping from the stacks. "You have a few minutes."

"Do I? Oh." She seemed to relax a bit and gave him a quiet smile. "I haven't taken many voyages."

Come to Papa, sweetheart. I'll take you on a voyage.

Her gaze had shifted to his hands, which were still gripping her waist, then with an unsettling frankness, she looked him square in the eye again.

He released her, then touched the brim of his priest's hat and gave her his best "The Lord be with you."

She smiled again, and he stifled a deep groan. *Whoa, boy.*

She had started to turn away.

In an old habit borne from too many years spent in rum joints, he raised his hand to swat her on her sweet butt.

She paused midturn, snapping her fingers as she murmured, "Oh! I knew I forgot something." She glanced up.

His hand was level with her nose.

She grabbed his hand and shook it vigorously. "Thank you, Father!"

A second later she had whipped around and was rushing toward the gangplank.

Hank stared at his right hand, then at the back of her tall figure as she ran up the ship's ramp. He grinned, then called out, "May He shine His countenance upon you."

She stopped halfway up the ramp and waved, then turned back around.

"And give you peace!" His gaze shifted to her ass. *What a piece . . .*

He just stood there, even after she had disappeared onboard. Legs, he thought. Beneath that skirt were yards of long legs. He shook his head and gave a short whistle.

A moment later he felt the nudge of the crowd that still milled around the dockside. He turned back and looked.

No dogs. No guards.

No French militia.

Nothing but the crowd.

He grinned, stark and white and full of the devil, then strolled toward the gangplank. He shoved his right hand back into his pocket. In his left hand, he casually tossed a small leather pocketbook he'd picked from her purse.

He approached the crewman. "The young woman who just went on board dropped her pocketbook in the crowd."

The man appeared to listen with only half an ear. He cast a quick glance at the small purse, then at Hank. "Yes . . . yes, Father." He waved Hank aboard the steamer. "Go aboard and find her."

Hank walked up the ramp toward his freedom, whistling a barrel house rendition of *Ave Maria*. He handed the pocketbook to a steward and waited until the man disappeared in the passage, then casually made his way along the railing toward the stern.

He slipped up a stairway to the upper deck and moved toward the closest lifeboat. Covertly, he unsnapped the tarp, glancing left, then right. The crew was busy readying for departure.

In a flash he stowed under the tarp. He quickly refastened the tarp snaps.

Canvas life vests were clipped to rings in the lifeboat and oilskins and blankets were wrapped in an extra tarp. A tin box of supplies, a lantern, and a container of water were wedged into the bow. He pried open a can of potbeef and devoured it, the other stolen bananas, and a few crackers, then washed them down with some of the water. The bread and cheese he'd swiped from an outpost the night before had been a better meal. Probably because he'd washed that down with three stolen beers.

He took a few of the life vests, blew them up, and lay back, using them as pillows and the tarps and blankets as a bed, and he waited. Before long the steamer whistled and moved away from the dock. The ship rocked on the sea, slowly, like the hips of a native girl.

Hank took a deep breath, the first one he'd taken in a helluva long time. One more breath of freedom, and it all caught up with him, the torture, the running, the isolated hell of the past four years.

God . . . He rubbed his face with a hand and let his head sag back against the vests. He took in deep chestfuls of air. Sea air, not the heavy tight air of a cell. He closed his eyes, and before long every muscle in his hard and tense body had relaxed.

His days were his again. His alone. His nights, too. No more bars. Except those that served cold beer and strong whiskey.

No more stakes, just beefsteaks, thick and rare.

No chains. No pounding the rocks. No stifling cells where sleep was impossible. Sleep was possible. Real sleep. Not those catnaps he'd taken for so many years. He had the freedom to sleep.

For the first time in too long he felt as if life had dealt him an ace.

⊷ 3 ⊶

By midnight, he'd been dealt his deuce.

The ship had pitched and rolled in a brawl with the sea. Hank had gripped the rim of the lifeboat at least a hundred times, cursing every time. After an endless hour of bad weather, the wind stopped howling as suddenly as it had all begun, and the sea grew calm.

He lay back in the boat and listened. He could hear the crew rushing on the deck to secure things. He heard their laughter and a few bawdy jokes, the sailors' way of dealing with the aftermath of fear.

Soon it was calm and quiet again, so he closed his eyes.

He awakened with a start, his pulse racing like someone in the throes of a too-real nightmare. He jerked up, fist swinging. An old reflex. His fist connected with the tarp, and he stared at it for a disoriented second. He rubbed a hand over his face, then shook his head. He remembered where he was.

He listened again, his senses alert. There was nothing. He didn't know how long he'd slept. It felt as if it had been only a few minutes, but it could have been a few hours.

He lay back on the life vests, his hands still clammy, his pulse still racing. Uneasy. The air was absolutely still. Absolutely silent. Yet he was as tense as he had been in prison.

With his next breath came a deafening blast. The whole ship shook. Hank swore. He'd heard a steam engine blow before. He knew that sound.

The ship's bow shot upward. It seemed to freeze for an agonizing instant, then its steel hull slapped back into the water. Momentum slammed him against the bottom of the lifeboat.

There was a loud rumble, as if the deckload in the bowels of the hold had shifted. The ship lurched.

He could hear the shouts of the crew. He swore when their words sunk in. The hold cargo had shifted and thrown the ship off balance. Then he heard the distinctive, echoing sound of water rushing inside the hold.

He pulled at the tarp snaps.

The ship listed again suddenly. Too suddenly. The lifeboat snapped from its winch and fell through the air.

Down . . . Down.

Christ! he thought, and instinct kicked in. He quickly curled into a ball.

The lifeboat hit the water. Right side up. He

slammed upward into the canvas tarp. Some of the snaps popped free, but the tarp kept him from flying out.

The lifeboat shifted on a swell. He gripped the rim, jerked loose the tarp snaps, then sat up, shoving the tarp out of his way. He looked at the steamer.

Flames shot like rockets into the night sky. There was a burning hole where the engine room had been. The seams of the ship cracked open a few feet, and water rushed inside.

His lifeboat rocked against barrels that had fallen from the deck. Hank struggled into one of the life vests and clipped it together.

There were screams and shouts and a horrific howling noise from the fire.

He looked up.

A hollow steel echo belched from within the bowels of the ship, and it rolled heavily toward its port side. Smoke coughed from the stacks. Men shouted and scurried like rats while debris fell into the sea.

Then he saw her: the blonde. Stranded on a small part of the port deck that hadn't blown apart. She hugged what was left of the rail. To her right was a gaping hole filled with flames; to her left, a few feet of deck and nothing.

He grabbed another life vest and dove into the sea. A second later he was swimming toward her. The water all around him rippled an orange color, an eerie reflection of the ship's flames. He could smell the fire and the oil and the black taste of coal.

The steamer groaned and slipped lower.

He was only a hundred feet away. The ship had listed to almost a forty-five-degree angle over the water.

The woman wore a dark coat and had one leg hitched over the lower bar of the ship's rail. Her arm was wrapped under and over the upper rail so that she was half sitting on the lower rail, clinging to it and using it to keep her from falling into the sea.

By the time he was in shouting range, the ship had shifted again lower, and the main deck and its railing were barely fifteen feet above sea level.

"Jump!" he bellowed, treading water and gripping the other life jacket.

She whipped her head around.

"Jump!"

"I can't!" she screamed.

"Jump, woman!"

She shook her head and huddled into more of a ball.

A burst of flames exploded behind her. She turned her head. It was then he saw the children. Two small, terrified faces peered down at him as they clung to either side of her.

She looked back at him and shouted, "Baby!" She had a dark bundle cradled in her lap, and he realized that in all the racket there was the sound of a kid wailing.

He swore and scanned the sea while he slung the other life vest up his arm.

A garbage can floated nearby. He swam to it, dumped it out, and kicked back to a position just beneath her, the can floating next to him. Only twelve feet of air separated them.

"Drop it!" he yelled, reaching up.

She stared at him. Frozen.

"Drop the kid! I'll catch it!"

She unwrapped the baby. It was a toddler. She leaned out, her arms over the rail, struggling to lower the screaming little kid by its hands.

He reached up and out. She let go.

Screaming, the toddler fell into his hands. He stuffed the kid in the can and clamped one arm around it to keep it from tipping and filling with water. The can amplified the kid's crying. It was noisier, tinnier, and so loud he felt the sound in back of his teeth.

"Toss me the life ring!" he bellowed, his free hand cupped around his mouth.

She leaned across the rail and fumbled with the life ring hooks. A second later the ring fell into the sea.

"Now jump!" he shouted.

She moved quickly and pulled both children by the hand to an open section in the railing. For an instant she stood there. The fire roared behind them and framed their silhouettes, making them look like black figures against a wall of blue orange flames about to swallow them.

"Jump!" Hank shouted.

A second later she did, pulling the kids with her. They splashed into the black water a few feet away.

He held his breath. *Surface, sweetheart. Come on, baby. Come on . . .*

Her head burst out of the water. So did the heads of both of the kids. The older one—a girl—screamed that she couldn't swim, then she panicked, struggling and crying.

With his free hand, Hank grabbed the closest kid—a small boy who had begun to sob. "Hang onto my neck!" The kid stopped sobbing and did what he was told.

The little girl was still screaming and struggling, half pulling the blonde under. The coat she wore wasn't helping. He shoved the vest at the woman.

"Get out of that coat and put this on."

She tried to put the vest on the hysterical girl.

"Put it on yourself!" he yelled.

"But I can swim! She can't!" she screamed back, trying to stay above water.

"Put the vest on and you hold her!" He shouted, adjusting the boy's hands around his neck. "Are you strong enough to keep her head up?"

The blonde nodded, finally shrugging out of the coat and doing exactly as he had said. He spotted the life ring behind her. He couldn't let go of the can.

"Grab that life ring!"

She clipped the vest, then looked around in front of her.

"Behind you!"

She reached out and snagged it, then she placed the girl's hands on it and used her own body to trap the girl to the ring. The youngster had stopped struggling and just laid her head on the life ring and cried hysterically. The woman spoke to her quietly.

"You okay?" Hank yelled.

The blonde looked up and nodded.

"I'll be back!" He gripped the base of the floating can and shoved it out in front of him, then kicked as hard as he could, pushing it along. The little boy on his back had a death grip around his neck. But the life vest and the buoyant can kept them above water. The baby was howling, which was okay with him. As long as it howled, it was alive.

But the boy was too quiet.

Hank kept kicking. "Say, you hanging on, kid?"

"Yes, sir," he said, his words little more than a half sob next to Hank's ear.

"Good."

A few more strokes and Hank asked, "What's your name?"

"Theodore."

Before he could respond, the can clanked against the lifeboat and the baby screamed again. He put the can inside, then tossed in the little kid. "Hang onto the can!" he ordered, then grabbed another inflated vest and swam back.

The woman and the young girl were clinging to the life ring. The girl was still crying.

"Oh, shut up or I'll drown you myself!" He jerked the girl's hands from the life ring and shoved her arms into the vest. She blubbered the whole time. As he struggled with the vest clips, he glanced up at the blonde. "You still okay?"

"Yes."

He could see that the woman was good and scared, but she had control. He wrapped his arm around the girl, who, with the life vest on and three more threats, had finally stopped struggling. He glanced back at the blonde again. "See the lifeboat?"

She shook her head and searched the water.

"Swim that way." He nodded toward the lifeboat.

"I see it!"

"Let's go!" He flipped the sobbing girl onto her back and pulled her with him as he swam back.

With almost every stroke, he checked on the woman. She was swimming right with him. She had strength, probably generated from pure fear. He knew all too well that I'll-be-damned-if-I'll-die kind of will. He'd lived with it for too many years. And both he and the blonde were living it now, he thought, then his hand struck the side of the lifeboat. The baby and the kid were still in it.

He got the sobbing girl inside, then the woman.

He took a breath and turned back around. He scanned the water, but he couldn't see anyone else. There were barrels and scattered pieces of the ship.

But no crew. No people.

He treaded water for a moment, trying to get his wind. Debris and cargo floated all around them, but no other survivors.

Hank looked at the ship. He could see the other lifeboat and human figures struggling to get inside while the steamer burned. Every so often, he could make out a member of the crew working to try to save the ship.

Fools to the end, he thought. Gripping the rim of the lifeboat, he watched them a second longer, then turned to the blonde. "I'm going back!"

The ship moaned a steely, grating sound.

"Wait!" she screamed and grabbed his hand.

He looked at her, then followed her horrified stare.

The funnel stacks buckled, then crashed through the flaming deck. They took the other lifeboat with them. Men screamed. There was a loud moan of iron breaking apart. The ship split open like a cracked egg, spilling every burning thing into the sea.

It took barely a moment, an empty moment, to realize they were the only survivors. They sat there, unable to do anything but watch as blue orange flames shot into the night sky and the ship gave one last aching creak.

A few seconds later the bow pitched upward, then slowly slid down. There was a sizzle as the flames hit water. The hull of the steamer sank slowly as if being swallowed by the sea.

And the last thing to disappear was the ship's name written plainly across the bow, only two words: *The Deuce.*

The lifeboat floated on the dark and quiet sea. Hank worked the small fuel pump on the lantern. It was one of those pressure lamps that, when they were in good working order, could stay lit in a full gale. He'd seen men gut fish in a storm by the dependable light of a tilley lantern. He lit it with a safety match.

"I'm Margaret Huntington Smith."

He glanced up at the blonde.

Three names . . . Now there was trouble.

He didn't respond, just lifted the lantern up and stared at her. She was a looker, even soaking wet. Especially soaking wet. He could see right through her thin clothing.

However, any bright ideas he had for taking Madame Smitty there on a few hot voyages had gone straight to hell when those kids had peered down at him from the ship.

He looked from her to her children, who were wrapped in the tarps and blankets. The baby cuddled inside a dry blanket in her lap. The lantern cast a shallow amber glow on their upturned faces, all looking at him expectantly.

He looked away, watching the dark sea and night

sky that surrounded them. He saw nothing but black, as if fate had pitched them into a deep hole to see if they could survive.

He knew how to survive. Hell, he had been doing it long enough. Yes, he could take care of himself just fine. But a woman and her three kids? They were not part of the plan.

"Father?" She was waiting for an introduction and giving him one of those direct looks again.

He silently swore. He'd forgotten about the priest's clothes. He fiddled with the lantern and pretended he hadn't heard her.

She waited, then glanced around at the sea. "This was supposed to be a holiday," she said, almost as if she were speaking to herself alone.

He gave a bark of sharp laughter. "I suppose you might say I was on a holiday myself."

She looked back at him, then glanced at her children. There was a lost look about her, a sense of helplessness when she looked at her children.

A vulnerability he noted and stored away. He unclamped the small mast from its fittings and mounted it into the mast hole. He spent a few minutes with the sail lines, then nodded at the kids. "Where's their father?"

"Dead," the little girl answered in a bitter tone he knew only too well.

Hank gave her a sharp look.

She stared right back at him.

"How old are you, little girl?"

"I'm Lydia, not little girl," she said, her chin in an angle of so-what's-it-to-you. "I'm eleven." She pulled her blanket tighter around her angry, childish face, then averted her eyes from his and stared at the bottom of the boat. "Our mother's dead, too. Everyone's dead."

So their mother was dead, he thought. He glanced at Miss Smitty, who had just become fair game again.

"Their parents were killed in an accident," she

said, placing her arms more tightly around the children. "A matron was taking them to an orphanage on Cook Island. We became friendly on the voyage between island stops."

She paused, then glanced out at the sea for a moment. "She was trapped inside the stateroom next to mine. I managed to get to the children, but . . ." Her voice drifted off, and the young girl began to sob again. The woman turned back to the girl. "I'm sorry, Lydia." She put her arm around her. "It's okay. Get it all out. Go ahead and cry."

Hank looked away and rolled his eyes. He didn't think Lydia needed any encouragement. All she had done was cry.

The little boy, however, was sitting very quietly. He stared at Hank with wide and curious eyes. There was something grounding in those eyes. An odd mixture of innocence and caution, like someone who been hit for no reason.

The kid had gotten his first bad taste of the life Hank knew. He'd been younger than this kid when life had dealt him a bad hand. He hadn't been innocent for very long. But he did remember the feeling of confusion. He looked at the boy again. "You wanna help me, kid?"

The kid bobbed his head. "I'm Theodore."

"I remember." Hank pointed to the bench in front of him. "Come here."

The kid shrugged out of the blanket and sat on the seat, his look serious.

Hank looked down at him. "How old are you?"

"I'm five," he said, then added quickly, "but I'm not the baby. Annabelle's the baby 'cause she's not even two yet." He pointed to the bundled baby in Smitty's lap.

Hank handed him the ends of the lines. "Here. Unwrap these from the sail."

"Father?"

Hank looked at the blonde. She was still holding the baby and trying to soothe Lydia.

"Perhaps you can say a prayer for them," she suggested.

He froze.

"A prayer for the matron and the rest of those people onboard."

He paused for the second it took him to think, then pulled the rosary from his pocket and knelt over the edge of the boat. He dipped the beads in the ocean a couple of times as if he were baptizing them. "The Lord give them peace," he said, making his best imitation of the sign of the cross, then he stuck the beads back in his pocket, staring at the water. "Amen."

"Amen," she repeated, then whispered, "Thank you."

He felt a brief stab—very brief—of something deep in his gut. He'd eaten those bananas too fast.

It couldn't have been guilt. Hank didn't feel guilty about anything. Never had. Never would.

His words didn't do those victims much good now. And he doubted a priest's would either. No one could bring them back.

He turned back and opened the small sail, then showed the kid how to work the lines.

Smitty spoke quietly to Lydia and played with the baby's hands, then her blond head shot up. "What was that?"

"What?" He threaded one of the lines.

"That sound," she said. "There it is again! Listen."

There was a loud, grating noise, and Hank whipped his head around.

"Look!" She pointed northeast. "In the water! Over there!"

The children's heads perked up and turned.

"It's a goat!" Theodore shouted, his voice excited.

There, in the water, was one of the goats Hank had

seen being loaded on the ship. The animal was swimming, its head disappearing, then reappearing with a bleat.

"There it is!" Smitty had turned from the goat toward him. "Sail over to it."

He frowned at her. "What for?"

"Why . . . to save it, of course. The poor thing."

"Look! Look!" Theodore was leaning half out of the boat.

Hank grabbed the seat of his pants to keep him from falling in.

"It's drowning!" He looked to Hank. "Save it! Hurry!"

He stared back at the three faces watching him and waiting expectantly. The baby suddenly poked its little head out of the blanket, looked around, then grinned right at him.

"Save it?"

They nodded in unison.

Calling himself every kind of fool, he wrapped the lines back around the sail and unhooked the oars. A minute later he was rowing toward the animal and muttering about the likelihood of surviving with a goat in the lifeboat.

It took him five minutes and two hooves slamming into his gut to get the frightened goat inside. He locked the oars back in their safety clamps on the inside of the boat, sat down on a bench, and untied the sail again.

"Look! What luck!" Smitty said in a bright tone.

He just looked at her.

"It's a nanny goat." She waited, and when he didn't respond, she added, "We'll have milk for the children."

Hank grunted some response and busied himself by adjusting the lines, then he glanced up. All of them were fussing over the stupid goat. "Hand me the compass. It's behind you in that tin supply box with the matches and food."

Smitty turned slightly and rummaged through the box.

Fate had doomed him. Again. After being locked in a French hellhole of a prison for four years, he was now suddenly in a lifeboat with a prime dish who had a sweetheart of a body. And she thought he was a priest. Hell, he'd better act like a priest. Along for the ride were three orphan children and a noisy goat, all of them floating somewhere in the South Pacific.

Ain't life grand?

She handed him the compass. He didn't say anything, just stood and turned around, bracing one foot on the plank seat while he bent to secure the lines.

"Look out!" Smitty screamed.

Too late he realized she meant him.

The goat butted him. Hard.

The compass flew from his hand, and Hank sailed over the side headfirst.

He swore. Very loudly. Very graphically.

The worst word in his vocabulary . . . and five more just like it.

The compass hit the water first. He hit the water second. He surfaced ready to kill the goat. Seeing red and a dead goat, he swam to the lifeboat and climbed inside, cursing the air blue.

The children cowered in their seats, their eyes wide and their mouths hanging open. Smitty pulled the baby closer to her just as he spat his last "Damn that goat to hell!"

He shook the water from his face and head. Glaring, he reached for the goat, which was innocently chewing on a banana peel.

"Muck! Muck! Muck!" The baby chanted, then pushed the blanket away from her bright face and repeated, "Muck, muck, muck, ssssi-it!"

They all stared at little Annabelle, who was grinning proudly.

"Daaaaamn goat!" she added and clapped her hands

There was a full minute of silence.

"Colorful language, *Father*," Smitty said knowingly.

He looked up at her.

"Colorful enough to melt those rosary beads."

He clamped his mouth shut on his next curse.

She pinned him with a narrowed look. "Just *who* are you?"

⇜ 4 ⇝

He was no priest.

Margaret sat there, watching the man's face for some clue to who or what he was. All she saw was a calculating edge that did little to put her at ease. He's going to lie to me, she thought. After a long minute of silence she said, "I assume you have something to hide."

He laughed at that, loud and cynically, then he sat down on the plank seat behind him and eyed her from a ruthlessly ridged expression that gave nothing away.

She waited.

So did he.

"Who are you?" she repeated.

"I'm the man who saved you and those kids."

She never took her eyes from his, a maneuver her father had taught her. *Look people square in the eye, my girl. You'll be surprised what you'll find out.* She waited a few long and silent seconds in which she realized that from this man's eyes she would find out little or nothing.

None of her usual methods worked. He didn't seem to mind the long lapses of silence that bothered most people into saying something just to fill the awkward moment.

"I asked you a question."

Putting him on the defensive didn't work either. He said nothing.

She changed tactics. "I'm supposed to just accept the fact that you are disguised as something you are not and blindly trust you with my life and the lives of these children?"

"Blind acceptance?" He rested his elbows on the rim of the boat. His mouth quirked slightly. "Sounds good to me."

"I want an answer."

"Yes," he shot back.

"Yes to what?"

"Yes," he said. "You can blindly trust me with your lives."

"That's not the question I wanted answered."

"Well, sweetheart, that's the only answer you're gonna get." With that he swung his feet over the plank seat in front of her, then dropped them on top of it and crossed his ankles. He gave her a cocky look.

She stared at his feet for a second. Around both ankles was a strip of skin that was paler than the skin on his tanned feet. She glanced up and caught his gaze as it flashed up from his feet to her face, then narrowed ever so slightly.

She waited to see if he would say anything. He didn't, but that cocksure look of his faded ever so slightly.

"Ankle cuffs," she said, fishing for information.

He returned her stare.

She hugged the children a little closer. "You're from that French prison I heard the crew mention before we docked at Dolphin Island."

He said nothing.

"I assume, since you are dressed as a priest, that they didn't release you."

He continued to stare.

"The crew said no one had ever escaped from there alive."

He laughed, crowed actually, as if what she'd said were a fine joke. "I didn't escape alive."

She frowned, refusing to look away.

"They thought I was dead."

"But you're not dead."

"No, and since your sweet butt's in this lifeboat instead of bobbing along like shark bait, you should be damn glad I'm not dead."

She knew he was trying to get a reaction from her, anger or fear or both, but she wouldn't react. Because despite his disguise, despite the fact that he was a convict, despite his bitter tone and hard looks, he had saved their lives. It didn't make sense that he would save them only to turn around and harm them. So very calmly she asked, "How long were you there?"

"Too long."

"Why were you there?"

"No place else to put me."

She tried another angle. "What did you do?"

He didn't answer.

After a long, tense few seconds that stretched into minutes, she exhaled. "You're not going to answer me."

He just gave her a long and cold stare.

"Considering our situation"—she gestured to the small lifeboat—"I'd appreciate an answer."

"Yeah, well I'd like a million dollars, a steak dinner, and a wagon load of beer, but I'm not gonna get those things anymore than you're gonna get an answer."

She shook her head. "I don't see why you just won't tell me. What am I going to do? Turn you in? Notify the authorities?" She glanced out at the dark sea. "Hardly."

"It wouldn't matter if you did." His eyes narrowed, but he wasn't looking at her. "I won't go back."

"Since you escaped, you'll get a tougher penalty. It would have been easier to just serve your sentence."

He gave a long look she couldn't read. The silence went on and on. He nodded slowly, then said in a quiet and pensive tone, "Easier." He glanced out at the black water and didn't speak. The lifeboat bobbed on the sea, and a small swell slapped against the side of the boat. He turned back to her. "So, Margaret Whatever Smith . . . where are you from?"

"San Francisco."

He didn't look at her but through her. "I've been in San Francisco." He paused. "Nice place."

"I like it."

He let his gaze rove over her slowly and assessingly. "Nob Hill, right?"

"Russian Hill."

"Close enough. Nice weather. Great town, San Francisco." He paused, seemed to let the moment hang there, then asked, "What was that railroad slogan about California?"

"Take a golden ride to the golden state. The land of plenty."

"That's right. The land of plenty," he repeated. "Plenty of food. Plenty of water."

He wasn't looking at her. He sat straighter, his look intent, and he rested his elbows on his knees, then slowly moved his face closer to hers. "So you think it would have been easier to serve my sentence?" he asked pointedly, clearly not wanting an answer. The anger on his face became more vivid and a little frightening the closer his face came to hers. "You, a woman from San Francisco, some . . ."—he paused and looked her up and down—"thirty-year-old—"

"Thirty-two."

"A thirty-*two*-year-old woman from Russian Hill in San Francisco thinks you know what prison is like?"

"That's not what I meant."

"I wonder how long you would last on a chain

gang." His voice was calm, but there was nothing calm about the tension emanating from him. He pinned her with a cold look then. "Have you ever been hungry? Had no food and no water for days?"

His face was inches from hers. She said nothing.

"Ever been locked in filthy black cell, Miss Margaret Whatever Smith, and been afraid to sleep for more than a few minutes at a time? I'd bet you don't have any idea what a man has to fear in a prison."

One of the children edged closer to her, and in reaction she glanced down. His hand shot out, and he grabbed her chin, forcing her to look at him again.

"Do you?" He paused, and she could see his scorn. "I don't think so, sweetheart."

Lydia began to cry.

He pulled his gaze from hers, then released her chin and shifted back. He gave Lydia a dark look, then glanced toward Theodore. His look didn't change.

Margaret hugged both the children a little tighter.

"When you're me." He jabbed his finger against his chest. "Hank Wyatt. And you've lived my life. Then you can tell me what the hell is easier."

"You're frightening the children."

He gave a caustic laugh. "They'd better learn now what a hard life they've got ahead of them."

"They're only children."

"They're orphans," he said coldly. "The orphanage I grew up in wasn't much better than that prison."

"You are a cruel and bitter man."

"Life's cruel and bitter. They can learn that lesson now while they're young. No one's gonna look out for them. Believe me, I know. They'd best grow up damn fast."

She looked from the children, whose faces had paled, back at him. "Why did you save us?"

He wouldn't look at her. "Don't ask me that."

"Why not?"

"Because I just might tell you the truth."

"But—"

"Trust me, sweetheart. You don't want to know."
He wrapped the lines around the sail. After a moment
he stopped and looked at her again. "You just worry
about those kids." He turned his back to them.

Theodore shifted, then stood up and wobbled a
little from the motion of the boat. Margaret grabbed
his arm to steady him, and in a cracked voice he said,
"Mr. Wyatt?"

The man grunted something.

"Mr. Wyatt?"

The man turned around. "I'm just Hank."

Theodore nodded, his small face serious. "You said
I have to grow up now. Because I'm an orphan."

Margaret covered her mouth with one hand.

The convict said nothing.

Theodore puffed out his bony chest and said very
seriously, "Thank you for saving us."

Margaret sat powerless as she watched Theodore
stand there, trying to be brave in front of this crude
and formidable man. A convict.

The man just looked at him for long seconds, then
stared at Theodore's outstretched hand.

She held her breath, afraid of what the convict
named Hank might say or do to this little boy who'd
already seen more pain than any child should have to.
She started to reach for Theodore to pull him back.
Then she saw his small pale and childish hand covered by a rough, tanned one. She exhaled a breath she
hadn't even known she was holding.

There was no cockiness in the man's manner, no
cruel look of challenge.

"That's okay, kid." He shrugged and looked up.

His gaze met hers over the top of Theodore's head.
She could see nothing in the convict's expression to
give away what he was thinking, but he was tense. He
sat more erect. She had seen something he wanted
hidden.

He dropped Theodore's hand. His face grew harder and his mouth tight. Theodore stepped back and sat down next to Lydia. They began whispering.

His back to her, the man tied off the sail lines, then sprawled out in his end of the boat and crossed his feet again. He looked at the kids, then gave her a warning look.

This time she said nothing.

He looked away.

After a moment she quietly said, "Thank you."

They both knew exactly what she was thanking him for.

"Don't go getting all gushy, sweetheart. I did what I did because I did it." He plopped his hat over his face and rested his arms on his chest.

"Certainly," she said in a wry tone, staring at the black hat.

He tilted the hat back and scowled at her from beneath the wide brim.

She smiled sweetly.

He nudged the hat back over his face and grunted something.

She should have had Theodore question him, she thought. The boy might have gotten some answers out of him. She watched this Hank Wyatt person for a long time, then frowned slightly when she realized he was sprawled in the boat like a man who hadn't a worry in the world. His breathing had evened out like someone who was almost asleep. "What are you doing?"

He didn't say anything.

She looked at the sail, uselessly wrapped around the small mast and tied with the rigging and lines. "Mr. Wyatt?"

He groaned.

"I asked you what you were doing."

"I'm going to sleep," he said from beneath his hat.

She looked at the dark sea, first left, then right. "But shouldn't we do . . . something?"

"Like what?"

"I don't know. Sail somewhere. Do something other than just sit here."

"I'm not doing anything until morning."

"There's a map in the tin box. I saw it." She reached around Lydia and Theodore, who were playing with Annabelle, and pulled out the map, shaking it open with a crackling snap. She shook the creases from it a few times.

He tilted back his hat and scowled at the map, then her. After a moment he said, "We'll have to wait till sunrise."

"I realize it's still dark and the print is small. But with the lamplight . . ." She raised the map close to her nose. "I can read it if I hold it very close, like this."

"You can read the map," he repeated as if it were a joke.

"Yes." She lowered the map slightly and peered at him over the top.

He almost smiled.

"Yes, I have the capacity to read a map." She raised her chin a notch. "I have a brain." She snapped the map. "And right here, on this map, it shows east, west, north, and south. And here"—she poked her finger at the map a couple of times—"is the Pacific Ocean."

"Well, Smitty—"

She cringed at that name.

"—there is one small problem."

"What?"

"Show me where east is."

"Here." She stabbed a finger on the map.

He shook his head. "No, sweetheart. Not on the map. From our perspective. Where is east?"

She stared blankly at the ocean around them. There was no moon, no stars, just a dark and cloudy night sky.

"The compass is gone. Thanks to the goat." He shot

a look down at the goat that should have scared it. But the animal just continued to lie innocently beneath Theodore's small feet. "That's why I didn't open the sail." Hank looked back at her. Very slowly, very distinctly, as if he were talking to a simpleton, he said, "You cannot use a map if you don't know where the hell you are."

A reference point. She sat there for a full minute, frozen, feeling more than a little stupid, then she folded up the map in neat creases. Of course he was right. She turned and tucked it back in the box, then looked everywhere but at him. It wasn't a comfortable feeling, being wrong, especially in front of this man.

"I'm going to sleep."

She looked up then.

He had pulled his hat back over his face and again crossed his arms on his chest.

She sat there feeling uncomfortable and too helpless, things she wasn't used to feeling.

"Hey, Smitty!" he said after a few minutes.

She looked at the hat again. "What?"

"You might want to rest that brain of yours." He laughed obnoxiously.

She looked away, then jerked a couple of the life vests free and covered them with the blankets. "Lie down here, children, and try to go to sleep."

Theodore looked to be already half asleep. Lydia slid under the covers but scooted as close as she could to the goat, which was curled in a small space near Theodore. The animal shifted slightly, then rested its bearded chin on her narrow shoulder.

Margaret settled down herself beside Lydia. She cradled sleeping baby Annabelle into the crook of her arm. She sighed, then stared up at the black night sky where the clouds grew spotty and a thin slip of a new moon shone for a brief instant. Before long, the clouds thickened again.

She'd been wrong, not something Margaret accepted from herself. She knew how to read a map and should have figured out that they needed a reference point. Her thinking was off, which bothered her because she wondered what else she would misjudge.

"Smitty?"

She ignored him and chose to wait silently.

So did he.

Finally she gave in and said, "What?"

"Wake me up when the sun rises." He paused for a full minute, then added, "You know . . . in the *east.*"

Something poked him in the foot. Hank stirred slightly.

"Mr. Wyatt?"

He took a deep breath and grunted a what.

"Mr. Wyatt! You said to wake you up."

"I changed my mind."

"The sun's up."

"Well, I'm not."

"Mr. Wyatt?"

He ignored her.

"Are you awake?"

After a few minutes he heard her sigh, then mumble something under her breath. She shifted around the boat, banging this and moving that. He blocked out the noise and was just about asleep again when he heard the irritating sound of paper crackling. Over and over.

He groaned silently. She was at that map again. Rattling it.

He took a deep breath. Let her play Captain Cook. He'd sleep for a few more minutes.

Much later, he awoke to the sound of a loud *klunk* and an even louder goat bleat near his ear. The children began to chatter excitedly, and the boat shifted and rocked as they moved positions.

"There it is! It's closer now!"

He tilted back his hat. The goat stared at him, its muzzle about a foot from his face. He swatted it with his hat and glanced up.

Bright sunlight almost blinded him. After a sea of flashing stars, he squinted in their direction and his vision cleared.

The first thing he saw was Smitty's butt. She had one knee on the bench, and she was half bent over the back of the lifeboat with an oar in her hands. She was banging it against something hard and hollow.

"You've almost got it!" Theodore shouted, kneeling next to her while Lydia sat on the bottom of the boat holding the baby and trying to peer around Smitty's thin white skirt.

He watched them, then heard her bang the oar again. "There!" she said, then dropped the oar back inside and looked to be tying something. Her butt wiggled the whole time.

Hank dropped his hat beside him. He locked his hands behind his head and took in the view. *Nice . . . really nice.*

Finally she straightened. "That makes seven." Dusting her hands together, she turned, and her gaze met his. She stiffened slightly.

He yawned, then scratched his head and stretched. When he looked at her again, she was frowning at him.

He frowned back. "What the hell are you doing?"

She raised her chin. "Salvaging things from the shipwreck."

He sat up and looked behind her.

Hitched to a mooring chain at the other end of the lifeboat was a rope caravan made up of floating trunks, wooden boxes, and barrels. The garbage can, which was still in the bow of the lifeboat, was filled to the brim with glass bottles, pans, and a kettle.

He glanced out at the smooth silvery water, where the bright sun reflected back. He blinked, then saw the ship supplies and wreckage that floated on the surface.

Something knocked against the stern of the boat a couple of times. Hank leaned over and squinted down. A small silver flacon was floating nearby. He fished it out and looked at it.

Smitty glanced up. "Oh. What's that?"

"Nothing. Just an old perfume bottle."

She held out her hand. "Oh. It looks lovely. May I—"

He tossed the bottle over the side. "The last thing we need is more crap in the lifeboat."

He stretched and yawned again, then flexed his arms and legs and grunted and groaned a few times. Out of the corner of his eye he saw her shake her head. He ignored her and frowned up at the clear blue sky to get his bearings, then sat up and began to unwrap the rigging.

Smitty whipped out the map and plopped down on the seat, pressing the map open with her hands and a few irritating crackles. She leaned down and burrowed through a box, then pulled out a twin compass, protractor, and a pencil.

"Where'd you get those?"

She looked up, distracted. "Hmm? Oh. These?" She held up the plotting compass and pencil. "From one of the trunks."

He watched her for a moment.

"I've been studying the map."

She'd been rattling the map.

". . . and the way I have this plotted we should sail . . ." She poked the compass into the map and swiveled it around. "About, hmmm, yes, that's it . . ." She lay the protractor on the map and said, "Forty degrees south. Or perhaps it should be sixty degrees?" She paused and looked up, then looked back and studied the map. "No, no, I was right. Forty degrees southwest, not south." She pulled the pencil from the compass slot and jabbed it behind her ear before she looked at him.

He didn't say anything, just adjusted the sail lines and checked the wind.

"We were traveling west when we left Dolphin

Island and here on the map is Cook Island. It's southwest of Dolphin." She chattered on about how she had figured their correct course taking into account the time past and direction, never realizing that current and wind were involved.

He yawned again while she yammered about how she had calculated her course until his eyes began to glaze over.

She finally shut up and tilted the map toward him, then scratched her finger over it, pointing at a chain of islands. "See? Forty degrees southwest."

Hank trimmed the sail, looked up at the sky for a minute, then turned the lifeboat sixty degrees northeast.

She watched him, frowning. She glanced down at the map in her hands, then looked at the sun, at the sail, and again in the direction they were headed. "I believe you're going the wrong way."

He gave her one of his universal grunts meant to cover a whole wealth of responses from "Yeah" to "Who cares?"

She crumpled the map in her lap. "You are not going to listen to me, are you?"

"No."

"I am an intelligent adult, Mr. Wyatt, and I should have something to say about how we proceed."

"Think so?"

"Yes," she said emphatically.

"What happened to blind acceptance?"

"What happened to democracy?"

"I run a monarchy. Besides, you're a woman." He grinned. "You have no vote."

Her mouth fell open and her eyes narrowed.

He didn't smile, though he wanted to. She was angry. He stared out at the sea. "Don't go and get your knickers in a knot there, Smitty. Women have their uses."

She grew angrier. Her knuckles were white, and her

lips thinned. But he had to give her credit; she didn't snap at his bait. He could see her thinking.

She glanced at the children who had been watching their exchange with avid interest and leery eyes. Then she stared out at the sea for a minute. When she turned back toward him, she appeared to be biting back a smile.

Not the reaction he expected.

A second later she began to laugh, honestly and clearly, which surprised him, although he didn't show it.

She stopped laughing after a minute or two. "Now I understand you."

"Think so?"

"Yes." She paused, then beat her fist against her chest and lowered her voice to deep tone. "Man hunt! Ugh! Woman cook!"

He stared at her, then rubbed his beard. "I'd say that about covers it."

She gave him a look that said she wasn't fooled or angry. "Does that tactic work often for you?"

He gave a sharp bark of laughter. She did have a brain. He watched her for a minute. "You are quick, Smitty." He paused. "For a woman."

"As you said." She gave him a sugary smile. "We do have our uses."

❦ 5 ❦

"Hey, Smitty! Make yourself useful and hand me that can of water."

Margaret slowly looked up from bouncing the baby—an attempt to keep her happy. Annabelle didn't want to be held. She didn't want to play. She wanted to crawl all over the boat. She wanted to throw handfuls of soda crackers. She wanted to do anything but sit still.

Lydia and Theodore had had two arguments over who got to sit by the goat, another about who had asked first, one about who was hogging the other's space, and three more about who touched who. Now Lydia was pouting, and the goat brayed with obnoxious regularity.

It was hot, and Margaret was sweating. The air was thick enough to swim through, and her head ached from the heat of the sun. She had draped a tarp over her head and over the children to block out the sun.

Her sweat-damp hair hung in her face, and she had Annabelle's soda crackers crumbled all over her. In her mind, they were hopelessly lost and His Majesty, king of his little monarchy, wished her to hand him the can of water.

He had stripped off the black tunic and was lounging in his end of the boat in what must have been his prison clothes: a pair of filthy cotton pants with a rope belt and a cotton shirt with only one button left. The shirt gaped open and showed his tanned chest and washboard-flat stomach, both of which were covered with black curly hair.

At one time—perhaps a year ago—his clothing had most likely been white. Now it was gray. He held the sail lines in one rough hand; the other hand was tapping an irritating tune on the rim of the boat.

His hat cast a shadow over his face. She couldn't see it until he tilted the hat back, stretched, and gave a jaw-cracking yawn, then scratched his hairy, tanned stomach. Next he jutted his chin out and scratched his beard and neck with such vigor she was surprised he didn't use his foot

She watched him, completely amazed.

After a minute he looked at her expectantly

48

She smiled innocently.

"Well . . ."

"Hmm? Did you want something?"

"The water. Hand me the water."

"Oh, certainly." She clamped one arm around Annabelle and grabbed a tin cup from behind her. "Let me pour it for you."

He frowned at the cup. "Where'd you get that?"

"This cup? From one of the trunks."

She spun around on the seat so her back was to him, and the baby giggled and clapped her hands. "Fun! Fun!"

Yes, Annabelle, Margaret thought, this is going to be fun. She glanced over her shoulder and saw that Hank was looking off in the distance, whistling. She tapped the water can with her foot to rattle it and quickly dipped the cup in the ocean, then covertly dried the outside with her skirt.

She turned back, gave him another honeyed smile, and handed him the tin cup. "Your water."

He grunted something, then raised the cup to his mouth and swilled down a nice big Neanderthal-sized gulp.

Water sprayed everywhere, and he roared one of those foul words. He swiped the back of his hand over his mouth. "That's seawater!"

"I know."

"What the hell did you do that for?"

"The peasants are revolting."

He stood up, rocking the boat, and stepped around the mast, then crawled past her. He grabbed the can, grumbling a string of foul words before he moved back to his end of the boat.

Annabelle looked up at him and said, "Hi!"

He frowned.

She grinned and waved her hands. "Sit, sit, sit, sit!"

"No, Annabelle." Margaret shook her finger. "No. No. That's a bad word."

He raised the can and gulped down some water, then screwed the cap back on the can and set it down between his feet.

"Shouldn't we be rationing that water?"

"Worried, Smitty?"

She scanned the horizon on all sides, then gave him a pointed look. "Do you know where we are?"

"I don't have to know where we are."

It was like talking to a brick.

"Men have instincts. Think of it as a sixth sense."

"What? Ignoring women?"

"That, too." He waved her off with one rough hand, then added, "I know exactly where I'm going."

"Without the map or a compass."

He tapped a finger against his temple and gave her a cocky I-know-everything look. "It's all in here. A natural gift, sweetheart. Like knowing the exact moment to pick a pocket."

She shook her head. "You have no scruples."

He grinned as if she had just complimented him. He propped his arms on the boat rim and nodded at the trunks behind her. "Any cigars in those trunks?"

The look she gave him was meant to tell him exactly what he could do with his cigars.

"Beer?"

"No. No cigars, no beer, and no hoochy-koochy dancers either."

He grinned and stared at her legs. She looked down. Her humidity-drenched skirt clung to her like a second skin.

"I don't suppose . . ." He raised his head and looked her in the eye, then shook his head. "Nah . . ."

After a few minutes he began to whistle and tap out another tune on the boat rim. He sighed and glanced around him. "This is the life. Fresh air. Sunshine . . ."

Annabelle hit her in the face with a handful of sticky soda crackers, then giggled. Margaret blinked, then brushed the crumbs off her face and took the cracker tin away from her. Annabelle let loose with a howl that raked down her spine, then the baby began to squirm and twist.

Fifteen torturous minutes later Hank glowered at her for the hundredth time. "Can't you shut that kid up?"

"I'm trying . . ." she gritted, frustrated and edgy and feeling completely disarmed by one little baby, who was howling like a banshee, trying to squirm off her lap and succeeding. Margaret tried to give her back the cracker tin, but she batted it away and screamed louder.

Margaret blew a hank of limp hair out of her face. "I don't know what to do."

"Christ! Do something."

Lydia looked up from beneath the shadow of the tarp and said quietly, "My mama used to rock her."

"Yeah, Smitty. Listen to the girl. Go on." Hank waved his hand and acted as if it were his idea. "Rock her."

She counted slowly to ten.

"What are you waiting for? Rock the kid!"

She shifted, holding Annabelle who screamed and squirmed and kicked.

Margaret leaned forward. She plopped the crying baby in his lap. *You* rock her."

"Like hell!" he bellowed and froze. "Get her off me!" He sat there, his arms spread out as if little Annabelle were something untouchable.

An instant later, Annabelle stopped crying so suddenly that everyone stared at her. She sobbed once, then hiccuped. She tilted her small, wet face up and stared at Hank.

He was eyeing the baby the way some of the opposing attorneys—the men—eyed Margaret.

The baby hiccuped once more, then stuck two fingers in her mouth and curled her small, pudgy body closer to his big, tanned one. She sighed and snuggled her head against his dark chest.

A moment later she was sound asleep.

The mournful sounds of an old freedom song rode slowly on the thick, stagnant air. The notes sounded sadder than Hank remembered. He stopped playing and tucked the harmonica away, watching Smitty stare out at the water. The children had fallen asleep, and the goat was eating the hem of her skirt.

It was suddenly quiet, the only sound that of the water lapping at the sides of the boat. After a few minutes she turned back and looked at him.

"We're lost," she said abysmally.

"We are not lost."

"Do you know where we are?"

He looked left, then right, then skyward. "We're floating in the middle of the Pacific."

"Funny," she said under her breath. "Very funny." She dipped a handkerchief in the water and swabbed her neck and cheeks. "I know we're lost." She slicked her hair back from her face with the damp cloth.

"You women are always worrying about something. Everything's a big deal to you."

"Oh, I see. Men are calm and rational and understanding."

"We don't get our knickers twisted over stupid things like women do."

"Stupid things?" She wrung out the handkerchief with a firm twist.

He gave the cloth a pointed look. "Primping."

"I'd hardly call cooling myself off primping." She swabbed her neck and hands. "However, I don't expect you to understand that."

"Knowing how to stay alive is a helluva lot more valuable than sewing samplers and drinking tea."

"I don't sew samplers and drink tea. I have a profession."

"A profession," he repeated mockingly, then laughed. "A professional female?"

She looked at him as if she wanted to say something, but she remained silent.

"So what is this *profession?* Tea tasting?" He laughed again.

She eyed him for a long time, then said, "I don't think I'm going to tell you."

He shrugged as if he could care less. After a minute or so he looked at her. "I know one thing."

She sighed. "What?"

"This profession of yours can't be in navigation."

"Goad all you want, I still say we're lost."

"Which is why I'm sailing the boat and you're not." He locked his hands behind his head and watched as she dipped the cloth again and wiped her arms.

"There's a whole ocean of cool water out there, Smitty. Don't let me stop you."

"Pardon me?"

"Just strip and jump in."

"You expect me to jump in the ocean."

He shrugged. "It's cool. Think of it as bathing."

She dipped the cloth in the water again. "This is sufficient, thank you." She rubbed the handkerchief over her arms.

He snorted.

She looked up. "What was that for?"

"You women and all your little niceties. Just take off your clothes and jump in the water."

She eyed him suspiciously. "I'm supposed to believe you wouldn't look."

"I didn't say I wouldn't look." He winked. When she said nothing, he added, "What's the matter? No guts?"

"Give up." She turned to look out at the sea. "Your tactics don't work with me."

"Yeah . . . I have to say, you don't take the bait often." He paused, then began to tap out a tune on the boat rim because he knew it annoyed her. "Tell me something."

"What?"

"What do you call that thing you're wearing anyway?"

She looked at him, frowning. "What thing?"

He waved his hand at her clothes. "That thing."

"A dress," she said with enough sarcasm that only a deaf man could miss it.

"Not much to it. Looks pretty thin and cool to me."

"It's imported cotton. From France."

"That explains it."

"Explains what?"

"I've been to Paris." He gave her a lascivious grin.

"What are you talking about?"

"Well, Smitty . . ." He waited for a moment. "That cotton thing you're wearing sure didn't cover much when it was wet." He shook his head, then he gave a short, sharp cat whistle. "Helping you inside the boat was, well, it was almost like looking at a French postcard."

Her back went ramrod straight. She was silent, her eyes looking anywhere but at him.

Before he had time to gloat, the wind picked up as quickly as it had died. It almost seemed to come out of nowhere. A small gust blew the tarp back and her hair from its topknot. Another stronger gust buffeted the sail. The boat rocked on a shallow swell, and the air began to cool a few degrees.

Frowning, Hank glanced around, then looked behind them.

Rolling into the horizon was a fast-moving cluster of dark storm clouds. He whipped back around.

Smitty was looking at the clouds, too. "That's a storm coming."

He grunted something noncommittal.

She folded her hands in her lap. He saw that she clasped them so tightly that her knuckles were white. She bent and lifted the blanket tented over the sleeping kids.

Theodore woke and sat up. He rubbed his eyes, then looked at Hank. He blinked a few times, then he pointed skyward. "Look! It's a seagull!"

Hank glanced up, then turned back to Smitty just as she did the same double look. They stared at each other, then both said, "Land!"

He scanned the north.

She looked toward the south.

"There it is. Look!" She pointed toward the southeast.

Hank turned.

At first glance, the island looked like the dark edges of the oncoming storm, brooding purple and gray and misty. But as the winds picked up and the small boat cut through the rising swells, there was no doubt that there was land ahead.

Land. An island.

They could survive.

Hank stared at the horizon. Yes, there it was. He could see the high volcanic mountains rising from the sea like an angry bruised fist.

He looked up at the sky. Between the island and their boat was a storm—dark and roiling and high as the eye could see. That meant only one thing in the tropics. It was one helluva storm.

The lifeboat pitched into the air and slammed back on the wake of a swell. Margaret's stomach lurched. Lydia screamed.

Margaret held her hand more tightly. "It's okay. We're okay." But as the boat pitched again, she wondered whether she was reassuring the children or herself.

She, the children, and the goat lay in the bottom of the boat. Oilskins covered them, and the tarp cover was snapped closed over their section of the lifeboat, an attempt to keep the children as safe as possible.

She could see Hank's knees just a few feet in front of her. He had tied himself to the plank seat with a piece of rope and was trying to keep the boat afloat with the oars. She couldn't see his face, only a glimpse of his forearms jamming an oar forward as another big swell sent the boat into the air.

A barrel and the garbage can clanked together in the bow and some tin cups floated in the rain and seawater pooled in the bottom of the boat. There was enough water to slosh over her and the children and to slap repeatedly at the sides of the lifeboat.

She was really scared.

The waves kept hammering at them. The storm roared and rushed around them while Hank cursed and swore. The goat cried out and tried to stand up. Lydia and Theodore pulled it back down and clung to the animal's neck.

Margaret buried her head under the oilskins and tried to logically think the situation through. Don't panic, she told herself.

Hank was shouting. Then he kicked her hard in the backside. "Woman! Are you deaf?"

She turned around just as he shouted her name again.

"Come here, dammit!"

She turned to the frightened children. "Lydia! Theodore! Here!" She put Annabelle between them. "Hang on to each other and stay down under this seat!" She slid along under the tarp. "I'm coming!"

He grunted something.

She had to poke her head up in between his splayed knees. The rain pelted her cheeks, stinging. The wind howled and whipped her wet hair against her face.

She heard a roar that seemed unreal. She turned and looked around them. She didn't know if the sound was from the ocean or the storm, but it was loud and doubly frightening. She could see swell after cresting swell coming toward them and little else.

Hank bellowed her name again, and she whipped her head back around.

"We're close to land! I need you to watch for rocks ahead!"

Still kneeling, she turned back and scanned the horizon but couldn't see much, only the rising sea and sheeting rain. Another swell hit and sent the boat into the air again.

Her stomach rose. Sea spray washed over her, and rain stung her cheeks and neck.

She heard Hank curse. He shoved the handle of one oar beneath his hip and grabbed her by the shoulder. "Hang on to my leg!"

She clasped one of his thighs in both arms and held on. He locked the other oar. The boat slammed back into the trough of the wave. Saltwater slapped her hard in the face, burning into her nose and eyes. Momentum sent both of them upward.

The rope that anchored his hips to the seat held, and they slammed back down. She clung onto his leg with all her strength, then she felt him grip her shoulders with one hand. He shoved her down. Her knees hit the boat bottom so hard she cried out.

"Sit!" he yelled, forcing her down lower until her backside hit and she was sitting on the boat bottom.

She could hear Lydia and Annabelle crying underneath the tarp. "The children!" she screamed and tried to move toward them.

"No!" he shouted and held her down.

Another swell hit. An angry squall. Harder and higher and stronger than the last time.

Above the roar of the sea and storm she could hear the crash of water. She spun around, bracing her hands for another swell. More water doused her and foamed into the boat. She swiped it from her eyes, and for a second, the driving rain let up. She stared ahead for a frozen moment.

"The rocks!" she screamed. "Oh, God . . ."

The boat shot across the curl of a huge wave straight at a sheer wall of black, jagged rocks.

❧ 6 ❧

Smitty screamed at him, then buried her head in her knees.

Hank looked up and saw the rocks.

This was it. Good-bye . . .

He closed his eyes and waited for the impact.

A wall of water smacked the boat so hard it snapped his neck back as if he'd been punched by God. He shook the water from his head and looked where that last wave had come from. It had ripped in from the opposite direction.

Before he could think, another wave hit, its foam spilling over the tarp. The rocks were still ahead, but the crosswaves had shoved them back. The boat rose with the scend of a new wave, then jerked back as if a giant hand had just grabbed it.

Waves washed over them, one after another. But the boat didn't move forward. It sloshed back after each swell drove past them.

Hank shook more water from his face and turned around.

He caught a glimpse of a rock reef behind them. And the trunks—Smitty's trunks—one of which had caught like a grappling hook in the rocks. He turned back around and stared at the wall of dark rock in front of them, the headland on the island, then he looked back at the trunk line, not believing what he saw.

The waves must have been high enough to send the boat over instead of into the natural breakwater. And the trunks, still chained to the lifeboat, had snagged on the reef.

"No shit . . ." he muttered as the next wave filled his mouth and nose.

The boat twisted, almost turning over.

He cut the rope that anchored him to the seat and heard Smitty scream something and felt her grab at his leg.

There wasn't time to stop. He crawled toward the chain that held the line of trunks. *Hold, baby, come on, hold . . . just a few more minutes . . .*

He stretched forward and gripped the line, then braced his feet against the plank seat. He pulled, hand over hand, using his strength to try to pull the boat toward the rock reef.

His hands gripped the slippery chain, pulling inches at a time. The swells hit again and again. He didn't know how long the line would hold. If the line would hold. If the trunk would stay snagged. One wave could slam them loose and send them crashing into the headland.

The boat banged against the rocks, and another swell washed over them. He coughed and gasped for air.

His hands slipped. The chain slid like kelp through his palms. He cursed and shouted and yelled. Anything. Everything. He held it as tightly as he could.

Then Smitty was there beside him, her hands gripping the chain behind him. She pulled and screamed, "Don't stop!"

They pulled together harder in spite of the surging swells. Hand over hand to bring the boat in closer.

A breath later the boat knocked into the rocks again. Another swell hit, but they held tight. Hank pulled his body over the edge of the boat, onto the rocks. He turned and gripped the cleats on the stern. A swell lifted the lifeboat just as he jerked back with a bloodrush of power that came from the sheer need to survive. The last punch of a fight.

The lifeboat surged forward and wedged into a cleft in the rocks.

"Grab the kids and get out!" he shouted, trying to fight the sea for control of the boat.

Smitty shoved a screaming Lydia at him.

Two threats from him and the girl crawled out and into a protected nook in the rocks. "Stay down there and stop blubbering!"

Smitty pushed Theodore, who clung to the braying goat, toward him. Hank swore and reached for the kid, who shoved the goat in his face. He jerked the goat out and dropped it next to Lydia. The kid crawled out onto the rocks and went down into the crevice beside his sister and the goat.

Smitty moved closer and held the baby in her arms. Another wave hit hard. He held onto those cleats with every bit of strength in his body. He couldn't see anything but heard the screams—Smitty and Annabelle's garbled cry.

He shook the water from his head. They were still in the boat, lying flat, half under the tarp and half covered in water. The baby was screaming and coughing.

"Smitty! Get up!"

She moved upward, Annabelle hugged to her chest. *Come on, sweetheart.*

She crawled—he didn't know how—over the edge. A second later she was huddled between the rocks with the children.

Another swell hit, and he jerked the empty lifeboat back. It shot over them, twisted on the wave. Upside down, it jammed to a stop on the rocks.

The anchor flew past him. Cold, wet metal hit his head. Pain shot through his forehead and scalp. Something warm flooded his right eye.

He swiped it away only to see the rusted links of the anchor chain hanging down before his eyes. He looked down, still stunned, and picked up the anchor, raising it over his shoulder like a sledgehammer. With every ounce of his strength, he slammed it into a rift in one of the rocks.

The boat sat over them like a cocoon, protection, small as it was, from the angry churning of the storm.

The waves battered into the lifeboat, rocked it hard, rattled it against the rock, but the anchor and the trunk chain held the boat in its place.

Hank fell back against the jagged edges of the rock, his breath tight and fast, bloodrush speeding through him. He swiped at his eye again and looked up.

Rain pelted the boat bottom, sounding like shots from the prison Gatling gun. But under the protective cover of the boat, nothing hit them but some sea spray and the foam that swelled between cracks in the rocks.

He turned toward the others, huddled safely down between the rocks. He saw looks of horror on their faces as they stared up at him.

"You're bleeding!" Smitty shouted, her hand reaching toward him.

Then everything went black.

Margaret pulled hard on the anchor. It wouldn't budge. She stared at it, then dropped the chain and wiped her hands on her dress. She didn't have the strength to loosen the anchor or the trunk line. She crawled back into the crevice where Hank was still unconscious and the children were huddled with the goat.

The storm had stopped sometime earlier, but she had no idea when. She had no concept of time past. All she knew was that she needed to do something. They couldn't just stay there.

She needed to think.

Lydia was playing with Annabelle. She stopped and looked up. "What are we going to do?"

"I don't know. I can't move the anchor, so we're stuck here." Margaret settled down next to the children and put Hank's head in her lap.

The children were staring at the small stream of dark blood dribbling from the gash in his forehead.

She dabbed at it with the ragged hem of her dress.

"I think he'll wake up soon, then we'll be fine." But she was only reassuring the children. She wasn't sure they would be fine, but at least they were alive. And though Hank was bleeding, he was alive, too.

She watched the heave of his chest just to make certain. The gash ran from one black eyebrow, up his forehead, and disappeared into his hair. The deepest part of the wound was near his hairline. His tanned skin was too dark to be pale, but his lips were grayish and she felt that wasn't good.

Then he groaned softly.

"Mr. Wyatt?"

Nothing. No response.

"Hank?"

He moaned again.

"Can you hear me?"

He turned his head so his mouth was against her midsection. Through her thin wet dress she could feel the heat of his breath.

She glanced at the children, then back at him. If he was unconscious much longer, she would have to do something. Think of something. "Hank?"

His breathing was slow and even.

She pressed her hem at the trickle of dark blood, then pressed harder, worried that she needed to apply pressure to stop the bleeding.

"I don't know what your profession is, sweetheart, but you're sure no Florence Nightingale." His nose was about three inches below her bosom, and his eyes were locked on the thin white pintucks of her bodice. Her thin cotton dress was the only thing between his face and her skin.

"I was right." He gave an exaggerated squint. "You can see right through this cotton stuff." His sly gaze shifted to her face from her bosom, and he winked.

"You have two seconds to move your head."

"Or what?" He didn't move but just grinned up at her.

She leaned down a bit closer and whispered, "Or I'll punch you in the nose."

"You know what, Smitty? I believe you would, too." He laughed in that wicked way he had. The sound of it gave her the same sensation she got when she banged her crazy bone.

He sat up quickly and winced. He grabbed his head and muttered something vile. He pulled his hand away and scowled at the blood on it. "What hit me?"

"The anchor," she said, taking Annabelle from Lydia and rocking her. "Luckily, it hit you in the head, otherwise it might have killed you."

He gave her a narrowed look that promised retribution.

She smiled innocently and rocked the baby.

He looked around for a moment. "When did the storm stop?"

"I'm not certain. It's been a while."

She watched him brace his feet on the rocks and push hard on the lifeboat. It rocked, and he kept rocking it until the anchor she couldn't budge began to loosen. He gripped the chain in two hands and pulled the anchor free almost too easily, then tilted the boat over to one side.

A snatch of pinkish sky was all she could see, but it was a welcome sight. Not too long before, she'd been certain that wall of rocks was the last thing she'd ever see.

While Hank crawled up onto one of the high rocks, she turned to the children. Theodore and Lydia were in deep conversation with the goat, assuring it like worried parents that everything was safe.

"Hey, Smitty."

She turned back and looked up. The sunlight grew a little brighter, and it took a moment for her eyes to adjust. She could hear the waves against the shore, the caw of gulls. She caught the sweet tropical scent of something wet and green.

"Take a look at this," Hank called down to her.

She crawled up the rocks, hugging Annabelle to her chest. She knelt on a flat rock and froze. Everything froze—her ability to speak, her breath, for an instant, her heartbeat.

Spread out before her was the broad cove of a tropical inlet, entirely arched in a thick rainbow of pink, purple, blue, and yellow. Beneath the rainbow were lush green hills. In the distance was the high, dark cone of a volcano. A small cloud of mist ringed that tall peak and made the island look as if it touched heaven.

The water in the cove bled from deep aqua blue to pale green to a brilliant silvery color just before it foamed like spun sugar into the wet sand. Spiky pandanus palms and bushes thick with flowers the color of the tropical sunset spread from the green hills all the way down to the edge of the beach, where the white sand took on pink tints from the cast of the slowly setting sun.

Even the sky was different here. The late afternoon sun was a yellowish-pink ball in the west, where clouds strolled by wearing colors of gray and lavender. It was the same sky, the same earth, yet it seemed too brilliant to be earthly. Perhaps it was because this island's beauty was something she had never before experienced.

Like yesterday's dream, the rainbow faded. A cloud blocked the sun, but there was still enough tropical warmth to cause steam to rise up from the sand and from the lush green ferns and bushes behind the beach. Tall coconut palms waved in the trade wind like welcoming hands. Their color turned from green to violet to purple while the gleam of the sea blended from silver to pink.

Surprised that something could touch her as deeply as this place did, Margaret stared at the changing colors so real, yet so unreal. She had seen islands, had seen the setting sun and pink skies after a storm. She'd seen many beaches. The northern coast of

California was one of the most majestic sights in the world.

But this was so different it was hard to believe it was the same Pacific Ocean that she had known all of her life. There was more than just a sense of peace about this island. More than a place saturated in beauty. It was untouched, isolated, as though the world had passed it by. Not forsaken, but hidden. A treasure so precious, nature had protected it.

Silently, the children joined them, first curious, then chattering. They pointed at the flowers and birds and shoals of bright swimming fish spread before them. Annabelle tugged on the neck of her dress and tried to squirm her way down. Margaret hugged her tighter.

Annabelle patted her shoulder to get her attention, but Margaret couldn't bring herself to look away at that moment. All she could do was whisper, "This is paradise."

❧ 7 ❧

"This is stupid."

Margaret raised her chin and looked Hank in the eye. "What is stupid? The fact that I made a suggestion or that you don't agree with it?"

"Look, sweetheart." He dropped the trunk he was carrying, and it hit the sand with a heavy thud. "You just worry about those kids and let me handle everything else."

Margaret turned away from him and watched the children for a second. Not because he'd said to, but because she'd momentarily forgotten about them.

Luckily Annabelle was curled underneath a palm

tree, sleeping on a tarp near the tilley lamp. It wasn't quite dark yet, just dusky and shadowed. Theodore was digging in the wet sand. Nearby, the goat ate a clump of tangled kelp. Lydia was bent over, her hands pressed against her knees and her blond hair hanging in the sand as she stared at the goat's belly. There was a tin cup underneath the animal's udder. It looked as if she was trying to milk it.

"Lydia! Wait!" She turned to Hank, who was looking at the girl, too.

They both started walking toward her at the same time.

"Hey, little girl!" he bellowed. "You trying to milk that thing?"

Lydia looked up at him and nodded.

"Just grab it by the tits."

"That's *teats.*" Margaret jabbed her elbow into his ribs.

"Hell, Smitty." He scowled at her. "It's the same thing."

She leaned closer and whispered, "You're talking to an eleven-year-old girl."

"Yeah, well she's gonna have 'em someday. She might as well know what they're called."

Margaret looked down, her hand rubbing the throbbing spot between her eyebrows.

"Nothing's coming out." Lydia frowned up at them for answers.

Hank hunkered down and reached out toward the udder. The goat turned its head and bleated in his ear.

"Damn!" He sat back in the sand and clapped a hand over his ear. The goat trotted down the beach until it found some new kelp to nibble on.

Margaret put her arm around Lydia's shoulders, and the girl stepped away, her head down.

"I don't think she wants to be milked right now, Lydia. Would you go keep an eye on Theodore and see that he doesn't get too close to the water?"

Lydia nodded and ran off.

She took a deep breath and turned back to Hank. "You can't talk that way to a little girl."

He sat in the sand, his wrists resting on his splayed knees. "What way?"

"So . . . hard. She's just lost her mother and father, been through the trauma of a shipwreck, and now here with us—two strangers. She must be scared to death."

"Yeah, well, she'll get over it."

"You have the sensitivity of a rock."

"You think so, Smitty? Let me tell you something. Sensitivity and a nickel will get you a cup of coffee." He stood up and swaggered over toward the trunks and barrels.

She leaned against the rough armored trunk of a tall coconut palm and watched him lug another trunk over and drop it with the other supplies. "You are making our situation difficult and it doesn't have to be."

"You're right. Things can be easy. Just be quiet and do what I say." He turned around and strode down the beach.

The urge to throw something at him, something big like the trunk, came over her so swiftly she just stood there. By the time he dragged two more trunks over, she decided to change strategy. "Give me five good reasons why we should make camp here . . . instead of there." She pointed to the lovely, peaceful spot she'd suggested, which was hidden from the shore by a cluster of rocks, yet one could see the lagoon.

It was a spot that in addition to being attractive took the best advantage of the island's closest resources. Her location was near a stream of fresh water and a rock pool that was fed by a waterfall directly behind a grove of hibiscus bushes, a few banana plants, and two mimosa trees. The sound of rushing water was peaceful and idyllic, and they would have easy access to water and food.

Her plan was based on simple logistics. She'd spent

quite a bit of time analyzing their situation while Hank had maneuvered the trunks, lifeboat, and what supplies they could salvage to the edge of the lagoon. She had a well-thought-out plan with the best and most sensible conclusion. It made perfect sense.

He looked at her, then shook his head. "You never give up, do you?"

"Changing the subject isn't going to work."

"What will?"

"Answering me." She repeated her challenge. "Give me five reasons why we should settle here."

"Okay. Number one." He waved his thumb in front of her face. "Because I said."

She rolled her eyes.

"Number two." He raised his index finger. "Because I have experience in surviving."

She'd give him that one.

He waved two fingers and a thumb in front of her face. "Number three—"

"Wait!"

He stopped talking.

"What are you doing?" She stared at his fingers.

He scowled at her, then popped off with, "I'm counting off the reasons I'm right and you're wrong."

"You're not counting correctly."

"One, two, three." He held up his thumb first, then his index finger, then his second finger. "You know some other way to count? Two, nine, seven?" He flicked his thumb, then his fingers up again.

"The index finger is standardly used to signify one, two is the second finger, and so on. The thumb is number five."

His eyes narrowed for a second, then he flipped up his middle finger and held it in front of her face. "And *this* is number three."

If he thought she'd offend that easily, he could think again. She gave a small sigh and looked away.

"Number three," he continued. "Because I run a monarchy."

68

She'd love to crown His Majesty, except that if an anchor hadn't knocked some sense into him nothing else would.

"Number four, because *you*, a woman, haven't got a vote . . ."

She could feel her jaw tighten. Her foot was tapping with impatience. She pulled it back so he wouldn't see her reaction.

"And number five, because I'm a man and what I say goes." He turned back to the trunk, dismissing her because he must have believed his words were absolute—his final argument.

It was worse than talking to a brick. She watched his broad back as he tried to unhook the other end of the mooring chain from a trunk handle. "And to think I insulted bricks everywhere," she muttered.

He stopped and glanced up. "Huh?"

"Nothing. Just an observation."

"Good idea, Smitty. You observe. That means look, not talk." Then he chuckled.

At that same moment, the goat looked up. Its gaze shifted to Hank. A second later it charged.

She really should warn him, she thought. She looked from the goat, its head lowered and its hooves eating up the sand. She looked at the target: Hank bent over the trunk, laughing obnoxiously.

Yes . . . She sighed and looked up at nothing in particular. She really should warn him.

She closed her eyes instead. A second later she heard the smack. Then the curses. There was a distinct echo to his vitriolic language, she thought, her eyes still closed, as she tapped a finger against her lips. Yes, it was almost as if his swear words were slowly flying away.

The words stopped abruptly.

A new sound. Muffled, yes, that was it. Definitely muffled. She opened her eyes.

He lifted his face out of the sand. From his forehead

to his whiskered chin, pearly white sand clung to him. His eyebrows were dusted with it and looked like two plump sand caterpillars. It clung to the scab where the anchor had hit him. A thick mask of it cupped his jaw and turned his lips ghostly pale. His eyes were narrowed, the sockets the only places on his face free of sticky sand.

The goat, however, couldn't have cared less. It just belted out a bleat and moved down the beach where a long rope of kelp held more interest than Hank's backside.

Hank pushed himself up.

"Wait!" Margaret held up her hand.

He froze, his body taut, his forearms supporting his weight. He started to say something but spit sand instead.

"Don't move."

That sandy face stared at her. He spit again. "Why?"

"Because I want to remember you just as you are." She tried not to laugh. Really. And failed.

The sun was lazy in the tropics. It rose and set slowly as if the thick and humid air affected the passage of time in the same listless way it did man. This morning was no different. The sun crawled up the eastern horizon and painted the Pacific sky pink and blue and silver—the colors of an abalone shell.

Hank stood on the edge of the headland, scouting the lay of the island. The northeast coast was a sheer drop of limestone cliffs with jagged coastal rocks and strong current—too strong for the lifeboat. It had been the same to the southwest. Nothing but walls of untraversable rock protected the small lagoon and beach.

From the coned peak of a distant volcano spread corrugated slopes of solid lava, which weather and air had turned black as loam. Those rivers of black flowed into a dense green jungle, thick, lush, seemingly untouched by humankind, and inaccessible.

Uncivilized.

He turned and crawled down the rocks to the isolated white sand beach below. He took a deep breath, then stretched and bent to work out the stiffness of a long night spent on the damp ground.

Above him gulls flew from their cubby nests in the sheer face of the headland and cawed like roosters at the rising sun. One wheeled sharply, then swooped toward a wave, gliding over the sea and the air with soaring freedom—something most of the world took for granted.

He stripped and walked into foamy waters of the surf. He dove under a clear blue-green wave, swimming along the idle trench of the next swell with the seabirds flying above him.

The water was cool and clearer than a Pacific sky, the waves and swells gentle and low in the morning tide. He swam, stroke after long powerful stroke through the same distant ocean he'd heard from his cell.

Within a few minutes he was past the surf and swimming along a sand bar. He stood, his feet sinking in the soft sand. The water hit him at his waist.

He walked along the sand bar looking down at the water as small swells drifted by. Yellow and orange fish darted past him between the rocks that littered the ocean floor.

At the western edge of the lagoon, he dove down and caught the flash of something that glittered up at him from underwater. He surfaced, took a breath, and stuck his head under, trying to focus on the spot where he'd seen that flash of metal.

He'd lost it. He came up for air, then went under again and swam down until he was almost lying on the ocean floor. A mass of kelp wavered in the current, and as it moved, he caught the flash again. He pushed aside the seaweed. There was something metal there behind the seaweed. A large lump of something hard that wasn't a rock.

With a fistful of sand, he rubbed it until he recognized the small brass lock. A trunk lock. He shoved the sand and kelp away. The trunk sat half against the sand bar and the rock.

His chest burning for air, he surfaced, took in deep breaths, and dove again. He kicked at the trunk a few times until it loosened from the sand bed. He gripped the iron trunk handle and pulled.

Over and over he pulled the trunk. Into the trench, then closer and closer to shore. Five more times he had to take in air, but he finally got the trunk to the shallow water and dragged it onto the beach.

Winded, he dropped the trunk handle and bent over, his hands on his knees as he gulped in big chestfuls of air. After a minute he straightened and looked at the trunk.

It was made of japanned iron, with nailheads that had oxidized in the brine of the sea. The lock was brass.

He eyed it closely. A Yale lock? He wasn't sure. But he was sure of one thing: trying to break a brass lock was like expecting to have fun with a virgin—a complete waste of time.

Hank scoured the beach until he found a broken board with a rusted nail. He hit the board hard against the trunk of a palm tree and drove the nail up. He stood on the board and yanked out the nail. He squatted and worked in front of the trunk. About a half a minute later, the lock popped open.

He grinned and snapped his fingers. Like good liquor, some skills just get better with age. He rubbed his hands together and opened the trunk.

The strong scent of cedar and flowers filled the air. There were clothes inside, formal clothes.

Helluva lot of good some monkey suit and a ball

gown would be to him out here. He dug through, looking for jewelry, something of value, but there was nothing.

No jewels. No gold. No treasure.

Figured.

Disgusted, he sat back in the sand and rested his arms on his sandy knees. He turned and shot a scowl at the trunk. Completely worthless. He slammed it shut.

The muffled sound of glass clinked together. He frowned and reached over and opened the trunk again. Something rolled inside the lid.

Kneeling, he scanned the cedar and found a small catch and opened it. Stored in the dark recesses of the lid were five bottles wrapped in felt bags. He took them out one by one and whistled in appreciation.

Inside were two bottles of dark rum, one of Scotch whiskey, and two squat bottles filled to their sweet golden seals with fancy-schmancy French brandy. He grinned. Now *this* was worth something.

He sat in the sand, his knees up, and leaned back against the trunk, then broke the seal on the whiskey and took a swig. "Ahhhhhh." He toasted the rising sun. "Good stuff. Burns all the way down," he muttered, then took another long pull. He coughed and wiped his mouth with the back of his hand. Things were looking up.

"Whatchadoing?"

He whipped his head around.

Theodore stood behind him, about ten feet away, eating a banana and rocking on his bare toes.

The trunk blocked the kid's view, but Hank shoved the bottle in the sand and stood up anyway. He didn't want him coming closer. "Where are the others?"

"By the coconut trees." Theodore finished the banana and craned his head to see better while he chewed. He swallowed, then asked, "Where'd you find the trunk?"

"In the water."

"What's in it?"

"Nothing." Hank slammed the lid closed.

The kid's eyes grew wide and round. "Why are you naked?"

Hank looked down and mentally swore. He shoved the lid back up. "I was swimming. Say, kid, wanna do me a favor?"

He nodded.

"My clothes are down the beach. Behind you. By that grove of coconut trees. Go and get 'em for me."

"Sure!" Theodore spun around and ran down the beach.

Hank gathered the bottles in his arms faster than he could deal himself an ace and shoved them under a thick hibiscus bush near the rocky edge of the beach. He covered them with some sand and then rushed back in big, loping steps.

By the time Theodore had returned, clothes flapping behind him, Hank sat on the trunk, trying to breathe slowly and evenly.

The kid handed him his clothes. He took them, turned around, and stepped into his pants. He heard the kid gasp.

"What are those purple marks on your back?"

Hank tied a knot in the piece of rope he used for a belt. "Whip marks."

"They whipped you in prison?"

"Yeah."

"Do the marks still hurt?"

"Not anymore."

"Did it hurt then?"

He shrugged into his shirt and buttoned the second to the last button, the only button. "Yeah."

Theodore was quiet for a minute, then asked, "Why did they whip you?"

"Nothing better to do." Hank started walking down the beach. "Let's get outta here."

"What about the trunk?"

He turned around and scowled down at the kid. "What about it?"

"Aren't you gonna take it back?"

"No."

"But Miss Smith said we need to gather everything we can because we might could use it."

We don't need a monkey suit or a ball gown. And I gathered exactly what I need. "Just leave it there."

"But what if a wave comes in? See? The water's almost hitting it now."

Yeah, the tide'll take it, which is fine with me.

He glanced at the kid's worried expression. He reached out and ruffled his red hair. "I'll get it later, kid." He turned away and strode down the beach, knowing he wouldn't come back for the trunk. He would, however, come back to dig up those bottles.

He could hear the kid running to catch up, could hear Theodore's rushed breaths. Out of the corner of his eye, he could see his small arms churning and his feet scampering in an effort to match his own long strides. He slowed his steps until the kid was keeping an easy pace with him.

"Hank?"

"Yeah?"

"You said you were an orphan."

"Yeah."

"I was wondering . . ."

Hank stopped and looked at him.

"What was the orphanage like?"

Hank squatted down and absently poked at a pile of kelp with a stick.

"Hank?"

He looked at the kid, then stood and faced the sea. The kid was beside him, waiting.

"Cold." Hank stared at the waves, then he turned and pitched the stick into the water. "It was cold."

"You mean they didn't have any blankets or fires or anything?"

He looked at Theodore, and for a minute, he saw

himself some thirty-five years before. Naive years. He didn't explain but just turned away. "Look, just because I had it tough doesn't mean you will."

"You said orphanages are like prisons."

He shrugged. "It was a long time ago."

"How long?"

"Long," Hank said. "Enough questions, kid. Come on." He started back down the beach, heading for the clearing beneath a cluster of palms where they all had slept. He was halfway there before he realized the kid wasn't dogging his steps. He turned back.

The boy was standing where he'd left him, staring out at the ocean with his back to him.

"Hey, kid! Did you grow roots? Come on!"

The boy swiped a hand across his eyes a couple of times, turned, and ran toward him. A few feet away, he stopped running. His eyes were red and his face was blotchy. He didn't look up at Hank, just stuck his hands in his pockets and stood there, staring at a piece of slimy kelp.

Hank looked down at the kid's bowed head. "I have a riddle for you."

Theodore looked up. "What's a riddle?"

"A question game."

"How do you play?"

"I give you a question and you have to tell me the correct answer."

"Okay." The kid's voice was barely a whisper.

"What is the best thing about being on a deserted island?"

The kid looked all around them. "The beach?"

"No."

"The sand?"

Hank shook his head.

"The sunshine."

"Uh-uh."

"The bananas?"

"Nope."

Theodore's face puckered in thought.

"You give up?"

He appeared to think about it, then nodded.

"On deserted islands there are no orphanages . . . *or* prisons."

Theodore gazed up at him. A few seconds later, his freckled face brightened.

"Now let's go. I need you to help me."

"You do?"

"Yeah, kid. We have a hut to build." Hank turned and walked up a short sand bank.

A few seconds later Theodore was dogging Hank's steps again.

"Hank?"

"Yeah?"

"What are those?" Theodore pointed at a green coconut lying in the sand.

"A coconut."

"Oh."

"Where'd it come from?"

Hank stopped and pointed. "See those palm trees. The tall ones?"

"Uh-huh."

"There are coconuts high in the branches. Look closely."

The kid smiled. "I see 'em!"

They walked along a few more steps, then the kid asked, "What's a coconut?"

"Food."

"What kind of food?"

"A coconut."

The kid frowned up at him. Hank grinned and nudged the kid's arm. "You're supposed to say 'What's a coconut?'"

"Why?"

"Just say it."

"What's a coconut?"

"Food."

The kid stopped, thought about it for a long few seconds, then said, "What kind of food?"

Hank grinned. "A coconut."

The kid looked up at him, then asked tentatively, "What's a coconut?"

"Food." Hank laughed.

"What kind of food?"

"A coconut."

By the time they reached the clearing, the kid was laughing, too.

❦ 8 ❦

She'd misplaced the baby.

"How the hell can someone lose a baby?"

Margaret crawled out from beneath a clump of oleander bushes and glared up at Hank. "I don't know," she snapped. "I've never lost one before!"

She stood up and dusted off her hands, her eyes scanning the area. Lydia was crying. Hank was swearing. And Theodore was gazing up at Hank. Annabelle was nowhere.

Margaret felt the most consuming sense of failure, compounded by guilt and anger, all directed at herself. One second Annabelle had been toddling in the sand just ten feet away. A few minutes later, she was gone.

"For Christ's sake!" Hank turned and bellowed at Lydia, "Stop that blubbering and help find your sister!"

Lydia's head shot up, and she stiffened. Her mouth clamped shut, and the sobs stopped. Through stunned and damp eyes, she stared at Hank.

"Get up!"

Lydia scampered up and stood at attention.

"Go search that area!" His hand shot out, pointing at the stream and the waterfall. "Theodore! You go with your sister."

Without a word, the two children scurried off toward the stream.

He turned back to Margaret. He didn't say anything for a long moment. He just gave her that hard stare of his. "I'll search the beach." He paused. "And the water." Then he left.

Margaret stood rooted to the ground. She thought she might vomit. Annabelle couldn't swim. She doubted the child was a year and half old yet. The toddler could drown in one wave.

A surge of panic hit her so hard that when she took a step, she stumbled slightly. She braced her hand against a tree trunk for support, and she stared at the sand, seeing nothing. Her mind flashed image after horrid image. A few seconds later, she took a deep breath. "Annabelle!"

There was nothing.

"Annabelle . . ." Her voice grew smaller. She could hear the distant sound of the others calling the baby's name. She could hear the waves, a sound that suddenly had no soothing peace to it.

Think. Think! Use your head.

She covered her mouth with her hands and paced, then moved to the spot where Annabelle had last been seen. There were no signs of her. Margaret's hands fell to her sides, and she took another deep breath. Annabelle had been looking up at the sky, pointing up at the birds and giggling as she watched them fly.

Slowly, Margaret searched the ground, looking for a trail. There was little sand here, just thick short clumps of monkey grass. She began to walk in concentric circles, moving outward, examining every inch of grass until she finally reached the sand. Still nothing.

She stopped and glanced back to the area already searched, just in case. The front of the clearing led to the beach and the other three sides were framed with thick bushes and tropical flowers. To her right, rocks were scattered between three coconut palms that made spotty shade on the nearby sand. The landscape was empty. There was no Annabelle.

She moved out farther, expanding her search. A few more circles and she spotted round and deep hoof marks from the goat and a scattering of small w-shaped gull tracks, but nothing human except her own footprints.

For eternal minutes she kept looking, moving farther outward. She swiped the hair from her face repeatedly as the warm breath of the trade wind continually ruffled it into her eyes.

She looked toward the stream. Lydia and Theodore were searching the bushes and climbing between the rocks. Without thought she glanced back at the shoreline, not realizing until she saw Hank wading in the water that she was terrified of what she might see.

She looked back at the sand, driven to find something. And when she did find some little marks in the sand, she was so desperate that she thought she'd imagined them. But there they were . . . barely. Footprints with little baby toe marks.

Ready to call out to Hank, she looked up. Her words froze in her throat like winter air. Out of the corner of her eye she saw their blankets hanging from a rope tied from a thick guava tree to a spiky pandanus palm. Hank had rigged the line the night before.

She stood in the spot where they had slept last night. She looked closer. All around her were footprints from each of them, Hank, Lydia, Theodore. Everyone's prints were scattered between the trunks and tarps and ship's salvage. Last night's footprints. Not today's.

"Annabelle!"

A warm, thick breeze drifted by and made the damp blankets snap.

"Annabelle! Annabelle . . ." Margaret's shoulders fell slightly and her hands hung uselessly at her sides. The breeze died as suddenly as it had begun. The air felt stiller here, heavier. With one hand she shielded her eyes from the glare of the new sun and looked down the beach.

A dull tapping sound broke the stillness.

"Annabelle?" Margaret spun around, looking this way, then that way. "Annabelle!"

One of the large wooden trunks behind her wobbled.

She ran over to it and threw open the humped lid.

A little head with bright red curls popped up. "Hi!"

Margaret slumped to the ground. Her relief was fierce. It sped through her in a bloodrush that made her face feel hot. She sat there trying to take in a deep breath, but she was shaking so badly she couldn't.

Annabelle was grinning. She gripped the edge of the trunk in two chubby fists and pulled herself up until she was peeking over the edge of the trunk. "Peeeekaboo." She ducked her impish head down and giggled.

Margaret had the completely insane urge to cry. To blubber like Lydia. She reached over and lifted the baby from the trunk. Annabelle kicked her feet and laughed. "More! More!"

Margaret clasped her to her chest and rocked her for a minute, until Annabelle stopped squirming, popped two fingers in her mouth, and nuzzled comfortably against her while she played with the fingers on one of Margaret's limp hands.

She placed her cheek on Annabelle's soft baby hair and closed her eyes. Margaret held little Annabelle tighter than she had ever hung on to any single living thing.

And that was how Hank found her.

* * *

"Are you crying?" Hank scowled down at Smitty. She looked up at him from eyes that were damp. "No."

He gave a snort of disgust and strode past her, then stopped and cupped his hands around his mouth. "Hey, kids!" He waved at them. "Come on back." He watched them jump down from the rocks, and he muttered, "The sun is barely up and already she's lost and found the kid. Instead of telling anyone, she sits there blubbering."

He turned toward her just as she put the baby inside an open trunk. She bent over and dusted the sand off her backside. Hank stood watching as Annabelle crawled over the rim of the trunk and toddled off toward the coconut palms where that damn goat was grazing. He kept an eye on the kid and waited.

Smitty straightened, turned around, and looked in the trunk. "Oh, my God!" She whipped around.

Hank didn't move. He just pointed.

"Annabelle!" Smitty raced over and plucked up the giggling baby. With the kid balanced on her hip, she marched back and pinned him with a hot glare. "You let her run off again? After what just happened? Why didn't you say anything?"

He shrugged. "I knew where she was. Besides, the kids are your problem."

She looked at him as if he'd grown horns and a tail. "What a perfectly horrid thing to say."

"What? That they're a problem? It's true. They are a problem. But they're your problem. You're the woman."

"Sex does not define responsibility."

"No. But sex is a helluva lot more fun than playing nursemaid."

She rolled her eyes at him. "This is serious. It's only fair that we both be responsible for them until we can get help."

"There is no help. The island's deserted."

She looked around. "Are you certain?"

"Yeah, except for the jungle, and you can't take three kids into that." He started to turn, then played an ace. "Some of these islands have never seen a white man or woman. Just other natives." He paused for effect. "And cannibals."

"That's absurd."

"You think so? Well, sweetheart, I don't intend to be anyone's Sunday pot roast."

"You're not joking." She frowned, then shivered slightly and looked over the landscape with a wary eye. "What are we going to do?"

"I'll run things, and *you* take care of those kids." He turned and took a step, then stopped again. "And after what just happened with that baby, I'd say you need some practice."

Smitty spun around and opened her mouth, but before she could say anything Theodore and Lydia came running back.

"You found her!" Theodore skidded to a stop in front of Smitty and stuck his face up toward Annabelle while he petted her small arm.

But Lydia stopped at the perimeter of the clearing, about ten feet away. The look on her face made Hank take pause. He watched her standing there. Outside the scope of the rest of them.

Lydia looked at him, then quickly averted her eyes. She started moving again, walking past him with stiff forced steps. She stopped in front of the group. After a second, she said, "I'll take my sister."

Smitty handed her the baby.

Hank exhaled, shaking his head. He knew trouble when he saw it. He started to walk away, but Smitty touched his arm.

"We need to talk."

"About what?"

She glanced back over her shoulder at the children,

then looked him straight in the eye and said quietly, "About caring for the children."

He held his hands up in front of him and shook his head. "No." He backed up a couple of steps, then turned and walked away.

"Hank!" She scurried to catch up with him, kicking up sand behind her.

He ignored her. He had bottles to dig up and a hut to build.

"Hank!" She tapped him on the shoulder, but he kept walking. She kept right up with him. "I don't know anything about children," she said in a harsh whisper.

"Try paying attention."

"What?" She grew roots. And he wouldn't say she had shrieked, but the noise she made was close to it. He stopped and turned to face her one last time.

She stood scant inches from him, her hands planted on her hips. Her expression reminded him of the prison mule.

"For Christ's sake, woman! How hard can it be to watch a little kid?"

It was harder than trying to reason with Hank Wyatt. Margaret spent a couple of minutes retying the knots in the rope around her waist. She turned and walked toward the banana plant. As Margaret reached for a banana, the rope went taut as a clothesline.

"Not again," she muttered. For what seemed like the tenth time in the last hour, Margaret turned and followed the thirty feet of rope. This time, it was threaded like Maypole ribbons around and through three hibiscus bushes and two spiky pandanus palms.

Right in the middle of everything stood Annabelle, the opposite end of the rope tied securely around her waist. She grinned at Margaret, then on chubby feet she began to weave in and out of the bushes, tangling the rope and poking her head out. "Peekaboo!" Then she laughed and laughed and did the same thing all over again.

The rope tugged at Margaret's waist again and again. Annabelle seemed perfectly happy to tangle the two of them to anything and everything nearby.

Margaret's neighbor's two pet pugs had been easier to care for than this one child, and those dogs had half dragged her down Taylor Street chasing an alley cat.

There was a logical way to handle this. There had to be. She thought about it for a few minutes. Her leash idea had made sense, but now? She glanced at the rope twisted through the trees and bushes. It looked like a game of cat's cradle.

Lydia ran up the beach with a bucket. Margaret looked up, the rope looped at her feet, and waved. Lydia slowed down, looking at her sister, then at the rope. She set down the bucket filled with mangoes. "My mama used to play with her."

"Did she?"

"Yes."

"How?"

"You know, fun little games like all mothers do with children."

"I don't know, Lydia."

The girl cocked her head and stared at her as if she were an oddity. "Why not?"

"I haven't been around children much."

"Don't you like children?" There was a challenge in her tone, as if she expected Margaret to admit she didn't like her.

"It has nothing to do with liking or disliking anyone or anything. I just don't know any children. I don't know how to entertain a baby."

Lydia turned away and seemed to think about that for a minute.

Margaret stood there equally quiet. She didn't know how to make Lydia understand that they weren't opponents. Or how to reach across the awkwardness of the moment.

Theodore called out to Lydia. She muttered something and ran off down the beach, seemingly eager to leave.

As Margaret watched her run away, she wondered what it was Lydia expected of her. There seemed to be a challenge to everything she said, as if she thought Margaret didn't measure up to what an adult should be.

Margaret plopped down hard in the sand, hugged her knees, and rested her head on them, feeling like a failure for one of the few times in her life. She sat there thinking, unable to reach a plausible solution.

When faced with a dilemma in her work, she had made notes, analyzing the problem from every angle, listing all possible solutions. This method forced her to view all sides of a problem. The process opened her mind while the words kept her focused.

She looked down at the sand and began to scribble words with her finger. Girl. Anger. Loss. Orphan. Child. Mother. Baby.

Nothing came to mind. No word triggered an answer. She glanced up, frowning. Then she saw Annabelle, and any thoughts she had went off with the wind.

The child was curled beneath a hibiscus bush, a bright orange flower clutched in one small hand and two fingers of the other hand in her mouth. She looked to be sound asleep.

Margaret stood and walked over to the child, squatted down and untied the rope. Annabelle was asleep. Margaret reached out and slowly pulled her fingers from her small mouth. Annabelle sighed but didn't wake.

Her skin was so soft and pale, unlined by time. Her cheeks were bright pink, her curly hair as deep an apricot color as the hibiscus blossom clutched in her pudgy fingers.

Her head rested on one plump arm, and her fist was next to her mouth. Her little bare toes were curled into the pale sand and waxy green hibiscus leaves clung to the ragged hem of her pique gown. She looked utterly at peace.

How could one small and happy little child create such havoc? Margaret was fast gaining a new respect for motherhood, something she hadn't thought much about until now.

She had never watched a baby sleep. What amazed her was how quickly children could fall asleep. One minute they were running and laughing and playing and the next minute they would be asleep. Sound asleep from what she had seen in the last couple of days.

She reached out and stroked Annabelle's forehead. Margaret had no idea how long she sat there. Her mind was far away in thoughts so foreign that it seemed as if her mind were not her own. Because for the first time in her adult life she wondered what it would be like to give birth to a child.

❦ 9 ❦

Muddy's bottle had hit land the night before after being tossed about during a violent and rocky storm. But with two thousand years' worth of experience, he'd weathered worse—floods, hurricanes, a tornado in some place called Kansas.

Sometimes, idiots who found the bottle heaved it away. He wondered how many people over two thousand years had thrown him away or passed him by and lost the chance for three golden wishes.

He had known the moment he'd landed. It was like

riding a bounding camel and suddenly slamming into a stone wall. And something else was always the same. The inside of the bottle was a mess.

His gold silk pillows were everywhere. Leather-bound books and a stack of yellowed newspapers littered his Persian carpets. Everything he owned from an ancient brass hookah to a baseball bat and cap had toppled in a jumble on the floor. He was sporting a large knot on his head from the bat.

Each new master and new decade and new place brought with it new inventions. Muddy had managed to slip many of the more fascinating items in his bottle.

In recent years, he had collected quite a library of the latest dramatic adventures; an ivory chess board, and checkers, but he had to play by himself; a badminton racket and birdie, which he frequently batted about the bottle; his baseball paraphernalia; and some photographic equipment.

He sat cross-legged on the floor of his bottle and placed his spilled chess pieces back in their box. For just a moment he looked up at the stopper. If wishes and prayers helped, someone would find him soon.

Margaret set the sleeping baby in the makeshift crib she'd made from a trunk and turned around. She raised a hand to shade the glare of the sun and looked at the beach.

Earlier, Hank had sent Lydia and Theodore to gather driftwood. They were stacking wood on the beach. The goat stood by Theodore, probably because Hank, the goat's target, was nowhere nearby.

Now that she thought about it, she hadn't seen much of Hank, not that that particularly bothered her. Asking for Hank's company was like wanting to dine with the devil.

A second later she heard the devil whistling.

He came swaggering out of the thick jungle, his arms loaded with a bundle of green and yellow bamboo. He was whistling something that sounded like *Home on the Range*. He walked past her, stopped, and looked around, then dropped the bamboo.

Margaret stared at the pile of green sticks. "Are those for the hut?"

"Yeah."

"Why did you put them there?"

"Because this is where we are going to build the hut."

Margaret pointed to the spot she had chosen. "Not there?"

He shook his head.

She took a deep breath. "I realize that we've had this argument before, but I think you should be aware of the fact that I have given this project quite a bit of thought."

He looked at her as if she couldn't possibly know what she was talking about.

"It seems most reasonable that we should build closer to our water and food supply."

He squatted down and began sorting through the bamboo. "We'll build it here." He started whistling again.

She changed arguments. "Look. You've said this island is deserted, so we are stuck together. It's less than an ideal situation."

He grunted.

"I would like you to treat me as an equal and consider my opinions and suggestions. It's only fair and right. I am not a man, but of course there is no scientific proof that men are superior to women in anything other than brute strength and muscle capacity. And since I am an educated professional woman who thinks things through thoroughly and analytically, I believe my opinion benefits us all. I make no rash decisions and believe that we should have a fair and equal partnership on everything that affects us."

He stood and walked a few feet away, then stopped.

"Yeah, well, I'd like to find buried treasure but that's not bloody likely." He began to coil the rope she had gathered into a pile.

She watched him for a moment, her arms crossed. "Just what makes you so certain that your way is the only way?"

He glanced up from coiling the rope around his elbow and over an open hand. With that male cockiness that set her teeth on edge, he tapped a blunt finger against his temple. "Instincts. I get by because of mother wit."

"And I suppose it was mother wit that landed you in prison."

"Yeah, well, I wouldn't have been there if it weren't for some stupid pissant attorney." He jerked the rope into a tighter coil, his movements angry and stilted as if he were throwing punches or wanted to.

She didn't say anything.

He tied off the rope and tossed it to the ground. "And those guards called convicts scum of the earth. They ought to put the attorneys in cells and let the prisoners free."

She waited, then said, "I expect you've known your share of attorneys."

"I know attorneys. The most idealistic, word-twisting, egotistical, and argumentative group of horses' asses alive."

She chewed on her upper lip as she watched him storm around in front of her, moving a trunk and then opening and closing it for no reason. She sighed. "And I suppose you've never done anything illegal."

"Laws were made to be broken."

"You believe that?"

"Yeah."

"Yet you blame your attorney for your situation."

"I told the little paper shuffler that there was no such thing as a fair trial in an island court." He threw down the lid of a trunk and stomped past her, muttering, "Fool."

"You are innocent," she said in a wry tone.

He stopped in front of her and scowled down. "I'm innocent."

"Hank Wyatt is innocent." She tapped a finger against her cheek. "Now why does that sound oxymoronic?"

He looked at her for a minute, then went over toward the bamboo. "Yeah, well, I'm not half as stupid as an attorney."

She looked at him, blinked once, then burst out laughing.

Squatting on the ground, he glared up at her.

She laughed harder. She couldn't stop.

"You're crazy," he said.

She shook her head, then took a deep breath. "An oxymoron is a phrase of incongruous words."

He was rigidly silent.

"You know . . . two contradictory words?" She bit back another smile and explained, "The last thing I'd call you is innocent."

"Yeah, maybe I've had my share of trouble, but I am innocent."

"There is a saying that in prison all convicts are innocents."

"I didn't kill anyone," he shot back so quickly that they both fell silent. He looked as if he wanted to eat his words.

She just stood, frozen. But her mind was not frozen. Murder meant a life sentence or death.

"Were they going to execute you? Is that why you escaped?"

"My attorney said I was lucky. I got a life sentence." He looked up at her from his squatting position as if he expected her to scream and run.

She wouldn't run.

Finally he said, "You have nothing to fear."

"I know that." She reached out and touched his shoulder. "A murderer doesn't risk his life to save three children and a woman from a sinking ship."

He looked at her hand on his shoulder with a confused and wary expression. She'd once seen the same look on a Chinese client who didn't speak English. Then Hank slowly rose from the ground.

She let her hand fall away.

He watched her a long time as if making a decision about what it was he saw. He stepped closer, giving her the same direct look she gave him.

She waited.

"You are a smart woman." He paused, then turned and slowly walked away. After he'd gone a few feet, he turned around and said, "Another oxymoron."

Margaret persisted.

He refused to compromise.

For the last hour he'd oxymoroned her to death. He wouldn't listen to her suggestions, and he spent a wealth of time tossing off a plethora of rude comments about attorneys, judges, prison guards, and the law in general, all things he held in contempt.

"Look, sweetheart. I'm not going to agree with you. Give it up. I say we build the hut here and here is where we will build it. A smart woman would have figured that out by now."

There were moments when she actually liked sparring with Hank. This was not one of them. She waited, then casually strolled past him. "Actually, I'm more than just a smart woman."

"Yeah," he said with a laugh, "I forgot. You have a profession."

"Yes, I do."

"And a brain," he added as if it were another joke.

"I think we need to work on your attitude."

"You can do me a big favor, Smitty."

"What?"

"Don't think."

"I'm paid to think."

"Then don't talk."

She laughed and walked around him. "Actually, I'm paid to talk, too."

He gave her another long look that said he didn't believe anyone would pay her to do anything.

She refused to make this easy for him.

They played a waiting game. He raked her with a hot look she saw for exactly what it was. A look that reduced the two of them to a man and a woman. An elemental look that cast her into the weaker role.

"I don't offend that easily."

"I'm learning that, Smitty."

And you're going to learn another lesson, she thought, but she remained silent.

"So," he said after a few moments, "what is this profession?" He stressed the last word as if it were a joke.

She crossed her arms and gave him a look that said he could figure it out.

"Ah, I get it." He stepped closer and stared down at her. "You're not going to tell me."

He was trying to intimidate her, standing close and using his height to his advantage. She used a square look and stubborn silence to hers.

"Okay, I'll bite. I'll play your guessing game." He began to pace in the sand. "You can't be a nurse." He turned and paced back. "Your touch is about as soft as cement." He stopped and turned again, then gave her a narrowed look. "What was that you just muttered about my head?"

"Nothing." She gave a dismissive wave of her hand.

"I can figure this out. You said you're paid to talk," he repeated.

She nodded.

"A schoolteacher?"

She shook her head.

His cocky expression should have warned her. He glanced at the rope looped around the trees and bushes, then he shot a look at Annabelle sleeping in the trunk. "After this morning, I'm certain of one thing. You're not a nanny."

If she hadn't already known she was going to come out the winner in this contest, she might have done something rash and emotional. Instead she gave him a blank and unaffected stare.

"A librarian."

"Not even warm."

"A seamstress."

She rolled her eyes. She couldn't sew on a button.

"Hatmaker? Nah." He shook his head and rubbed his hairy chin thoughtfully. "I remember that ugly brown hat you had on in the marketplace. Couldn't possibly be a hatmaker."

"You are *so* witty."

He smirked at her. "I try."

"You need a shovel, Hank."

"Why is that?"

"So you can dig that hole you're standing in a little deeper."

"Which hole?"

She strolled past him. "I'm neither a teacher, a nurse, nor a *nanny*." She gave him a pointed look. "Nor a librarian, a seamstress, or a hatmaker."

He snorted.

She paused and turned. "I am . . . let me see if I can remember the more polite words. Ah, yes. I am"— she stopped right in front of him and looked him square in the eye—"an idealistic, word-twisting, egotistical, argumentative"—she took a deep breath, then smiled—"attorney."

He stared at her. His usually tight jaw went completely slack.

"With the law firm of Ryderson, Kelly, Huntington, and Smith."

He frowned as if he couldn't believe it.

"Sutter Street, San Francisco."

One could have heard a bird's heartbeat, it was so absolutely and utterly silent.

Then he said that truly foul word again.

❧ 10 ❧

By late that afternoon they had reached an agreement not to kill each other. Hank was building his hut on the best spot while Smitty was building hers on the worst spot.

"Hand me that rope, kid."

Theodore shuffled over and handed it to him.

"Now hold this," said Hank, showing the boy how to hold the canes of bamboo and then wrap them together with rope so that the hut would have a solid frame.

Hank tied it off and glanced at Smitty. She was trying to hammer a rod of bamboo into the sand with a rock. Annabelle was running in circles around her, twisting the rope that kept them tied together around Smitty's knees.

He crossed his arms and watched, thinking it was a fitting situation for an attorney, being tied up with rope. Now if he could only find a way to gag her.

She fussed at the baby, then tried to unwrap herself. Her blond hair hung down her back in a loose knot, and as she bent down, her ragged skirt went up high enough so he could see her calves.

He exhaled in a half whistle. She had great legs. Hell, she had a great body and a great face. She also had a big mouth.

And he had a big problem. He was an escaped convict, and he was stuck on a deserted island with a female attorney. Hell, he didn't even know women could be attorneys. Didn't say much for the state of the world.

Theodore tugged on his sleeve. "What do we do next?"

"Suicide," he muttered, never taking his eyes off Smitty.

"Huh?"

He looked down at the kid. "Nothing." Hank glanced around the bamboo frame of the hut. It was sturdy and secure. "We need to gather some filler for the walls."

"What's filler?"

"Palm fronds. Big leaves."

"I saw some really big leaves on a bush by the stream." The kid took off running.

Hank started across the clearing. He stopped a few feet away from Smitty. She had three bamboo rods stuck at cockeyed angles from the soft wet sand. If he walked by too fast, the draft might blow them over.

He stood, waiting for her to turn around. Two of the poles began to tilt slowly toward each other. He fought back a grin.

Muttering, Smitty grabbed them. Annabelle crawled between her legs, and the third pole rattled against the other two.

He gave the poles a pointed look. "Building a tepee?"

She glanced up at the bamboo poles, cringed slightly, then gave him a cool look just as Annabelle let out with a holler. The kid was caught in the rope knotted around Smitty's ankles. Smitty dropped the poles. "Now, Annabelle, just hold still, and I'll fix this."

"Annabelle stuck!" The kid cried and struggled.

Smitty was stuck. He chuckled to himself and moved on. When he was a few feet away, he stopped. The kid had quit hollering. He looked back. Smitty was sitting in the tangle of rope and bamboo, the kid in her lap.

"Hey, counselor!" he said.

She looked up.

"I hope you build a legal case better than you build a hut." He walked away laughing.

She didn't build a case.
She didn't build a hut.
She built a tepee, as he had sarcastically suggested.
Margaret stood back and appraised their work. Not bad. For a frame she had tied the poles together at the top when the dratted things refused to stay upright in the sand. She and Lydia had woven wide flat leaves into mats, then she'd tied them together in a thatched covering.

She stepped back, then walked around and eyed it from a couple of directions. It wasn't exactly symmetrical. But it worked. She looked at Lydia. "What do you think?"

Lydia shrugged. "It's okay."

Margaret dusted her hands together, then wiped them on her skirt. "I think we did a good job." She smiled at Lydia. "Thank you for helping."

Lydia didn't respond. She was watching her brother and Hank. Margaret turned and looked across the clearing. Hank was lifting Theodore in the air so he could lay palm fronds on top of their square hut. It looked very sturdy. The walls and roof were stuffed loosely with palm fronds between the bamboo frame.

She looked back at the tepee. She thought their thatch looked stronger. She laughed. "I'll have to thank Mr. Wyatt for his suggestion." She looked at Lydia, who just shrugged.

Margaret thought of Hank's nasty words as she studied the tepee. "The perfect rebuttal," she mumbled to herself.

Lydia looked at her. "What's a rebuttal?"

Margaret hadn't thought she was paying attention. "In court, when someone raises an assumption of a fact, the opposing argument is a rebuttal. Proof they are wrong. It is like winning an argument. A way of showing that something is true or false."

Lydia seemed to think about that, then after a moment she looked at Margaret strangely. "Are you really an attorney?"

"Yes, I am."

"You go to a court and everything?"

She nodded.

Lydia bent down and picked up Annabelle, hugging her sister tightly. "My mother stayed home with us."

"Many women stay home with their families. But more and more women are working and quite a few are professionals. Doctors, lawyers, journalists. We have a woman editor on the paper at home."

Lydia bounced Annabelle. "Mrs. Robbins, who lived next door, was a teacher. I asked Mama once if she ever wanted to be a teacher or something like that. She said we were enough for her." There was a note of challenge in her tone.

Margaret was used to arguing with hard-headed men. Hank wasn't the first one she'd encountered and he probably wouldn't be the last. Most men thought the world was theirs alone to manage. She had learned a long time ago that her father and uncles were the exception rather than the rule.

Under their tutelage, she had grown up believing that she could be anything she wanted to be as long as she earned it. Her father respected her mind and helped her sharpen it, and not once had he said she couldn't be or do something because she was female. If she worked hard, she could become anything. She had lived thirty-two years exactly that way.

She could hold her own with other women, too. Make them understand her desire that the world be fair and equal and just for everyone, male or female. Only her colleagues, father, and uncles understood her absolute love of the law. It was her life.

But she wasn't certain she should or could defend her choice to this quiet young girl. She certainly wasn't going to contradict the girl's dead mother.

She needed to think long and hard about how to

deal with these children. She knew she had to understand them, to be able to think like them and see the world through their eyes or she'd never be able to help.

Yet with them, she felt completely unnerved, like she was walking into court unprepared. She felt responsible for them. They had no one else but her.

She watched Lydia play with the baby. Even now she didn't smile. Margaret realized that she'd never seen Lydia smile.

Lydia picked that moment to look up.

She has old eyes, Margaret thought. Too old for a young girl. Margaret nodded at Annabelle. "I'll take her for you."

"No." Lydia stepped back. "She's *my* sister."

Margaret was caught completely off guard by the sharpness in the girl's voice. Lydia turned away, pointedly ignoring Margaret. She began to sing a silly song to Annabelle.

A minute or so later, Lydia took Annabelle's hand and walked slowly away. Margaret saw that Lydia was putting distance between them for a purpose. And although it was only a few feet, at that moment it seemed like miles.

"Miss Smith! Miss Smith! Something's wrong with Hank!"

Margaret grabbed Theodore as he barreled into the tepee. "Calm down, Theodore. Please."

"But Hank's sick. Hurry! Please. He might die! Please." He looked up at her. "Everyone dies."

Margaret turned to Lydia. "I'll be right back." She took Theodore's hand, and they ran across the clearing toward Hank's hut. The sun had just set, and there was nothing but a small pink and gold glow in the purple sky. She stepped inside the dark hut.

Hank lay in the corner.

She moved swiftly, Theodore right behind her.

"See?"

Margaret squatted down and looked at Hank. He was frighteningly still.

"Is he dead?"

She lay her ear to his chest, which suddenly shuddered as he inhaled in a loud snore.

Theodore jumped.

"It's okay. Stand back a bit." She crawled forward, and squinting, she brought her face close to Hank's. Her eyes teared from the whiskey fumes.

He's dead all right, she thought, sitting back on her heels and waving his breath away. Dead drunk.

She leaned over him and spotted a half-empty bottle of whiskey clutched tightly in his hand.

Theodore shifted closer.

"He's asleep," she lied, prying the bottle from his rough hand.

Hank snorted like a pen of hungry pigs and flung his other hand over his head, then muttered a string of words that turned her face bright red.

She carefully hid the whiskey bottle in the folds of her skirt. She placed her hand on Theodore's shoulder and blocked his view of Hank. "Come along. You can stay with us. We should leave Mr. Wyatt to his *rest.*"

"But I was s'pposed to stay here tonight."

She couldn't see the boy's expression, but she could hear the disappointment in his voice.

"He said I could 'cause I helped build the hut. He said he'd let me play his harmonica."

"I know." She slid her arm around his shoulder and gently guided him from the hut. "Another night, okay?"

There was a loud snore from behind them. She wanted to clobber Hank Wyatt.

Theodore walked quietly beside her, his head down and his feet dragging through the sand. Again she felt a rush of anger at Hank.

Kicking sand in front of him, Theodore scuffed

over to a palm tree where they had tied up the goat for the night. He talked quietly to the animal.

She took a deep breath and looked around, because she knew that the anger she felt wouldn't help any of them.

There was no moon yet, and just a few stars had begun to glitter in the vast blue-black sky. In the nearby bushes, night bugs chittered while the waves methodically pounded the beach like war drums.

She watched Theodore say good night to the goat and reluctantly enter the tepee, his hands shoved into his pockets and his shoulders sagging. It just ate at her to see disappointment in a child, especially a little boy who already had more pain than any five-year-old should.

Pausing at the entrance, she looked across the clearing to the hut. How could anyone be so selfish? She lifted the half-empty whiskey bottle and stared at it for a long time, then shook her head in disgust. What a complete waste.

By the time the moon had risen, the temperature dropped by several degrees and the wind had picked up. The cracks in the thatch of the tepee glowed with golden light from the tilley lamp. Inside Margaret sat with Annabelle in her lap while Lydia and Theodore were huddled under blankets.

According to Theodore, it was story time.

"And then the wolf said"—Theodore lowered his voice—"'Open up, little piggy, and let me in or I'll huff and I'll puff and I'll blow your house in!'"

"Assault, unlawful entry," Margaret murmured.

Theodore nodded. "He was a bad wolf."

"Bad wolf!" Annabelle said. "Sit! Sit! Sit! Bad wolf!"

"No, Annabelle, that's bad *word,* not bad *wolf.* Wurrr-da." Margaret sounded it out. "Word."

"Sit!" Annabelle grinned.

Margaret gave up and prayed the child would not be able to pronounce the *h* anytime soon.

"You wanna know what happens next?"

Margaret looked at Theodore. "What?"

"The wolf blew down the house of sticks like the house of straw and both piggies had to run and run and run to their brother's house of bricks. And the same thing happened again."

Margaret looked at him. "You mean the bad wolf—"

"Sit!"

Margaret ignored her this time and continued, "He blew down the house of bricks? He must have some powerful breath." Margaret thought one whiff of Hank's breath could have melted a few bricks.

"Nope." Theodore grinned.

"He didn't blow down the brick house?"

"Uh-uh. He tried and tried, but the smart little piggy had built a strong house. Finally the wolf climbed up on the roof and jumped down the chimney. And you know what happened next?"

"What?"

Theodore moved his face really close to Margaret's. She waited while he grinned. She sensed he was building up to the dramatic ending.

"The pigs put a big kettle of boiling water on the fire, and the wolf fell into it." His eyes grew big, and he wiggled his fingers at her. "And they cooked him and ate him all up!"

"They *ate* the wolf?" Margaret made a sick face. "That's horrible."

Lydia looked up and scowled at her. "My mother used to read us that story all the time. From a book of fairy tales. It's Theo's favorite story."

Margaret looked at Theodore, who was frowning thoughtfully, then at Lydia, whose look hadn't changed. Margaret closed her eyes and wanted to kick herself. At that moment she was certain she had disappointed the kids—Theodore in particular—just as much as Hank had.

In the wee hours of the morning, before the birds had wakened, before the tide had waned, and when all were sound asleep, another storm hit the island. It swirled in from the west with rain and clouds and wind. The rain pattered on the sand and on waxy tropical leaves. The clouds blocked the moon and the stars. And the wind blew in a howling wail that sounded like a wolf. Then it huffed and puffed and blew their huts down.

❧ 11 ❧

Hank awoke to the smell of wet goat hair, which was about the same as sticking his face in an old prison work boot. He quickly turned his head away, and immediately regretted it. He had one mother of a headache.

He closed his mouth tightly and regretted that, too. It felt as if a thousand woolly sheep had stampeded through his mouth. The goat shifted closer and shoved its stinking, wet muzzle in his face, then bleated loudly.

With a moan of pain, Hank rolled away, his head throbbing like a hammer on quarry rock. He held his head in his hands and waited for the pain to subside. After a few deep breaths, he squinted, then cracked open one burning, bloodshot eye.

Bright sunlight almost blinded him. He flinched and rubbed his face with his hands but quickly pulled his hands away and stared at them, scowling.

They were wet. He raised his head a few inches off the ground, an action for which he deserved a medal, and looked down at his clothes. He was soaking wet.

He sat upright slowly, very slowly, so his head could keep up with him. His eyes focused gradually. The goat stood a few feet away, staring at him while it chewed on something.

Hank watched it for moment, then saw some metal sticking out of its mouth. He frowned. What the hell was that blasted animal eating now? He started to crawl toward it, and the goat took two steps backward.

"What have you got there?"

The goat backed up again.

Hank muttered a few choice names and crawled forward.

The goat stepped back, still chewing.

"Here, goat. Come here."

The goat blinked.

"Come to Papa."

He shifted slightly, and the goat moved back again. He froze on his hands and knees, his gaze locked with the goat's.

One . . . two . . . three!

He shot forward.

The goat shot backward.

Hank landed face down in the monkey grass. He could feel the goat standing over him. Taking deep breaths, he slowly lifted his head.

Something hard conked him on the back of the head. He sucked in a breath of pain through gritted teeth and looked up.

The goat had trotted away.

Hank glanced down at the grass. A silver bottle was lying next to his head. He sat up, one hand rubbing the sore spot on his head.

Frowning, he picked up the bottle. He turned it one way, then the other. It had a few nicks and some teeth marks on it. But it was just an old perfume bottle, like the one he'd thrown overboard. Not a jewel or a stone on the worthless thing.

He took a deep breath and looked up, then froze. He dropped the bottle and slowly scanned the area around him. "What the hell?"

His hut was gone. The roof. The walls. Gone. All that remained was the bamboo frame.

He got up, and his feet sank in the muddy grass. He looked around for the first time and saw the remnants of a storm. Outside the bamboo frame, the palm fronds and leaves that had last night been his walls and roof now littered the ground and were sticking out from bushes and shrubs. Fresh rain dripped from the trees and bushes, and steam was beginning to rise from puddles of rainwater in the grass and sand.

He spun around and looked toward Smitty's tepee. There was nothing left standing. Only a huge messy pile of thatched matting that lay atop some of the trunks and crates she'd salvaged.

He swore and ran across the clearing, thinking she and those kids were somewhere under it all. He was a few feet away when he realized they weren't there at all.

He took off running down the beach. When he'd gone about a couple of hundred feet, he heard squeals of laughter and stopped.

Smitty stood in the shallow tide holding onto Annabelle's hands. Whenever a small wave would drift in on the low morning tide, she would fling the baby up like a swing, just letting her toes brush through the seafoam.

A few feet back, Theodore was burrowing in the sand. He looked up, then began to holler and jump up and down and point. Lydia rushed down from the bank, her arms filled with bananas.

Hank shielded his eyes from the bright sun and looked out toward where the kid was pointing on the eastern side of the water. Every few seconds, a group of porpoises arced one by one over the glassy sea, making white, foamy sea spray when they hit the water.

He remembered the first time he'd ever seen a school of porpoises leap from the sea like that. There was something sobering about it; the realization that other things lived on the same earth, an awareness that humans weren't the only things trying to eke out a life. Some long-buried part of him had reacted just like Theodore.

Watching them now, he still felt that same sense of awe. And he relished it because he hadn't felt that way for so long. Too long.

He stood there, soaking up the freedom to do whatever the hell he wanted. He watched the porpoises, something that in the past few years he'd forgotten existed.

With an overwhelming sense of bitterness, he wondered what else prison had stolen from him. In the distance he could hear sea auks crying from the cliffs. Their keening didn't sound like the call of birds but of men who had been condemned.

Men cried in prison. He had cried in prison. When no one knew.

He threw his head back and took in deep breaths of sea air. He was free. He wouldn't hear the loud and brittle clank of the cell closing tonight. He wouldn't have heard it last night either, but the whiskey he'd drunk was a little insurance. It gave him one night of sound sleep, something he felt as if he'd never get enough of.

He opened his eyes and looked above him, reminding himself he wasn't staked. He wasn't locked in a box in the scorching sun. His ankles weren't chained together, and he wasn't in a cell.

Overhead, gulls soared across the blue sky and circled above the dancing porpoises, swooping down, teasing. Off to the right, a waterspout shot up from a group of rocks near the edge of the headland, and its spray picked up rainbow colors in the bright morning air. The sea was easy; the waves drifted in instead of beating the shore.

And Smitty and Annabelle were laughing.

He looked back at them. Smitty stood in the shallow water, Annabelle propped on her hip while the tide lapped at her calves and sprayed water up her thin, ragged skirt. He could see through it.

"Hank! Hank!" Theodore ran up the beach. He skidded to a stop in front of him. "Look!"

Hank looked in the kid's outstretched hands. Bits of blue, green, and amber glass polished smooth and round by the force of the sea were stuck to his small palms with globs of wet sticky sand.

"You know what these are?"

"Pieces of colored glass."

"Uh-huh. Miss Smith said that if you melt the sand on this beach and then let it cool, you know what you'd have?"

"What?"

"You would have glass."

Hank watched Smitty laughing at Annabelle. "She said that, did she?"

"Uh-huh."

A wave splashed on her, and she raised the squealing little girl high in the air. From this distance Hank could see those incredible legs of Smitty's limned by sunlight through the wet, flimsy cotton of her dress. With her arms raised, her whole figure from her breasts down stood in silhouette.

He forgot to breathe. Hell, he couldn't breathe.

Spilling down her back was a thick wad of tangled blond hair, damp and curling and so damn female that even for a wagon load of gold he wouldn't have pulled his gaze away.

"And look at this."

"Yeah, kid." Hank watched her. If he moved just a little closer and to the left, he could get a better view.

Theodore tugged on the tail of his shirt. "You're not paying attention."

Hank grunted, his gaze stuck on Smitty.

The kid tugged again. "Hank?"

Nothing.

"Hank." Theodore's voice had grown smaller. And in that sound Hank heard something he hadn't thought about in too many years to count. The pain of being ignored. He knew what it was like to be treated as if he didn't exist.

He glanced down. Theodore looked back at him with such awe and expectancy that Hank felt a small twinge of that guilt he had told himself he never experienced.

Theodore quickly dumped the bits of glass in his pants' pocket and pulled out something else. He raised his sandy hands higher. "See?"

He looked at the kid's hands. Cupped inside them was a small but perfect sand dollar.

Hank stared at it and laughed to himself. It hadn't taken a wagon load of gold to rip his gaze away from the most incredibly carnal sight he'd seen in years.

It had taken one small white sand dollar.

Only a sucker could be had that cheap.

He shook his head. His life story.

The salvaged trunks turned out to be more than a godsend. To Margaret, they were as welcome as buried treasure. And something that was just as handy was Hank's skill at picking locks, although she didn't tell him so. She was busy going through one of the two trunks he'd unlocked.

She gasped loudly and straightened, then realized Annabelle was asleep nearby. She cast a quick glance at the baby. She hadn't moved. Clutching her prize find, she turned back. "Look," she said in a loud whisper and held up a small bar of French-milled soap.

Lydia and Theodore blankly stared at her. The

same way they had when she'd found the tooth-brushes and tin of toothpowder.

She held it out. "See? It's soap. Real soap! We can bathe and wash our hair." She closed her eyes briefly. "A bath. A real bath." She sighed and gripped the soap a little tighter.

"Yuk!"

She crossed her arms and gave Theodore a direct look. "A bath wouldn't hurt you, young man."

He shivered and wrinkled his freckled nose.

She felt Hank's look and glanced up at him. He was eyeing her soap.

"I believe I'll keep this," she said pointedly and tucked it into the deep pocket of her skirt, the same safe place she'd put a toothbrush and tooth powder.

She and Hank had spent the past half an hour arguing over what was important to their survival. Margaret had gathered clothing, toothbrushes, a hair brush, and something that caught Lydia's attention—satin hair ribbons.

Hank had a pocketknife, tools, and a flint. He just finished picking another of the locked trunks and opened the lid. She watched him pull out a man's cap with a long brim, look at it, then put it on. It fit perfectly.

Must be a large size, she thought.

Then he bent over and began to randomly toss things aside as if they were completely worthless.

The goat came trotting by and dropped something at Hank's feet. He scowled down, bent over, picked it up, gave it a disgusted look, then pitched it toward the water. The goat brayed and trotted after it.

"What was that?"

"Some old worthless bottle." He bent over the trunk and threw out something else.

"You keep throwing things away."

"Worthless," he muttered and stuffed something back inside the trunk.

Margaret propped her fists on her hips. "What was that?"

"This?" Hank held up a corset by its tape strap.

She raised her chin. "I'll take that, please."

He stared at her, his gaze on the area below her chin. After a few seconds, he pointedly looked at the corset, held it up, and turned it this way, then that, eyeing it. He looked back at her figure and frowned. "Think it'll fit?"

She snatched it away. "You are so very witty."

It took a minute or two for him to stop chuckling. "Now here's something useful." He held up a deck of playing cards and shuffled them with the ease of someone born with a deck of cards in his hand. He did a fancy shuffle by arching his hands.

Theodore looked up at him with awe. "Can you teach me to do that?"

"No!" Margaret said.

"Sure," Hank said at the same time.

She gave him a pointed look. "He's a child."

"The best time to learn." He handed the cards to Theodore, who sat in the sand and tried to shuffle them. Cards flew everywhere. A chagrined Theodore picked them up and handed them back to Hank.

"Like this." Hank bent down and fit his hands over Theodore's. He cupped the cards and let them shuffle into a neat stack into the boy's fingers.

She didn't say a word. She couldn't, not when she saw Theodore's delighted face turn up to grin at Hank. She cast a glance at Lydia, who was also watching them. "Perhaps you can show Lydia, too."

"I don't want to shuffle any silly old cards," Lydia said and walked toward the goat.

She waited until Hank straightened, then looked him in the eye. "You toss away clothing, a hair brush, combs, and ribbons, claiming they are useless. But you keep a deck of playing cards?"

He shrugged. "I don't need hair ribbons."

"But Lydia does."

Hank looked at Lydia. "What's she blubbering about now?"

"She's hurting."

"Yeah, well, she'd better learn to get over it."

Margaret shook her head in disgust. He wasn't going to help her in that quarter. She looked at the girl standing beside the goat, stroking its coat.

Margaret started toward her but stopped when Lydia turned to look at her. They watched each other for a moment. As if Lydia could read her thoughts, she stiffened, then she spun around, presenting her back.

It stopped Margaret in her tracks. She wanted to help but didn't know how. She decided to give the girl a little time alone and herself some time to try to analyze the situation and come up with some way to try to reach the girl.

Margaret glanced back at Hank who was tossing things into piles so swiftly she had to blink. She moved closer. In his keeper pile were dice, a flint, a pistol, a pocketknife, a pair of black pants, and a belt. All but the dice were useful items.

It still annoyed her that he'd tossed aside things she and Lydia could have used. She started to turn back but stopped when she saw another stack of things. "What's that pile for?"

"You."

"Pardon me?"

"It's your stuff. Things women need."

There were a few pots and pans and some skillets, a scrub brush, and a small hand broom—the type a maid used to brush clothing—a flat iron, a sewing basket, and a cap and apron.

She crossed her arms. "I don't clean. I can't sew and I can't cook."

"You're a smart woman. With a brain *and* an education. You'll learn." He paused. "Remember, counselor, in your own words: Man hunt. Ugh! Woman cook."

"I'm used to having my words thrown back at me by men who think they are superior."

"I don't *think* I'm superior." He stood there rubbing his black beard. "I know it."

She watched him for a moment. He scratched his neck again.

"You know, a little soap might help."

He looked at her. "Might help what?"

She gave his beard a pointed look. "Your itch."

His cocky gaze poured over her slowly, then he gave her a perfectly lascivious grin.

She cast a quick glance at the children, who were a small distance away, then leaned close enough for him to hear her whisper. "Don't say it."

"Say what?" His voice was dripping with feigned innocence.

"Whatever it was you were thinking."

He laughed obnoxiously. "You think enough for all of us. I don't think, sweetheart. I *do.*"

She could have sworn she saw his chest swell. No doubt his head did.

She reached into the trunk she'd been going through and whapped a leather case into his hands. "Then here. *Do* this."

He stared at the case.

"It's a shaving kit."

"I can see that." He opened it.

"There's a straight razor, a mug and brush, a comb, and a toothbrush."

"Yeah." He scratched his beard again even harder. Then he shrugged. "No lather." He turned toward the pile of things he'd tossed aside and started to toss it away, too.

"Wait! Here!" Without thinking, she plopped that wonderful little ball of soap into his hand.

His fingers closed around it so quickly she blinked.

"Thanks, Smitty." He tossed it in the air in front of her nose, then snatched it out of midair. "I never even had to ask." He started laughing, a sound she could only describe as crowing.

She stared at him.

"Think I'll go take a bath. A *real* bath." He sauntered off toward the stream. "Have fun here, sweetheart."

She just stared at his back, wanting to slap herself in the forehead.

He began to whistle a tune that sounded suspiciously like *The Old Gray Mare*.

Better yet, she thought, she would like to slap *him* in the forehead. He was heading off to bathe with her soap.

Very simply, very easily, he'd outmaneuvered her.

Hank learned a few things about Smitty that morning as he strolled off to take a bath, casually tossing that ball of soap. She could whip past him, and from right beneath his nose, she could snatch a ball of soap out of midair. She also ran a helluva lot faster than he'd thought she could.

He stopped and watched her race toward a wall of rocks that protected a pool beneath the waterfall. She had her ragged skirt hiked up around her knees, and he had a great view of those long legs.

Hank discovered something else. Smitty jiggled in all the right places.

She looked over her shoulder once as if she had expected him to be right behind her. He waved, then sat down on a rock and waited.

It only took a few minutes for her to poke her head out from behind the rocks.

"I can't take a bath. I don't trust you."

He didn't say anything, just picked a banana from a nearby plant and began to peel and eat it.

She climbed out from behind the rocks, tucking a

toothbrush and the tin of tooth powder back into the pocket of her skirt. She plopped down next to him, and took the ball of soap from her pocket. She held it in one hand and looked at it for a minute. Then she glanced at him. "I don't suppose you'd give me your word you'll stay away, will you?"

He finished the banana. "Nope."

"I didn't think so." She stared at the ball of soap with a covetous look. After a minute of silence, she sighed and held out the soap to him. "You win."

He tossed the banana peel away and took the soap, laughing. "You're a good loser."

She watched him laugh. "It figures you'd be a poor winner." Her tone was resigned. She rested her chin on one hand. "I suppose it was too much to hope that you would accept this without braying like an ass."

"Never give up hope, Smitty." He stood and lightly tossed the soap in the air just to tempt her. "A smart woman like yourself should know that." He started to walk around the rocks but stopped halfway and looked back at her. "And while you're at it, you might want to hope for a fairy godmother to magically appear. Or a guardian angel. Leprechauns? Maybe even a genie in a magic lamp!" Chuckling, he rounded the rocks, then leaned back out and said, "Or Santa Claus!"

A banana flew past his head.

❧ 12 ❧

A good hour later, Hank stood waist deep in a small pool near the base of the waterfall. He'd lathered himself three times. Smitty had been right. This was great.

No routine. No schedule. No guard with a club or a whip waiting to beat him if he thought Hank took a minute too long. He didn't have to soap up, rinse, and get out before the guard beat the crap out of him.

He rubbed Smitty's soap over his chin and neck until his face was thickly lathered. He dunked the razor in the water and began to shave one side of his face.

"Hank!"

He glanced toward the dense wall of lava rocks that shielded the pool from the beach. Smitty's voice had come from the other side.

"Hank?" She called out again. "Can you hear me?"

"Yeah."

"Are you decent?"

He laughed loud and hard. "I'm never decent, sweetheart."

There was a lapse of silence.

He could picture her on the other side of those rocks, her hands on her hips as she muttered something. He chuckled again and drew the razor over his upper lip.

After another second he shouted, "You say something?"

There was a pause.

He shaved his jaw line.

"I've been thinking."

God, now we're in trouble. He glanced up at the sun and figured it was about midmorning sometime. "So early?"

"What?"

"Nothing." He shaved the other side of his face.

"Did you hear me?"

"You've been thinking," he repeated, listening with only half an ear.

"That's right. I still believe that we should work together."

He drew the straight razor over his chin again and

down his neck. His mind flashed with something they could do together. *If she didn't think or speak.*

"Regarding this shelter we need to construct. I spent most of the early morning assessing the situation . . ." She rambled on.

He rinsed the lather off the razor, splashed water on his chin, and rubbed his fingers over his jaw. Smooth.

"If you'll just listen . . ."

He ducked underwater and surfaced, then shook the water from his face and head.

"Of course it is the most fair decision and logical compromise we can reach, considering our situation . . ."

He ran his fingers through his hair to slick it back from his face. He got out of the pool, brushing off the water that clung to the hair on his chest and stomach before he stepped into a pair of black trousers and buttoned them.

"If one has no defense, then one should consider settling. For the sake of the children and for our own benefit, if we pool our efforts, we can successfully . . ."

He slung his dirty clothes over a shoulder and walked toward the rocks while he put on the belt. He rounded the rocks just as he was tightening the buckle over his pants.

"I'm certain that you will see that we can all gain from this propos—" She stopped talking so swiftly it caught him off guard.

He jammed the belt through the catch and looked up.

Smitty stood there, staring at him. Her mouth hung open. And she was silent.

He looked behind him, then next to him, then back at her. "What's wrong?"

Her mouth snapped shut. She didn't say anything, which made him immediately suspicious. He crossed his arms over his chest and pinned her with a dark look meant to intimidate.

After a tense second or two, he noticed she swallowed thickly as she averted her eyes and stared at his feet. "I was just suggesting that we should pool our efforts."

"Why?" He stared at the top of her head.

She looked up, blinked once. "To build a chest together."

"Huh? What the hell are you talking about?"

"Hut," she said in a rush. "I meant build a *hut* together."

"Why?"

"That's why." She pointed at the clearing.

Hank and Margaret stood side by side, staring at what was left of their shelters.

"Your frame is still standing even after the storm."

"Yeah."

"The thatch Lydia and I made stayed together in spite of the winds and rain. But our frame collapsed. Your walls blew away, yet your frame withstood the weather. It makes perfect sense to rebuild with your frame and our thatch. A group effort."

He gave her a long look, then glanced back at the remains of the huts. He rubbed his smooth jaw, then looked back at her. "We'll build where I decide."

"But I truly believe it is most beneficial to have the hut near water."

"So it can flood whenever it rains?"

She glanced from him to her spot. He followed her gaze. He knew the ground was too low, and when it really rained, the monsoon rains of the winter, that stream and pool would flood the area where she'd built that tepee thing.

He turned back and caught her staring at his chest.

"Monsoons," he said before he realized she wasn't paying attention. Her mouth was open slightly, and he realized why she was acting so strangely. He wasn't the only one feeling those mating howls.

He didn't grin, but it was an effort not to. Instead, he closed the distance between them. She shook her head, then looked up at him. Her eyes widened just slightly, and she took a step back. He watched her for a moment and had to give her credit. She was giving him one of those direct looks of hers. But she was breathing through her mouth, and he'd bet she didn't know it.

He took another step forward. "A partnership? You and me."

She took a step back and nodded. "Equal partners."

"A woman partner?"

"Exactly." She took another step back and butted up against the rocks.

He shrugged and closed the last couple of feet separating them. He looked down at her.

"Is that a yes?"

He nodded.

"Well . . . then." She stiffened slightly and looked around them for a second. As if she wanted to shove him away and run like hell. She took a deep breath, squared her shoulders, and stuck out her hand. "Agreed."

He stared at her outstretched hand. His hand closed about hers.

He smiled down at her. She relaxed her guard slightly and gave him a tentative smile.

He jerked her against him, clamped one hand on the back of her head and the other on her butt. His mouth closed over hers.

In the most perfect reaction, she gasped. He filled her mouth with his tongue and tightened his hold.

Her arms fell to her sides, and she went limp. If it weren't for his hand on her butt, holding her up against him, he figured she might have sunk into the sand. Hell, from the deadweight feel of her, she might have sunk through to Argentina.

As suddenly as he had kissed her, he pulled back and looked down at her. She gained her balance and stared up at him in stunned silence. Not moving.

Amazingly, not talking. And from her dazed expression, she wasn't thinking either.

He let go of her. "Sure, sweetheart." He raised his hand and gave her a light swat on the backside.

Her gaping mouth snapped shut, and she went as stiff as a palm tree.

"You've got yourself a deal." He gave her a wink and he strolled away. Whistling.

There was an old Hebrew proverb Margaret had read once: When a rogue kisses you, count your teeth. She still had thirty-two teeth left, but she wasn't certain she had any sense left.

She walked down the beach toward Lydia and the baby. Annabelle toddled alongside her older sister. The baby sat in the sand, then picked up a banana and held it up to her sister.

Lydia stared at the fruit with a weak look. "I'm sick of those."

"I'm sick, too," Margaret muttered as she plopped down to sit in the sand near the water. She had to be sick, she thought and pinched the pounding bridge of her nose, trying to will herself to forget Hank Wyatt existed.

But her mind flashed with the image of the man emerging from behind the rocks, his head bent and chest exposed while he buckled the belt on his pants. There was something wickedly private about that image as if she'd been part of an intimate moment.

It hadn't bothered him. But it bothered her just as much as how he looked cleaned up. He had a strong square jaw, hair as black as the devil, classic features. A handsome man.

She *was* sick.

Frowning, she stared at the sand and watched the waves slosh near her bare feet. She poked her lips with a finger, then licked them. They tasted like banana and tooth powder. And Hank.

119

There had to be something wrong with her. Shock. A delayed reaction to the trauma of being shipwrecked. Something. Some perfectly logical reason why she would feel something so incredibly illogical.

She put her palm up to her forehead. Perhaps she was fevered. She felt her cheeks and face. They didn't feel hot. She wondered if malaria could make a person go numb like she had.

With a sudden sense of desperation, she searched her body for mosquito bites. There were none. Just as there was no logical reason for her reaction to Hank.

He'd kissed her, an act she certainly had experienced before. She *was* thirty-two years old. But she had acted like a young girl, standing there without a coherent thought in her head.

She rested her head in one hand and took a deep breath. Nothing was making sense. It was almost as if she had stepped into another world, an odd underworld, like Lewis Carroll's Alice. A world where she didn't even know herself. She closed her eyes and saw the foolish image of herself playing croquet with a flamingo. Then she imagined Hank standing behind her, his hands on hers, helping her hit the croquet ball.

Her eyes shot open. She was almost afraid to close her eyes again, afraid of what her mind might come up with next, so she stared down the beach.

Hank and Theodore weren't in sight. They had gone to search the north end of the beach, combing the beach for anything they could use.

"No, Annabelle. I don't want it."

She looked up at Lydia, who was pushing away a banana that Annabelle was trying to stuff in her face. "I'm sorry. What did you say?"

"I'm sick of bananas. Isn't there anything else to eat?"

"Breadfruit. Those large round things, but Hank said they have to be cooked." She paused. "How does one cook a breadfruit?" She gazed off at one of the breadfruit trees.

Lydia didn't respond.

Margaret sighed and turned back to look at the sand. After a moment, she picked up a black shell and held it up. "There are plenty of mussels."

Lydia wrinkled her nose.

"Mussels are wonderful." She opened one of them. "Especially these little ones with the green tips."

Lydia groaned.

"Really. There's a little Italian restaurant back home in North Beach. They serve the best mussels in white wine." Margaret stared at the black shell in her hand. She turned it this way, then that. "If I could only figure how to cook these things." She looked at Lydia. "I'm not much of a cook."

"Mama was a wonderful cook."

Margaret saw an opening. She looked at Lydia and smiled. "Was she?"

Lydia nodded.

"What did she cook?"

The girl shrugged. "Stuff." Lydia started to walk away.

"Where are you going?"

"Hank said we needed driftwood. I see some down the beach."

"I'll help." Margaret stood up.

"That's okay," Lydia said. "I can do it by myself." She kept on walking.

Margaret sat on a rock, her chin in her hand, her elbow propped on a knee, thinking about everything and concentrating on nothing. Annabelle plopped down next to her and was getting ready to eat a handful of waxy kelp leaves.

Margaret snatched the leaves away. "No!" She shook her finger. "No."

Annabelle blinked at her, then frowned at the leaves.

Margaret picked up a banana and peeled it. "Look,

Annabelle. See? Bah-nan-nah. A banana. Here. Eat this." She held it out.

Annabelle stared at her.

Margaret took a big bite and made her eyes go wide. "Mmm, good."

Good grief, I sound like a moron.

Annabelle must have thought so too because she was busy playing with her own feet and completely ignoring her.

Margaret tossed the banana over her shoulder. Lord, how life could change almost overnight. Here she was talking baby talk, thinking unfathomable thoughts about a convict, a man who held in contempt everything in which she believed. She was trying desperately to communicate with a young girl who wanted nothing to do with her.

She picked up Annabelle, then stared bleakly at the ocean. Nothing was right, she thought. A few minutes later, she walked down the beach.

On the north side of the lagoon, Hank walked down the stretch of sand pulling along a makeshift wagon—a wooden crate with a piece of rope. It was half filled with stones, rope, and driftwood—anything that they could use to build a better shelter on the island.

He figured last night's storm should have stirred up the seas and washed up plenty of debris they could put to good use. So he walked along the section of fine sand that was still wet from the rain but fast growing warm and steamy in the bright sun.

"Hank! C'mere! Here's one! Come see!" Theodore stood a few yards away, his shirt flapping in the slight breeze and pants rolled up like Hank's. He'd tried to make a cap from banana leaves and kelp, but the trade wind had loosened his childish weaving and the leaves were trailing down the sides of his head like lop ears. His bare feet were half covered by the foamy tide and a long, wet piece of old weathered rope dangled from one hand.

He walked over to the kid.

"See?" He held the rope up proudly.

Hank ruffled his red hair, and more banana leaves slipped free. "Yeah. You did good. Put it in the crate with the driftwood."

Before he had finished his sentence, the kid put the rope in the crate and was back at the tide line, bent over, and rummaging through the kelp and shells that littered the beach.

"Hank, c'mere! Look at this!"

At this rate, he thought, he would only find enough wood to build a small fire. He moved over and looked at the seashell that the kid wanted him to see. It was just like the last twenty he'd showed him.

Hank stood there for a moment, then said, "Listen, kid."

Theodore looked up from kneeling in a bed of kelp, his fists filled with seashells.

Hank nodded down the beach. "I'm going to walk down that way and search that section of beach. You stay here and go through the seaweed. Make a pile of anything you find."

"Okay!"

"And don't wander off. Keep me in sight. You understand?"

Theodore nodded seriously.

And Hank moved on.

Muddy lay inside his bottle, three plush tasseled pillows behind his head, the sound of waves crashing in the distance. No bouncing around. No flying through the air. Just peace and quiet. Everything was in its place. And he was reading a dime novel.

Terrible Tom Torture was about to abscond with brave lawman Bowie Bradshaw's horse *and* his woman, Clementine Purdy, in *The Adventures of Bushwhacking Bowie Bradshaw*. It was one of the small books he had slipped inside his bottle before he had granted his former master his last wish.

He was just reading the part where Tom had raised his Colt to shoot Bowie in the back when Muddy heard something and looked up, listening.

Thud . . . thud . . . thud!

He dropped his book and stared up at the stopper way up in the top of his bottle. Had he heard footsteps?

Thud . . . thud . . . thud . . .

There they were again. They were clearly footsteps.

He shot off his bed and leaped up and down. His purple turban slipped over one eye, and he shoved it back on his head. The bells on the curly toes of his shoes tinkled, and he waved his hands frantically.

Here I am! Here I am! Find me!

He stopped and held his breath, listening, waiting, hoping.

There was no sound but the surge of the sea.

A moment later, the footsteps just walked past.

Muddy stood staring at his stopper, then he looked at his rug for a moment, sighed, and sagged back against the cushions. The same thing had happened so many times over the years that disappointment was becoming a natural emotion.

He glanced back at the novel, but he'd lost interest in Bowie Bradshaw's troubles. He rested his chin on his hand and wished for a little luck and excitement in his boring and lonely existence.

A second later the bottle tilted suddenly, then shook up and down. Muddy flew back and forth, tumbling upside down and sideways. He bounced on the cushions and pillows and ducked when the cursed baseball bat flew past his head.

Then it happened.

The stopper popped open.

A shaft of bright golden sunlight pierced the bottle's interior.

In a cloud of purple smoke, Muddy blasted upward. Like the suction in a waterspout, air pulled at his silk turban and sucked on his golden earrings. A cloud of magical purple smoke swirled around him, and he passed through the mouth of the bottle into the thick, sweet-smelling air of the tropics.

He curled in a smoky circle and spiraled to the ground. His feet hit the sand. He put his right hand to his forehead and bent low in a salaam while the cloud dissipated.

The ancient lines of the genii ran through his head by rote. He had said the words *Greetings, oh master* enough throughout the centuries. But in a moment of whimsy, his mind flashed with the image of hero Bowie Bradshaw.

Muddy dropped the salaam and raised his head. He tugged on the waist of his billowing pants. "Whoa . . . Howdy there, pardner! This here's yor lucky day!"

He heard a loud gasp. It was always the same. Disbelief. Skepticism. Cynicism. He waved the smoke aside and blinked a couple of times.

The bright sunshine turned his vision into a blur for a second. He shook his head slightly and rubbed a hand over his eyes, then stared at the face of his newest master—a little red-haired boy.

❧ 13 ❧

"You're a child."

"You're a genie!"

Muddy clamped his gaping mouth shut. The boy's speech was American. He was red haired, freckled, and small, barely three feet tall. He was dressed in ragged brown pants with the cuffs rolled up and patches of damp sand on the knees. Sticks of driftwood and bits of mossy rope stuck out of his baggy pants' pockets.

He wore no shoes, and his bare toes curled in the

wet foam of a receding wave. Next to the boy's right foot, the silver stopper from his bottle lay amid a scattering of spilled seashells and bits of cobalt glass.

A rope of kelp the color of Greek olives hung around the open neck of the boy's dirty white shirt. Low on his forehead he wore a crown of floppy waxy green banana leaves artlessly woven into a makeshift cap that looked like a tropical version of Nero's olive wreath.

"A real honest-to-goodness genie," the boy said with such utter belief and awe that Muddy wanted to prostrate himself at the boy's bare feet.

A believer . . . a believer! Praise Allah and belly up to the bar, boys!

The boy looked from him back to the silver bottle. He raised the bottle to his eye and squinted inside for a second, then stared at Muddy. He frowned. "How'd you get through there?"

Muddy watched the boy closely. "The same way St. Nicholas comes down the chimney."

The boy's eyes grew as big as golden dinar. "Do you know Santa Claus?"

Muddy crossed his arms over his chest. "Do reindeer fly?"

"Santa's reindeer do." There was no doubt in the child's voice.

Yes! Yes! Yes! A true believer!

The boy looked inside the bottle, turning it this way and that way.

"As surely as reindeer fly, I"—Muddy thumped his chest with a thumb—"know Santa Claus."

The boy gave him a freckled grin.

Muddy took a deep breath and tapped together the thick gold bracelets on his wrists three times. He placed his right palm on his forehead and bent low. "Greetings, oh master!" He turned and peeked out from beneath his arm at the boy staring at him in rapt wonder. "I am Muhdula Ali, ancient purple genie of Persia. As a reward for freeing my most humble and subservient self from the lonely and desolate confines of my sadly unadorned silver bottle—"

"Huh?"

Still bent in a salaam, Muddy turned his head slightly and winked at his new master. "Give me a minute. I haven't gotten to the important part yet. Now where was I?" Muddy stared at the sand and mouthed the ancient words. "Ah, yes, my sadly unadorned silver bottle, I, the most gratefully indebted purple genie, bondaged slave to—" He paused and shot a quick look back at the boy. "What's your name?"

"Theodore."

"To my master, Theodore, hereby grant him three wishes." Muddy dropped the salaam and straightened. He crossed his arms over his chest and waited.

"Wishes? I get wishes?"

Muddy nodded. "Three wishes."

"Holy cow!"

"Yes, they are."

"Huh?"

"Cows are holy. But I wouldn't wish for one. They can start fires."

The boy's face creased into a confused frown.

Muddy gave a wave of his hand. "Never mind."

"I know my wish, I know, I know!" Theodore hopped up and down in excitement. "I wish my mother and father were alive again!"

Muddy should have explained the limitations first. He dropped his arms at his side. "I'm sorry, Master Theodore, but my powers cannot bring back those who have died."

"You can't?" The boy's face fell.

Muddy shook his head.

"Why?"

"I can only fulfill wishes in this life."

The boy just stood staring at the sand. A lazy wave sloshed over his bare feet and ankles, but the boy didn't look up or move. In a moment thicker than the tropical air, he squatted down and picked up a couple of the seashells near his feet, then turned one over in his small hand. Muddy had the feeling he wasn't seeing the shells. When the boy finally looked up at him, it was through the damp eyes of a wounded child. "That was the only wish I had."

A little while later Margaret was crouched down on all fours, her cheek pressed to the sand as she stared at a pile of wood that refused to light. She struck another safety match just as the rope at her waist jerked her back.

She turned. "Annabelle! Come here." She waited. "Annabelle!" The match singed her fingers. "Ouch!" She dropped it and stuck her burned finger in her mouth.

Annabelle was running in circles again.

She sat back on her heels. "Come here right now, Annabelle. Annabelle! I'm talking to you."

The baby stopped and looked at her, then plopped down in the sand and grinned. After a long pause, she waved her tiny hand. "Hi!"

"Come here, please." Margaret patted the ground next to her. "Come here."

The baby stuck her two fingers in her mouth and grinned.

Margaret plopped down in the sand herself and rested her arms on her raised knees. About twenty feet separated them.

Annabelle watched her as if doing so were the most important thing in world.

Margaret returned her look. "Why won't you do what I ask? Why? I've tried talking to you. I've been patient. I've asked nicely. I've asked repeatedly. This is getting absurd. You know that, don't you?" Margaret poked herself in the collarbone with one finger. "I'm the adult here. Do you understand? Me. You are the child."

Annabelle raised one hand and wiggled her fingers at her. "Hi."

Margaret sighed. She couldn't reason with her. When could one reason with a child? Wasn't everyone born with the ability to reason?

It was as bad as talking to Hank. And she got the same results. None.

Margaret cast a quick glance at the pot of mussels she had gathered from the beach. Cooking them couldn't be that difficult, she thought.

Lighting the fire was another matter. She stared at the pile of driftwood. It was too damp to catch from just the small quick flame of a match.

She thought about it for a moment, then picked up a piece of wood and broke it in half. It wasn't soaked through, just damp from last night's rain. She tossed it on the pile and tried to light the dry center of the wood with a third match, something she knew she shouldn't be wasting.

Still nothing. She stared at the wood for a minute. She needed something she could burn long enough to make the wood catch. She looked around for something useless to burn without the worry that she'd be sorry later.

After going through all their supplies, she gave up. There wasn't one thing she felt she could burn.

The rope yanked on her waist again. She'd had enough. She whipped her head around. "Annabelle!"

The baby was toddling toward her, Hank's whiskey bottle in her small hand.

"Oh, you brilliant child. There is something completely useless." Margaret smiled and reached out her arms. Annabelle toddled into them and sat in her lap and let her take the bottle away. "What a good little girl you are." She gave the baby a gentle pat on the head.

Margaret pulled out the cork, lifted the bottle to her nose, and shuddered. It was strong. She read the label.

One hundred and twenty proof, which as she recalled meant it was sixty percent alcohol.

She smiled.

She got one of the pots and pans Hank had given her—bless his cocky black heart—and she dumped the rest of the whiskey into it. She tossed a lit match in the pan. And whoosh! Blue flames danced around the pan.

She laughed rather wickedly as she stuck a piece of wood into the flame.

A few minutes later she had the perfect fire. She picked up the empty bottle and grinned, then tossed it over her shoulder in the same who-needs-it kind of way Hank had tossed away things. Then she sat there, Annabelle in her lap as she watched the fire lick into the air.

She gave a big sigh. Cooking might not be so difficult after all.

Hank walked back up the beach and felt someone's stare. He looked up, and he saw Lydia standing there, her arms loaded with driftwood.

Odd, he'd have thought she would have stayed with Smitty. But she was looking off in the distance, toward the thick jungle and the volcano.

He closed the distance between them, then stopped when he was a few feet away from her.

She glanced back at him, then said, "I found some driftwood."

Hank nodded at the crate. "Drop it in there."

She started to take a step but stopped. "Do you think anyone will find us?"

He shrugged. "I don't know."

"Hank! Hank!" Theodore came running up the beach. "Look what I found! Look!"

Another seashell, Hank thought with an internal groan.

Theodore tripped and fell, then quickly scampered up. He ran toward them with something in his hand.

Lydia touched Hank's arm. "How do you know when a volcano erupts?"

Hank glanced back at her. "There's smoke and ash in the air. Why?"

"Look." She pointed toward the west. "Is that a volcano?"

Hank turned around. Above a thick grove of trees and bushes near the sand, a large and billowing black cloud rose into the air.

"That's no volcano. That's coming from the beach!" He dropped everything and took off running, the children following after him.

Muddy had completely forgotten to explain to Theodore that he shouldn't run. So he clamped a large pillow over his head and hung onto the bed, which he'd long ago bolted to the base of the bottle. A good thing, too. When Theodore ran, everything flew.

His head jiggled and bobbed and his knees banged against the divan. The bells on his shoes rang like sleigh bells, and the sound of his things crashing together echoed a hollow sound throughout the bottle.

At one point, the bottle slammed so hard he lost his grip and tumbled head over heels against the opposite wall.

Stunned, he sat up, his vision a gallery of blinking stars. He wobbled slightly and shook his rattled head.

Thankfully, the bottle had stilled. He stared at the mess, then planted his fists on his hips and said, "And Bowie Bradshaw thinks he's got trouble."

He heard a loud shout from a vaguely familiar voice. Actually, what he heard was a loud curse. Then it started all over—the running, then jostling.

Pillows sailed through the air. A wine jug broke loose from its fitting in the wall and spiraled toward him, crashing right above his head. A cupboard opened and fruit spilled out. Pomegranates, figs, kumquats, and dates rolled like billiard balls across the carpets.

His turban flew one way, he flew another. He smacked against the floor. Dazed, he struggled to sit up. A second later an ancient brass hookah came at him, tumbling end over end. He saw it coming. Fast.

The hookah slipped over his head, banging against his noggin with a loud *bong!* It was like having a palace gong clang through his head.

He sat there, somewhat lightheaded, and tried to push the blasted thing off. It was stuck.

He blinked but couldn't see anything but the dark interior of the brass hookah. He raised a hand and felt around the opening. The water pipes were tangled around his neck like tentacles of an octopus.

He spat a healthy curse on the descendants of the idiot who invented the hookah, only to have his words come back at him in an irritating brass echo. He reached up and grabbed the brass handles and tugged.

His head was stuck in a hookah.

He sat there, hardly realizing that the bottle had ceased its wild motions. He had other problems.

He pulled and pulled. It wouldn't budge. *May Allah banish the cursed thing to the hottest and most desolate desert!*

But first, he thought, let him get his cursed head out of it.

❧ 14 ❦

"Smitty! What the hell are you doing?"

Margaret adjusted Annabelle on her hip and looked up. There was a wall of black smoke between them and the sound of Hank's bellowing voice. "I hear you, but I can't see you." *President Cleveland could hear him.*

"Dammit, woman!" Hank was suddenly beside her, grabbed her arm, and pulled them away from the smoke to an area where the air was clear. "Are you trying to burn down the whole island?"

Annabelle started to cry. Margaret started bouncing her on her hip and scowled up at Hank. "Stop shouting." She looked down at the baby. "It's okay, Annabelle, he just doesn't think before he shouts."

Annabelle continued to sob. Hank scowled at the baby, then looked at Margaret as if he expected her to shove the baby at him as she had in the lifeboat. He stepped back, out of reach, and glowered at the fire as if he were trying to make sense of it.

Theodore stepped closer to her and tugged on her skirt. "I found a genie."

Annabelle was still fussing loudly. Margaret brushed her tears away and continued to bounce the baby on her hip. "I don't know anyone named Jeannie, Theodore." Margaret stepped around him.

"His name is Muddy."

"No. It's not muddy, dear." Margaret gave him a pat on the head. "The sand soaks up the rain." She placed her hand on his shoulder. "Stand back, Theodore. The fire's spreading."

Hank kicked sand on the flames. "What the hell are you doing?"

"Cooking."

He looked down and scowled in the smoking pot. "It's blacker than lava rock in there." He straightened and turned back to her. "Are you cooking or burning?"

Margaret raised her chin a notch. "Mussel shells are black."

"I know that, Smitty, but they don't smoke."

"That's steam. I'm steaming them."

"Steam is white. Smoke is black." He used his

shirttail to pick up the handle on the hot pan—something she couldn't do because the fire had been a little bit bigger than she'd planned. He turned the pan upside down and shook it, then looked up. "Stuck like tar."

She had two choices: to continue her argument, which she knew was fallacious at best, or to capitulate. She stared at the fire. Cooking hadn't been so easy.

Before she could say anything, Hank dropped the pan and bent down. He picked up the empty whiskey bottle, looked at it for a very tense second, then faced her. "What happened to my whiskey?"

"I needed fuel to start the fire, so . . ." Her words just hung there.

"You used my whiskey to start a fire just so you could burn a pot of mussels?"

"No. I used the whiskey to make a flame that would burn long enough to light the wood—which was a shade damp from the rain—so *then* I could *steam* a pot of mussels."

He was looking at the empty bottle as if he wanted to throw it somewhere, perhaps at her.

"Lydia is sick of bananas and if the truth be told, I am, too."

He muttered something vile.

Theodore shifted closer to her and tugged on her skirt. He whispered rather loudly, "Why is Hank's face so red?"

"He's just hot, Theodore."

"You're damn right I'm hot!"

"Please stop shouting and swearing."

"Like hell I will!"

"I wonder if the genie in the bottle is hot," said Theodore. "I didn't ask him. I shoulda asked him."

"Yes, Theodore, that's nice," she said with a cursory glance. "But right now Hank and I are having a discussion." She turned back to Hank. "You're behaving poorly. I just used a little whiskey for a better purpose."

"Little? This bottle is empty!" Hank tipped it upside down and shook it. "Empty!"

Theodore moved to stand between them and held up the silver bottle. "My bottle's not empty. It has a real honest-to-goodness genie inside. Wanna see?"

Margaret didn't pay any more attention to Theodore than Hank did. They were locked in a battle, and Margaret didn't want to give in anymore than he did. Hank could be stubborn. She could be persistent. "Yes, well, I wasn't certain how much of those spirits I needed," she said.

"I had my own use for those spirits."

"So I saw last night." She looked him square in the eye, knowing her tone left no doubt as to what she thought of his drinking. She waited, then added, "My use is more logical and of benefit to all of us. I'm certain that if you would just stop shouting long enough to actually think about it, you'd find my use of that liquor logical, fair, and equal."

"You think too blasted much." Hank began to pace and muttered something about driving a man to drink.

"I could wish for something to drink," Theodore said, still holding up the bottle so one of them would look.

Margaret crossed her arms. "There's plenty of water."

"The genie gave me three wishes. Real wishes."

"There's no one named Jeannie on the island, Theodore. No matter how hard you wish for it."

"But I found a genie in a bottle! A real genie! Look!" He pulled the stopper out of the bottle, and a cloud of bright purple smoke billowed out in a spiral.

The clearing was suddenly silent.

In the distance, waves still washed the shore and the seagulls cried out, but those sounds were continual. Utter silence between the castaways was not.

Purple smoke flowed upward from the mouth of the silver bottle the way one imagined a ghost would materialize. It curled and wound upward, then seemed to flow in a circle above them like a hawk circled for food.

Margaret and Hank exchanged a stunned and wary look. Lydia gasped, and Theodore jumped up and down, saying, "See! See it!"

The purple smoke spread out like a fan, then drifted to the ground where it billowed, then faded slowly.

"What the hell?" Frowning, Hank stepped closer.

Margaret hugged Annabelle a little tighter. She stared at the smoke, then at the odd image before her. And she whispered, "Oh, my God . . ."

Muddy stood in the open, outside his bottle. But he was unable to see anything with the hookah on his head. Well, he thought, this ought to be interesting.

A woman screamed, "No, Hank! Not the knife!"

Muddy screamed. "Knives? Where?"

Instinctively he turned his head, forgetting he couldn't see. The hookah pipes flew left, then right, and the brass pipe tips hit the base and rang like finger symbols in his ears.

"No knives!" he shouted and stuck his hands high into the air quicker than Bowie Bradshaw could draw his gun. He just stood there, his heart and head pounding and his knees knocking together like cracking walnuts.

"Muddy?"

"I'm here, Master Theodore." Muddy paused, then whispered, "Are the knives gone?"

"I don't know what kind of scam this is, chump," said a man's voice, "but you hurt this kid and I'll use this knife so fast you won't know what gutted you."

Muddy forgot to breathe.

"No, Hank!" Theodore cried.

"Hank, please," the woman said. "I don't think he . . . it will hurt anyone. Look, its hands are in the air."

"Yes, Hank." Muddy stretched his hands even higher in the air. "Look. See? My hands are in the air."

Muddy heard someone take a step. He flinched and sucked in a breath of fear. His eyes tightly closed, he waited.

Nothing happened.

After another endless silence, he heard a deep male voice. "What the hell is it?"

"I'm a genie!" Muddy yelled so loudly the reverberation made his eyes cross and he wobbled drunkenly.

"Yeah, and I'm Aladdin."

"Hank," the woman warned.

"He *is* a genie," Theodore said stubbornly. "And he knows Santa Claus, too."

Muddy mentally groaned. Now there was an argument that would help convince them. He wanted to drop his head into his hands, but he was scared to death—*not a good choice of clichés, you idiot*—too scared to lower his hands.

"He is a genie!" Theodore said, his small voice panicked. "I know he's a genie. He gave me three wishes 'cause I let him out of the bottle." He began to cry.

"Theodore . . ." the woman said calmly, apparently trying to soothe the boy.

"He is! He is! Tell 'em, Muddy." Theodore cried harder. "Tell 'em who you are."

"I am Mudhula Ali, purple genie of Persia . . ." Muddy bent over in a salaam and immediately regretted it.

He fell forward, face forward, and the hookah landed in the sand with a dull *thong!* "May Allah curse this thing!" He lay there, flat on the ground, muttering, his face smashed against the rough brass wall of the hookah. "This is worse than riding a drunken camel." His voice sounded as if he was pinching his nose.

"Theodore, stay back!" the woman warned. "Hank . . . please."

"I'm harmless!" Muddy yelled. "No knives!" His voice rang around him in a full minute of echoes. He lay there and groaned.

Then there was nothing but silence.

"Muddy?" Theodore asked quietly. "Are you okay?"

"Yes, master. I just have a slight problem." He paused, then asked, "Is that Hank fellow still there?"

"Yeah. This Hank fellow is still here. And so's his knife."

Muddy swallowed hard, then said, "I'm not going to hurt anyone. I'm just going to try to get up." He waited, then said, "Pax? Truce?"

Hank didn't respond, and the seconds seemed to stretch into minutes.

"Just make sure to move slow," Hank finally warned. "Real slow and easy."

Muddy got to his knees, but the weight of the hookah kept his head tilted on the ground. He grabbed the hookah handles, and as he straightened to his knees, he lifted his head upright with a grunt.

Theodore asked, "What's that thing on your head?"

"It's a hookah, master, a water pipe, and I cannot get it off." Muddy pulled as hard as he dared, then moaned and sucked in a sizzling breath of pain.

"Does it hurt?"

Muddy nodded—a foolish move. His forehead banged against the hookah twice. Startled, he fell backward this time. He lay there, sprawled on his back, seeing an ocean of stars flash before his eyes like fireflies.

After a dizzy second or two, he answered in the quietest voice he could, "It only hurts if I try to pull it off, speak, or fall on it."

It was tensely quiet, too quiet, which made Muddy wonder exactly where Hank and his knife were.

"I wish . . ." Theodore cried out suddenly, "I wish the hookah was off Muddy's head!"

A second later, the hookah disappeared in a puff of purple smoke.

Hank stared down at some crackpot wearing earrings and stupid pants. The man was lying face up in the sand. He looked up at everyone, one by one, then lifted his fingers and wiggled them. "Howdy, folks."

"Don't move," Hank warned, shifting closer and slowly waving the knife with the street skill he'd learned some thirty years before.

The man looked at Hank, then at the knife blade, which caught a flash of sunlight. His stunned eyes filled with fear and grew huge. He shook so hard that the small golden hoop earrings he wore in each ear quivered.

He was dark skinned and big nosed, with thick eyebrows, dark eyes, and a pointed chin covered with a small black goatee—the same color as his hair, which stuck out from his head like the spiky leaves of an island pineapple.

Even though he lay flat on the ground, his stomach was paunchy. He wore a spangled multicolored vest that Hank couldn't imagine any man coming near— even for a bucketfull of sawbucks—and a wide sissy belt that went with those fluffy purple pants.

It got worse. His shoes were some shiny green and blue fabric, like a woman's fancy dress, all froufrou and shimmery. Hank looked down at the chump's feet and almost groaned aloud. The toes of the shoes were curled up. And if that wasn't bad enough, bells dangled from the tips like brass dingleberries.

Hank stared at the man's wrists, which were banded with wide bracelets made of what was, to Hank's practiced eye, eighteen-karat gold and worth at least a few months of living expenses. High living expenses.

Hank took a long and assessing look back up to the genie's face. His dark eyes were wide and cautious, watching every motion Hank made. The guy's face and neck were red from holding his breath.

"Stand up." Hank gestured with the knife, and the chump was on his feet before those bells on his toes could ring.

Even though he looked like a nut, there was something harmless about him. Probably because he was shaking so badly his earrings and gaudy vest shimmied. It was hard to believe there could be any imminent danger from someone who wore the same pants as the belly dancer at Club Morocco.

Hank raised the knife and cast a quick glance at Smitty. She sat on a rock, her mouth open and her face pale. He turned back. "Okay, chump. Spill it."

"What?"

"Your game."

The guy frowned. "Chess? Badminton? Base—"

Hank took a step closer. "I'm no fool. What are you? Some kind of mesmerist? Magician? What?"

"I told you. I'm a genie."

"Yeah and I told you I'm Sinbad."

"Actually, you said you were Aladdin—"

Hank pressed the knife against the man's neck.

"Sinbad," he babbled in a rush. "I'm an ignorant fool who must have heard you wrong."

"Don't hurt him! Please don't!" Theodore began to cry again, and he ran over and tugged on Hank's shirtsleeve.

"Stand back, kid."

"Muddy won't hurt me. He's a genie. He gave me wishes."

"Don't be stupid. There's no such thing as a genie, kid."

"Hank." Smitty said his name in a warning tone.

He looked up at her. She frowned at him and gave Theodore a pointed look.

"Well, hell, there *is* no such thing, Smitty. You know it, and I know it. He might as well know it."

Lydia looked up and spoke for the first time. "But then how did that hula thing get off his head?"

"Tricks, slight of hand, mirrors," Hank said.

"It's not a trick! I wished it. I used one of my three wishes."

"Thank you, Master Theodore. That was very generous."

Hank watched the exchange, listening, but still trying to figure out where the chump had hidden the hookah.

"If you'll remove your knife from my neck, I'll prove that I am what I claim. A genie."

Hank's laugh was bitter. "Right."

"Skepticism is as old as sand." The chump sighed as if this were a tired argument. "I've had two thousand years of proving who I am to skeptics."

"Just remember, one move that threatens any one of us"—Hank held the knife in front of the guy's face and smiled without humor—"and I'll be your last skeptic."

Hank slowly backed away. He grabbed Theodore's hand and pulled him back to the rock where Smitty still sat, silently and appearing thoughtful. She held the baby in her lap, and Lydia sat next to her. Hank watched for just an instant.

"Holy cow! Look!" Theodore began to jump up and down. "Look at Muddy!"

Hank whipped back around, the knife raised, and stared at the empty spot where the crackpot had been standing.

He quickly scanned the nearby bushes, thinking the guy had gotten away. Then he heard Smitty and Lydia gasp together.

"I'm up here."

Hank looked up and swore.

"Sit!" Annabelle mimicked.

He didn't look away. He couldn't. He just stared up at the sky.

The crackpot was flying.

❧ 15 ❧

"This is not happening," Hank said.

Margaret watched Hank continue to deny what they were seeing.

"It is not there." He closed his eyes and shook his head.

"I see it! It's magic!" Lydia said. "He is a genie!"

Hank opened his eyes, looked at Lydia, and frowned. His gaze shot to Margaret. He was still frowning. "Do you see it?"

With ironic timing, the genie flew right past Hank's nose, leaving a trail of purple smoke. Hank blinked, shaking his stubborn head. "I didn't see that."

"I did," Margaret told him.

"You, the educated, logical attorney, Miss It-Makes-Perfect-Sense, sees some crackpot in purple pants and earrings flying around us?"

She nodded.

"You know as well as I do that genies do not exist!"

"I see him. The children see him. You see him. We all see him. Therefore, he must exist."

"This is not happening," he repeated, then muttered, "Mirrors. Where are the mirrors?"

The genie buzzed around him like a bee, hovered over his head for a moment, then soared straight upward.

Hank scowled so hard his black eyebrows almost touched.

"It is not logical to assume that the existence of anything can be understood rationally in a world that is consistently irrational," Margaret explained.

He stared at her as if he'd been clobbered in the head. His gaze cleared, and he seemed to think about what she had just said. He stared at the sand for a long time, then he looked back to her and waved the knife. "You actually believe this crap?"

"I have to believe it. It would be illogical not to believe what I can see." Margaret was watching a purple genie fly. She turned back to Hank, who sat down on a nearby rock. He rested his wrists on his bent knees and stared down.

"I can see him flying, Hank."

He slowly looked up as the genie flew over the tops of the coconut palms, then soared downward purposely close to Hank's head. To Hank's credit, he didn't duck.

On the genie's next flight past, he snatched the cap from Hank's head.

"Give me that back! You little . . ." Hank shot up and tried to grab Muddy. He missed.

A few seconds later the cap came floating down next to Hank's feet. He stared at the cap lying in the sand, then grabbed it and jammed it back on his head. "Let me see that bottle, kid."

Theodore handed Hank the bottle. "I found it and got three whole wishes."

Hank lifted the bottle close to his eye and examined it the way a jeweler looked at a stone. The only clue that he recognized the bottle was the slight tightening around his mouth.

"It looks exactly like the bottle you threw away," Margaret said as casually as she could.

His eyes narrowed with the promise of retribution.

She gave him an innocent smile, then added, "Actually, you threw it away twice."

They argued for almost an hour. Muddy sat on a nearby rock, his chin resting in one palm, while his gaze darted back and forth, like someone watching a long volley in a game of lawn tennis.

"Now, Theodore," the woman named Margaret said, "don't worry. Hank doesn't mean to yell at you."

"Like hell!"

"Please stop bullying him. He's only a little boy. I'm certain he doesn't understand how important this is." Margaret turned back to Theodore and squatted down so she was eye level with him. "You understand that you are the only one who has the power to get us off this island."

"I understand," he said sullenly.

"One wish and we can all go home."

He stared at his bare toes. "I don't have a home."

Muddy saw her flinch. She straightened, took a deep breath, and pinched the bridge of her nose. She'd stepped right into that one.

"Look, kid." Hank barged in front of her. "I'm telling you. This is the way it is, understand? You have to wish us off this island."

Theodore looked at Hank for a long, drawn-out minute, then his small jaw became as rigid as Hank's and he was stubbornly silent.

And Muddy had thought camels were stubborn. He shook his head and looked at the baby, a bright and happy little thing with a crop of orange curls. She sat on a rock. She looked at him and grinned from around the two fingers stuck in her mouth.

Muddy waved.

She waved back, then dropped down from the rock and walked toward him. She was about three feet away when she ran out of rope. She tugged on the rope, but it wouldn't give. She looked at the rope, then said, "Sit!"

Muddy bit back a smile, then looked back at the others. They certainly weren't what he was used to. He'd never had a family in two thousand years, even if they weren't in truth quite a family. They were an interesting group.

Theodore stood next to his sister, a quiet and complicated-looking girl named Lydia. The children talked while Hank scowled and paced. Margaret, who had more beauty than Paris's Helen, stood with her arms stubbornly crossed.

Finally, Margaret cocked her lovely blond head and gave Theodore a direct look. "Well?"

"I don't want to leave."

"For Christ's sake!" Hank bellowed.

Muddy winced.

Margaret jabbed Hank in the ribs with her elbow. "Stop shouting at him. You'll only make things worse."

"Things can't get much worse."

Theodore stood there, even more straight and determined. He looked at Hank, then at Margaret. "I like it here."

Hank groaned.

Theodore stepped up to him. "You said deserted islands were the best places."

"What are you talking about, kid?"

"Remember the riddle?"

Hank looked as if he wanted someone to punch him.

"There are no prisons or orphanages on deserted islands," Theodore said by rote. "Hank said so."

Margaret looked as if she were ready to give Hank exactly what he wanted.

"I don't want to live in an orphanage. They don't give you any blankets, and Hank said it was cold and as bad as prison," Theodore spoke in a rush to get out all the words. "Hank has purple marks on his back 'cause they beat him in prison, an' he said it was 'cause they didn't have anything better to do. I don't want anyone to beat me or my sisters."

Margaret spun around. "Why on earth did you tell him those things?"

"I didn't tell him."

"I suppose he imagined it." Her eyes narrowed in accusation. "Oh, forgive me, I forgot. Five-year-old children always know about prisons and orphanages."

Hank began to pace in the sand. "He kept asking questions. Hell!" He waved his hand in the air. "I just answered him!"

"Well, you certainly picked a fine time to suddenly become Mr. Honesty."

"Let me handle this." Hank elbowed past her.

"Oh, yes, I forgot that, too. You're the man," she said in a deep and mocking tone.

As Hank walked past her, he said under his breath, "At least you understand your place."

Muddy whistled. She should have punched him. A fool with a big mouth, he thought. Based on his past experience, Hank should have been the one to find his bottle.

"I wish my father had taught me how to throw a punch instead of how to create a brief," Margaret said to Hank's back, then glanced at Muddy. Hank towered over Theodore. "Look, kid, I'll make you a trade."

"What kind of trade?"

Hank took off his cap and flipped it over. He pulled out a harmonica and held it up, turning it enticingly before the boy's serious face. He dropped the harmonica in the crown of his cap.

Theodore watched his every move, his expression curious but cautious.

Hank held the cap out to Theodore. "My hat and harmonica for the genie and the bottle."

Muddy stood quickly. "Wishes are nontransferable. Theodore is my master. He must make the wishes. Him and only him."

Hank and Margaret were quietly thoughtful. Muddy watched them for a moment, then added, "And you can't have Master Theodore make his three wishes and then one of you take the bottle. No one who knows I exist can become a future master."

Hank swore under his breath and cast Muddy a look that was hot enough to cook him. Margaret gave a resigned sigh.

Muddy sat down on the rock, crossed his leg, and rested his chin in his hand again.

"Okay, kid, here's the deal," Hank continued. "We need to get off this island. You understand?"

Theodore nodded.

"You have three wishes."

Muddy raised one finger and stood again. "Excuse me. Master Theodore only has two wishes. He generously and unselfishly used one to get rid of the hookah."

Hank's look said exactly what he thought of Theodore's wish.

Muddy sat down, crossed his leg, and began to swing it back and forth. His bell tingled like wind chimes.

Hank swung back around and gave his foot a pointed glare.

Muddy froze.

Hank looked down at Theodore and raised his thumb and forefinger. "Two wishes."

Margaret made an odd snorting sound, loud enough for Hank to glare at her, too. He continued, raising his hand even higher, "You can wish us off the island and still have a wish left. You can use that wish for anything you want. Understand, kid?"

Theodore stared at the sand for a moment, then looked at him. "I tried to wish for what I wanted."

"What do you mean you tried?" Margaret asked.

"I want my parents back, but Muddy can't bring them back. It breaks the wish rules. He can only give wishes in this world."

No one said anything for a long time.

Theodore looked at Hank, then at Margaret. "I don't want anything else except to stay here."

Margaret stepped in front of Hank. "Let me handle this." She stood near Theodore, who had his head bent. He was drawing designs in the sand with a bare foot. She knelt down so she was eye level with him. "Theodore."

He looked up at her.

She placed her hands on his narrow shoulders. "I realize how very apprehensive you must be. But I am an impartial party, since I haven't been associated with any orphanages. I can assure you that I will aggressively seek the best possible institution for you and your sisters. Now if you will just think about this from every angle, you can *clearly* determine the best possible course of action. It is a rare occasion that this method doesn't work for me." She smiled.

"We just have to introduce all the facts and your concerns, then weigh each option, decide which are the most significant points and why you are apprehensive. With some deliberation and good positive analytical thought, we can come to a mutually satisfying settlement that is in the best interests of all parties."

He stared at her for a moment, then said, "I like parties, especially birthday parties."

Hank laughed. "Clear as mud, Smitty."

She looked from Hank to Muddy. The genie still sat on the rock, his head hanging down. He gave a short snore, then he straightened, startled and wide-eyed. He blinked twice.

"Theodore, I was trying to explain that if we talk about your fears and about our situation, then perhaps you will see that the most logical thing you can do is to wish us off the island."

"But I don't want to leave here. It's fun."

"I think we should consider everyone, your sisters, too."

"Leedee?" Theodore tugged on Lydia's hand. "Do you wanna go to an orphanage?"

She shook her head. Her hand closed protectively around his. Brother and sister looked up with the same stubborn looks on their faces. Together they said, "We want to stay here."

Hank shuffled the cards. "It's called poker, kid."

Cards sailed through the air like feathers on the wind and lit in perfect fan sequence on the sand.

"Holy cow! Can you teach me to do that?"

"Sure, kid." He looked up at Smitty who was trying to get Annabelle to eat a banana. "But first I'm going to teach you how to play a man's game."

Smitty's head whipped around. She looked at Hank, then rolled her eyes just as a banana peel hit her in the shoulder.

He laughed. He had already explained to her that this was the way to get the kid to give them the wish. She was skeptical. But Hank knew this was one thing he could control.

Distract the kid with a game, a game he could manipulate, and *bam!* they'd be home faster than he could pick a pocket. He looked back at the kid, who was eagerly waiting. Hank smiled and began to explain the rules.

An hour and a hundred or so questions later, they finally picked up their cards. Hank's jaw was tight from gritting his teeth, from answering the same questions, and from restraining his urge to yell at the kid.

The first rule of a smart grifter: gain the trust of the patsy.

Hank laid down his hand without looking at it. He grabbed the brim of his cap and twisted it around so it was on backward.

Rule number two: don't underestimate good ol' lady luck.

Theodore watched him intently. "Why'd you do that?"

"For luck."

"Oh." He was quiet, then looked up. "I don't have anything for luck. Except my sisters."

"I'm not very lucky, Theo." Lydia sighed but perked up a minute later. "You have Muddy and the bottle. You could use them for luck."

"That's right!" Theodore took the stopper out of the bottle and a stream of purple smoke drifted out.

Hank shook his head and tried to forget what he was seeing.

"Yes, Master Theodore."

The crackpot was back with bells on his toes. And a purple turban.

"Muddy, you're gonna be my luck, okay?"

The genie's eyes darted from left to right with a baffled expression. "Whatever you say, master."

Hank stared at the guy's clothes and shuddered slightly. He looked away. It wasn't a pretty sight.

He shifted his gaze to Theodore. The kid was staring at his cards and chewing on his lip, his forehead creased in thought.

"I forgot. What beats what?"

Hank began to mentally count. At fifty, he said, "A straight flush is tops. Got it?"

The kid nodded.

"You're sure?"

"A straight flush is tops," the kid repeated.

"Four of a kind beats a full house."

"Uh-huh."

"A full house beats a flush. A flush beats a straight. A straight beats three of a kind, and three of a kind beats a pair."

"Okay."

"You got it all this time?" Hank's jaw was tight.

"Theodore." Smitty stepped between them and knelt in the sand next to the kid. "Can you read?"

"Uh-uh." He shook his head. "But Leedee can." He turned to his sister. "Can't you?"

Lydia nodded.

"I'll write them in the sand, and Lydia can read them for you. Then you won't have to ask Hank anymore."

They spent another five minutes writing lists in the sand, while Hank twiddled his thumbs for a while. He watched them, then found himself staring at Smitty. She had smashed bananas in her blond hair, but that wasn't what he found interesting. He let his gaze rove down over her, then stopped.

She had great legs.

She was kneeling in the sand, and as she wrote in it, she would move back. Her dress was bunched up at her knees, exposing her lower legs. They were pale and long and sleek.

God, but he loved a woman's legs. He had always been a sucker for a woman with legs that went on forever.

He watched her stand up, then walk back over to the baby, her hips moving in that natural rhythm of a woman. Kind of slow and . . . come to Papa.

"Hank?"

He pulled his gaze away and looked at the kid.

Theodore grinned. "I'm ready."

Hank gave a quick sigh. "Good."

"An' aces are the highest cards?"

"That's right." Hank nodded.

"An' I can take new cards."

"Yeah. How many do you want?"

"I don't know." The kid spent another five minutes frowning at his cards. Finally, he looked at Hank. "Four. I want four cards."

Hank laughed to himself wickedly. He gave the kid four cards.

"How many are you taking?"

"One."

"Oh." The kid paused, then asked, "Only one card?"

Hank shrugged. "I play the long shots."

"What's a long shot?"

"Nothing you have to know, Theodore," Smitty called out over her shoulder.

Hank looked at his cards—a king high full house. He managed a good healthy scowl when he looked at the kid, who gave him a blank but thoughtful stare. Then the kid looked at the list Smitty had written in the sand. "I forgot. What's a flush?"

The genie, who had been silent until then, groaned quietly.

Hank almost crowed.

"All one suit or group, Theo." Lydia pointed to her brother's cards. "Like those two black clover things in your hand."

The genie closed his eyes as if he couldn't bear to watch.

"I bet my harmonica," Hank paused for dramatic effect. "And raise you my cap." He tossed them into the pot filled with seashells and sand dollars.

Smitty turned around and looked at him. He gave her a quick and covert nod while the kid was looking at the harmonica as if it were candy.

Hank could see her shoulders relax slightly. He waited, then said, "You'll have to call my bet, kid."

Theodore laid his cards face down in the sand and dug through his pants' pockets. He looked up, frowning. "I haven't got anything left to bet."

"You don't?"

He shook his head, his expression childishly serious.

Hank counted to fifty again, then looked up at nothing and counted to ten. He faced the kid. "I guess . . ." He stopped, then shook his head. "No, that wouldn't work."

"What?" the kid asked eagerly.

"I was just thinking that you could bet a wish."

Theodore frowned and looked at the genie. "Muddy said I can't give you my wish."

"Yeah, he did." Hank pretended to be thinking. Made a big deal of it, too. He rubbed his chin for a good two minutes. "Tell you what, kid. You can bet the wish, and if I win, you have to wish for anything I ask. If you win, you get my cap, the harmonica, *and* you get to keep your wish."

Theodore's tongue curled out of the side of his mouth, and he chewed on it. After the long and tense few minutes, he looked at the genie. "Can I do that?"

"Yes, Master Theodore. As long as you make the wish, it doesn't break the rules." But the look the genie gave Hank said he knew his game.

Theodore looked at Hank. "Okay. I bet a wish and yell at you."

"Call, not yell."

Lydia and the genie leaned forward, waiting.

"Okay, I call you," Theodore said.

Hank laid his cards down. "King high full house, kid. Read 'em and weep!" He laughed and laughed, rubbing his hands together.

The genie sighed and shook his head. Lydia sagged back, her expression lined with disappointment.

Theodore stared down at Hank's hand, lying in the sand, then he looked at the words written next to him in the sand. He frowned, then looked at Lydia. "What beats a full house?"

"Four of a kind," she said, reading the list.

"An' aces are the highest?"

She nodded.

Theodore looked at Hank, then at Muddy. He looked down at his hand again.

Hank picked up the pot, then paused and looked up.

The kid's face suddenly brightened. He looked at the genie and said, "I wish my hand had four aces."

❦ 16 ❧

The sharp, piercing sound of an off-key harmonica cut through the air. Muddy winced, then tapped the heel of his hand against his ear. He looked up.

A hundred or so feet away, Theodore skipped across the sand. He was wearing Hank's cap backward and playing the harmonica loudly.

Hank scowled at Theodore and muttered to Margaret, "I think my ears are bleeding."

She plopped down next to him on a rock and rubbed her eyes as if they were tired. She gave a defeated sigh. "At least with the harmonica in his mouth, he can't say 'I wish.'"

Theodore hit a high and off-pitch note.

Everyone flinched.

"God . . . ," Hank groaned.

Squinting, Margaret looked at the boy. "His talents must lie elsewhere."

"Yeah. In poker." Hank ran a hand through his hair.

"I can't believe he wasted a wish on a card game." Margaret stared at the ground. As if talking to herself, she added, "I should have realized that was a possibility."

Hank absently shuffled the deck of cards in his hand a few times, then frowned at them. "It was a masterpiece."

Margaret looked up. "What was a masterpiece?"

"The rotten hand I slipped the kid. The worst set of cards I've ever dealt anyone."

Her face creased with disbelief. She looked at Muddy. He shrugged, feeling his policy of noninvolvement was still safest.

154

She turned back to Hank. "You were cheating with a five-year-old boy?"

Hank looked at her like she had rocks in her head.

Here comes another argument, Muddy thought.

"Hell, yes, I was cheating!"

"Oh. Excuse me. I foolishly thought an adult could beat a child, especially at a 'man's game.'"

The blast of the harmonica blared through the air and drowned out Hank's response. Muddy figured it was best that none of them heard it. He could read lips.

Theodore blasted the mouth organ again three more times. Muddy could feel the notes in his teeth. He looked up just as Margaret's mouth fell open, and Hank muttered, "Sounds like a thousand dying geese."

"Hey, Hank!" Theodore came running up to him, waving the harmonica.

"Yeah, kid."

"Listen?" Theodore blasted five bad notes. "How was that?"

Hank blinked, then looked at Margaret, who gave him a shrug that said he was on his own.

"Am I getting any better?" Theodore looked at Hank as if he'd hung the stars.

Hank was silent as stone. He just looked at Theodore the same fatalistic, yet perplexed way that Mrs. O'Leary had watched Chicago burn.

Theodore gave the harmonica a look of youthful longing. "I wish—"

Hank and Margaret shot off the rock at the same instant. Each reached for Theodore. "Don't wish!" they shouted together.

Hank's hand clamped over the boy's mouth first.

Theodore looked at them from eyes that were wide and white above Hank's tanned hand. The boy blinked a couple of times.

"Understand, kid?"

Theodore nodded.

Hank carefully drew his hand away.

"I'm sorry," Theodore said, looking down. "I forgot. I almost used up my last wish, huh?"

Margaret put an arm around his small, hunched shoulders. "Theodore, you gave us your word that you would talk with us before you made another wish. I know you'll work very hard to keep that promise."

His small, freckled face turned serious. He nodded.

"And, in turn, we promised we wouldn't ask you to wish us off the island again. That was our agreement."

"I remember."

She patted his shoulder. "I knew you wouldn't forget."

"Is my song better?" He whipped the harmonica in his mouth and blew so hard his cheeks and face turned red.

Margaret shuddered, and Hank turned away. His shoulders were hunched and his head was down and resting in one hand.

"Does that sound good, Hank?"

Hank turned around slowly. His eyes took a minute to clear. He stared at Theodore.

"I'm wearing your cap backwards for luck and trying real hard. Does it sound better?"

"Yeah, kid."

"Leedee got mad. She said I was playing so loud that I made the coconuts fall off the trees. And one just missed her head."

After an awkward few seconds of blessed silence, Hank reached out and gave Theodore's cap a tug. "We'll work on it, okay?"

Theodore grinned up at him. "Good. 'Cause I thought I sounded awful!" He turned around and started to run, then stopped suddenly and turned back to Muddy this time. "You're yawning."

"Yes, master."

"You wanna get back inside your bottle?"

"Yes, master." It was quiet in the bottle. Peaceful. No arguing. No harmonicas.

Theodore dug the bottle out of his pants' pocket and held it up.

"Leave the bottle here, Theodore," Margaret said. "I'll keep it safe." Theodore looked at the bottle, then at Muddy, who nodded because he trusted the woman.

Theodore set the bottle on the rock next to Muddy. He grinned, waved, and took off down the beach, the harmonica in his mouth.

Muddy sighed and began to levitate toward the mouth of the bottle.

Home, he thought. Where peace and quiet and a good book all awaited him. His purple smoke began to billow and swirl. A heartbeat later he passed through the mouth of the bottle.

And the last thing he heard was a flat, dull note of a harmonica echoing in the distance.

Margaret sat on the hard rock, staring at the white sand beneath her bare toes. The air had grown thicker and the sun higher, more intense. She felt the heat of it on the back of her neck. Thankfully, the air had also grown quieter.

"He's not a kid," Hank said.

She looked up.

He was staring down the beach at Theodore. "He's a fifty-year-old midget."

She understood how he felt. She was fast learning that children were another species altogether. "It's not easy to admit that a five-year-old can get the best of you, is it?"

He didn't say anything. His demeanor made him look about as flexible as the rock they sat on.

"I forgot. It's not easy for you to admit anything."

He turned, pinning her with a sharp look. "I can admit things."

"Oh? Like what?"

"Like I'm right and you're wrong." He gave a wicked crack of laughter.

"I walked right into that."

"Yes, sweetheart. You sure did."

She stood and walked over to the bottle sitting abandoned on the rock. Three wishes, she thought. She picked the bottle up and turned it slowly in her hand.

She was holding a genie bottle. She wondered briefly if anyone back home would believe this. If she ever got back home.

Now there was a depressing thought.

She turned to Hank. "What if we're stuck on this island for a long time?"

"Then we're stuck. I've been in worse places."

She looked at the tropical paradise around her. She paused, suddenly a little shaken. The words *twenty years* or *thirty years* came to mind.

"Oh, my God . . ." She sat down hard on the rock, her whole body suddenly limp at a horrid but real possibility. What if they were never found at all?

Hank stared at Margaret's stiff back. She marched down to the beach with the determination of a German kaiser. And the energy of a German shepherd.

Hell . . . She'd been thinking again.

He slowly followed her, then leaned against the armored trunk of a tall sago palm and watched her.

Like a beaver intent on building a dam, she dragged pieces of driftwood down the beach and piled them on the crest of a small rise, where the ground was dry and a rocky cliff jutted out toward the sea.

The longer he watched, the higher the stack of wood.

She gave him a glance but didn't stop for a few more minutes. Finally she stood back, her hands on her hips, and she cast a critical eye on the wood.

"Having fun?" he asked.

She rearranged the wood a few times until she had it the way she wanted—God only knew why.

"If you want to build something, Smitty, we have a hut to build."

She stopped fiddling with the wood and apparently decided to look at him. "If a ship passes, we have to be prepared." She bent over and adjusted the wood again.

"Uh-huh."

She was in the midst of digging a shallow ring around the pyre with her foot, and she stopped suddenly and looked up, her eyes narrowed. "Don't use that condescending tone with me."

"All I said was uh-huh."

"It was the snide way you said it." She straightened and then searched the beach, tapping a finger against her lips in thought. "I wonder if I should build another one." She turned around and raised a hand to block out the sun. "Perhaps over there."

He crossed his arms. "You want to tell me what brought all this on?"

She looked over her shoulder. "All what?"

He waved a hand. "This sudden need to build signal fires?"

She stood there for a very long time, having some kind of internal battle. He could see it on her face and in her stance. Her arms were clasped tightly to her as if she were suddenly chilled.

"Nothing" was all she said.

He didn't turn away. "I built a pile of driftwood for a beacon fire on the ridge the first morning on the island."

She turned around, her hands still hugging her elbows. "You did?"

He nodded.

Her arms fell to her sides for a moment, then she rubbed a hand across her forehead. With a sigh, she walked down to the sand. She stood near him but didn't look at him. Her attention was on the vast ocean beyond their lagoon. "What if no one finds us?"

So that was it. He squatted down in the sand and picked up a tiger shell, then turned to look at the same distant horizon. "Someone will come eventually."

"But there's no guarantee. It could be twenty years."

"It could be tomorrow."

She didn't say anything for the longest time. There was only the distant noise of Theodore's harmonica, the crash of a wave on the rocks near the headland, the nearby lapping sound of the water as it licked the edge of the beach.

"Do you have anyone waiting for you?" she asked.

"Me?" He laughed and tossed the shell a couple of times. "Like who, Smitty, a lover or wife?"

She shrugged.

He looked out at the sea, then tossed the shell in the water and straightened. "There's just me. No one else." He waited for her to look at him.

She didn't. She sat down in the sand and hugged her knees to her chest, staring out at the sea.

He sat down next to her just to see what she'd do. She didn't move, which surprised him.

She stared at the silver bottle. "Look at how old this is."

He gave the bottle a cursory glance.

She held it up in the sunlight. "See these carvings and designs? They weren't made by a machine. They are too imperfect. Something made by human hand is never perfect."

He didn't respond. He wanted to know what she was getting at.

She hesitated, then asked, "What would have happened if we had found this?"

He gave a wry laugh. "We'd be off the island."

"Yes, I suppose we would. I'd be back in San Francisco." She paused and dug her feet in the wet sand. "Home," she said wistfully. "Where would you be?"

He shrugged. "Somewhere in the States."

"Isn't there someplace you could call home?"

"I grew up in Pittsburgh."

"What brought you to the South Seas? Seems like an odd choice."

"You're here."

"On a holiday only. At least it was supposed to be a holiday." She gave him a wry look. "Somehow I don't think you came here on a holiday."

He looked at her then. "What is this, a cross-examination?"

"No," she said with a sharp laugh. "Just plain old curiosity. No need to put up a defense."

"I heard there was a lot of money here—gold, pearls the size of your eye. Men were coming here to find treasure."

"So you came to hunt for treasure," she repeated.

"Yeah, you could say that." He laughed.

She turned, frowning. "What's so funny?"

"I wasn't planning on hunting for it." He held up the deck of cards. "I had big plans to fleece it from the suckers who did."

"But you got caught and ended up in prison," she said knowingly.

"No. I didn't get caught." He couldn't keep the bitterness out of his voice. "There is no such thing as innocent until proven guilty in these islands." He threw the seashell into an incoming wave.

"Napoleonic law," she murmured and absently drew one finger through the sand. "Sometimes it's the things we Americans take for granted that are the things we should value the most."

They sat in companionable silence, something new for them, while the trade wind ruffled the leaves on a nearby palm. A sand crab skittered across the shoreline, then disappeared into the deep safety of the wet sand, a small bubble the only sign that it had ever been there.

After a few minutes Smitty looked back at the bottle. "If you had found this"—she turned it in her hand again—"and were given three wishes, what would you wish for?"

"Freedom," he said without a second of thought.

He could feel her stare and knew what she wanted. She wanted to ask him about his prison sentence. He turned and gave her one of those direct looks she favored. He saw curiosity, interest, and intelligence in her face. But he'd volunteered enough. "How about you?" He picked up a small stick and jabbed it into the sand a few times, then looked back at her, waiting for an answer.

"I'm thinking," she said after another stretch of silence.

He laughed to himself. What a surprise. Smitty thinking. He tossed the stick in the water and watched a wave catch it and tumble it back toward them. "What does a woman attorney wish for? To win every case?"

"No. I love the challenge of the law. The way it always changes. It fascinates me." She paused. "There's something special about trying to make the world a fair place."

"That sounds like one of your oxymorons, sweetheart. The world can't be a fair place."

"I believe it can be fair and equal."

"You're just chasing rainbows."

"The law is there for all of us. Think about it. Without laws we have chaos."

"With laws we have chaos." He laughed more caustically now. "What the hell is the world going to be like a hundred years from now?"

"A better place to live. More fair. More equal. Closer to perfect."

He just shook his head. A perfect world, what an

idealistic joke. He looked at her. Yeah, he thought, she is an attorney. "So what about those wishes, Smitty? What does an attorney who works to make the world perfect wish for?"

"I was a woman before I was ever an attorney."

"What does a woman wish for?"

She shook her head. "I can't speak for all women. Only me. I would want to go home."

"You have three wishes. What about the other two?"

"I don't know. I really don't know," she said almost as if she were talking to herself. She looked at him. "That sounds strange, doesn't it?"

"No." He waited, then added, "You probably haven't *thought* about it long enough."

She slowly turned to look at him.

He tried to keep a straight face.

She burst out laughing. "I walked right into it again, didn't I?"

"Yeah, Smitty, you sure as hell did."

Her laughter died as easily as it had come. The wind whipped her hair loose and strands of it stuck to her face. He watched her pull the hair away from the fullest set of lips he'd seen in years.

She had a face and body that were what men in prison dreamed of—knock-'em-dead looks, full chest and hips, a small waist, legs that went on forever.

And he was intensely aware of her. But not as he would be about just any female, which seemed odd to him. He watched her a moment longer and became aware of a few other things, too. Aware that they could be on this island for a long time. Aware of how goddamn long he'd gone without a woman.

Mixed with the scent of the sea and the heavy air was the soft musk scent of her. That woman-smell men knew so keenly. The scent that could drive some men to cross the line and take what they wanted.

He'd never forced a woman. Never had to. Didn't think much of those men who did. He had always been able to talk himself into walking away from any woman. And it hadn't been too tough either.

But now, as he stared at her profile while she drew something absently in the sand, he felt a restless need to touch her. He shifted closer, casually resting one hand in the sand behind her.

She turned. Her eyes widened when she saw how close he was. Her gaze dropped to his lips, then back up to his eyes. Her lips parted, and she took one deep breath through her mouth.

With his free hand, he brushed another strand of hair from her lips and cheek, then slid his hand behind her neck. Before she had a chance to think, he kissed her.

⇒ 17 ⇐

There were times when reality was far worse than anything imaginable. For Margaret, reality came in the form of a wave—the cold wet slap of an ocean wave.

The water washed over her, and a second later she realized that she was rolling in the sand with Hank. Her tongue was in his mouth, kissing him back. He was on top of her, pinning her to the wet sand, one hand holding her head to his, his other hand between her legs.

She opened her eyes and blinked up at his face, then shoved him off of her and stood so quickly she saw stars for a second. She covered her eyes with a hand and took a deep breath to calm herself down.

Water dripped from her face and hair and pattered on the sand. Another wave sloshed over her ankles and calves and the sand sucked at her feet. The sea was pulling her one way. Her body pulled her another. Her head resisted them both.

Hank stood and moved closer to her, his shadow blocking out the warmth of the sun.

She didn't want to look at him. This wasn't happening. She took another deep breath, then without a word she turned and took a step.

He grabbed her arm and made her turn back around. "Running away?"

She stood there stiffly, embarrassed, confused, angry. "No."

"You're a rotten liar."

"Let go of me."

He didn't.

"Please let go." Her voice was almost a whisper.

He swore and released her hand.

From somewhere she gathered the strength to look at him.

He was angry, too. His eyes were black with it. He gave her a mock bow and flung his hand out. "Go ahead. Run as fast as you can. But remember. I'm still here. And you're still here. That isn't going to change anymore than you can change what just went on between us."

"I don't want anything between us."

"Believe me, sweetheart, neither do I." He ran a hand through his hair and wiped the water from his face. Even with the anger and embarrassment of the moment, she could feel something pass between them. Tension and more—something neither wanted.

But even she couldn't deny it. He'd been right about that. She turned her back to him and clutched her arms to her. After a minute, she said quietly, "In a perfect world, you would be a doctor . . . a judge or a professor. Anything but a crook."

He shifted even closer, and a long dark shadow spread over the sand. "The world isn't perfect and I'm no doctor or professor." His voice was harsh and low and right next to her ear. "But it takes a crook to know the world will never be fair. And you want to know why?"

She shook her head. She didn't want to hear this.

He grabbed her shoulders and spun her around. "This is why." His mouth hit hers hard.

She stood there stiffly, refusing to respond. Her hands were clenched at her sides, her lips tightly sealed, her eyes open and angry.

His eyes were open, too. His look was coldly cruel, penetrating, as if he could somehow force her to see things as he did.

He let go swiftly, half pushing her away. But he never broke that hard look. "Use that brain of yours to think about it. Too many men are like me. Out to get what they can. Any way they can. Accept it, sweetheart."

She watched him walk away. She brought a hand to her head and just stood there. Something was wrong with her.

She had no idea how long she stood there, staring at the horizon, then down at the water. After a few more minutes she sank down onto the sand, just sat there thinking.

Suddenly she felt more alone than she had in a long time. Alone and confused. Nothing made sense.

She began to draw in the sand a list of words, single, disjointed words. Hank. Man. Margaret. Kiss. Love? Sick! Blame? Humidity. Hot. Sun. Trauma. Something . . . Anything.

She stared at her list. A second later, she frantically rubbed out the words.

Two hours later, Margaret swept a strand of hair out of her face and stared at the burnt remains of three fish. They had been a good ten inches long. Now they held a striking resemblance to small, black goldfish.

She picked up one of the smoldering sticks Hank had carved as a spit. It broke in half. The stick and the fish crumbled into the fire. She just stared at it, unable to believe that she could possibly have burned another meal.

"Are those fish done yet?" Hank and the children walked toward her.

She looked at the fish, then up at him. "Yes. I'd say they're done."

"Good!" He stepped around her, took one look at the fire, and bellowed, "Dammit, Smitty!"

With an uneasy sense of failure and embarrassment she looked at their hungry faces. She gave them a forced smile. "Anyone else for bananas?"

The day only got worse. It was one of those days that had all the earmarkings of being so rotten that one looked forward to night. She busied herself with the children, made Theodore bathe, then sent him on his way while Lydia took her turn at the pool. The girl finished and changed into a small flannel nightdress they had found in one of the trunks.

In the bright afternoon sunlight, Margaret had brushed Lydia's hair back and tied it with blue ribbons. In between grabs at Annabelle to keep her from falling in the water—and a few close calls when the baby had tried to eat a butterfly, two beetles, and leaves from all the surrounding bushes—it had taken almost an hour to get Lydia's hair dry and silky.

"All done." Brush in hand, Margaret stood back, waiting to see if Lydia would smile. Even just a look of pleasure or delight would be enough.

Lydia knelt at the edge of the pool and frowned down at her reflection. She stood up quickly. "I'll take Annabelle so you can bathe now" was all she said.

No "Thank you" or "I like it." Nothing. Lydia handed Margaret the ball of soap.

Margaret felt like a complete failure. She watched the girl walk toward the arm of rocks that hid the pool and called out. "Lydia!"

She turned around.

"Do you like your hair?"

Lydia shrugged. "Mama always used yellow ribbons." And she and Annabelle disappeared around the rocks.

Shaking her head, she set down the soap, stripped, and walked into the pool. As the water lapped around her, she made a mental note to let Lydia pick her own ribbons in the future.

Margaret stared down at her reflection. She looked like something the cat dragged in. Actually, she looked worse.

She ducked underwater and surfaced. She looked at herself again and wondered who the woman was that looked back at her.

She was an attorney, not a mother.

An intelligent and fairly talented woman to whom most things had come naturally, easily. It had always amazed her father and uncles at how she had grasped the intricacies of the legal field as easily as someone born with the knowledge. She could usually think her way out of any sticky situation.

But here on this island, with the children and Hank, nothing seemed to work right. She didn't understand children any more than she understood Hank.

And it wasn't only her inability to do something as simple as cook. That just seemed to symbolize everything she couldn't grasp.

Babies seemed to know no schedule, something that made a mess of her methodical routine. In her role as a mother she had almost no time alone. She wondered how on earth the mothers of the world got anything done with all the interruptions.

A fact that was driven home to her again less than five minutes later.

Annabelle began to cry. She could hear her. She waded over to the side of the pool where a pea-sized sliver of soap sat abandoned on the rocks.

The baby was crying "Mama!"

She tried to make lather from the almost nonexistent sliver of soap.

Annabelle cried out over and over.

Margaret scrubbed her body harder, telling herself that Lydia was with her and she'd be fine. She washed her hair and dove under the water. But even underwater she could still hear Annabelle's wailing.

She climbed out and dried off, then put on another flannel nightdress that was about a foot too short in the hem and sleeves and an inch too tight in the chest.

"Ducky," she muttered, shoving up the sleeves to her elbow as she rounded the rocks. The baby was screaming and kicking to get Lydia to let her go. She took one look at Margaret and cried, "Mama!"

Lydia's face paled.

"Ma-maaaaaah!"

Margaret reached for Annabelle. "I'll take her."

Lydia looked down at her sister, who was sobbing and twisting and crying so hard she was hiccuping. The girl handed her to Margaret as if she were being forced to give away her heart. Lydia turned and stiffly walked away.

"Lydia, please wait!" Margaret bounced the sobbing baby on her hip.

The girl kept walking.

"I'm sorry . . . I . . ."

Lydia disappeared around some rocks at the other side of the clearing.

Margaret stared at the spot where Lydia disappeared, feeling a complete failure. She asked herself how could an intelligent and educated woman make such a mess of everything.

She looked down at Annabelle. The baby was sound asleep in her arms.

And at that moment Margaret, an intelligent and educated woman, realized something else. She had absolutely no talent for instant motherhood.

Muddy awoke to someone knocking on his bottle. He wiped the sleep from his tired eyes and stared up at the stopper. If he were given three wishes, one of them would be for a door.

He swung his feet off the divan, his bells tingling. He stood and stretched.

"Muddy?" came a loud whisper. "Are you awake?"

Muddy cupped his hands around his mouth and shouted, "Yes, master!"

The stopper popped open, and a big, blue eyeball stared down at him. "You coming out now?"

"Yes, master, just as soon as you move your eye."

"Oh." The eyeball blinked and moved back. "How's that?"

Muddy's feet left the carpet, and a second later he passed through the opening of the bottle. The smoke dissipated, and he saw that Theodore was back to squinting into the bottle.

He looked up. "Whatchagot in there?" Then he looked back inside.

"Would you like to see?"

Theodore jerked his eye away from the bottle and looked up, his face showing how badly he wanted to see inside. "Can I?"

Muddy uncrossed his arms—a stupid stance that some moron back at the beginning of time thought was geniesque. May Allah save him from the ludicrousness of ritual.

He looked down at Theodore, who had begun to fidget from anticipation, and extended a palm. "Just take my hand, master."

Theodore ran over and took Muddy's hand. A second later purple smoke began to swirl like a small whirlwind, and they both levitated up with the smoke.

"Holy cow!"

They circled over the bottle like a bird of prey. Theodore giggled, then laughed, and Muddy took him for an extra few laps around the bottle, the smoke following in their wake.

They had just made the last lap and were hovering over the bottle when Lydia came walking around some rocks.

"Look, Leedee! Look! It's me! I'm flying into the bottle!" And they disappeared inside.

"Where's the kid?"

Margaret placed a sleeping Annabelle into the trunk-bed and looked up.

Hank was scowling at her.

"Theodore? I haven't seen him."

"Me either." Hank turned, his gaze scanning the area. "Where's the other one, Lydia?"

"She wandered off a few minutes ago."

"For Christ's sake! Can't you keep an eye on them?"

She turned slowly, her hands clenching into fists. "Now wait just a minute—"

"Go get her."

She counted very slowly to twenty-five, then she said calmly and reasonably, "I can't leave the baby. She just fell asleep."

He swore loud enough to wake the baby. And he did.

Annabelle began to cry.

His expression turned cocky. "Well, now she's awake."

Margaret looked from him to Annabelle, and she took one short step backward. "Fine." She spun on one foot and marched off toward the rocks. "I'll go look for Lydia."

"Where the hell do you think you're going?"

She never looked back, just grabbed her flannel skirts and broke into a full run.

"Smitty! You can't leave this kid with me! Godammit! Come back here!"

She tightened her grip on her nightdress and took a runner's shallow breaths. Now here was a natural talent she hadn't lost. No, siree! Her long legs ate up the ground like an antelope——her nickname on the ladies' field and track team at college.

"Smitty, dammit!"

She laughed with wicked glee and hot-footed it the last hundred feet, then whipped around the bend before one could say Hank Wyatt was a sucker.

❧ 18 ❧

Annabelle stared at Hank from over the rim of the trunk with a look so serious and intimidating she should have been a judge. He ran his hand through his hair and swore under his breath.

"Sit!" she repeated, then stuck two fingers in her mouth and stared at him again.

He stood there scowling.

She ducked down and then poked her head up. "Peekaboo."

"Yeah, yeah, kid, peekaboo to you, too."

She ducked again.

He rolled his eyes. *Great! We can sit here and play peekaboo all damn day.*

A red curly head slowly rose above the edge of the trunk and two bright eyes sparkled at him. "Papa!"

"Oh, no! No way!" His hands shot up, and he backed up so fast he bumped into a tree trunk. "No Papa!" He jabbed a finger in his chest. "Hank! Got it, kid? I'm Hank."

She grinned around her fingers, then took them out of her mouth and gave him a childish wave. "Hi!"

While he was pacing, running his hand through his hair and mentally spouting every curse in his vast knowledge of them, Annabelle climbed out of the trunk and ran toward him on short, stubby little legs.

He turned and froze. She was holding up a banana.

They eyed each other, a meeting of innocence and cynicism. Hank squatted down in front of her, and she handed him the banana. "You hungry, kid?"

She just grinned at him. He peeled the banana, and she edged closer, then poked her finger on his nose.

"Nose," she said as clear as could be.

That surprised him.

"Hank's nose."

He laughed. "Yeah. That's my nose."

He sat down in the sand and held out the banana. "Here, kid."

She grabbed it and squeezed so hard the banana mashed through her fingers. She looked at it, then looked up at him and said, "Sit!"

"That's what it looks like all right. You're a smart kid." She crammed some banana in her mouth, licking it off her palm, and crawled into his lap, then settled in, her back to his chest and her squat legs casually slung over one of his.

He stared down at her. She swung one foot back and forth. She had fat feet, fat hands, and fat legs that looked too short to support her. "So, kid . . . where are your knees?"

"Kneezzz." She pointed to her nose and wrinkled it.

"Nah. That's your nose."

"Kneez."

"Nose."

"Kneez," she insisted, then blew air out her nose twice.

He laughed then and nodded. "Sneeze."

She blew out her nose again and laughed with him.

He looked at those squatty legs for a second and said, "Yeah, well, you probably don't have to know what knees are until you grow your own."

She wiggled into a standing position and brought her face scant inches from his. She lifted a sticky finger and started to poke it in his eye.

He grabbed her wrist. "No, you don't."

"Eyez."

"Yeah, those are my eyes."

She wiped her sticky hand on his hair. "Hair."

"Yeah."

"Muck, muck, muck!" She poked her finger at his mouth for each word.

He stared at the kid. She reached down and took another mashed handful of banana. "Smitty's right there, kid. You shouldn't say that one. That's a bad word."

"Bad wolf." She puffed her cheeks up and blew banana out of her mouth.

He flinched, then wiped it from his face. "Yeah, well here, kid." Hank handed her another banana. "Eat. We'll talk later."

She threw the banana across the sand.

He scowled down at the kid. "You don't want it, huh?"

"No."

"Yeah, I don't blame you. I think we're all tired of bananas." He looked around, but all he saw was a pile of the green fruit. He scratched his chin for a second and set her on the ground, then stood and reached for her hand.

It was gooey with smashed banana. He used his shirttail to wipe her hands, then swung her up onto his shoulders.

She laughed and slapped his head. "More!"

But before he could swing her again, he spotted the damn goat moseying up the sand and chewing on some monkey grass near a bright red ginger plant.

He studied the goat for a calculating minute, then looked at Annabelle. "How 'bout some milk, kid? You don't cook milk, so Smitty can't burn it. . . . Although she might try."

The goat looked up and bleated. Hank studied it. The goat appeared unfazed. It just lowered its head and went back to eating the grass.

Hank looked around, then set the kid down on a rock. "Don't move. Got it?"

She grinned up at him.

He watched her for a moment, then shrugged. "Yeah, what the hell, I guess that means yes."

He crossed the clearing and picked up one of Smitty's iron cooking pots, then he moved in on the goat. When he was about three feet away, the goat looked up. They stared at each other.

The goat blinked, then ate some more grass.

Not bad, he thought and moved closer, slowly sliding the pot under the goat's udder. Very carefully he squatted down. He rested his hand on his bent knees and looked at the goat.

It just chewed on the grass, not even bothering to look at him.

He reached toward a tit.

The goat shifted so its butt was in his face. Hank swore.

"Sit!"

He scowled at the kid. She was still sitting on the rock, watching him as if it were the most important thing she could do. *And Smitty acted as if taking care of a kid was hard. Women. . . . Everything's a big deal.*

He turned back, and the goat kicked him right in the gut.

The air left his lungs, and he doubled over. "God . . ."

He shook his head and focused just as the goat shifted out of reach. Hank drew a deep breath. An instant later he vaulted toward the goat.

The damn thing ran almost as fast as Smitty. He chased it all over the clearing, through trees, around bushes, down the beach, and around the rocks.

For the next five minutes, the goat outmaneuvered his every move, and the kid clapped and laughed and echoed every curse he hollered. He rounded the rocks and made one last leap for the goat. It darted back, and he missed.

Hank lay face down in the sand, trying to catch his wind. It took a while. Hell, he was getting old.

He lifted his head up and watched the goat's butt disappear into the jungle.

The kid clapped her hands. "Fun!"

He glowered at her. "You think this is funny, don't you?"

She grinned.

"Yeah, well, I know when to throw in my cards." He pushed up to his knees, took another breath, and stood. He turned and walked over to pick up Smitty's cooking pot.

"Hi!"

"Yeah, yeah, kid. I know you're there." He bent down and grabbed the pot handle.

"Damn goat!"

Hank paused, half bent down, and turned to look at the kid. "What?"

And the goat nailed him right in the ass.

Margaret walked into the jungle beyond the beach. It was like another world. Fern fronds and climbing pothos webbed a narrow path that twisted where the jungle grew deeper and darker and the bamboo more dense. As if weighed down by the monsoonlike humidity, the air turned thick and heavy.

The sounds even changed. The birds whistled their songs and the insects hummed and clicked and chattered in nimble tunes dichotomous with the sluggish air. Looming like pillars at a courthouse were tall, ribbed ebony trees, their lower branches matted with dense jungle vines. Orchids in rainbow shades dripped from the dark creeper ivys and thick waxy leaves. Pockets of mist and fog lingered like forgotten guests, untouched by the heat of the island sun.

On the flowers and plants, leaves and bushes, dew glimmered in minute rivers and trickled down the veins in the foliage the same way the humidity ran down Margaret's skin. As she walked into the interior, the path grew wider and darker. Because the rain forest was covered with a lush canopy, entering it was almost like being swallowed by dark green night.

There was a sudden stillness here, a perfectly frozen world. No motion, no breeze, just jungle.

She moved more slowly. Then, as if a giant hand had carved out a small piece of Eden, she entered into the fringes of a clearing where fuchias, orchids, and stephanotis dangled like a socialite's jewels from the tree branches and creepers overhead.

Sunlight sliced through the crowns of the trees like prisms on the most exquisite crystal chandelier, spilling rainbow colors on the moss- and lichen-covered ground. It was a world of color, all colors of the spectrum.

And there, sitting on a fallen hollow log of an old tree, was Lydia. Her back was to Margaret, and there were quivers of movement about her shoulders.

Margaret stood silently, afraid to move.

Lydia was crying. Her head was buried in smooth hands too young to have to cope with mourning.

Yet Margaret knew the desolate feeling well enough herself. She remembered being scared and feeling alone even though she was with her father and uncles. She remembered crying like Lydia, that empty aching sound of the lonely ones the dead left behind.

Instinctively she reached out a hand toward the girl but stopped, uncertain of what she should do. How could she explain to Lydia that time and age would lessen the confusion and turn it into acceptance?

To Lydia, her loss was all still too fresh and too painful.

From behind Margaret came a thrashing sound, someone running through the jungle. She shifted back behind a tree laced with vines.

The goat trotted up the path, then moved into the small clearing.

Lydia looked up and turned. The goat and the girl

eyed each other. Lydia wiped her eyes with the back of a hand. "Come here, goat. Come here."

No one, not Hank, not Theodore, not even Margaret, had been able to coerce the goat to stay near enough to even make the slightest attempt to milk it.

The goat gave a bleat, then trotted over to Lydia just as merrily as a lapdog. Lydia reached out and petted the goat, which shifted closer and nudged the girl with its muzzle.

"Good goat," she murmured and laid her head against the goat's neck. Lydia began to cry again, hugging the goat and sobbing, sputtering words broken and lost and desolate. Disjointed words that made no sense, but somehow Margaret understood.

The girl talked to the goat through her sobs, telling it how scared she was and lonely and sobbing that no one could understand. Lydia finally held the goat so tightly that it bleated but didn't move away.

Lydia moved back and stroked the goat as she tried to catch a breath. "I'm sorry," she told the goat. "I hugged you too hard, didn't I? I didn't mean to hold you so tightly. I guess . . . I guess I'm just scared . . . because there's no one left to hold me anymore."

Margaret leaned against the tree and rubbed her forehead, trying to think. She waited a few minutes, then took a deep breath and called out, "Lydia!" Then she tromped toward the clearing with as much noise as possible. "Lydia!" She stood on the fringes of the clearing. "Oh, here you are."

This time the girl's back was straight and stiff as an ebony tree.

Margaret stood there a second longer. "This is a lovely spot."

Lydia said nothing.

Okay. . . . Now what?

The girl began to fiddle with the goat's beard.

Margaret took a deep breath and walked into the clearing. She stood over Lydia. "What are you doing?"

"Braiding the goat's beard."

"Oh. Why?"

"Because she's a girl. My mama always said girls should wear braids."

Margaret sat down next to Lydia. Their arms brushed slightly, and Lydia jerked a few inches away. She looked at the girl's hair, the side sections tied back off her troubled face with blue ribbons. "I never learned to do that."

"What?"

"Braid hair." Margaret gave a short laugh, hoping she might break the ice between them. "For the life of me, I can't do it."

Lydia didn't say anything.

"We need to name that goat. I don't think it's fair to keep calling it 'goat.' Do you?"

The girl shrugged.

"You can name her," Margaret suggested.

"I can't think of anything right now." Lydia let go of the goat's beard.

Margaret stared at the vines twisted into knots on the moss-covered ground. She felt just as choked as they were because she was so unsure of what she could say to help Lydia. Some part of her needed to help the girl, for herself as much as for Lydia. Finally she cocked her head and looked at the girl. "Why are you here?"

"No reason."

Margaret made a big deal of looking around the jungle. "It's rather quiet and secluded, isn't it?"

"I like to be alone." Lydia folded her hands in her lap.

"Do you? I never did." Margaret turned toward Lydia. "After my mother died, it took a long time before I could stand to be alone."

Lydia's knuckles were white because her hands were so tightly knotted. She turned toward Margaret. Her cheeks were blotchy, her lips and eyes slightly pink and swollen. "Your mother died?"

Margaret nodded and stared at the lines in her palm. She realized that Lydia wouldn't truly listen if she were looking at her. "I never wanted to be alone after that. I think I was always afraid that if I wasn't with the only family I had left, that they would die, too." She paused, then admitted, "I was more afraid of being left alone than almost anything I could imagine."

"I'm not alone," Lydia said defiantly, as if she wanted to fight with the world. "I have Theodore and Annabelle."

"That's right. You do."

The silence just hung there.

Finally Lydia spoke. "Who did you have left?"

"My father and my uncles."

"No brothers or sisters?"

Margaret shook her head.

"Oh." Lydia pulled an orchid from a nearby stem and absently twisted it in her hand. After a moment, she began to pluck off the thick pink petals, letting them drift to the jungle floor. "Did they know you were scared?"

"I don't know. It must have been difficult for my dad. He had to worry about me when he was still grieving himself."

"Did he cry for her?"

"I think so."

"Did you cry?"

"Yes. Sometimes I still do."

"You do?" She sounded surprised at that. "How old were you when she died?"

"Seven." Margaret looked off at the flowers around them. "Too young to remember very much about her and too old to forget she had been there."

"I'll always remember them," Lydia said with quiet fierceness. "Always."

And Margaret sat there, a little raw and open herself. In trying to make Lydia see a pathway out of her grief, she understood the path her own had taken—the knowledge that the memories were still there soothing the loss after time. A dead parent was never truly gone because they lived forever in your memory.

She looked at Lydia as something kindred passed between them. "Yes," she said with a quiet certitude. "You always will remember."

❦ 19 ❦

"Let me see if I have this straight. You want me to hold hands with a guy in earrings, purple pants, and toe bells, then fly around in a cloud of smoke and shrink so I can fit inside this bottle?"

Muddy kept a straight face, but it wasn't easy. Hank was making his mastership more interesting than most.

"I don't know what else we can do." Margaret threw up her hands and watched Hank pace. "Theodore won't come out."

Hank ran a hand through his hair and turned, winced once, then slowly began to walk a new path, favoring one leg.

Margaret frowned at Hank. "Are you hurt?"

He stopped suddenly and pivoted with the rigid motion of a German soldier. He gave her a black look. "No."

"Then why are you limping?"

His look turned incendiary and shifted to the goat gnawing on some grass behind Margaret. Lydia stood over the animal, stroking it like one stroked a pet cat.

"I'm just stiff," he barked, then glared at all of

181

them, his expression warning them to drop the subject.

Not that Muddy was foolish enough to bring it up. He had survived for two thousand years, after all. Besides which, Hank could barely look at him without getting a wild look in his eyes that warned Muddy to stay away.

"Hank, we need to find out why Theodore refuses to come out of the bottle. He told the genie he wants you. You have to go into the bottle with Muddy. The only way to do that is to take ahold of his hand."

"If you're lying, chump, it'll be your last lie." Hank gave him a hard stare.

Muddy remained silent.

"Why would he lie?" Margaret asked.

"I believe Hank is afraid that all I truly want is to hold his hand." Muddy kept a perfectly straight face even though Hank's was red.

"Do you think he's afraid?" Margaret asked with enough exaggeration that Muddy wanted to congratulate her. He winked at her instead.

"I'm standing here, dammit. And I'm not afraid of a chump in purple pants."

"Oh, that's good." Margaret appeared to be biting back a laugh. "Then just pretend you're giving a handshake."

After a few minutes of grousing and swearing, Hank stepped in front of the genie and stuck out his hand.

Muddy grabbed it. The devil in him wanted to tickle Hank's palm, but he was afraid he might get punched. Instead, he donned an appropriately serious look. "Tell me when you're ready."

Hank scowled at all of them but especially at him.

"You want to say your last good-byes?" Margaret laughed a little as she bounced Annabelle on her hip.

"Cute, Smitty."

"No last words, huh?" She had a wicked glint in her eye.

"Yeah, I have something to say. Tie that damn goat up while I'm gone."

She looked at him, then at his backside. "Did the goat butt you again?"

Hank's silence gave them the answer.

"Oh! I thought of a name!" Lydia said, showing the first bit of excitement anyone had seen. They turned and stared at her.

"For the goat! We can call her Rebuttal!"

Margaret smiled at the little girl. "That's a wonderful name."

Lydia gave them her first smile, bright and filled with pride. And Muddy saw a look that was part happiness and part relief cross Margaret's face.

"Let's get this the hell over with," Hank groused.

Muddy glanced at Margaret, and she rolled her eyes. He looked at Hank, who cringed slightly, then eyed him the way Paris should have eyed that Trojan horse.

"We must face the east," Muddy told him in a very serious and deep monotone.

"It's a good thing you're not going, Smitty. You'd have a helluva time figuring out which way to turn."

"That's the east," Margaret said, pointing north.

Hank snorted and turned.

"May Allah bless this flight," Muddy prayed aloud with what he thought was just the right touch of melodrama. Then he added in a stage whisper, "And please don't let that most horrid . . . gory . . . and bloody of all accidents happen *again*."

Hank looked sick. His jaw tightened until he had a tick in his cheek. He glanced down at the ground and rubbed his forehead with his free hand.

Muddy cast a quick glance at Margaret and winked, then turned to Hank. "Okay." He paused for a full minute. "Get ready." He paused again.

Hank looked up, his expression that of a man on his way to the executioner.

Muddy held Hank's hand firmly and warned, "Hang on . . ."

Hank's eyes narrowed.

". . . chump!"

And up they flew. Straight up.

"Sonufabi-i-i-itch!"

A good five hundred feet.

Hank blinked for a minute to get the purple smoke from his eyes. It didn't help. The interior of the bottle looked like a junkman's heaven. He'd been in pawn shops that were less cluttered.

Contraptions sat in every corner, some with cogs and belts and strange mechanics. An ancient battle ax and a bowl of figs and dates sat next to a fat clock filled with water and sand and a series of chutes that looked like a rat's maze.

There was a camera and tripod, a powdered wig, shoe buckles, and a collection of vests, each more gaudy than the last. A fancy board game like checkers sat next to a hand organ that was propped against a bed warmer and bellows.

Hank shifted, and his elbow hit a tall Greek urn filled with—he frowned and picked up a small book—dime novels? He glanced at the genie, who sat on the edge of an orange-and-red-striped bench seat with feet shaped like dragons. The genie's legs were crossed, and he rested his chin on one hand while he swung one foot to the tune of his toe bell.

Hank couldn't get used to this.

He looked down and saw stacks of newspapers, pamphlets, and scrolls piled beneath the seat.

He looked up. Silk drapes in purple and red and yellow hung like tents in a carnival nightmare from the sides of the bottle and a thin film of mosquito netting was hooked over brass wall hooks that were in the shape of pythons.

There were pillows, fancy tasseled pillows in every color and style, strewn over a collection of small but old Persian carpets. A gong went off near his right ear, and he turned just as a carved wooden clock chimed a stupid tune while a small wooden man and woman with finger cymbals for hats rolled out of doors in the face of the clock, rode along a small track where they met, then bent and banged their heads to the count of the hour.

He turned away and froze when he saw something he hadn't seen in years. Leaning against a gaudy red wall was a baseball bat, a black Al Spalding glove, and a ball.

He took a couple of stiff steps closer and picked up the baseball bat. The wood felt heavy, and he slid his hands to the grip, instinctively testing the bat for weight and balance. He held it in front of him and stared at it.

His mind drifted back to a time when he had one foolish dream—well, not a dream, but a chance. And now, after so many years had passed, it seemed as if that chance hadn't been a moment from his past, but one from someone else's life, some tall tale he'd heard another man telling, a story, a lie, an excuse—like the big fish that got away.

He looked at the bat in his hand. Perhaps because he'd been locked away for the last four years, perhaps because he was getting older, whatever, he stared at that damned baseball bat, and it stood for everything he'd thrown away over forty years, every door that might have opened and shone a crack of light on the dark path he'd chosen for himself, chosen because he was so damn afraid that life might not really be as bad as he thought it was.

He closed his eyes for a moment and saw himself running fast and hard with fists flying away from every opportunity. Ready to lose, because deep inside him, he was too damn scared to try to win.

"Hi, Hank!"

He whipped around. Theodore stood a few feet behind him. Hank stared at the kid for second, caught in a confusing lapse between the past and the present. He leaned the bat back against the wall, then faced Theodore.

As if fate were jeering him, the kid was wearing a

Chicago White Stockings baseball cap. A wreath of olive leaves hung around his neck, a toga was fitted over his clothes and hung on the floor next to a half-burned fiddle. The kid had a badminton racket slung over one shoulder. The white feather birdie was clutched in his fist. He lifted the hand with the badminton racket and waved.

Hank glanced at the genie, who sat on that divan watching him with great interest. Hank scowled.

The genie's eyes grew larger, and he snatched a novel from the Greek urn. "Don't mind me," he said too casually. He lay back on the divan, crossed one leg over the other, and began to read.

Hank waited, but Muddy didn't look up. "Come here, kid."

Theodore cocked his head at him but didn't move. "Am I in trouble?"

"Yeah."

"Oh."

"I said come here."

"I don't want to."

"If I have to walk over there, I'm going to be even madder."

"I wish—"

"Don't wish!" Hank dove for the kid, his hand reaching.

The kid clapped a hand over his mouth and gave him a sheepish look. The kid didn't say anything. Hank thought he heard a snort of muffled laughter and shot a look at the genie. He still lay there, seeming absorbed in his book.

Hank shook his head and looked back at Theodore. "Why wouldn't you come out of the bottle, kid?"

"'Cause."

"I want an answer."

Theodore looked down at his feet. "'Cause I wanted you to see it, too."

"So you wouldn't leave?"

The kid nodded.

Hank watched him. "Did you think about just asking me?"

He nodded again. "I didn't think you'd come."

Well, hell, he thought. The kid was right. He wouldn't have come. "Look, kid, you can't go through life manipulating everyone to get your own way." He could just hear Smitty if she'd heard that one. She'd have made some remark about the black pot talking to the kettle.

"But it worked."

"This time, maybe, you got away with it. But next time? No way, kid."

"Are you gonna give me a licking?"

That took him aback. "Did your father?"

"Sometimes."

Hank clasped his hands behind his back and looked away just as the genie whipped his nose back into the book. Hank looked back at Theodore. "Well, I'm not your father, kid."

Theodore was quiet for a long time, then whispered, "Could we pretend you were?"

"You want me to take a switch to your butt?"

"No."

"Good. 'Cause I don't hit kids."

The kid mumbled something.

"I can't hear you."

He looked up at Hank, his face serious. "I'd take a licking if it meant you could . . . someone would—" Theodore stopped, then blurted out, "I just want a dad."

He heard a sniffle and shot a quick glance at the genie. The book was shimmying in his pudgy, beringed hands.

Hank looked back at the kid; his face was turned up as if he were waiting for him to say yes. Hank shifted his gaze away and stared at that stupid clock. "I'm not dad material, kid. Sorry."

"What is dad material?"

Hank laughed a bitter laugh. "Hell if I know. I

never had a father." He looked at the kid but could tell his words hadn't satisfied him.

"Do you have to have a father to be a father? Can't you learn?"

Hank rubbed his chin and realized he had no answer. He paused, then squatted down so he was at eye level with him. "Look, I was an orphan and you're an orphan. We have something in common, so how about we just be buddies instead?"

The kid was quietly thoughtful. "I've never had a buddy. What do they do?"

Hank shrugged. "What we've been doing. You can help me, like you did with the sail and the hut."

"Do buddies do things together?"

"Sure."

"Like fishing?"

"Yeah, kid, we could do that."

"Swimming?"

"Yeah."

"I don't know how to swim."

"You can learn."

"If I can learn to swim, then why can't you learn to be a father?"

He could have sworn he heard someone mutter, "Answer that one, chump." But when Hank looked at the genie again, he hadn't moved.

He turned back to the kid. "Because it's easier to learn things when you're young."

Theodore was thinking. "Oh. I guess that has something to do with your ways."

"What ways?"

"I don't know. Smitty told us you were set in your ways."

"She did?"

He nodded.

Hank supposed that was better then telling the kid he was a pigheaded bastard, which both he and Smitty knew was true.

"Will you teach me how to play baseball?"

Hank spun around. "How did you know—" He cut himself off.

The kid had picked up the bat, and he was looking at Hank with a startled expression.

Hank realized with a sudden uneasiness that he had yelled at the kid about something the boy knew nothing about. No one here knew.

He looked over at the genie. He wasn't reading the book. He was watching Hank with penetrating interest. Hank scowled at him, but it didn't do any good this time, so he took the bat from the kid and tossed it on some pillows. "Let's get outta here, kid."

"But—"

"Now." Hank held out a hand. "Let's go."

The kid looked him, then set down the badminton racket and birdie. He took off the cap, wreath, and toga, solemnly handing them to Muddy. "Thank you. We have to leave now."

The genie set the things on the divan before he came over to Hank, the kid's hand held in his. Without a word he extended his other hand to Hank.

A second later they blasted out of the bottle.

Margaret knelt over Hank. He lay flat on the sand. Around him, a misty ring of purple smoke was slowly fading. Theodore, Muddy, and Lydia, who was holding a sleeping Annabelle, stood nearby and leaned over.

"Is he dead?" Theodore asked her.

"No, dear."

Hank moaned.

Margaret looked up at the others. "He's coming around." She placed her hand on his chest. "Hank?"

"Did I make it?" he asked in a distant voice. "Am I safe or out?"

"You were knocked out for a few minutes."

He groaned, then opened his eyes, which were

disoriented. He looked at her, at the children, then his dull gaze shifted to Muddy.

Hank blinked up at the sunlight from a face that looked as if it had sucked on bad pickles. He rubbed a hand over his eyes and swore like a sailor.

Margaret looked at the others and rolled her eyes. "He's all right, children. I told you there was nothing to worry about. He probably fell on his head. Run along now. Muddy will go with you."

"Wait!" Theodore paused and poked his red head over Margaret's shoulder. "You okay, Hank?"

"Sure, kid," he said in a raspy voice.

"Good! We're still buddies?"

"Yeah."

And he spun around and ran off. "Leedee! Wait for me!"

Hank scowled up at her. "What the hell happened?"

"When you shot out of the bottle, you let go of Muddy's hand."

He cursed again.

"Too bad you didn't fall on your mouth."

His eyes narrowed. "If I'd fallen on my mouth, then I couldn't have done this." His hand shot out, and he pulled her head down. He kissed her hard.

She shoved at his chest and jerked her head away. "Stop it!" She turned and spotted the children standing by the palm trees, gaping. She could feel her face flush bright red—at thirty-two years old.

"Hey, Leedee! Muddy! Stop!" Theodore hollered. "Did you see that? Hank and Smitty are smooching!"

"Curse your black heart, Hank Wyatt," she said in a hiss.

"I don't have a heart, Smitty." He sat up. "I'd have thought a smart woman like you would have figured that out by now."

"They're children."

He glanced at the children, then bellowed, "Smitty was just helping me catch my breath, kid! You go on."

He looked back at her. "Unless you wanna get kissed again, sweetheart, you'd better move your butt."

He slowly stood, muttering that he was getting "damn old." He rolled his shoulders, then rubbed the back of his head. He winced, then wiped his hand across his chest and reached for a banana growing nearby. He peeled it and began to eat.

She watched him for a second. "If Charles Darwin could see you now."

"Who?"

"Charles Darwin. The naturalist who theorized that we are descended from apes."

He gave her a long, unreadable look. "My education came from the streets, Smitty. There were no Charles Darwins." He stood straight and tall, his look challenging. "I don't use my mind to question life. I use it to stay alive."

She watched him and realized he was truly angry, and his voice was even more bitter. She moved toward him, then placed her hand gently on his arm. "Hank?"

He stared down at her from a face that gave nothing away.

"You have no reason to be ashamed."

He looked at her hand, then stared off some place over her head. "The children need you."

She'd been dismissed. "Hank . . ."

He turned and said nothing, just walked past her and across to a brow of rocks that jutted out over a crescent of white beach sand. He jumped down into the sand and stood there, his back to her, his hands shoved into his pockets, staring out at the lagoon.

"Hank, please . . ."

"Who the hell said I was ashamed?"

She'd said exactly the wrong thing. She stared at his hard back and took a couple of steps. "I'm not trying to fight with you."

"Good. Because you'd lose. Now get the hell outta here."

Over the next few days, the weather was their friend.
The winds had been only light island breezes, and to
Margaret's relief, there had been no rain. They had
started the new hut—a combined project. Within a
couple of days, the hut had a frame sturdy enough to
withhold the monsoon storms Hank grumbled about,
and it had strong walls of woven leaves and tied
bamboo.

Like a neutral country, the new shelter sat in the
clearing on a spot exactly halfway between the original huts. It was a long and narrow bungalow-type
structure with window shutters that could close the
hut off tightly from the driving tropical rains, yet
could be propped open with levers of bamboo to let
the sunshine and trade breeze through.

There was one door, and like the shutters, it was
made from rods of strong bamboo tied tightly together. A barrel filled with freshwater sat near the door.
There were hammocks woven of copra for sleeping
and mats for sitting.

A flat-topped trunk was a table and smaller barrels
served as stools. The tilley lit the hut, but the fuel was
quickly disappearing. They had little in the way of
comforts.

There was some argument about a kitchen. A
comment from Hank about needing a volunteer fire
department. Margaret conceded when she burned five
mangoes, then spent an hour making notes in the
sand about what island foods were eaten cooked and
what were eaten raw.

Hank's dark mood hadn't much changed. For some
reason, Margaret was certain that their Darwin conversation wasn't the reason for his brooding.

His resentment wasn't against her, but at the world in general. He remained silent, a man who looked as if he wanted to pick a fight with anyone who would oblige.

In an angry, cutting voice, he'd told Theodore to keep the genie inside the bottle, blustering that Muddy got in the way and distracted everyone—everyone being Hank, who groused about all that damned purple smoke.

But Hank had worked hard, and finally, because they all hounded him, he even let Muddy out of the bottle to help with the roof thatching. That was, however, after Hank had fallen through the roof twice. Purple smoke was nothing compared to the blue air around Hank.

At night, though, he would disappear. In the morning, when Margaret awoke, he would be asleep in one of the hammocks they had made, snoring and sleeping off a binge of drinking.

By the third night she decided to follow him. She figured luck was in her favor since she had only burned half the fish and three breadfruit that evening.

Margaret stepped outside the hut and walked toward the beach. A quarter moon hung high in the black sky, making the sand a little darker and the sea more gray than silver.

In the distance the waves rumbled against the rocks. But other than the booming sound of the sea and the slosh and sizzling sounds of the water hitting the sand, there was nothing else. No gulls, no clicking of the insects, no human voices, just the powerful voice of the Pacific Ocean.

She walked along the beach, her feet padding silently on the spongy sand. The wind picked up and whipped her skirt and hair. She searched the high beach and the rocks. She searched the dark corners where the coconut palms looked like open hands against the night sky.

Finally she climbed up onto a stack of rocks near the end of the cove and she saw him sitting on a small crescent of beach, hemmed in on every side by either rocks or sea. There was sheen of moonlight on him and she could see his black hair flow back in the night breeze. He sat in the sand, his arms resting on his bent knees, staring at the black miles of the Pacific.

She didn't move. Some sixth sense warned her. There was something bleak about him, something that hadn't been there before. Or perhaps she hadn't noticed it before.

For a few minutes, he looked as if he were part of a vast and distant place. She could see his face, just the outlines, the hard ridges of his jaw, neck, and shoulders. He was like a silhouette on glass—only the solid black outline and no clue as to who or what the person was. Just lines that drafted one's shape but defined nothing.

She took a step, and some pebbles rattled down the face of a rock.

He turned sharply, his posture suddenly guarded.

She stepped down into the soft, dry sand cooled by the night air and approached him. "What are you doing?"

"Celebrating." He lifted a bottle to his mouth and took a drink.

"More whiskey?"

"Rum."

"Where did you get it?"

"Buried treasure." He laughed and lifted the bottle to his mouth again. He took a huge swig, then wiped his mouth with the back of his hand. He held up the bottle. "Have a drink, sweetheart. You look like you could use it."

She shook her head.

"No guts?"

"I don't need liquor to color the world."

"I do."

"Perhaps you just think you do. It's a crutch."

He looked at her for a long and angry moment. "A crutch? Yeah, it is." He drank some more.

"You don't care?"

"Nope."

"But it's such a waste."

"That all depends."

"On what?"

"On whether you're talking to me or you." He laughed.

"You're impossible."

"Yeah, I know. But I'd bet if you drank some of this, you'd be possible."

"What's that supposed to mean?"

He didn't say anything. It was times like this that his silences were worse than his words.

He stared at the bottle as if his mind were a million miles away. Then he laughed a self-deprecating laugh and shook his head before he took another drink. She stood a few feet away and watched him, wondering what kind of life would bring a man to this point.

There was a taint about Hank as if each of his years had slowly decayed him. No one could miss it. At times like this, he wore it like a hero wore his medals.

He was a rugged, cynical man with a distant isolation about him, a part of him that wasn't open to the world. A part of him that said keep away. Hank Wyatt had all the scars and bruises of someone who had gone through hell at an early age and was still trying to get even.

"I'm sorry," she said softly. And she was sorry not for how she felt, but sorry for him.

He looked up at her as if he just remembered she was there. He took another drink, then stared out at the sea. "Me, too, sweetheart. Real damn sorry."

She shook her head, turned, and walked away.

Maybe it was the booze that made Hank think. Maybe it was the trip inside that bottle and reminders of his past. But each night he had sat here on this small plot of beach. Alone. He'd recounted the years in his mind, drowning the memories with enough booze to make him forget who he was or who he could have been.

Whiskey and rum could drown both dreams and failures.

So he drank, a kind of self-persecution for every goddamn mistake he'd ever made. And over forty years he'd made plenty. As a kid he'd been warned, heard the words but didn't heed them—that he was someone bent on destruction. "You'll never be anything, Henry James Wyatt."

He'd heard similar warnings when was an angry, young kid of fifteen, and the grizzled old owner of a baseball team had bellowed at him, "No one can destroy your life but you, you hardheaded bastard."

And Billy Hobart, that grizzled, old owner, had been right.

Hank was forty years old, and there wasn't much left of him. He wondered what else he had destroyed inside of himself. Or, he thought, had there ever been something to destroy?

He had fought so long against being what everyone else was, telling himself they were the world's suckers. But he wondered now if the only sucker out there was him.

He held the bottle to his lips and took a long drink, not because he needed it or even because he wanted it, but because it dulled his mind, dulled the truth he had to face. He was a man who had been throwing himself away for so damn many years that he didn't know how to stop.

Hank awoke to a loud crash. He groaned and turned over. His head felt like it was about to explode. He opened one eye, then the other. The sunlight made his head throb and about killed him.

Smitty's shadow came past, and a loud clash of

metal against metal echoed through his head and down into his teeth.

"God," he groaned and clapped his hands over his ears.

She walked past him, pausing at the doorway. "Good morning," she said brightly.

He scowled up at her from his hammock. "Don't you ever sleep?"

"I'm a morning person."

"She's a morning person," he repeated as she disappeared through the door. He flung an arm over his eyes and lay there. His mouth felt like something had died in it.

Another crash echoed through his pounding head. It sounded like a train wreck. He staggered to his feet.

No, the train wreck was in his head.

He sucked in a breath of pain, then blinked and stumbled toward the water bucket they kept inside. He looked at the cup hanging next to it, ignored it, and picked up the whole bucket. He chugged down half of the water, then wiped his mouth with the back of his hand. His mouth felt half human again.

He went outside, stood in the doorway, and watched her. Smitty was whipping around like a busy little beaver, clanging pots and pans and clattering seemingly anything and everything that was metal against metal.

He'd never flinched so much in his life. "What the hell are you doing?"

"Cooking." She hammered some more pans together.

"Cooking what? A train?" He ran a hand through his hair and kept it there when she tossed an iron lid against a kettle.

"Fruit." She held up a bottle and dumped it into a pan.

"Sweet Jesus! That's my rum!"

She looked up. "Oh, it is?" She held the bottle up

again, eyed the last two inches of booze, and dumped the rest of it in the pan. "Thank you for sharing it." She gave him a sugary smile that made him itch to do something to her. But he couldn't think of anything terrible enough with his head pounding and his ears ringing. Even his teeth hurt.

She lit a match and dropped it into the pan.

He groaned and swayed. His rum turned orange and blue and went up in the air with loud whoosh!

He was going to kill her, but later, when he felt human again. He was going to do it with his bare hands.

She frowned and stuck a stick into the pan, then whipped it around as if she knew what she was doing. She grabbed one of the sticks he'd sharpened to use for spits and jabbed it into the pan, then pulled out something brown and black and slimy. She walked over and held it in front of his face.

The sweet, sickening smell of burnt rum hit him like a hard pitch to the gut. His stomach turned over. He could feel his blood drain from his head. His hand shot out and gripped one of the door's support poles.

"You look a little wan. Probably from lack of food." She waved it near his nose. "Want a bite?"

He lurched past her and stumbled across the sand, almost running over the children. His hand over his mouth, he staggered to the oleander bushes and heaved his guts out.

"What's the matter with Hank?" Theodore asked.

"You know, Theodore, I'm not really certain." Smitty's voice dripped with feigned innocence. "I guess Hank doesn't have the stomach for bananas flambé."

Muddy asked himself if kismet truly existed.

It was difficult to believe anything or anyone would have had a hand in stranding Margaret Smith and Hank Wyatt together anywhere, let alone an uninhabited Pacific island. Either fate was cruel or had a wickedly black sense of humor.

Over the next week, Muddy had watched Margaret develop the hunting skills of a ferret. She'd managed to find two more bottles of Hank's liquor. She'd come running back to the hut in the middle of the night, the bottles hidden in her skirts as she sneaked inside the hut and tiptoed over to a dark corner.

She'd cast a quick glance at Hank snoring in his hammock, then she'd hide them in an iron cooking pot and slide the lid quietly in place. The next afternoon, while Muddy was on the roof finishing the last of the thatch, he caught a glimpse of her laughing with wicked glee as she dumped a fortune's worth of Napoleon brandy into the fuel base of the tilley lamp. The lamp burned freely for two straight nights.

The third night, Hank caught on.

He stormed into the hut. "Where the hell's my booze!"

Margaret closed the bamboo door behind him and turned away. "I can't imagine."

"Listen to me, Smitty. You'd better come clean."

"I just took a bath this morning."

"Cute." He closed the distance between them and scowled down at her. "Look. Don't pretend you don't know what I'm talking about. We both know I buried the bottles and you dug them up. Your sneaky footprints were all over the sand. So don't play the innocent. Now where's the brandy?"

"I put it to good use." She turned up the lamp, smiled calmly, then turned around and crossed her arms. Lined up along the wall like trophies were two squat brandy bottles and one tall rum bottle—all empty.

Hank looked at the bottles, then said, "There's one bottle left and I'll be damned if you're going to get it." His look turned retributive. He drove his hand through his hair, something he seemed to do a lot around Margaret. "This is war, Smitty." He stormed out the door.

She stared at the door, her expression thoughtful. She looked down for a second and turned around.

She caught Muddy's look. "You are a brave woman, Margaret Smith. Braver than most. He won't rest till he gets even. Revenge was in his eyes."

She shrugged, but she stared at the doorway for a moment and rubbed her arms as if she were uncomfortable. "Better that he be good and angry than drunk and feeling sorry for himself." She looked back at Muddy. "I'll take the brunt of his anger if it will help him."

A few minutes later Muddy went back inside his bottle to the peace and quiet and familiarity of his home. He settled down with a new novel: *The Story of the Wild West: Campfire Chats* by Buffalo Bill. He opened it and read a page, then put the book down on his chest and locked his hands behind his head. Over the last few days, Western folklore had lost its appeal.

He stared up at the mouth of his bottle. The stopper was out and he could make out the glow of the tilley lamp. Muddy lay there, grinning. Perhaps the fates knew what they were doing after all.

The next morning Hank was sitting on a rock near the hut. He had spent the whole night plotting revenge. He just couldn't think of the exact way to get even with Smitty. Whatever he did had to be the perfect thing.

So he figured he'd keep thinking, just lull her into a sense of security. Then *bam!* He'd give it to her.

Whatever *it* was.

He rubbed his stubbled chin, then went back to cleaning the pistol—a navy Colt .38, six-shot. But there were only five bullets and no more ammunition in the trunk.

He cleaned the barrel, made a big deal of it, too, because he'd caught Smitty eyeing him and the pistol as if she expected him to use it on her. He wouldn't, but a little intimidation couldn't hurt. Might even win the war.

He set the pistol aside and began to work on sharpening the knife with a lava stone. A man was only as good as the quality and care of his tools. Or weapons.

He heard a loud bleat and looked up just as Rebuttal came trotting by with his last bottle of whiskey in its mouth, the frayed ends of a chewed rope trailing limply behind her.

Hank did a double take. "Goddammit! How'd you get that?"

He dropped the knife and dove for the goat, but it trotted off down the beach.

Hank got up and took off after it in a cloud of sand. Rebuttal began to run. He didn't know a goat could run that fast. It could turn on a dime and dodge him better than a batter could dodge a wild pitch. The damn thing ran right into the thick jungle with his last bottle.

He went after it.

Not that he really wanted the whiskey, although having to put up with Smitty could drive a preacher to drink. Now it was the principle. Damn females—human and animal—kept swiping his booze.

Fifteen minutes later, Hank came stumbling out of the jungle, sweat pouring from his hair and down his face and neck. His shirt was soaked, his pants had fern fronds and flower petals clinging to them along with a few gnats and bugs. He took deep breaths, and his chest burned like hell, but it didn't matter.

He had the whiskey bottle in hand. He broke into the clearing and held up the bottle as if he'd just caught a fly ball and expected cheers.

Smitty stood alone near the doorway of the hut. She looked at him from narrowed eyes.

"The last bottle, sweetheart." He crowed. "And I

got it. You lost the final battle." He bent over, one hand resting on his knee while he caught his breath. He was still laughing when he straightened.

"Drop the bottle, Hank."

"Like hell! Give me that gun, Smitty! You might hurt someone."

She shook her head.

"Well, then, you're just going to have to shoot me, sweetheart, 'cause I'm not letting go of this bottle."

"Fine." She raised the pistol.

He laughed. "Oooo-whee! I'm scared." He took a step.

She held the gun with two hands.

"Hey, sweetheart. You almost look as if you know what you're doing." Then he laughed again.

She aimed, and he watched her finger slide to the trigger.

"Wait a damn minute, Smitty. I—"

She shot the bottle.

Shattered glass and whiskey flew like winter sleet. He froze. He looked at his right hand.

Whiskey dripped from it. All he was holding was the glass neck of the bottle. "No shit . . ." He clamped his gaping mouth closed and looked up again.

She smiled, blew the smoke from the pistol like a gunfighter, and calmly went back inside the hut.

❧ 21 ❧

Margaret tied the last ribbon in Lydia's braids. "There. All done."

Lydia turned around. The part in her hair was off by a good inch. One loose and lumpy braid was in front of her ear and the other started two inches higher, was too tight, and stuck out from behind her ear at a ninety-degree angle.

Margaret chewed her lip for a second. "I think they're a bit lopsided." She reached for the hairbrush. "Let me try again."

Lydia sighed and sat back down on a barrel. She sat there utterly silent while Margaret brushed her dark blond hair and divided it into sections.

She cast a quick glance at Annabelle. She was asleep on a nearby mat.

Lydia was absently staring at her hands. After a minute she asked, "How did you learn to swim?"

"My dad taught me."

"Oh."

"Why?"

"I just wondered."

Margaret continued to brush the girl's hair and she waited.

"Do fathers usually do things with their daughters?"

"Some do."

"What else did your father do with you?"

"He taught me to roller skate and to jump rope."

"He did?"

Margaret laughed. "He had my uncles turn the jump rope and he showed me how to jump double time. Right out in the middle of the park, where everyone could see him. He's very tall. Now that I think about it, it must have looked pretty odd, a tall, distinguished lawyer in that park jumping rope." She smiled at the memory and wondered what her dad was doing right then. If he knew yet about the ship.

"He's a lawyer, too?"

Margaret nodded, then took a deep breath and said, "And he's a state supreme court judge."

"What else did he teach you?"

"He took me skating at the roller rink once and fractured his arm. He taught me to ride a horse, and when I was thirteen, he taught me to shoot a pistol."

Lydia was quiet. "My papa was a botanist. Mama said his work was important so we had to understand that he couldn't be with us much."

"I don't think that's unusual, Lydia. My dad and I, well, we only had each other after my mother died."

After a few minutes Lydia asked, "Can you still remember what your mother looked like?"

Margaret paused. "She was tall, like I am. And she had dark hair and eyes and the most beautiful smile." She looked at the braid and realized she'd lost count. It was falling out. She brushed it out and started again. "What did your mother look like?"

"She had red hair like Theo and Annabelle and blue eyes."

"Like yours."

Lydia leaned her head back and looked at Margaret. "I think so. I don't remember." She was quiet, then she asked, "When people die, do they become angels?"

"I don't know."

They were both pensive.

"Do you believe in heaven?"

"Yes."

"Do you think people in heaven can see us?"

"I'd like to think that my mother can see me and that your mother and father can see you. We're the part of them that's still here. Perhaps they're keeping an eye on us."

"Like guardian angels?"

"Um-hmm." Margaret stopped, then said, "I'll tell you something I've never told anyone, but I'd like to keep it between us. Our secret, okay?"

Lydia turned around and nodded.

"I remember once when I was about your age I was playing with some other children at a birthday party, and we were chasing after a barrel hoop. It went down the hillside, and the kids wanted me to run after it. I was always running, racing the boys and winning, so I ran after that hoop. It rolled and rolled down through some trees and over a few grassy hills. I ran faster and faster, because it was rolling toward the cliffs at the edge of the bay.

"The hoop finally stopped rolling right at a high cliff. I slowed down to a walk when I saw that I wasn't going to lose it after all. When I was a few feet away, I took a step toward it, and someone grabbed my arm and pulled me back. It happened so suddenly that I was scared. I looked up, but there was no one there. I turned around. I was all alone. Not a soul anywhere.

"A second later, I turned back, and the place where I was going to step just literally crumbled away. The ground, the dirt and rocks and the hoop, everything tumbled down the cliff side onto the rocks below."

Margaret paused again. "If I had stepped where I was going to, I would have been killed."

Lydia looked up at her. "You think it was your mama?"

"I don't know."

"I think it was," Lydia said with more surety than Margaret had ever felt about that incident. To this day she could still feel that touch on her arm as vividly as if someone had just touched her again. And since it didn't make logical sense, she never spoke of it. Until now. But she'd felt it as surely as she'd seen Muddy fly.

She looked down at Lydia and sighed. Both braids stuck out like cattlehorns. "I think I'm still not doing this right."

Lydia reached up and felt the braids and frowned. "Want me to take them out?"

Lydia shook her head and one braid drooped. But it didn't matter. Because Lydia reached out and slid her arms around Margaret's waist, hugged her, and said, "Thank you."

Hell, she'd been thinking again. Hank recognized that walk. He stood in the waist-high water after his morning swim and watched her march down the beach toward him. Smitty stopped at the waterline and crossed her arms in that annoying way she had when she was about to start a stupid argument or demand equality or tell him he was wrong.

"We need to talk about the children."

"What about them?" He slicked the hair out of his face and wiped away the water that was running into his eyes.

She wasn't looking him in the eye. She was staring at his chest. He looked down, wiped it a few times, but didn't see anything.

"I think we need a chest—" She shook her head a second, muttered something he didn't hear, and pinched the bridge of her nose. "Let me start over." She looked up at him.

He waved her on. "Go ahead."

"We need a schedule, an agenda so to speak. To both spend time with the children individually and together. I think we need a plan."

He crossed his arms. "Theodore and I already have plans."

"But Lydia needs to be involved, too. She needs to be included as much as Theodore, maybe more so."

"She's a girl."

She arched a brow at him "And . . ."

"You're a woman. She should be with you."

"She lost her father, too."

"I'm no father substitute, Smitty. I told the kid that and I'm telling you that. No way."

"You can't make her feel excluded because of sex."

He gave her a wicked grin. "Sex includes, it doesn't exclude. Want me to show you, sweetheart?"

"I'm trying to have a rational conversation, and you are being purposely obtuse and lewd."

"Well, Smitty, let me tell you something for a change. I'm no chump. You're asking me for help after you stole, burned, and shot my booze. You're the one who wants the world to be fair and equal." He laughed. "That's like you scratch my back and I'll scratch yours. No backscratch. No deal."

"I'm thinking of Lydia, not myself."

"And that's your problem, Smitty. You think too much."

"You're better off—we all are—without you being drunk."

"If I were drunk, I might be less obtuse and lewd."

She muttered something just as a wave broke near her bare feet, then gave him one of those direct looks, her chin high and challenging.

He crossed his arms. "I didn't hear you."

She sighed as if her patience was running out. After a moment she said, "Please come out of the water so I don't have to stand here and shout."

He made a mock bow. "Sure thing, Smitty. Whatever you say." And he walked out of the water.

"Ohmygod!" she shrieked and spun around. "You're naked!"

"What's the matter?" He held out his arms. "I'm just doing what you told me." He grinned at her back.

"Intimidation isn't going to work," she called out over her shoulder.

"Then how about compromise, sweetheart?" He paused on purpose. "Let me *think*. Hmmm ... I suppose you could take off your clothes. Then we'd both be naked. If that'd make you feel better, go right ahead."

She shook her head and walked up the beach, not looking back.

He cupped his hands around his mouth. "Anyone ever tell you, Smitty, that you're no fun?"

"I wasn't put on this earth for your amusement, Hank!" she hollered back without stopping.

He shook his head, then said under his breath, "That's what you think, sweetheart." He strolled over to a palm tree and picked up his pants. He looked at them for a moment and grinned like the devil.

He glanced back to the beach, but she was gone. He rubbed his chin with one hand. Well, well, he thought, she's cooked her own goose.

Then he remembered it was Smitty. She hadn't cooked it. She'd probably burned it. He glanced down at his clothes again and laughed. Revenge was going to be sweet.

He swiped her clothes.

Got up bright and early just for the occasion and waited until she went to take her bath at the freshwater pool near the waterfall. He slunk along, his back pressed to the rocks that walled off the pool. As he moved, he rubbed his hands together and grinned.

Life was grand.

She was in the water. He could hear her splashing around and humming. He chuckled to himself and waited. He figured if he could get an eyeful while he was getting even, then what the hell?

He peered over the edge of the rock wall. He could make out the reflection of white female skin under the water and long sleek legs. He gave a quiet whistle through his teeth.

He took a few more minutes and caught a sweet glimpse of the finest ass this side of heaven. Then he waited until she was across the pool, swimming on the other side.

He whipped around the rocks and snatched up her clothes. She was leaning back and dipping her hair in the water, her arms raised and her cleavage exposed.

He stood there, because it was too good to pass up. He moved toward the rocks with all the stealth he could muster. He paused for one last look.

Whoa, boy.

Then he disappeared around the rocks before he could say Smitty's goose was burned.

It was his lucky day. He had an eyeful of woman and a bucketful of oysters. After stealing her clothes, then leaving them in the hut, he'd gone diving and found an oyster bed.

He brought up a bucket of oysters, his mind thinking of pearls more than of food. He trudged onto the beach, dropped the bucket, and pulled on his pants and shirt.

Come to Papa, all you sweet island pearls.

He took out his knife and sat on the beach, opening the rough-shelled oysters one by one.

Oyster after oyster. After empty oyster.

He stared at the bucket filled with oysters as pearlless as he was. This was the South Seas, home of the most magnificent and valuable pearls that had ever been found. And not one bloody pearl in any of these oysters?

He swore and tossed the last oyster back in the bucket. Something small and white ricocheted out and pelted him in the arm. He dug around in the sand and found it.

One small milky pearl. He held it up to the sun. It was still frosty and light shone through it, meaning it wasn't worth much, for in truth it was barely a pearl. Hank picked it up and tucked it in his pants' pocket anyway.

"Whatchagot?" Theodore stood a few feet away.

"Food."

"Oh." He rocked on his toes. "What kind of food?"

"Oysters."

"Oh." He stepped closer and frowned into the bucket. "What are oysters?"

"Food."

"What kind of food?"

Hank grinned. "Oysters."

The kid giggled. "What are oysters?"

"Food." Hank reached out and ruffled Theodore's hair. "You're getting it, kid!"

Theodore grinned back, then shifted his look to the bucket.

"Oysters are like mussels," Hank explained.

"Yuk!" The kid wrinkled his nose. He leaned over farther and frowned at them, then looked up again. "Do they smoke?"

Hank started laughing. He stood and picked up the bucket. "No. That's just the way Smitty cooks everything." He paused, then he grinned and poked the kid in the arm. "Hey. Here's a riddle for you. What should you do if you're ever lost?"

The kid shrugged. "I don't know."

"Just wait until suppertime. . . . Look for the smoke, then follow it back home."

"Like smoke signals!"

"Yeah, kid." Hank chuckled. Now where was Smitty when he was being so damn witty?

But Theodore just stood there, his hands locked behind him. He stared at Hank from a face that had serious thoughts—too serious for a little kid.

Hank nudged him in the arm. "Why the long face?"

He shrugged.

"I thought we were buddies."

"We are."

"Then spill it."

"I heard Smitty say she was gonna learn to cook even if it killed her."

She might take all of us with her, Hank thought, remembering the previous night when she had cooked the breadfruit so long it had actually disappeared.

"I don't want Smitty to die like everyone else."

"That's just an expression. Cooking can't really kill her." Hank looked down at him for a second, then said, "As for dying . . . You have to face facts, kid. Nothing lives forever."

"Why?"

"Because death is part of life."

"Why can't we live forever and ever?"

"Because everything has to die, then something else can live."

"I don't want to die."

"When we die, there is part of us left behind."

Hank squatted down until he was eye level with Theodore. "You know that word game we just played where we end up asking the same questions? It's like a circle, right?"

"Uh-huh."

"Life is like that, too." Hank drew a circle in the sand. "The earth starts off as dust and then man is born, lives his life, then he dies and becomes dust, part of the earth again. You understand?"

"Sort of."

Hank grabbed a handful of sand. "Hold out your hand."

The kid did, and Hank poured the sand into his hand. "Feel the sand."

Theodore rubbed it around in his hand, running his thumb over it and closing his palm tightly.

"Tell me what it feels like."

"Little rocks."

"That's right. That handful of sand used to be rocks—big rocks. Like those over on the cliffs."

"It did?"

Hank nodded. "But the sea and wind and time turned the rock into this sand. The sand you're holding could have been rocks that were all the way across the world."

"Really?"

"Yeah."

"Like China?"

"Sure, kid. Remember what Smitty told you happens when you melt sand?"

"It becomes glass."

"That's right. And you can mix sand with special kinds of chemicals you get from other rocks and dirt and mountains. If you mix them all with water, you have cement or concrete. They use concrete for buildings—"

"And statues in parks and stuff like that."

Hank nodded. "So life works the same way. Even though something is gone suddenly, like the big rock.

It's not really gone. The rock is always there as sand or glass or concrete. It never goes away completely." Hank pointed at the circle in the sand. "Just like this. You understand?"

"Then part of Mama and Dad are still here?"

Hank nodded and pointed to the kid's chest. "You were part of them; so were your sisters. And you're still here."

The kid nodded, then waited a second. "But what happens when we die?"

"Your children live on."

"Do you have any children?"

Hank laughed. "No."

"How come?"

Hank shrugged that one off.

"Then what happens when you die?"

Hank gave him a long look. "I expect I'll be buried, turn to dust, then I'd like to think maybe a big wind'll come by someday and blow me somewhere real special."

"What about heaven?"

Hank looked at the kid, then touched his temple. "In here"—and he touched his chest—"and in here. That's what goes to heaven, kid. You understand?"

Theodore nodded.

"Here's another question for you, like the riddles." Hank picked up a shell and tossed it into the ocean. "That shell was an oyster, which used to be a sea creature, then it died, and now it's a seashell. The water and sand will break it up, and eventually, after a long, long time, what will happen?"

Theodore's face brightened. "It'll turn into sand!"

"You're a smart kid, you know that?"

He grinned.

"Come on." Hank straightened and picked up the bucket. "Let's take these back." He started up the beach, and a second later the kid was dogging his steps. Hank glanced down and shortened his strides.

Theodore slid his hand around one side of the

bucket handle so they both were carrying it. He looked up at Hank. "Will the oyster go to heaven?"

"Yeah, kid."

"How do you know?"

Hank stopped, set down the bucket, and pulled the small pearl out of his pocket. "See this? You know what it is?"

"A pearl?"

"Yeah. Pearls come from oysters."

"They do?"

"Yep. Hold out your hand." Hank dropped the small pearl in the kid's palm. "You know anything about heaven?"

"God lives there and so do the angels."

Hank picked up one of the oyster shells and set it in his palm. "See the shell, kid?"

He nodded.

"It's rough and ugly on the outside, but look at the inside." Hank turned it over so that its pearlescent side was showing.

"It looks like a pearl."

"That's right." Hank grinned. "Ever heard of the Pearly Gates?"

Theodore looked from him to the shell and then to the pearl in his hand. His face lit up, and he laughed.

Hank looked down at him and winked, then picked up the bucket again. "Let's go."

Theodore dogged his steps. "We're buddies, Hank, aren't we?"

"Yeah, kid."

"Yeah," Theodore mimicked in a deep voice that made Hank grin. The kid took hold of the other side of the bucket handle again as they walked up the beach.

Hank watched Theodore try to ape his walk. "Say, kid?"

"Hm?" He missed a step, then looked up.

"I'll take this." He shifted the bucket to his other hand.

The kid frowned. But before he could say anything, Hank nudged him in the arm, then took off running. "I'll race you back!" He called out over a shoulder.

Theodore charged after him. "You cheated!"

"Nah . . . You just gotta give the oldest buddy a head start."

"Hey, Smitty! We brought you something new to burn!" Hank chuckled and walked through the door of the hut with the kid in his wake. He looked around the inside.

There was a low moan from a lump in the dark corner.

Hank set down the bucket of oysters and crossed the room. "Smitty?"

"Go soak your head, Hank Wyatt." She was huddled in a knot in the corner, her knees pulled against her chest and her head turned away from him and resting on her knees.

"What the hell are you doing?"

"Trying not to shoot you."

"Ah, yeah. The clothes." He gave another wicked laugh. "Snuck those suckers right out from under your nose, sweetheart." He looked at her clothes. "I see you found them."

"But not for hours," she said weakly, then looked up at him.

Hank looked at her and froze.

"You got sunburned," the kid said.

It was an understatement. She was sunfried.

Her face. Her neck. Her eyelids and lips and cheeks. Her arms and hands were all bright reddish pink. She had little tiny white creases in the corners of her eyes. It was one helluva burn.

She looked down at herself and muttered, "I don't need whatever you have in that bucket. I already found something else to burn."

He felt about as low as a person could. He wanted to say something. But the right words escaped him—

if there even were right words for a time like this. So he just stood there, not knowing what to say.

She shifted and tried to get up, then gasped.

"I'll help." He reached out.

She turned too fast and flinched, her eyes moist with pain. "Don't you think you've done enough?"

"Yeah, sweetheart. I guess I have." He put his hands on her waist and lifted her up.

She only moaned once.

"Can you walk?"

She nodded and waddled like a wind-up toy for a few feet.

"Smitty . . ."

"I can't watch the baby."

"Where is she?"

"Asleep, over there." She tried to raise her arm. She sucked in a breath of pain and bit her lip.

"Where's Lydia?"

"I sent her to get some more fruit."

Theodore ran over to the flat trunk they used as a table and he picked up the bottle. "I can get Muddy out—"

"No!" Hank bellowed, then ran a hand through his hair. "I told you. Just leave that bottle alone."

Theodore looked at Hank from a sulky face. "You don't like Muddy."

Hank didn't say anything. He just spun around and strode toward the door.

"Hank!" Smitty called after him.

"I'll be back!" He called out over a shoulder.

"Where are you going? Wait please! I can't take care of Annabelle. I can't even lift her!" Her voice was almost a moan.

He stopped in the doorway. "Stay here and help Smitty, kid. I'll be back in a few minutes."

It was a few hours before Margaret could move without feeling as if her skin was going to burst.

A shadow loomed over her. "Feeling any better?"

She looked up at Hank. "Just ducky."

He stood there looking like someone who thought his feet and hands were too big. He looked away for a tense moment, then turned back. "Did the stuff I gave you help?"

"Yes. It doesn't hurt as much."

He had came back to the hut a short time after he'd left, his arms filled with a thick waxy-leafed plant. He'd squeezed juice out of it and gave it to her to rub on her skin. Some concoction he said they used in the prison rock quarry when inmates got badly burned or exposed.

He gave her a long once-over look. "You need to go down to the beach."

"Now there's something I could use. A little more sunshine."

"I'm trying to tell you what you should do."

"Oh, forgive me, I forgot. I'm the woman. You're the man. Please tell stupid little me what I should do."

He rubbed the back of his neck with one hand and shook his head. "God but you can be a sarcastic b—"

"Don't say it!" She held up her hand. "Don't."

"Oh, hell! I'm sorry, dammit!" He ran his hand through his hair, then jammed both his hands in his pockets and began to pace—all gestures that she had come to realize meant Hank Wyatt was feeling some uncomfortable emotion.

"Stealing my clothes was a cruel trick, Hank."

"How the hell was I supposed to know you'd go and get yourself sunburned?"

"I didn't 'go and get myself sunburned.' I didn't have any clothes."

"Well, hell. What did you do, just stand there buck naked in the hot sun?"

"Yes, and in the water," she whispered.

He said nothing, just gave her that you're-out-of-your-mind kind of look.

Very softly she admitted, "I thought you'd be waiting if I came out."

"I wasn't there." He gave her an odd look.

"So I realized . . . two hours later."

"I didn't think of it," he muttered, staring thoughtfully at the ground.

She hurt too much to throw something at him and didn't feel up to sparring with him anymore. "Just go away. Please. Go and watch the children. I can't. I just can't."

He watched her for a second, then turned around. He started to take a step but stopped, his back to her and his hands still in his pockets. "If you go down to the beach and go in the ocean a couple of times a day, Smitty, the saltwater will help your skin heal."

"Right now, I just want to go to sleep," she whispered, gently laying her burning hot cheek on one sore arm. And she closed her puffy eyes.

Hank served the children oysters on the half shell. Lydia, Theodore, and Annabelle sat in a small circle on grass mats in the center of the hut. He set one of Smitty's pans, a big skillet, down in front of them. It was layered with fresh raw oysters.

He sat down next to them and picked up an oyster, lifted the shell to his mouth, and let it slide down his throat.

Ahhhhh. All it needed was a little Tabasco sauce. A few beers on the side . . . Yeah.

He ate three more before he realized the children were staring at him. He gazed back at them over the rippled, pearly edge of the oyster shell that rested on his lip. His gaze went left, then right, then back to them.

Three sets of wide and serious blue eyes watched him.

He swallowed, then waved a hand. "Go ahead. Eat."

"I'm not hungry," Lydia said quietly.

Theodore shook his head. "Me either!"

Hank looked at the baby. She reached out a hand and poked the oyster a couple of times, then stared at her finger and brought it slowly back to her nose. She made an awful face. "Sit!"

Hank scanned the group one more time, then crossed his arms. "Eat!"

They looked at the skillet as if it were a monster.

"Just try 'em! They're great. Go on."

Lydia stared at one, then slowly picked it up. She brought it to her mouth, looked cross-eyed at it, and swallowed hard. She looked up at him, then back at the oyster. She dropped it like it was on fire. "I can't. I just can't!" She shuddered and wiped her hand on her skirt a few times.

"Hey, buddy." Hank nodded at the kid. "You're a man. Go ahead. Show these sissy girls how silly they are."

The kid shook his head.

"Go on!"

Theodore picked one up, then quickly exchanged a worried look with Lydia. He brought it to his small mouth, his freckled nose wrinkled, and he paused.

Hank gave him a go-on nod.

The kid took a deep breath and gagged.

Hank shot across the mat, slammed his hand over the kid's mouth, and ran outside with him. He left Theodore at the same oleander bush where he'd lost his guts.

He stormed through the door and stood there, scowling.

Annabelle was rubbing oysters in her hair and ears. Lydia's gaze was locked on her folded hands.

"What's going on?" Smitty asked, yawning.

"I thought you were asleep."

"I was."

He picked up the oysters and walked over to her. "They won't eat!"

"Really?" She craned her sunburned neck a little, then flinched slightly. "What are you feeding them?"

"Oysters!" He shook the skillet in her face.

"You're making me dizzy."

"Oh." He stilled his hand. "Look at these."

"Ummm." Her eyes lit up and she reached for one. She had it in her mouth in two shakes. "Good," she said with her mouth full.

"You're damn right they are!"

She grabbed three more, popped them in her mouth one by one and nodded. "Mmmm. Mmmm."

She flinched suddenly. "Ouch!" Her eyes grew really huge, and her sunburned cheek bulged with the oyster.

Hank stared at her.

The lump of oyster shifted from cheek to cheek, then she raised her hand and spit into it. "Oh, my . . . Will you look at that!"

He blinked once.

"A pearl!"

He didn't breathe. He didn't move. He couldn't.

She held up the most perfect black pearl he'd ever seen.

❧ 22 ❧

"Did you say what I think you just said?" Margaret stared openmouthed at Hank. He held Annabelle, who was squirming and screaming and kicking for all she was worth.

"She's got the pearl up her goddamned nose."

Margaret blinked, then opened her mouth. "How—" She cut herself off, then shook her head. "Never mind."

He stared at the baby as if she had two heads, then he looked up, frowning. "Do you think it's dangerous?"

"No, of course not. It's perfectly normal to have a pearl stuck up your nose."

"Shit, Smitty! I need your help here. How the hell do we get it out?" He was agitated and began to pace even faster than before.

Margaret studied the baby's nose. There was a slight bulge high on the bridge. "Let's press on the side of her nose and force it down."

"I did that. That's when she started screaming and kicking."

"Hold her and I'll try. But first take her over to the trunk."

They walked across the hut and lay the baby down.

"Hold her down, Hank."

"She hates me," he muttered.

"Mama! Mama!" Annabelle tried to get up. Her small face was red and angry. Tears poured down her cheeks. She kept trying to reach for Margaret, kicking her feet when Hank wouldn't let her go.

Hank's tanned skin grew pale as if someone were sticking bamboo under his fingernails.

"There, sweetie. It's okay, Annabelle. It's okay." Margaret stroked her arm and leaned over her. She lifted her hand toward the baby's nose and Annabelle screamed as if she was dying, and she twisted her head and began to bang it against the trunk.

"Damn!" Hank's hands were shaking. "Can't you pry it out?"

"What a good idea. Get me a crowbar, will you? Then we'll just cram it up her nose. Babies and jammed doors are so much alike."

Hank swore under his breath.

Margaret tried to think, but she realized that they were both just standing there—two adults—staring at a screaming toddler and neither one of them having any idea what they should do.

"Just hold her while I think for a minute." Margaret stood back and began to catalog details, to analyze the situation.

Hank picked up the baby and held her out in front of him, staring at her nose and her teary face. He set her back down on the trunk, and they just eyed each other. He brought his finger up to wipe a gnat from her tear-streaked cheek, and she started crying again. Louder.

He stared at the baby with the same look the judge had given Margaret her first day in court.

A second later Lydia and Theodore came through the door. They looked at the baby. Lydia picked up a piece of fruit. "What's the matter with her?"

"Annabelle has the pearl stuck up her nose," Margaret told her.

"Oh." Lydia casually peeled the banana. "She does that all the time."

Hank's jaw jutted out like a mule, and he bellowed, "She sticks pearls up her nose?"

"Peas," Theodore said matter-of-factly.

Hank swore three choice words, which Annabelle repeated in a sodden voice.

"Once she put a rock up there," Lydia said with her mouth full.

"An' that Indian-head penny, too. Remember, Leedee?"

"How did they come out?" Margaret stared at the baby. Annabelle sat in the middle of the trunk, quietly sucking on her fingers, tears streaking her pink face. She eyed them suspiciously.

"Mama always made her sneeze."

"Sneeze?" Margaret nodded, tapping a finger against her lips. "Yes, sneezing would do it."

Hank picked the baby up so fast even Margaret was stunned.

"What are you going to do?"

"Watch." He sat down on the mats with the baby.

He set her in his lap, her back to him, and he held her feet in his big palms. "Where's your nose, kid?"

"Nose." Annabelle pointed to her nose.

"That's right. So . . . where're your knees, kid?"

"Kneez . . ." She wrinkled her face up and blew out her nose—one side of her nose.

"That's a good girl." He looked up at Margaret and mouthed, "Watch."

She nodded.

"Knees?" Hank asked again and gently slid his hand near her mouth.

"Kneez!" Annabelle's face puckered up.

Hank slid his hand over her mouth.

She blew a big breath out her nose.

The pearl shot out like a bullet from a .38.

"Got it!" Hank snatched it from midair. He sat, staring at it for a frozen instant. He took a deep breath and sagged back against the trunk. He studied the baby, his eyes a little glazed, then he glanced up at Margaret.

Sweat dripped from his forehead, nose, and upper lip. His shirt was drenched, and his jaw tense. He looked like a man who had just seen hell and lived to tell about it.

"Busy day, Hank?"

His eyes cleared and he seemed to weigh her comment, then drilled her with a look that spoke volumes.

"What's the big deal. I mean, really . . ." Margaret turned and stiffly waddled back to her corner. After two steps, she paused and turned back, an exact imitation of his own motions. "How hard can it be to watch a little kid?"

It was harder than trying to escape from prison.

Hank carried Annabelle on his shoulder whenever she wasn't asleep, and then he was always nearby. Nowhere within reach was anything that could fit up her nose. The other two kids had been fairly easy to deal with.

But fate played him for a sucker. It rained the next three days without stop.

Not light rain.

Not pouring rain.

Torrents and torrents of rain.

The first rainy day Lydia and Theodore argued, nagged, and pinched each other until Hank threatened that if they didn't stop, he would make them each swallow five raw oysters a day.

Theodore fidgeted and wiggled until midmorning, when he began to whine. First he wanted to go fishing. When Hank explained that you can't catch fish in a rainstorm, he wanted Hank to take him swimming. He didn't understand why they couldn't swim just because it was raining, since you got wet anyway.

So for the rest for the rest of the day, he whined because there was nothing to do. He whined because Lydia wouldn't let him pet Rebuttal. He whined because Hank wouldn't play poker with him. He whined because he had to stay inside. He whined because Hank wouldn't let him release Muddy from the bottle. And he whined because Hank only let him play the harmonica for ten minutes—nine minutes too long in Hank's mind, not that he had much of a mind left.

The second day began with Theodore staring out the door at the rain. He turned toward Hank, sighed with melodrama, and said, "I wish—"

"Don't wish!" Hank's hand was on Theodore's mouth in a blink.

Ten minutes later Hank gave in and let the kid release Muddy from that bottle. It turned out to be a relief.

The genie read to the kids from a Wild West book. Theodore and Lydia sat cross-legged on a mat in front of Muddy, their eyes wide and their breaths held.

The genie read, " 'Big Chief Golden Eagle looked at all his warriors. Then the Indian chief said, "We scalpum bad white men and we bring bad medicine down on all who hurt the tribe!" The Indians played their tom-toms, loud war drums that beat throughout the dark and starry western night.' "

Hank watched, then made a note about kids. As it turned out, that one bloodthirsty tale kept the rowdy little suckers occupied for the rest of the day and that night, talking about Indians and buffalo and war paint.

The third day Hank woke up to the sound of pounding—godawful pounding. Theodore had covered the iron kettle with a shirt, turned it upside down, and he was beating on it with one of Hank's shoes.

"What the hell are you doing?"

"Me Big Chief Fire in the Hair! Me on warpath!" The kid hammered the pot a few more times. "This my tom-tom drum!"

A second later Lydia screamed—that sound Hank had learned that only little girls had—the one that sounded as if they were being skinned alive.

Hank staggered to his feet and crossed the hut. By then she was crying, huge big sobs. "My goat! Look at poor Rebuttal!"

"What the—Theodore!" he bellowed.

"Me Big Chief Fire in the Hair." He puffed out his bony little chest and tucked his chin into his neck. "Me scalpum goat!"

Hank picked the kid up by the seat of his pants and held him up so they were eye level. "You wanna be Big Chief Fire on the Butt?"

"You said you didn't hit kids."

"That was four days ago. I changed my mind."

Theodore was chewing on his lip.

Hank gave him a hard look meant to make the kid squirm. "What did you use on the goat?"

"Scissors."

Hank set the kid down and held out his hand. "Hand 'em over."

For a kid who could shear a goat in a couple of hours, he moved about as quickly as time moved in a prison cell. He dug into his pockets, took out shells and rocks and pieces of colored glass, then dug through the other pocket and pulled out a wad of string, a broken piece of a sand dollar, two more rocks, a piece of a crab shell, and some funny-looking little scissors with handles shaped like hummingbirds.

Hank frowned down at the kid. "Where'd you get those?"

Theodore stared at his bare toes. "Leedee found them in the sewing basket."

"Go give them back and apologize to your sister."

He shuffled over to Lydia, who was sniffling. "Sorry, Leedee." He stuck out the scissors. "Here."

She took them and buried her head in the goat's bald neck.

"Now go sit!" Hank pointed to a corner. "There! And don't even think about moving until I say you can. Got it?"

Head down, feet dragging as if made of lead, Theodore trudged to the corner and plopped down.

When the sun broke through on the fourth morning Hank had a new understanding of kids—the clear understanding that he didn't know a damn thing about 'em.

A couple of days later Margaret sat on the beach, using a bamboo and banana leaf parasol, protection against the intense rays of the sun. Lydia and Annabelle were playing with the sand crabs a few feet away. Annabelle chased them, giggling when Lydia placed one in her cupped hands.

A childish war whoop fractured the peace, and a second later Theodore came tearing across the sand.

For an hour or two each day, Hank had been teaching him to swim in the freshwater pool near the waterfall. Theodore ran past her wearing a pair of men's drawers they'd found in one of the trunks. They were sizes too big, knotted at the back of the waist and the legs stopped midcalf. But he didn't care. His arms churned as he ran into the water, splashing everyone within a few feet.

Hank came walking over the dune in that loose-hipped stride he had. He'd cut the legs off his prison pants for swimming. His chest was bare. He walked past her and stopped, watching Theodore in the water. His back was crossed with scar stripes that were dark purple and welted.

She covered her mouth with a hand and closed her eyes for a moment. The whip marks Theodore had seen. She knew she had to keep the reaction from her face. Hank's pride wouldn't take pity from her or anyone else.

"Hank! I won!"

"You cheated, kid!"

"Come on in!" Theodore called just as a wave hit him in the back and almost knocked him down. He laughed.

Hank ran right past the girls and dove under a wave, surfacing on the other side, his black hair sleek as a seal and his body, scars and all, shimmering in the sun and sea.

She felt as if the breeze had suddenly stopped as she sat there, watching him teach Theodore how to ride a wave. For reasons she didn't care to analyze, she was unable to look away. She watched them laughing and racing, each trying to outride the other by selecting the wave that would push him farther up the sand.

She shook her head after a minute of silly ogling, and she turned to say something to Lydia. There was a look of quiet longing on the girl's face while she watched her brother and Hank laugh and ride the foamy crest of the waves.

Margaret stood and casually walked over to Lydia. "Would you like to go in the water?"

"I can't swim," she said, not looking at Margaret.

"You can still wade if you're careful."

She looked down at her dress, then shook her head.

"Are you sure?"

"Yes."

"Look at those sissy girls!" Theodore called out. "Can't swim! Can't swim! Too bad you're not a *him!*" He made a face at them and stuck his thumbs in his ears and wiggled his hands. Hank stood there, his muscular arms crossed. He laughed with Theodore.

Lydia looked at Margaret. She could see the girl wanted to go in.

"What would your mother do if she wanted to go in the water?"

Lydia looked up at her. "I don't know." Her face grew serious, then she gave Margaret a clear and direct look. "What would you do?"

Margaret dropped her parasol on a blanket in the sand. "I'm not going to take that from those two. I'm going in." She picked up Annabelle and set her on her hip, then she looked at Lydia. "Are you coming?"

The girl looked at her brother, who was being his most obnoxious, prancing through the waves as if only men could swim.

"I'll make certain you're safe. Here . . ." Margaret set Annabelle on her small feet. "Take one of her hands."

Lydia slid her hand over Annabelle's plump one, then she looked at Margaret.

"Ready?" Margaret asked her.

Theodore was chanting again.

Lydia looked at him. A whisper of a smile lit her lips and she nodded.

A few minutes later the three of them were wading into the water, lifting Annabelle over the small waves that slapped against their skirts and sprayed foamy saltwater in their laughing faces.

❧ 23 ❧

Muddy was free. Finally. And flying. Purple smoke trailing behind, he soared in the blue sky above the beach, the cooler air washing over his beard and face. His vest flapped against his bare ribs and chest as he spiraled up in the air like smoke from one of Margaret's meals.

He flew low over the beach where Theodore and Lydia were digging in the sand. They turned their bright faces skyward, pointing and laughing in that free way children had.

Muddy dove down and snatched Theodore's cap right off his head, then watched him jump up and down, before he flew back for another low pass and dropped the hat in Lydia's lap. She grinned and waved the cap.

He soared by again, then did a series of rolling somersaults in the air, the bells on the toes of his shoes tingling like wind chimes, and a second later he landed in the sand between the kids, his feet flat, his arms out, and a wide grin on his face. He'd always been a bit of a grandstander.

"Take me flying, Muddy! Please!" Theodore jumped up and down.

Hank stood nearby, his arms crossed like a palace guard. He drilled Muddy with a look of intimidation, then shook his head in disgust and walked into the water, diving under a wave. Muddy knew Hank still wouldn't accept him, that he hadn't acknowledged him as anything other than an annoyance.

Muddy stood between the two older children and held out his hands. "Come. I'll take you both flying."

"Me, too?" Lydia said in a voice that was almost a squeak.

"Do you want to come?"

"Leedee's a sissy."

"I am not," Lydia said firmly and took a hold of his hand.

"Hold on tight," Muddy warned, then he made one of the smoothest ascents he'd made in two thousand years.

A child holding each hand, he rode the wind, flew in smooth banked turns that cast lumbering dark shadows in the sand. Their hair flowing back and their cheeks fresh and rosy, they soared with Muddy as he flew over Margaret, who watched them with one hand shielding her eyes and one hand holding a makeshift parasol of banana leaves.

He flew over the tall coconut palms, ruffling the fronds, then swooped down toward the crystal sea where the bottom stared back at them. He buzzed in circles above Hank, just because Muddy had a little of the devil in him.

With an extra squeeze of their small hands, a tighter grip, and a wink, Muddy flew the children over a row of bumpy air drafts, then up . . . up . . . up . . . through a puffy and white cloud that cast its dew on their faces, making their cheeks sparkle when they were once again soaring in the bright sunshine.

Over the blue sea and across the wide Pacific sky he flew on an ancient gift of magic and, even better, on the smiles of two delighted and squealing children.

Margaret sat on the beach, a blanket wrapped around her like a burnoose. She twirled her makeshift parasol over her shoulder as if she were in an Easter parade.

She looked up and watched the children flying overhead. No one at home would believe it, she thought. Not even her dad, who thought her the most rational of people. She turned back and glanced at Annabelle, who was asleep on a blanket next to her, her pale skin shielded from the sun by a tent shade she'd made from one of the lifeboat tarps.

A refreshing breeze blew in from the sea and rattled the tarp a little, then ruffled the banana leaves and pressed the thick flannel nightdress she was wearing against her legs. Her knees were drawn up, and she hugged them to her chest, digging her feet into the sand.

The water was a deep aqua blue and in the distance she could hear the waves rumble against the reef. Closer, flies buzzed around the kelp on the shore where sand crabs skittered across the wet sand and burrowed deep before a wave could sweep them out to sea.

Hank staggered out of the rushing water and plopped down next to her. "You should come in the water, Smitty. It's great diving."

She looked out at the lagoon, at the cool water. But she didn't say anything.

"There are all the oysters you could ever eat down there, sweetheart."

She looked at him. "You just think I'm the one who can pick the ones with pearls."

He threw his head back and laughed. "You're right."

They sat there for a moment, then Margaret looked at him. "I need a favor."

"Yeah?"

"I'd like you to teach Lydia how to swim."

"You can swim."

"You're teaching Theodore. You can easily teach Lydia at the same time. And I'm still sunburned," she added.

"You don't look sunburned to me."

"Trust me, I am."

He watched her for a moment. "You went in the water this morning."

"You said the saltwater would help my skin heal faster."

"Yeah, but that was over a week ago."

"I was too sore to go in until now," she said, trying to sound tired. "I think I was in the sun too long again." She raised her hand to her forehead and heaved a big sigh. "I've been feeling rather light-headed."

He watched her for a moment, and she hoped he didn't see through her. After a minute, he said, "Okay, I'll teach her."

"Thank you," she said as weakly as she could.

"But only until you're able to take over. Got it?"

She nodded, pulling the blanket tighter around her. He was looking out at the sea so she took the opportunity to watch him.

Beads of saltwater shimmered on his tanned skin, and the remnants of sea foam still bubbled on his ankles. He raised his wet hands to his forehead and combed his fingers through his black hair, slicking it back from his tanned face.

Those cutoff pants hit him midthigh and were a concession to decency. But his body was still exposed—dark skin and the black hair that grew so thickly over his chest and down his rippled belly only to disappear into the waist of his pants where the fabric clung to the outlines of his form and the color of his flesh showed through the wet cotton. The black hair reappeared on his tanned thighs and calves. His legs were long and hard and thick with rippling muscles that looked like slithering snakes when he walked.

She watched the way his arms flexed as he leaned back on his elbows and stared out at the sea, the way the water trickled down his ribs and slid around to his back before it dripped into the white sand.

She didn't know how long she looked at his body. Time didn't enter into her thoughts, only an absurd fascination with the rugged look of him—of dark hair, tanned muscle and tendon that made his body male. Only an awareness of differences between them. That not only did they see the world from different perceptions and philosophies, but their differences were physical as well.

She looked away, uncomfortable with him so close and wearing so little. She touched her mouth, aware that it was suddenly dry. She glanced at him to see if he'd noticed her.

He was frowning up at the sky where Muddy was flying overhead with Lydia and Theodore. "I still don't believe what I'm seeing."

"Me either." She looked away, keeping her eyes on a spot in the sand.

"Doesn't make a damn bit of sense."

"I know." She raised a hand to the bridge of her nose and pinched it while she closed her eyes, trying to make the image in her head go away.

When she opened her eyes and looked at him, he was staring at her with a look she couldn't read. He looked away.

She sat there beside him, her hands clasping her knees. Her hem was up a bit, an inch or two higher than her ankles. She stared at her feet, then looked at the outline of her calves and knees. She longed to shed all that flannel and dive into the water. But she was bound and determined to get Hank to capitulate and teach Lydia to swim.

Annabelle stirred on the blanket next to her, then sat up blinking at them. She gave them the serious look of an army general, then grinned. "Hi!"

"Hi!" Margaret laughed. The silly look on Annabelle's face made her appear as if she knew something funny that no one else did—a child's secret.

A shadow fell over her. Hank had shifted and looked at Annabelle over her shoulder. She could feel his breath near her ear and hair as warm as the trade wind, but she experienced an odd chill and her arms broke out in goose bumps, even with all those clothes on.

"Hi there, kid." There was a smile in his deep voice.

Annabelle gave him a childish wave, and his laughter went right through her. The baby pushed herself up and walked over to him. He sat back, and she crawled into his lap and swung her small legs over one of his. She leaned back against his stomach and then tilted her head back and looked up at him, her apricot hair against the black hair of his chest.

"Hi!"

Margaret sat frozen, completely baffled. She had the most powerful urge to cry. She could feel the tightness in her throat, the ache of tears in her chest, and the pressure in her nose and behind her eyes.

She turned away and took a deep breath. Then she realized she truly did feel light-headed.

Within two days, Hank had Lydia dog-paddling across the freshwater pool while Theodore slid down the falls and taunted his sister into learning even faster. Hank swam over to the opposite side, where Smitty was sitting in the shade of a breadfruit tree, dressed from her ears clear to her ankles.

He rested his arms on a rock and looked at her. Sweat beaded on her face and dripped from her hairline. She swiped it away and fanned herself with a broad banana leaf.

"It's cool in the water, Smitty."

"Yes, I'm certain it is."

"You haven't been in the water since you took Lydia in."

She shrugged.

"Hell, just wrap something around your torso so you can swim freely."

She gave him a strangled look.

"You won't burn again. Your skin is used to the sun now." He pushed himself out of the pool and sat down near her; water spread across the rocks and near her feet.

She pulled back, but he shifted closer. "Look." He flipped her skirt up to her knees and put his tanned forearm against her calf. "Your legs are almost as brown as I am."

She jerked her skirt back down and hugged it to her ankles. "Don't you do that again."

"For Christ's sake, Smitty. You think I haven't seen a woman's legs before?" He shook his head and jumped back into the water.

When he faced her again, she was staring at his chest. She wouldn't look him in the eye. "I've seen everything there is to see of a woman."

He caught a flash of some emotion in her eyes, but she didn't say anything. "Believe me, sweetheart, your legs are no different than those of a thousand other women."

He turned and swam away, pulling his body across the cool water of the pool with long strokes . . . knowing he'd just told the biggest lie of his life.

It was a few days later when Hank strolled down a stretch of sleepy sunlit beach. Smitty was sitting alone and drawing something in the sand with her finger.

He stopped for a moment and just watched her. Her hair hung down her back, and the wind caught it. He crossed the sand, and she glanced up, then quickly smoothed out the sand. He wondered what she had drawn or written.

He closed the distance between them and stopped when he was only a foot away. She was dressed in flannel from her high neckline to her bare ankles. Her face, hands, and feet were the only things exposed. And she was sweating; it was beading on her cheeks and in her hairline, dripping down her neck.

And she called him stubborn.

He sat down next to her. Close.

She gave him a withering look, which made him laugh because she was the one about to wither.

He didn't say anything just to see if she'd speak first. He leaned back on his elbows in the sand, and he watched some gulls swoop down toward the sea. He felt her stare and turned.

Her gaze was on his chest. He glanced down but didn't see anything. When he looked up again, she was looking anywhere but at him.

"If you're just going to sit here and cook, we might as well call out the cannibals and let them have you."

"You are so witty."

"I try."

"Well, don't. I'm trying to think."

He laughed. "Nah. You? Thinking?"

She rolled her eyes at him.

He waited, and she was silent. He watched her, wondering how long it would take before she finally said something. Her hair had turned blonder as if the tropical sun had stolen some of its golden color. Her cheeks were tanned and flushed, and she had a healthier glow about her.

She was damn good-looking, he thought, one of the best-looking women he'd ever seen, but there was more to her than looks. She had a sharp mind, and even though he teased her about it, he liked it. He liked her sassy mouth. Liked the way she called his bluff all the time. She made him think, too, and he supposed that wasn't a bad thing.

He liked the challenge she offered, that she wasn't predictable.

"What's eating at you, sweetheart?"

"I'm not your sweetheart, Hank."

"You could be."

She turned slowly and gave him a wry look. "Be still my heart."

He laughed. "Well, if you don't wanna talk, we could just—" He started to say a crude word but stopped himself. For some reason he didn't care to think about, he felt saying it to her was somehow insulting. He wanted to tease her, not insult her. He looked away, pretending he hadn't spoken.

When he looked back, he saw the same emotion on her face that was eating at him. An awareness of the other. He sat up and twisted slightly, moving closer.

She watched him, then suddenly held up her hand as if to stop him or ward him off. He could see it was instinctive, her natural reaction. He didn't say a word. But he didn't move either.

Her hand dropped like a white flag of surrender, and he reached for her. An instant later, she was in his arms, and he lay back in the sand, her body along his.

He gripped her head in his hands and kissed her openmouthed and hard. She tasted better than anything he could remember tasting in a helluva long time. He'd missed this, the feel of a woman. Long, hot, tonguing kisses; the beading of a woman's nipple against his lips; and the flavor and smell of a woman. Hours in a bed just screwing real slow and easy.

"No!" she said and jumped back, sitting on her heels between his legs. She caught her breath, then stood up and turned around, hugging her arms to her and looking out at the sea.

He got up and stood behind her for an awkward moment. "Still thinking, aren't you, sweetheart? Don't you know by now thinking isn't going to solve what just happened?"

"Go away."

"I can leave, but that isn't going to fix things."

"Perhaps not, but it would be a decided improvement."

"Talk to me, Smitty."

She shook her head. "I can't."

"What the hell is bothering you?"

"I don't know," she said. "I can't understand why I feel these things. I—I don't love you."

He laughed. "Love has nothing to do with it."

"Have you been in love?"

"Me? In love?" He laughed really hard at that. "Only with my hand."

She looked at him then, her head cocked slightly.

"Don't think about it. That was a barrel house joke."

"Yes, well, I expect you've more experience than I have at those kinds of things."

"Yeah. Years of experience."

She stiffened and stepped away from him, and he realized she had no idea he'd been joking about his age as much as teasing her. Smitty, with her healthy sense of humor, had suddenly lost it.

He stared at the back of her stiff neck for a few seconds, then grinned. "No reason to be jealous, sweetheart."

She whipped around, her mouth hanging open. "What?"

"I told you before. No wife." He raised his arms out in surrender. "No lover. No reason to be jealous."

She snapped her mouth closed and gave him a long, narrowed look.

"I'm all yours."

She just stood there. A moment later she raised a hand to her cheek in mock surprise. "And to think they say there's no such thing as a miracle."

Even he had to laugh at that. But she wasn't laughing.

They looked at each other at the same time. The silence seemed to drag by as slowly as days in solitary.

He stepped closer to her. "What's wrong with just grabbing it, sweetheart? Take the chance for a little fun. I promise you'll have a helluva lot of fun." He drew his finger slowly over her stubborn chin. "Thinking about it will only complicate things."

She stiffened and shifted away a couple of steps. "Nothing seems to make sense anymore. You don't make sense. I *have* to think about it."

"You think enough for both of us. Hell, Smitty, you think enough for the whole damn world."

"Well, one of us has to use their head."

He laughed.

She gave him one of her direct looks. "Your head's too hard to be of much use."

"My head among other things," he muttered to himself.

She turned and started to walk away.

"Oh, no, you don't. You're not walking away this time." He grabbed her hand and pulled her to him so swiftly she stumbled. He was right there, ready, and he caught her before she could even blink and swung her up into his arms.

"If you think you can manhandle me, Hank, think again."

He didn't say anything.

"Put me down."

"I can't decide if you need heating up or cooling off, Smitty." He started walking out into the water. A small wave splattered past them. "My guess is you need cooling off. Especially since Lydia can swim like a fish now."

She gave a slight gasp. "You knew?"

He just laughed and tossed her in the air once.

"Put me down, Hank."

"I don't think so." He kept walking into the water. Deeper. "Remember my rum? Those bananas flambé? Remember the missing brandy? The whiskey bottle you used for target practice?"

"Hank . . ."

"Any last words?"

She looked at the water, then gave him a narrowed look. "Don't even think about it."

"I won't, sweetheart."

"You'd better not."

"I won't *think.*" He swung back and threw her into the next wave, then waded back to the beach and turned around, his hands on his cocked hips as he watched her surface, coughing and sputtering.

He stuck his hands in his pockets and walked up the beach, whistling. When he got to the rise, he stopped and turned back.

She was trudging out of the water, muttering.

"Hey, Smitty!"

She stood on the beach, wringing the water from her skirt.

He cupped his hands around his mouth. "I won't think. I'll leave all the thinking to you."

The following morning Margaret walked down the beach with determined steps. She was wearing a makeshift bathing costume. She'd tucked the tattered hem of her skirt into a belt so it fit her like gymnasium bloomers. She stood there, waiting for Hank to notice.

He rode a wave to shore, then froze in the waist-high water the moment he saw her. He didn't smile. He didn't say anything. He just looked at her as if he didn't want to stop looking for a long, long time.

Her mouth grew dry again. She wondered how she appeared to him. She wanted to look confident, as if she didn't care that half her body was bare.

After all, she wasn't some shy young girl. She was a woman. A professional . . . intelligent . . . woman. "Want some company?"

He laughed and began to walk out of the water.

She was no fool. She tossed him his cutoff pants. Then she turned her back and waited. "Aren't you finished yet?"

"Yes," he said so close to her ear that she jumped.

She spun around, half expecting him to be holding the pants. He wasn't. He'd put them on.

She looked up into those dark eyes, that dark smile.

She forgot what she was going to say. She took a deep breath, then blurted out, "I've got a craving for more oysters."

He cocked his head and crossed his arms over his chest, which she was staring at.

"Oysters, Smitty, or pearls?"

"Oysters, actually, but more pearls would be nice, too."

He held out his hand. "Then come with me."

She stared at his open palm, then slid her hand into it. She didn't move, just stared at their hands as his closed about hers. His was rugged and tanned, his fingers thick, and his palms huge. Her hands were paler, her fingers long and slim. So different, she thought.

"Come on, Smitty."

They ran into the water, holding hands even when the waves slapped against them. "We need to swim out a short distance, then walk along the sandbar, and I'll point out the oyster bed."

She nodded as another wave rolled past them. "Those oysters were marvelous. One of my favorite foods."

He laughed. "I could tell."

She followed him. "All they needed was a dash of Tabasco sauce."

He stopped and laughed harder.

"What's so funny?"

He shook his head. "You wouldn't believe it."

They moved across the lagoon as shallow waves slapped against them and the tide pulled at their feet and legs. Once she had to slip an arm around him to keep from slipping. He put one arm around her and lifted her in front of him as if she hardly weighed a thing.

It was a new sensation. Men didn't carry women who were almost as tall as they were. It gave her a small thrill when his hands spanned her waist.

Now though, he stood behind her, and whenever a

wave would pass, he was like a wall that kept her in place, his body there for her to lean against. And she did. She felt the brush of his body hair against the back of her arm, the firm, solid muscle of his chest and thighs whenever a wave would shove her backward. Once, a wave pushed her suddenly, and he slid his thigh beneath her bottom to keep her in front of him. Within a few minutes, they moved onto a sandbar, then walked along it near the edge of a jagged coral reef.

Hank gripped her arm. "This is it. You want to go down?"

She nodded.

"Ready?"

She nodded.

"Okay, sweetheart. Take deep breaths of air. Ten or more."

They both began to breathe together. Then he looked at her, squeezed her hand, and nodded.

And they dove deep, hand in hand, down the blue green waters that were clear as air. A whole new world opened up to her, foreign and fascinating.

Fish in a multitude of colors—yellows, reds, oranges, and violets—swam about them, dancing in and out of the rocks where red and purple anemones four feet in diameter lay like prayer blankets. Sea plants with pink and yellow and purple leaves waved with the lazy current.

He pulled her down with him, his hand tightly holding hers. As they moved through the water, he pointed at the white and pink and black coral that grew like giant mushrooms from the nearby rocks. Small fish of every color—thousands and thousands of them in fluid, rippling schools—darted around blue water that must have been the color of heaven.

Margaret and Hank swam into this other world—a world so magical it was impossible to imagine. They kicked downward into an underwater paradise that was like walking through a Milky Way of color, like being deep inside a rainbow. The sunlight would catch iridescent colors of the fish and the plants, making them shimmer and sparkle more than any jewel.

Hank stuck his thumb up and they surfaced.

Margaret gasped for air. "Let's go down again," she said, still gasping, and she started to dive.

"Not so fast, sweetheart. Give yourself a few minutes of air. Take shallow, deep breaths."

There was something mesmerizing about the sea that made one understand the myth of sirens. Such brilliance, such magic. It called to her in a special way that had nothing to do with common sense or intrigue or curiosity, but something more elemental, as if a small door had opened only now, just this once, into a world made for just her to discover. She was still panting, wanting to take air in faster so she could dive again.

Hank laughed. "Calm down. It's not going to go away."

"I want to see it all, Hank. Everything. Now."

"What about the oysters?"

"I want to see those, too. It's lovely down there." She looked into his face and placed her hand on his chest, right over his heart, and she smiled sincerely. "Thank you for taking me down there. It's the most beautiful place I've ever seen."

His look was somehow different out here, no cynicism, nothing but an intensity she could feel. He treaded water and looked at her that way for a long time. She ducked her head a little, embarrassed that she was affected by something as silly as a man's look.

Then he ruined the whole thing. Ruined it completely, because he reached out and pulled her to him. And he kissed her.

"I don't know what the hell you're so mad about." Hank followed her out of the water.

"You wouldn't!" She glared at him, slapped her wet hair out of her face, and marched on. "You're too thickheaded and single-minded to understand."

"It was just a kiss, dammit."

She didn't say anything.

"Hell, I didn't feel you up."

She gasped and spun around.

"I could have. I could have stuck my hand wherever I damn well pleased. Your tongue was halfway down my throat, sweetheart."

"I hate this. I really do."

He laughed and walked past her, then stopped. "No, you don't." He whacked her on her backside. "You don't hate this, sweetheart."

She almost took a swing at him.

"You love it."

He swaggered away, his handprint still warm on her behind, his taste still lingering in her mouth. She looked around for just a second as if she didn't know where she was.

Slowly she raised a hand to her mouth and took deep breaths. She couldn't do much else. She realized she knew where she was. She just didn't know *who* she was.

Because to her horror, to her dismay, to her regret, she knew he was right. She did love it.

For the next week Margaret set out to change things. She was going to learn to cook *and* she was going to understand why Hank Wyatt was affecting her so strangely.

A baptism by fire, so to speak.

And it was. She burned three fish, two pans of gull eggs, a coconut—Hank informed her that no one on the face of the blankety-blank earth would cook a coconut—four breadfruit, some yams, her skirt, a wrist, and three fingers.

Margaret had spent a great deal of time watching

Hank, searching for answers. Hank spent the next few days adding another room onto the hut—a room for the children when it rained or for sleeping. This was after Annabelle woke him three mornings in a row. She pulled his eyebrows the first morning, then giggled when he woke up yelling. She grabbed the hammock and dumped him out of it the second morning, and that very morning she had tried to stick a banana up his nose.

Actually, the room wasn't for the children. It was for Hank.

Margaret watched him work, watched him sweat in the sunshine, watched him play with Theodore. He included the boy in everything, even included Lydia.

One morning Margaret had been busy dousing their burning breakfast with handfuls of sand when Lydia came running past her, her dark blond hair in two perfectly even braids. Later that day, after Lydia and Theodore had ridden the waves with Hank, Margaret sat on the beach trying to hide her surprise as she watched him rebraid the girl's hair. Perfectly.

But it was the hug Lydia gave Hank that almost did her in. Margaret had had to look away until she was certain her eyes had dried and her face didn't give away what she felt.

He was incredibly good with Annabelle, too, carrying her on his shoulders, letting her touch the tree branches and lifting her high in his arms so she could pick flowers. He showed her birds. The hummingbirds that would flit from flower to flower. And he laughed when she screamed with childish excitement at the gulls and auks and terns that dove through the sky, and the pelicans that waddled along the sand with the pipers and other scavengers.

And even more unsettling was the way he would look at Margaret, as if he knew something she didn't. Instead of answers, she only found more questions.

Why did his walk fascinate her? She had never even

noticed a man's walk. Why did she stand on the ridge and watch him swim in the morning? Especially when she felt so uncomfortable afterward, as if she'd eaten bad food.

And now, why was she climbing the rocks and sneaking a peek at him shaving? She was thirty-two years old. She was an attorney. She was supposed to be rational and sane and logical. But her hands shook. There was this uneasiness about her—a restless feeling that nothing satisfied.

She stood on the rocks near the pool, thinking that she should leave but not moving. Listening for the sound of him diving in the water. But there was only silence.

Then it hit her. Hard. The embarrassment of what she was actually doing. She covered her mouth with one hand and shook her head. She needed to leave. This was . . . completely foolish.

She scampered down the rocks and paused at the bottom, her breath rapid. Her hand went to her forehead, rubbing the frown away. She asked herself what she had been thinking. Fool . . .

She turned around.

There he stood, leaning against a nearby rock as if he'd been there for a long time, his arms crossed and his smile cocky.

❧ 24 ❧

He stepped forward.

Margaret moved back, suddenly wishing the earth would just open up and swallow her.

He moved again. So did she.

"Have you been taking lessons from that goat?"

"What are you talking about?"

"Nothing. You had to be there." He took two more steps toward her. She backed up and hit the coconut palm. She shifted to the left.

So did he. "You game for a new partnership, sweetheart?"

She tried to sidestep him and bumped into a wall of rock.

Both of his hands flattened against the rock on either side of her head. She started to duck under one. He moved his arm down, still blocking her.

She gave him a narrowed glare. "Don't get cute."

He smiled, a catbird seat smile if she'd ever seen one.

She looked away.

He moved so close that she could feel his breath on her cheek. "We could build a chest together." He paused. His expression mocked her the same way his words did. "We need a chest—uh—schedule." He laughed. "How about your chest against mine, sweetheart?"

She felt her face flush hot and red. She just wanted to shrivel up right there. But what was worse than the embarrassment of her situation was the horrendous realization that she actually felt something for Hank—truly the last man on earth she should fall for.

She bit her lip and closed her eyes, knowing her humiliation was complete. Even worse than the situation, even worse than admitting she'd fallen for Hank Wyatt, was the knowledge that he knew it, too.

He had her. Hank laughed to himself, looking down at her. She wouldn't look at him. He waited. If there was one thing he'd learned with her, it was patience.

Suddenly, as if her legs had turned liquid, she slid down the rock and sat hard on the ground. She drew her knees up and buried her head in them.

He stared at her. What the hell?

"Smitty?"

She looked like she was crying.

Stunned, he just stood there, frowning. It wasn't possible. She couldn't be crying. She should be throwing his cocky words right back at him like she always did. He waited a minute, then scowled down at her.

Her shoulders were shaking.

"Are you crying?" He leaned closer, squinting at her. "You can't be crying." He heard a sob. "Shit! You are crying!"

She sobbed. He shifted uncomfortably, looked left, then right. No one was around.

"Smitty." He stepped back a foot and waved a hand at her. "Stop crying, okay?"

She cried even louder. It sounded like hell. No—hell couldn't be that bad.

"Hey, come on. I was just fooling around."

She still cried.

"Stop it, Smitty."

He began to pace. "Look. I didn't mean to—" He cut himself off. "Well, yeah, I guess I did mean to give you a hard time." He plowed a hand through his hair. "But hell! I've been giving you a hard time for a couple of weeks now. You didn't *cry*."

She blubbered even harder. Her shoulders jerked as she tried to catch her breath.

Watching her, knowing he'd brought her to that point was the most belittling feeling he'd had in years. He stood there, wondering what the hell he had become, asking himself if this was what happened when you'd spent so many years throwing your life away. Did you start looking for others to take down with you? He wiped his palms on his pants. He just stood there, his chest tight with some obscure emotion.

She really sobbed.

Christ! She was noisy. "Smitty . . ." He tried to

think. He tried to say the word he thought he needed to say. It wouldn't come.

Her hair hung around her face, and she clutched her knees. She clung to them as if there was nothing else in the world for her to hold. For an instant he had the stupid thought that she looked as if she were growing smaller.

"Stop crying, okay?" He rubbed his clammy hands on his pants again and took a deep breath, then exhaled. "Please."

He squatted down in front of her. "Look at me, Smitty." He paused, then added, "Please."

She didn't move.

"Please." There, he thought. Third time. It was getting easier. Then he looked at her still hunched in that position, still sobbing.

"Oh, shit!" He slid his arms under her and picked her up, then stood. She curled into him, her head on his shoulder, her whole body limp.

"I—I—I didn't w—want to . . . to fe-he-he-el this way." Her voice was weak and her words stuttered between her breaths.

"I know." He started walking her toward the hut.

"It . . . it . . . just happened. But it's so . . . so stupid, you know? Really stupid. It . . . it doesn't make any sense."

"Sure, sweetheart."

Her damp face was in his neck. "How could this happen?"

"Don't ask me."

"I'm trying not to care."

"I can tell that." He rubbed his chin against the top of her head.

"I didn't want to care. You—you're not the kind of man I should care about, you know?"

"I know."

She sobbed again.

He rubbed her back lightly with his hand.

"Oh, Hank . . . ," she wailed.

"What, sweetheart?"

"I don't even like you!"

"If I were you, I wouldn't like me either."

"You wouldn't?"

"Nah. I can be a stubborn bastard."

"Yes, you can."

She was quiet for a minute. He looked down at her. She was thinking again. But hell, it was better than her crying.

She took a deep breath and muttered into his neck, "Why? It isn't logical." She looked up at him finally. Her face was pink and blotchy and a godawful mess. "Why us?"

"Because, sweetheart." He looked down at her but kept walking. "Life deals you deuces."

By the time he carried Margaret through the door of the hut, she had regained control. Her face was still buried in his neck, but she didn't move it. She wanted him to keep holding her. There was something relaxing about not having to try so hard, accepting that she wasn't perfect and that just this once she didn't have to be. To let her emotions—illogical or not—rule her for just a little while.

He stood in the dark hut, then slowly let her slide down the length of his long body until she felt her toes touch the ground. Her arms were still linked around his neck and his warm hands rested flat against her bottom. He was breathing rapidly, the sound husky and abrupt. But he didn't move. He only stood there, still and silent.

She couldn't fight him any longer. She couldn't fight what was between them. And she didn't want to. She was tired of fighting something that felt so right inside of her heart even if it seemed wrong inside of her head. She looked up at him, wondering what he would do.

There was no answer in his expression. Nothing but

a hard and blank look. She sensed he was battling with something inside him, something that wasn't easy for him. His hands shook with it.

She whispered his name, and he closed his eyes briefly, then he reached up and took her hands from around his neck. He just held them at their sides for a moment. He was staring somewhere over her head, his eyes showing no sign of what he was thinking.

She leaned her head against his shoulder. "What are we going to do?"

He released her, then took a step back. "I'm going to leave."

"You're what?"

He stepped back again, then turned away.

She stared at his back.

Two long strides and he was in the doorway. "I'm leaving." He stood very still, the late afternoon light behind him. It was intimidating, the way he almost filled the doorway, like a portrait that takes up the whole frame.

She could see the tension in his stance and that his breathing was still not even. "Why are you leaving?"

After an awkward stretch of silence, he turned, his hand resting on the door.

"Because this time—for once—I'm not going to try to take something I want."

Her voice was a ragged whisper. "Why not?"

"Because it's just too damn important." A second later the doorway was empty.

Margaret sat inside the dark hut, her head buried in her hands. She tried to tell herself it wasn't true. She didn't have those kinds of feelings for Hank.

But she couldn't lie to herself anymore than she could lie to him. She felt open and bleeding and miserable. She thought she heard something and looked back at the doorway, part of her hoping he would be standing there.

But he wasn't. No one was there.

He didn't have to be there, though, because his image was still in her mind. The image of his tall body backlit by the setting sun. Like that of a visiting angel.

But she knew him for what he was.

He was no angel. He was a heartache.

Hank went swimming every night. He had to. It was the only way he could get any sleep, swimming in the lagoon lap after lap. It cooled his thoughts. It cooled the fire in his blood, a fire he had trouble controlling for the first time in his life. And he didn't much like that fact either.

Smitty avoided him. That was fine, considering. Over the last few days he'd spent most of his free time watching her, watching her do anything. Burn a meal, light a fire, chase Annabelle.

He'd even taken a page from Smitty's book and slinked up the rocks, lurking in the shadows to watch her bathe. God . . . He'd only done that once. There was only so much a man could take.

After that he'd only watched her brush her hair dry in the sunlight.

He'd had the same response.

One afternoon he'd watched her walk on the beach when she didn't know he was there. She had stopped and drawn words in the sand. And he'd gone back and read them after she'd left. Just single words strung together with no particular meaning: *sick, mind, heart, Hank, kiss, no, why?*

She was going through the same thing he was.

He wasn't certain how he felt about that, which was why he went swimming in the middle of the night. After a few more minutes, he came out of the water and pulled on his pants, then walked back to the hut.

It was past midnight. The moon was low in the west. He walked into the hut and quietly closed the door. He looked at her hammock, but it was empty.

He scanned the hut, letting his eyes adjust. He spotted her outline on a mat in the corner of the new part of the hut where Annabelle slept.

He moved quietly and stood over them. She was curled on her side, asleep, the baby sleeping in the crook of her arm. Her other hand rested lightly on the baby's chest as if she needed to feel Annabelle's heartbeat.

Some foreign emotion hit him, flooded into him. And he stood there, confused but compelled to watch them because doing so filled some empty need in him. After a few minutes he looked at Theodore and Lydia. They were sound asleep, too. He turned back to Smitty.

There had been a time when he had wondered how people could bring a child into the world. It had been something he didn't understand.

Until the past few weeks.

Standing in the dark and watching all of them, he realized that he had grown to know them as he hadn't taken the time to get to know anyone in a long time. He felt something so powerful that he couldn't name it.

He had an insane need to just watch them.

He had no idea how much time passed, but finally he went to his hammock, stretched out in it and rested his hands behind his head. He stared at the woven thatch above him.

The night was fading, he knew. Somewhere outside the moon was going down. Before long it would be that ink black part of night just before morning comes—the darkest part of each day. He'd heard it called the dark before the rising sun.

Hank knew that darkness as well as he knew his own name. He had carried it in his soul for years. But he looked at the children, then at Smitty and Annabelle. He turned back and closed his eyes. And for some reason, the darkness faded.

❧ 25 ❧

One large blue eye stared down at Muddy from the mouth of his bottle. He grinned and waved. The eyeball moved back, and he could see the distant features of Lydia's face.

With the tinkling of bells, he swung his feet off the striped divan and stood. He checked to make certain the bottle opening was clear, raised his arms, and blasted out.

Just to make the children laugh, he did a backflip, three aerials, and a spread-eagle landing, where he hovered over their heads for as long as it took the smoke to dissipate. He gripped his knees, spun, and landed on his feet, bells ringing in his wake.

Lydia covered her mouth and giggled.

Theodore's eyes crinkled. "Holy cow!" he said in a loud whisper.

Muddy looked around. They were inside the hut. He leaned toward Theodore. "Why are we whispering?"

"'Cause Annabelle's asleep. See?"

The baby was curled into a sleepy ball in the corner. Muddy smiled and thought, Ohhhh.

There was something about babies, whether they be human babies or bunnies, kittens, puppies, ducklings, chicks, and piglets and even baby elephants. For some odd quirk of nature, when one looked at them sleeping, there was this overpowering urge to say, "Ohhhhh . . ." followed by a tightening in one's chest—right near the heart.

Yes, most babies could reduce just about anyone to goo-gooing morons. It was a universal and timeless thing—something that had been true for over two thousand years and in any part of the world.

In fact, he remembered one baby in particular, a little boy that had been born in a stable. He smiled. Three wise men had traveled far, only to say, "Ohhhh . . ." when they saw the little boy in his bed of hay.

Babies held a sweet innocence that could grip the heart of the most cynical. Even Muddy.

There was one exception though.

Baby camels. Baby camels were nearly as obnoxious as adult camels. They were smaller, but they could spit just as far and just as frequently and with surprising accuracy.

"We're bored," Theodore told him with a sigh big enough to make his whole chest sag.

Muddy looked at him, then at Lydia. "Would you like to visit the bottle?"

"Me? Truly? I can go inside?"

"Is that a yes?"

Both the children nodded. He held out his hands and said, "Hold on tight and close your eyes."

A minute later, they were inside the bottle.

Hank grabbed another nut from a candlenut tree and tossed it onto a nearby pile. The nuts looked like chestnuts and contained a strong oil. When they were strung like beads on coconut fiber and lit from the bottom, candlenuts would burn upward and would give a few hours of flickering blue light.

They needed light. The hut was dark enough in the daytime, but at night it was pitch black inside. The last two nights had been too damn dark.

There was no fuel for the tilley lamp. Smitty had made the fuel they'd had last longer than he thought possible. Now Hank wanted the dim glow from the candlenuts so he could watch them sleep.

Every night, he just stood there as if he expected them to disappear. As if he were waiting to find out that it was all a big joke.

Ha! Ha! The laugh's on you, Hank Wyatt. Fool. You thought you could have it all? Ha!

"Hank! Hank! Lookit here!"

He shook himself a second, then turned toward the sound of Theodore's excited voice. And froze.

"Lookit! It's a baseball an' a glove an' a bat! Muddy said Leedee and I could pick anything from inside his bottle to play with. I picked the baseball stuff!" The kid thundered toward him until the baseball cap flew off, and he skidded to a stop. He turned around and grabbed the hat, then dusted it off on his pants. He plopped the hat back on his head and started running again.

He stopped in front of Hank and looked up at him from beneath the long brim of a hauntingly familiar cap. "Look!" His face bright and excited, he held up the ball and bat. "Remember the baseball stuff? Will you teach me to play, Hank? Please?"

Hank felt as if every ghost of his past were gathered around him, all chanting and chiding, there to make him remember things he wanted to forget. He stood there, feeling as if he had lost control and hating it.

He'd had enough trouble dealing with Smitty. Dealing with the stupid, pissant heroic reasons he'd walked away from her when every instinct inside him had been shouting "You're a chump! Take her! Hell, man, she's yours. Take her!"

Instead he watched her sleep. Go figure . . .

And now this.

"Will ya teach me how to play baseball, Hank?"

He turned back to the tree and reached for a nut. "I don't know how, kid."

"You don't?"

"Nah." Hank didn't turn around.

There was silence. "Haven't you ever seen a baseball game or nothing?"

"Can't do it, kid. Sorry."

There was no sound from the kid. Hank stood there, not wanting to turn around. Finally he gave in.

Theodore was looking the bat and the ball as if they had suddenly broken.

"Tell you what. Tomorrow I'll teach you how to fish." He reached for another nut from a branch just above his head. His fist closed tightly over the nut. "But when it comes to baseball, I can't teach you anything."

"Oh." There was a wealth of childish disappointment in that one word.

Hank tossed the nut on the pile without looking at the kid. He turned back to the tree. "You go on now. It's almost dark. You can't be running around in this jungle alone."

"But you're here. Can't I stay?"

Hank leaned down and picked up a couple of the nuts. "Here. Put some of these in your pockets and take them to Smitty. Tell her to light them. They work like candles and will burn for about fifteen minutes. I'll come back in a little while."

Theodore frowned down at the plump brown nuts in his hand, then turned them this way and that. "What is it?"

"A candlenut."

"What's a candlenut?"

"Smitty can figure it out."

Theodore gave him an odd look.

"You be a good buddy now and go on."

The kid stood there, looking as if he wanted to argue.

"Buddies, remember?"

Theodore looked down and crammed some nuts into his pockets, then picked up the bat. He gave it one last look of longing before he ran back through the trees.

And Hank stood there, staring at nothing but an old memory.

Muddy flew low over the jungle, darting in and out of the tall ebony trees and flying around a giant banyan with a crown as big as a mosque. He circled above a figure, a tall man with black hair, who stood near a candlenut tree as stiff and unmoving as a statue.

Drifting on the trade wind, Muddy circled, then flew down and lit on the upper branches of a nearby dragon tree with thick foliage, a squat shape, and a branch with a view of the clearing.

Finally Hank shifted, bending and picking up a broken branch from an ebony tree. He gripped the branch in two hands, then shook it slightly as if he were testing the weight of it. He rested it on his shoulder like a bat. And again he stood there, silent and looking angry.

He grabbed one of the candlenuts from the three-foot pile, tossed it high in the air, and swung. He hit it. The nut sailed over the trees like a home run.

He picked up another nut and slammed it east. Another and slammed it south. Another and slammed it north. He hit pop flies. He hit fouls. He hit every nut in the pile. Again and again, like fly balls.

When the nuts were gone, he let the branch drop to the ground. He leaned on it while he tried to catch a breath. Sweat glistened from his forearms, forehead, and face, and poured down his neck and temples.

Muddy heard a slight rustling and looked down. Margaret stood beneath the dragon tree with Theodore. Muddy watched them, wondering what they would do. She held onto Theodore's small skinny arm, then bent toward the boy and lifted a finger to her lips, signaling him to be quiet. She waved him back into the trees, taking easy, quiet steps backward. They just stood there, watching.

Hank didn't move. He was still bent over the branch like a tree broken by a wind too strong.

Theodore stared at him as if he'd lost his best friend. Very quietly he looked up at Margaret and said, "Hank said he didn't know how to play baseball."

She pulled Theodore back a bit closer to the tree

trunk and whispered, "Let's leave him alone for now, okay?"

"But he said he couldn't teach me. He said he didn't know how."

"I know, sweetie."

"Just like he said he didn't know how to be a dad." She looked down at the boy and held out her hand.

"And he forgot the question game. He forgot. He never forgets. It's like a circle."

"Hank has some troubles on his mind, Theodore. I don't think he forgot on purpose."

Theodore's expression said he didn't understand. He turned and looked back at Hank one last time, then, his head hanging down, he slid his hand into Margaret's and they turned and walked away.

Muddy watched them leave and quietly move into the dense thick jungle. They had only gone a few feet when Theodore began to cry.

❧ 26 ❧

The next morning Lydia announced that Christmas was four days away.

Sitting outside the hut, the group looked at her. Hank had been showing Theodore how to tie knots in a line they would be using to fish. Annabelle was tethered to Margaret while she tried to scrape burned breakfast from a skillet. And Lydia was playing with a clocklike contraption with sand and water vials, a maze, and a pulley. It made strange sounds—gurgles, the hiss of falling sand, and a *chink-chink* sound when one of the cog wheels turned. She had brought the gadget out of Muddy's bottle for entertainment.

"I figured out what it is," Lydia announced. "It's a

timepiece." She pointed to a wheel with levers. "Look."

Hank went over to her. Theodore tagged behind.

"Right there are the hours." Lydia looked up. "And here are the numbers from one to thirty-one. See? They spin around the numbers of one through twelve."

Hank looked at it for a minute, then looked at her, amazed. "She's right. According to this, it's December twenty-first."

"Four days till Christmas?" Theodore began to jump up and down. "That means Santa's coming!"

Margaret shot a quick and knowing look at Hank.

"Santa Claus is coming!" Theodore frowned down at his bare feet. "We need stockings." He was quiet for a second, then asked, "Does Santa come if there are no stockings?"

With that question, Margaret looked at Hank. He played the coward and stepped back a few steps.

She looked down at Theodore, her mind still seeing his teary face from the evening before. She had tried to make him understand that Hank hadn't been trying to hurt him. But little boys didn't understand complicated moods the way adults did.

For children, things were either black or white. Luckily, though, children were resilient, too. They seemed to bounce back quickly when something new caught their eye. Something like a promise by Hank to take Theodore fishing today and now something as exciting as Christmas.

She slid her arm over Theodore's shoulders. "I think I remember seeing some woolen stockings in one of the trunks."

"You did?"

She nodded, then picked up Annabelle. "Come along." She held out a hand to Lydia. "Let's go look."

Later that afternoon, Hank reached around Theodore's small shoulders and pulled the fishing line higher. "Let me show you how to do this." He looked down at the kid and winked. "It's easier to catch a fish with a long pole. The current pulls at this string."

"But you caught a bunch of fish this way."

The kid always had an argument. "Only because I didn't take the time to make a fishing pole."

A second later they got a strike.

The kid squealed like a pig and started jumping up and down. Hank grabbed the line and wrapped it around his wrist. It was a helluva good-sized fish. He dropped his hands so the line was in front of the kid. "Pull!"

And they did. A few minutes later they had a large grouper flopping in the sand.

The kid was still hopping up and down while Hank pulled the hook out and added it to the other two perch he'd caught.

The kid looked at it. "What is it?"

"A grouper."

"It's a big one, isn't it?"

"Yeah, kid. You did good."

Suddenly, without warning, the kid flung his arms around Hank's neck and hugged him. It caught Hank completely off guard. He just knelt there, his arms hanging at his sides with Theodore clinging to his neck.

Very slowly Hank rested his palms on the kid's bony little back.

"Thank you, Hank. I'm gonna make you the bestest Christmas present! You wait and see!"

"Christmas present?" he repeated, then he stared at the kid.

"Yeah! Smitty says we'll make each other Christmas presents. Can I go tell 'em 'bout my fish? My grouper?"

"Sure, kid. Go on."

Theodore took off running down the beach toward the others.

Christmas presents, he thought. Hell. There was something he hadn't thought about in years. Long minutes passed while he pretended to be fishing. He wasn't fishing. He was thinking.

Smitty had the children on the beach gathering shells for something. Probably gifts, he thought, the kid's words eating at him.

He heard their laughter. It was clear and shining, as bright as their faces, like dawn coming through the night. The children's cheeks were fresh and rosy. Lydia held out her skirt filled with seashells and other treasures while Theodore made them stop and look at everything he found. Annabelle toddled next to Smitty, who sat in the sand like a child rather than an attorney. She dug and talked about their treasures with as much excitement as the kids.

And he sat there, not caring much about anything but watching them. A moment when time held no importance. When nothing else mattered.

After a while he turned and looked at the Pacific. It was the same. The same rolling dunes and flat, wet shoreline spread in a crescent before him. The same coconut palms waved in the constant breeze. The same waves washed up on the shoreline. The same birds flew in the sky.

But somehow he knew things had changed. He didn't feel the same. And he wasn't certain if he liked that or not.

He knew the moment when Smitty looked at him. He could feel her look, as warm and fresh as the trade wind that brushed his face. He turned just as she got up. She said something to Lydia who nodded and took the baby. Smitty walked toward him with that long-legged, hip-swaying walk of a woman, the walk that made him want to be behind her, watching.

When she was a few feet away, she smiled. "We're gathering shells."

"I can see that."

She pushed a strand of wind-whipped hair out of her eyes. "I guess you can." She looked down, then asked, "You want to help?"

He shook his head and smiled with a touch of irony. "I have fish to catch." He pulled on the line for a moment. "You need something to cremate for dinner."

"Yes, well, at least I'm consistent." There was laughter in her voice. She glanced at the fish lying beside him. "How would you like them—charred, incinerated, or just plain scorched?"

He laughed with her.

"I intend to master that skill, you know." Her voice was filled with both humor and determination but no offense.

He had realized over the past few days that their goading and teasing had changed. From the first moments in the lifeboat and on the island, their conversations had been meant to irritate. Now the teasing was mutual and had become something to ease the tension between them. Something they could laugh at together. He wasn't certain there could be another woman like her—one he could talk to the way he could tease Smitty. She could laugh at herself.

She had her hands behind her as she stood next to him. The wind pressed her thin clothing against her figure. The ragged hem of her skirt showed her tanned legs and feet. He watched her dig her toes into the sand, a habit of hers he'd begun to notice.

He looked out at the water because he was struck by his reaction to her, a reaction that seemed to grow in intensity.

He wanted her. But he wanted her with more than just his body. He wanted her with his mind as well. And looking at her only made him more uncomfortably aware of it.

She cleared her throat, then cocked her head and gave him one of her direct looks. "We have a problem."

He waited, then said, "Yeah, sweetheart, I think we do."

"Good. I'm glad you realize it. We have to do something about Santa Claus."

That hadn't been exactly what he was thinking about. He looked up at her. "Like?"

"We need to make some kinds of gifts, toys, something to put in their stockings." She paused. "I think after all they've been through we should try to make this special. For the children."

He looked at her face, the perfection of it, the smooth honey color of her skin, her golden eyes, a mouth a man could die in and be happy. "I'll see what I can come up with."

"Me, too." She smiled. When she turned and walked back toward the children, he watched her walk the way he had wanted to watch her before. But what he saw wasn't her hips slowly swaying. What he saw was the image of her smile.

That evening, no one was more surprised than Margaret when Hank walked into the hut carrying a fresh island pine tree that was taller than he was. It was straight and lush and green, with a tinge of blue on the needles like the noble fir her father always had delivered to the house the day after Thanksgiving.

Margaret watch him maneuver the sturdy pine tree through the doorway and around Theodore. The boy was so excited he all but danced a jig around the tree and Hank.

The tree had that Christmas smell, the sharp, clean scent of pine. So despite the heat, despite the tropical humidity and the intensity of the sun, it only took a few minutes for the subtle scent of Christmas to fill the hut.

It was difficult for her to believe that he was the same man in the lifeboat. She looked at him for a moment and suddenly felt a sharp pang of guilt because she realized something else.

What she had just thought about him was incredibly unfair. Hank had saved their lives before they even got into that lifeboat.

She was guilty of doing to him what had been done to her. A preconceived notion that the outer shell was the person. Because Hank was rough, he couldn't have a heart. Because she was pretty, she couldn't be smart. Because he was poor, he didn't deserve respect. Because she was rich, she couldn't hurt. Because he was a convict, he couldn't be of value. Because she was a woman, she couldn't be a lawyer.

She had fought those prejudices by trying to be perfect. He fought those prejudices by trying to be exactly what they thought—trouble.

"Where do you want it?"

That deep voice caught her as it always did. The sound seemed to wash right over her skin. Margaret blinked, then his words actually registered. He was holding the Christmas tree and asking her opinion. She almost laughed at how things had changed. "Right there is fine." She stood and walked over to the tree. She ran her fingers over the fresh needles, then turned to him. "Where did you ever find it?"

He shrugged. "There are island pine trees all over the higher hills of the interior."

She glanced at the children, who were wide-eyed and excited. She placed her hand on his forearm. "Thank you, Hank."

He seemed a little embarrassed but didn't say anything. He turned to the kids. "Come on. I need some help." As he strode toward the doorway, Lydia and Theodore were right behind him.

They came back laughing and lugging a fat barrel filled with wet sand. He potted the tree, talking to both children, letting them help and telling them about island trees—how they grew and where they grew. He would turn every now and then and wink at little Annabelle, who touched the tree with a child's look of awe, who clapped her hands and giggled and laughed.

Margaret watched with a strange kind of comfort. This tall man with the massive shoulders, the back criss-crossed with whip marks, a man who in the beginning had all the gentleness of a runaway train.

He was a man who had value, who deserved respect even if he tried to make people believe it didn't matter to him. It did.

Looking at him now, she knew with certainty that he had a heart. No matter how hard he tried to hide it.

❦ 27 ❦

The morning of Christmas Eve arrived without fanfare. Another cloudless sky where the sun was a lonely stranger and a light trade wind rustled the leaves, cooling the sun's heat from humidity-dampened skin.

A few hundred feet inside the thick jungle was a small area where the ebony trees weren't as thick and a small brook of fresh water trickled down a rock wall.

Spread upon the thick tufts of monkey grass were a menagerie of handmade toys—the sort of stuff that might plump up Santa's bag were Santa stranded on a tropical island. Ball and cups were carved from ebony with long handles that had rocks attached to them by long pieces of string. Tops were not symmetrical, but nature-made from thick seashells with tiger stripes that blurred when they were spun on the shell tips.

Clappers weren't made of wood and colorful cloth but instead made of coconut shells and thick leaves. A flat plank of wood had little niches handcarved with a penknife—an island version of a Wahoo game—only since there were no marbles, small pearls made do.

Hank glanced at the board game. He figured it was worth a fortune. He and Smitty had dived for two days to get enough pearls in each color—blue, black, pink, and white.

He found none of them. She had found all of them, including the last pearl, which was too big to use in the game. It was a deep rose color, perfectly spherical, rare and huge, as big as his thumbnail.

She'd grinned and tossed it in the air while he'd buried his head in his hands and groaned. The woman had amazing luck.

Early that morning, she had brought him some things she had made for the kids. An Indian headband she made of woven grass with a thick row of gull feathers, a tomahawk made from a flat sea rock tied with coconut twine to a driftwood stick, and two dolls with coconuts for heads, coconut fiber for hair, seashells for eyes and noses, and pieces of string for smiling mouths.

Their bodies were squares of cloth filled with sand and tied to a stick that served as necks. Driftwood twigs formed the stiff arms and legs. Compared to the bisque dolls in the fancy city toy stores, these dolls were primitive. But they had been made with love by the hands of an attorney whose expertise lay in the courtroom, not in a toy workshop.

Hank picked up a canvas sack and filled it with the toys, then slung the sack over his shoulder. He stopped at a nearby rock and picked up the fishing pole he'd made for Theodore. He tied another knot in the line and tested it for weight, then set it down. Next to the rock was a spinning toy he'd created for Annabelle and a set of ebony combs he'd carved for Lydia. These were his gifts to the children.

He'd made an identical set of hair combs for Smitty. But even after he'd finished them, something told him that wasn't what he wanted to give her. The right gift, however, escaped him. He stared at the combs but still couldn't think. He shrugged, slung the sack over his shoulder, and walked back toward the beach.

Not too far from the clearing stood a large poinciana tree in full bloom. At first glance it looked like a giant red umbrella. The lush red blossoms parted like the Red Sea, and a purple turban poked through the blooms.

Muddy sat on a sturdy branch watching Hank pace and mutter in front of his silver bottle. It sat in the sand, isolated and alone. The stopper lay next to it.

But apparently Hank hadn't noticed. He stopped pacing and stared down at the bottle. He picked it up, his expression tense. "Hey, you!"

Muddy laughed silently and gripped the branch in his hands. He leaned slightly forward and waited.

Hank started to lift the bottle to his eye, then paused and swore. He looked left, right, then barked, "Will you get the hell out of there?"

Muddy crossed his legs carefully, so his bells wouldn't ring. He rested an elbow on a knee and his chin in his palm. *This ought to be interesting.*

Hank stood there, kneading the back of his neck with a hand. "Hey, you! Genie!"

Nothing.

"Uh . . . Muddy!"

Muddy waited.

"Dammit!" He raised the bottle to his eye and scowled into it.

"Looking for me?"

Hank spun around. He looked at the tree, then frowned down at the bottle. He dropped the bottle. "Yeah."

Neither said another word for a good three minutes.

Finally Hank broke the silence. "Are you coming the hell down?"

Muddy shook his head. "Don't think so."

Hank stalked over to the tree and looked up. After a minute in which he worked his tight jaw but didn't say a word, he barked, "I need a favor."

Muddy just looked at him. "No wishes."

"It doesn't have anything to do with wishes."

"I'm not taking you inside the bottle again."

"No thanks, ch—" He stopped. "No thanks."

Muddy rubbed his goatee. "What kind of favor?"

Hank began to pace. "Smitty thinks the kids need to have a visit from Santa Claus tonight."

Muddy wasn't going to make this any easier for him.

Hank crossed over to where he'd been pacing. He picked up a canvas sack, came back, and dropped it at the base of the tree. "I want you to put this stuff in their stockings and stomp around the roof tonight. You know, make a lot of noise."

"Like Santa's reindeer."

"Yeah. I can't do it. I'm too heavy. I'll fall through the roof and give it away."

Muddy waited, then took a phrase from Hank. "Let me see if I have this straight. You want me to fly up on the roof, pretend to be Santa and his reindeer, then fill the children's stockings."

"Yeah."

Muddy watched him squirm for a moment longer. It was just too good to pass up. "As a favor for you."

"For the kids."

Muddy waited, took a deep breath, and crossed his arms over his chest. "I'll do it."

"Good—"

"On one condition."

Hank's eyes narrowed. "What?"

"You must teach Theodore how to play baseball."

Hank swore viciously and began to pace again.

"I'll supply the bat and ball. You supply the know-how."

He stopped and glared up at Muddy. "You're a sneaky bastard, aren't you?"

"Me?" Muddy poked his chest, then he shrugged. "I just want to see my master happy."

"Yeah, and I want to eat this tree." Hank stood there for a long time, then turned back, his hands shoved in his pockets. He looked at the sack, then said, "You win. I'll do it."

"When do you want the performance?"

"I'll give you a signal."

"What kind of signal?"

"I'll whistle a song." Hank paused, then said, "Jingle Bells."

Muddy gave him a mock salute. "Okay . . . chump."

Hank stood there as if he wanted to say something, but he shook his head and started to walk away. He stopped at the edge of the clearing and grumbled, "Thanks." He walked a little farther. "Chump."

On Christmas Eve, the hut was aglow with over a hundred candlenuts, each one lit like Christ's candles. They sat on trunks used as makeshift tables, lighting up the tops with a warm glow. Candlenuts burned atop a squat barrel used for an occasional stool. They sat as clusters of golden light in what had been dark corners of the hut, flickered near woven mats and circled the base of the Christmas tree like a ring of stars, casting golden twinkling light on the gifts stacked beneath. And the gifts were many, wrapped in banana leaves with flower vines tied around them as ribbon, and bright fresh orchids served as Christmas bows.

Wreaths made of lush green ferns and bright red and pink flowers were sprinkled with sand that caught minute fragments of the light and looked like a dusting of tropical snow. Sand glistened from the tree branches, too—an island Christmas tree. Different, yet oddly traditional.

The tree was decorated with strings of seashells— conch and cockleshells. Coned shells of all sizes hung like island icicles from the plump ends of its branches. Sand dollars served as white snowflakes and bright flowers of red and purple, pink and orange, were arranged inside the branches like finely crafted German glass ornaments.

Orchid vines draped in luscious garlands and coconut shells held green angels shaped from banana leaves. But the crowning glory was a Christmas gift from the South Seas—a bright red and yellow starfish that hung from the very top of the tree.

Muddy lounged back on the hard top of a trunk, enjoying the most unique and comfortable holiday celebration he'd experienced.

There was a sense of peace and joy inside the hut, in the laughter and smiles of those within. He played the observer, as he was prone to do, just watched them while he relaxed, his heart and head light, his belly full.

For some reason, probably a Christmas gift from fate, Margaret hadn't burned dinner. They had eaten fish that Theodore had helped catch, fruit Lydia had gathered, and yams Margaret had accidentally baked to perfection before they gathered around the tree, and just sat there, watching it, each person lost in their own thoughts.

The peace of Christmas was upon them.

Then Theodore pulled the harmonica out of his pocket and held it up in the flickering holiday lights.

Muddy winced. *There went the sense of peace.*

Hank and Margaret exchanged a worried look. But Theodore got up, walked over, and handed the harmonica to Hank. "Can you play Christmas songs?"

Everyone sagged back for a relieved second, then Hank lifted the harmonica to his mouth and began to play "Silent Night." By the second verse, Margaret was singing in a clear and lovely voice. She waved to the children and to Muddy to join in.

So they sang Christmas carol after happy Christmas carol, each one louder than the last and each one making them laugh when they were done. Until they hit the one song with a happy melody that was clear and clean. Without a thought, they began to sing, "We wish you a—"

Hank dropped the harmonica and bellowed, "Don't sing!" He clapped his hand over Theodore's open mouth.

"Merry Christmas . . ." Margaret and Lydia's voices faded suddenly.

Theodore looked at them over Hank's hand, which was covering his mouth while Hank and Margaret both exhaled a large breath of relief. Hank slowly removed his hand.

Theodore blinked, then frowned at Hank. "I don't know the words to that one."

Hank rested his head in one hand, rubbed his forehead, then took a deep breath. "Let's try 'Jingle Bells,' then it's time to get some sleep."

"I'm not tired," Theodore informed him with childish indignation.

Hank nodded at Annabelle asleep in Margaret's arms. "It's time for bed, kid. The quicker you go to sleep, the sooner morning will come."

"Why? Does morning come faster when you're asleep?"

Hank and Margaret exchanged looks of how-do-I-answer-that. Hank turned back to Theodore. "Yes."

He played the last carol. The song ended, and Margaret went to put Annabelle to bed. Theodore was just getting his second wind, his eyes bright, warning that he was ready to stay awake all night.

There came a rustling on the roof. There was a loud thud and some of the palm fronds fell down to the ground.

Everyone looked up, suddenly silent.

"It's Santa Claus," Theodore whispered, the whites of his eyes as wide as gull eggs.

Hank stood up so quickly it almost made Muddy dizzy.

Margaret placed her hand on Hank's arm. "What's wrong?"

Hank stared at the roof with a look of amazement. He whipped his head around and gave a narrowed-eye look at Muddy, who didn't say a word. Muddy just slid his arm around Theodore's shoulder, crossed his legs, and stared up at the roof. His shoe bells rang as he nonchalantly swung his feet back and forth, and he quietly hummed "Jingle Bells."

Hank turned and ran outside so fast that Muddy gave a small chuckle.

A choice swear word echoed back into the hut followed by Hank's deep voice saying, "This is not happening."

In the distance, there was a new sound. Not the small tinkling of Muddy's bells, but the clean ringing of brass sleigh bells.

And if one listened very closely, if one tried really hard, it was there . . . a deep and jolly bit of laughter that drifted across the great Pacific sky.

Dawn came cool and early that Christmas day. Margaret lay in the misty morning world where one was neither asleep nor awake. She heard something and opened her eyes. Hank was slowly closing the door of the hut.

He'd been acting odd most of last evening, even after they calmed down the children. She had awakened in the middle of the night. Hank was standing over her. He held the ragged hem of her dress between his fingers, and he was silent. She hadn't let him know she was awake and had closed her eyes quickly, but she wondered what he'd been doing. It had seemed an odd thing, to feel someone's clothes when they were asleep.

She rose now and checked on the children. They were sound asleep. She crept to the door and quietly followed him.

He walked down to the lagoon, dove in the water, and swam out to the sandbar, like he did every day. But somehow, she had a feeling today was different.

Margaret stood there, wondering why she had followed him. It was almost as if someone had told her to, like some odd instinct. Or like the time she chased the hoop. He was swimming as usual, diving beneath the water a few times. She shook her head and took one last look before she started to go back.

Then she saw it, just a few hundred feet from his dark head. She looked again. It was a shark fin.

And she ran.

28

Margaret ripped open the door of the hut, grabbed the pistol, and tore back outside, running as fast as she could. Faster than she'd ever run.

Down the beach. Over a crest in a sand dune. Then she could see the water.

In the distance, the shark slowly circled over and over, its fin black, ominous, slicing through the blue water.

Her feet ate up the sand, her long legs fleet. Her heart pounded in her throat. She clutched the pistol tighter.

She blew out breaths as fast as her feet moved.

The range? How far? How close?

Am I too late? No . . .

She just kept running.

She stopped suddenly. Raised the pistol, shaking. She steadied it with the other hand, sighted, and pulled the trigger.

Four times.

Bullets and blood spurted in the thrashing water, which turned pink, then wine red.

She dropped the gun, standing frozen and panting, not knowing if it was Hank's blood or the blood of the shark.

Then she was moving, running into the tide. She stopped suddenly, staring down at the blood that rolled in with the lapping waves.

She looked up. Shaking. Panicked.

Hank's dark head bobbed near the inert carcass of the shark.

"Hank!" she screamed, then cupped her hands around her mouth. "Hank!"

He raised one hand, a signal that he was alive.

Her breath left her in a half cry, and her knees almost buckled under a strong wave.

She locked her gaze on him. Was there blood on his hand? On his arm?

Oh, God, there was.

He moved slowly as if one side of him wasn't functioning.

Had she shot him?

A ribbon of bright red trailed behind him in the clear water. Her mind flashed with the obscure thought of red ribbons and Christmas.

She closed her eyes. *You're hysterical.*

She looked again. The red trail was still there.

She had shot him. *Ohmygod . . .*

She ran farther into the water.

He yelled something at her.

She froze, her hands to her mouth, her breath static.

"Get back, dammit!" And he worked his way toward the shore.

She dove under a wave and swam, swam like she ran, fleet and right toward him.

He swore at her. Cursed loudly when she was only a few feet away.

"Let me help you, please, Hank."

"Dammit, Smitty, move!"

He was standing on the sandbar, his body twisted as if he were hiding his wounds from her.

"Don't be so blasted hardheaded," she screamed. "For once in your life, let someone else help you!" She swam closer, and a swell rippled past them.

She realized her feet could touch bottom, too, and she reached for him. "You're hurt. Did I shoot you? You're bleeding, Hank. Oh, God, you're bleeding."

He swore again, then jerked hard.

She stood there, stunned. He wasn't hiding a wound. He was dragging a trunk through the tide.

She gripped the other side and saw that one of his upper arms was bleeding and open. She grabbed the trunk handle and pulled with him until they got the trunk to shore, where they fell to their knees in the sand.

They were panting. Hard. As if the air was playing a game of chase with them.

She sat back on her heels while Hank leaned back against the trunk, his long legs sprawled out in front of him.

"You're bleeding." She ripped a piece of her skirt and frantically wrapped it around the gash in his arm. She kept glancing at him. He couldn't catch his breath from exertion and trauma. He tried to speak, but she saw that the words were fighting at his throat and lips.

He glanced at his arm, stared at it as if it wasn't his. He gasped as he tried to say something, but his teeth chattered.

She knew that reaction was from shock.

"The sonufabitch almost had me," he finally rasped, then took a couple more breaths. He looked at her and shook his head slightly. "Damn, Smitty, but you can run. Can shoot, too."

"What were you doing out there? Getting a silly trunk?" She tied off the strip of fabric and leaned against him for a moment. She was still breathing hard herself.

She pressed her cheek to his wet shoulder for

herself. She needed that one small bit of comfort. He was alive. She closed her eyes and the words just came. "We almost lost you. God, Hank . . . Almost."

"Needed the trunk," he muttered into her hair, and one hand came up to rest on her shoulder.

She looked at him. "Why?"

"For you."

"Me?"

He moved his hand from her shoulder and patted the top of the trunk. "Merry Christmas, sweetheart."

And he passed out.

"Did you really have a fight with a shark?" Theodore hovered over Hank and stuck his curious little head right in Hank's face.

He glanced up at the kid, whose nose was almost pressed to the small but deep wound in his arm.

"Move your head, dear, I can't see what I'm doing." Smitty waited before she took another stitch.

Hank clenched his jaw tight, but he didn't say anything or make a sound. He just let her finish stitching the small gashes in his upper arm.

"There. All done."

Hank exhaled hard, then took a couple of deep breaths. Theodore cocked his head and stared thoughtfully at his arm. "It looks funny."

Hank frowned down at it. "It does?"

He nodded. "None of your guts are hanging out anymore."

Hank laughed. "Is that good or bad?"

The kid shrugged. "Good, I guess." Then he went back over to the Christmas tree with his sisters and he sat down, no longer fascinated with the stitched gashes from a shark's jagged teeth. It was back to the Christmas gifts.

Margaret and Hank exchanged a look.

"Bloodthirsty little thing, isn't he?" She laughed then. "Full of tact, too. Reminds me of someone else."

"I have tact. Hell, Smitty, I have enough tact for a lifetime."

"Can we open the gifts now?" Theodore asked in a voice that could only be described as a whine.

"Yes." Margaret walked over and held a hand out to Hank.

He laughed. "I'm fine, sweetheart." He pushed himself up.

"Take my hand anyway," Margaret told him.

He watched her for a second, then slid his hand over hers. She uncurled her hand and let the rose pearl roll into his.

He looked at it, then at her.

She smiled. "Merry Christmas."

He grinned, tossed it in the air, and caught it. With a wink, he took her arm. Together, they joined the children at the tree.

Margaret glanced up. Muddy sat in a dark corner as if he wasn't certain he was wanted.

She whispered in Theodore's ear, and the boy went over and took Muddy's hand. "Happy Christmas, Muddy."

"Happy Christmas to you, master."

Theodore pulled the genie over to the tree.

Gifts were plenty and as whimsical as Christmas itself. Hank took a long string and wound up the toy he'd made for Annabelle. It spun and whirred and popped, and she giggled and laughed and chased it wherever it chugged.

Theodore was a fishing Indian, now known as Big Chief Catchum Grouper, and Lydia, half young girl and half child, wore all her shell necklaces, hair ribbons, and combs and strutted like a grande dame as she carried her coconut doll in one hand and pulled Rebuttal along in the other.

Muddy had disappeared inside the bottle and after a few minutes came blasting out in a puff of red and green smoke.

"Look! Everyone! Muddy's smoke changed colors," Theodore said, pointing.

The smoke dissipated, and Muddy stood there, his arms filled with gifts.

And they had Christmas all over again.

A badminton set for Theodore, a hand organ for Lydia, a golden cup for Annabelle, and a lovely silver frame for Margaret along with the promise of a photograph with Muddy's photographic equipment.

Then Muddy reached behind him, picked up something, and walked over to where Hank sat. The closer Muddy got, the more narrowed Hank's gaze grew.

Margaret wondered what would happen between those two.

Muddy handed Hank a long package wrapped with old yellowed newspapers.

Hank grumbled something, then walked over to the tree. He picked up the only bundle still wrapped in banana leaves and walked back over. He shoved it in Muddy's hands and said, "Here."

And everyone stood around waiting for them to open the gifts.

They both sat staring at the gifts as if they were snakes.

Margaret looked from one to the other. "Merry Christmas to both of you."

They looked at her, then back at the packages.

"You go first," Hank said.

"No. You first." Muddy crossed his arms as stubbornly as Hank's were crossed. They both looked at each other.

Margaret watched them. "I'll count to three and you both can open them."

They eyed each other, then nodded.

"One . . . two . . . three!"

Both sat there. A second later they muttered, "Chump."

"If you two don't open those gifts right now,"

Margaret said, "I'm going to ask Theodore to play a two-hour concerto on the harmonica."

They looked at each other, paled, and tore open the packages.

There was utter silence when they looked at their gifts.

Hank stared down at a baseball and a bat, a black Al Spalding glove, and a Chicago White Stockings baseball cap.

And Muddy? Muddy was holding Hank's shoes.

On the lively notes of a hand organ, the three-quarter moon rose high above a thatched hut that Christmas night. The sand around the hut was dappled with flickering light that shone between the cracks, and laughter rode outside on tinny notes of music.

Hank was leaning against a wall, watching Margaret's ankles and calves. She stood nearby, watching the children, her skirt in her hands as she swayed to the music.

He shook his head. He had a new appreciation for Christmas.

Theodore and Annabelle and Muddy were holding hands and dancing while Lydia cranked the hand organ and played a polka.

After a few minutes, Margaret moved over to the trunk, and she picked up the ball gown.

It gave Hank a warm sense of pride as he watched her run her hands over the silky rose-colored fabric. She smiled a misty kind of smile that made him a little crazy for her.

Then she turned and walked over to him, the gown clutched in her hands. She stopped in front of him, and the smile she gave him was just as soft and misty. "Thank you for this gown. It's lovely."

"You like it?"

She nodded, but then looked up, her face serious. "As lovely as it is, though, it wouldn't have been worth it if . . ." She stopped. Then she took one step closer and placed her hand on his chest. "If I'd lost you."

He glanced at the children, then placed his hand over hers. He raised his other hand and touched her lips with one finger. Neither of them said a thing. They didn't need to.

He slid his hand along her jawline and smiled, then gave the dress a nod. "Put it on."

She looked at him. "Now?"

"Yeah, now."

She laughed and moved closer. Covertly she leaned over and said, "You're always telling me to take my clothes off, not put them on."

"Put it on, sweetheart."

She cocked her head. "I'll put on the dress if you put on the tails."

"The monkey suit?"

She nodded.

"Hell, no. No way."

Her face fell a little. He added, "It wouldn't fit anyway. Too small."

"What makes you think the dress will fit?"

"I've got a good eye, sweetheart. It'll fit."

She set the dress aside and walked over to the trunk. She held up the coat. It was not small, even he could see that. "This coat does not look too small to me. Look." She turned around.

He stared at it.

"Please."

He rolled his eyes. "All right, dammit. But only because it's Christmas." He pulled the rest of the suit from the trunk. He paused and held up the pants, hoping for a new excuse. Dammit if they weren't long enough.

Her cool look said she knew exactly what he'd been thinking. He shrugged. "Can't blame a guy for trying." He went toward the door muttering that he was damn glad Christmas only came once a year.

* * *

"Wowie! Lookit Hank!"

Margaret spun around, and the silk of the ball gown rustled against her bare feet. He stood in the doorway dressed in formal clothes. She'd always thought a man looked more handsome in a white tie and tails than anything.

Hank looked better than that. He was tall, and the black coat made him look even taller, leaner. The white shirt against his tanned skin gave it a more rugged and earthy appeal. The white tie was slung around the shirt collar and the shirt was undone with buttonholes on both plackets. There were no studs.

It was an odd mix. The fine precise quality of dress clothes and the hard ruggedness of the man himself. Together they made a formidable presence.

He crossed the room and just stood in front of her. She smiled. "Hi."

He was staring at her dress. Actually, he was staring at her cleavage.

He gave a small whistle through his teeth. "They sure look bigger than they felt."

She took a long breath. "How perfectly romantic."

"Well, hell, Smitty, that's one helluva set of—"

She covered his mouth with her hand and shook her head.

Theodore was standing beside them, his curious eyes taking in every word, every look.

He frowned up at Hank. "What looks bigger?"

Hank looked at him and said as smoothly as a con man, "The dress sleeves."

"Oh." Theodore frowned at the sleeves and then joined his sisters.

"Nice recovery," she whispered.

"Yeah, I recover real fast. Wanna clock me sometime?"

"I have to assume from that lascivious look on your face that I don't want an explanation."

He gave her a long look. "You really don't understand?"

She shook her head.

"Yeah, well, never mind, sweetheart. You'll get it someday." Then he turned slightly and muttered, "Better damn well be soon."

"Dance with her, Hank! Dance with Smitty!" Theodore was jumping up and down.

And Lydia began to play a waltz on the organ.

No one was more surprised than Margaret when he held out his hand and pulled her into his arms. They danced, and he actually knew how. In fact, his steps were smooth and his hand on the small of her back guided her to each move, held her firmly for each swirling turn. She was aware of his scent, of the warmth of his body, and even more aware of him and of the dark promise in his eyes whenever he looked at her.

After a few dances, he surprised her and pulled Lydia out to dance while Theodore cranked the hand organ. The young girl smiled and laughed when he swirled her around, practically picking her up off her feet so she could keep up with him.

Even Annabelle had a turn at dancing to silly steps that bounced her in his arms and made her giggle and laugh and tuck her head under his chin. Something happened to Margaret, something warm and special as she watched them. She looked down at the lovely pink ball gown. It was the same color as the pearl she had given him. She ran her hand down the fabric and smiled.

The next thing she knew Hank had pulled her into his arms again. And they spun around a thatched hut on a wacky and wonderful Christmas, with a smiling genie watching and candlenuts burning instead of rich crystal chandeliers, dancing and twirling and falling in love to the tinny tune of a hand organ waltz and the sweet music of children's giggles.

⚜ 29 ⚜

By the time Hank and Smitty had stopped dancing, Annabelle and Theodore were sound asleep and Lydia's lids were heavy over her blue eyes. They put them to bed and stood there, together watching them sleep. Hank slid his hand around hers. Because it felt right. Because he didn't want to let her go. Not yet.

Muddy was lounging on a trunk, his head resting in one hand. Hank looked back at Smitty, who was staring up at him. The air was thick with more than just humid tropical air.

"You two can go for a walk," Muddy said nonchalantly. "I'll watch them."

Hank had her out the door before she could blink. He pulled her with him until they both were running down the beach in the moonlight. She laughed, and so did he. She shouted his name, and he called out hers to tease her as they ran in uneven speeds over the sand, each pulling at the other. But they both slowed down and stopped when they were near the water. Her breath was short and sharp, and she grabbed her side because she was still laughing.

He watched her smile. He almost laughed to himself, knowing what that smile of hers did to him. Part of him was glad she didn't understand the power she had with that one smile.

But after a moment, Hank's gaze caught hers. There was a long tense pause while they stared at each other. Her smile faded.

He knew. She knew.

Nothing else mattered. It didn't matter that the lagoon shone a lustery black in the night. It didn't matter that a breath of night wind made the palm fronds whisper. Nothing mattered then but what they felt for each other—something there was no word for. Emotion so strong it had no name.

They turned and walked in silence along the sand where the moonlight turned their steps silver. The waves were breaking with a bolder sound, a boom, a rush, and foamy whoosh. And as those waves broke, thousands of red sea creatures glimmered in the subtle light, glowed as if there were fire in the waves.

Hank just held her soft hand as they walked, with nothing around them but the wind and the sea and a wealth of emotion and awareness of the other.

His senses were keen. With each breath of the trades, her scent came alive. It was suddenly all around him, that female smell that made him damn glad he was a man.

He could sense it above the brine of the sea, above the earthy smell of the sand and the shore. He was aware only of her. Just Smitty.

Her touch. Her profile. Her walk. The way the ball gown rustled against the side of his leg.

He stopped and smiled down at her, then pulled her to him. He threaded his fingers through hers and held their hands up as he slid his other arm around her lower back.

And they danced in the moonlight. On silver sand and cool sighs of wind. The music was all around them—the rumbling reef, the wash of the waves, the rustle of palm fronds in the nearby coconut trees, the rapid and syncopated beat of their hearts.

They sensed when to stop, and both did at the same moment. Whether it was in their eyes or in their minds, they knew. Almost as if at that moment in time they were one.

Hank looked over her head and stared out at the sea for a moment that he thought he needed. It was a little confusing, all this . . . stuff in his gut that he'd never experienced. It wasn't an easy thing for him to accept either.

He looked at her, and his doubts washed away.

He touched her cheek, then let his hand drift to her neck. Her pulse pounded like the surf. He leaned down and kissed her gently in a way he'd never kissed a woman before. He wasn't taking anything. Just touching his mouth to hers. He pulled back and watched her.

Her breathing was husky and abrupt, like his. In her eyes he saw the same raw emotion that was eating at him. A need that was more than something physical.

It was hard to tell who made the first move. He reached out for her and she for him. He lowered his head. She stood on tiptoe. Then she was in his arms, her body, that soft, female body was against his.

He kissed her again. Kissed her as he'd never kissed a woman. Kissed her as if she mattered. Because she did.

He never gave Margaret a chance to say anything. She didn't have to ask him for what she wanted. And she hadn't known the words to ask anyway. But he did the most romantic thing he could have—he picked her up in his arms and carried her down the beach.

She felt his arms tighten around her, and he stepped over the rock to that isolated spot of beach where he'd lost himself in bottles of liquor. A small plot of beach where rocks and sea made it private.

He dropped her legs so he held her along his tall body with one hand cupping her head and the other hand on her bottom. Then his mouth covered hers so swiftly he stole her breath.

She slid her arms up over his shoulders and hung on for all it was worth.

And it was worth everything.

His tongue brushed her lips, then he was in her mouth, a hard and seeking kiss that demanded that she give in return. Her hands moved up his neck and onto his head. Her fingers dug through his black hair and clenched it in tight fistfuls.

He moaned her name over and over. She opened her mouth wider, sucked on his tongue and his lips the way he'd sucked on hers. She kissed him in ways she'd never been kissed, had never known existed. With him her motions were instinctive.

His hand kneaded her bottom, first one side, then the other. He pressed her hard against him and groaned when she dropped a hand to the small of his back and slid her fingers into the waistband of his pants. His hips began to move in a slow rhythm that she soon picked up. She moved with him. Circling slowly in a new dance.

Their motions grew hot and hungry, unguarded and free. He tore at the buttons on her dress and drew his tongue and mouth along her neck, over to her throat, and lower as he pulled the fabric down under one breast. His head nudged her back over his arm, exposing her, and his mouth closed over her breast, sucking as much of it into his mouth as he could.

She moaned and grabbed his head again with both hands, holding him there. His hips still rotated against hers, and he pulled one of her knees up and tucked it against his waist so he could rub harder against her.

Then he changed arms and breast, and his right hand drifted down to her other leg and slid around the back of her thigh. He pulled that leg high around his hips, and he moaned something low and earthy about what he would do to her, where, and for how long.

Somewhere in the back recesses of her conscious mind, she hoped he kept those promises. And she told him so.

He growled low in his throat and jerked her dress off so fast she was chilled from the air. He tore off his coat and dropped it in the sand. He pulled off the rest of her clothing, then ripped off his shirt and undid his belt and pants.

He pulled her against him, then swung her up into his arms again and knelt, laying her in the silver sand.

She stared up at him kneeling beside her, cast in a sliver of moonlight that sliced through a lonely cloud. He was long, lean, hard, tanned, and as rugged as his manner. There was something elemental about him, an earthiness that sparked a side of her she hadn't known existed.

He moved then to kneel at her feet, and he slowly massaged them, moving upward to her ankles. He slowly spread her legs.

"God, these legs . . . ," he rasped in a throaty whisper. His hands moved up her ankles, calves, rubbing them and stroking them, only inches at a time. It took forever for him to get to her knees, where he lowered his head and kissed the insides, then dragged his tongue down her calves and sucked on her ankles, only to move up and do the same thing all over again.

He kissed her legs for long eternal minutes, driving her mad with his fingertips, nails, lips, and tongue. Then he lifted her knees, settling her feet flat on the sand. He slowly moved down the inside of one thigh with his tongue, licking, only to stop before he hit the juncture of her legs.

Then he moved the other side and did the very same thing, only more slowly and more thoroughly, until her hips lifted up and she was calling his name over and over.

"Open your eyes, sweetheart. Look at me." He knelt back on his heels.

She opened her eyes, seeing at first only a mist of his silhouette.

He reached out with one finger and drew it over her there, where she craved his touch. He did it slowly. Then he stopped, and she moaned.

"Watch me," he said.

He tasted his finger and then did the same thing again. Over and over until she finally grabbed his hand and pressed it to her because she couldn't take it anymore.

He pressed a thick, rugged finger into her and slowly moved it in and out, his knuckle doing things that made her forget everything but the center of her body. He added another finger, stretching her wider and putting pressure so deep within her that she stopped breathing for an instant.

He spent long minutes thrusting his fingers in and out of her, and her hips rose higher and her knees began to shake uncontrollably. He stopped and slid his hands under her bottom, moving her knees over his wide shoulders, and he lifted her to his mouth.

The world disappeared, just faded into nothing but the hot touch of his mouth. He didn't kiss her there with the same hungry motions as he kissed her mouth. He traced her lightly with his tongue, then rubbed his lips against the core of her before he moved up and drew a small, sensitive point into his mouth and sucked.

And she throbbed hard over and over. He didn't stop.

"Again," he said against her. "Again, sweetheart. Do it again." And he buried his tongue so deeply inside of her that she did do it again.

She was crying when her body quieted. He lay her back down and rested his cheek on her belly. When her breath returned and her heart stopped pounding in her head and ears, he lifted his head, his look so hot her breath caught.

And he started licking her again. Everywhere.

Everything all over again. Only just before she would fall over the edge, just before her knees shook too hard, he would stop suddenly, calming her with his hands on her legs, soothing her until it passed. Then he built it again, only higher. Each time, he brought her close to that point again, but then he stopped.

And he talked to her, telling her he was teaching her the power of her body, showing her how men and women mated—Hank didn't use that word.

He crawled between her legs and lifted them and wrapped them around his hips. He pressed against her with his length, then tilted his hips and slowly inched inside, pushing her wider than his fingers could or had, filling her more deeply than he could with his tongue.

"Oh, baby. This is heaven. Hang on. Hang on tight, sweetheart."

Then he covered her mouth with his and thrust home. Pain shot through her belly and down her legs. She stiffened and moaned at its sharpness. She dug her nails into his bottom.

He swore crudely, then buried his head on her neck. "I'm sorry, sweetheart. Just lay still. Don't move." He gripped her bottom and refused to let her back away. "Easy. Just lay still for a minute."

She did. And the burning slowly faded.

He gave her time, then said, "Look at me, Smitty."

And she opened her eyes.

"You okay?"

She nodded, even though she could feel tears streaming down her temples and into her hairline.

"I'm going to move a little. Real easy."

She squeezed her eyes shut, gritted her teeth, and gripped his bottom even tighter. "Okay," she whispered, holding her breath.

He gave a bark of wry laughter and dropped his head on her neck. "Damn . . . I hope it's not going to be that bad."

Her eyes shot open. "Don't you know?"

"I'm not a woman, Smitty."

She blinked, then frowned up at him. "You mean to tell me it doesn't hurt you?"

He shook his head.

"God is a man," she muttered.

He laughed so hard his arms gave out and he lay on her.

She watched his shoulders shake. "It's not that funny, Hank."

He lifted his head off of her and looked down, still grinning. He shook his head. "I never knew I could laugh and screw at the same time."

"How perfectly romantic."

He eyed her the same way he had eyed the genie bottle. "You're mad as hell, aren't you?"

"Yes."

"Why?"

"Sex is not fair and equal."

"But it's a helluva lot of fun, sweetheart."

"That's because you're the man."

"Give me a little while and I'll make you eat those words, Smitty."

"How?"

"Did you like what I did to you? This?" he asked, then slowly dragged his tongue across her chest, watching her the whole time.

Her breath caught, and she whispered, "Yes."

He reached down and drew a finger around where they were joined. "Here?"

"Yes."

"If you don't like what I'm going to do, then from now on we'll just do that."

Now that was an offer that had promise.

The only thing that bothered her was his expression. His face wore the same look he'd had when he was playing poker with Theodore, a look that said he held the winning hand. "Agreed?"

She nodded.

"Relax, Smitty. I'll go slow and easy until you're ready." He shifted slowly, pulling back. "Does that hurt?"

"No. There's just pressure."

He moved again slowly and carefully for long

minutes, until she realized that he was right. She felt
no pain, just the fullness and size of him as he moved.
He seemed willing to take forever, to move slowly,
then build, stooping his shoulders and freezing if she
flinched or made a sound.

He looked at her. "You okay?"

She nodded, then slid her hands over his back,
liking the way his muscles contracted when he thrust
into her. She slid her hand to his bottom and felt each
of his motions by the tightening of his muscles there.

Before long she realized he was moving too slowly.
And she told him so.

He groaned a "Thank God" and picked up speed.
She moved with him, because she had to, because it
felt so good.

They rotated their hips in counterpoint. Then he
was moving harder and swifter, his lower body thrusting hard and strong. He had to grip her hips to keep
her from sliding away from him.

She could hear the waves and how they pounded
the shore, and she felt a rush like that of the sea, a
surge that was deep inside of her.

There was no pain, nothing but that thrill—the
same one that had happened when he loved her with
his mouth. Only with this, the friction was coming
swifter and deeper and stronger, as if everything
began and ended with his body.

"Come baby, come on . . ."

And he thrust three rapid and deep thrusts that sent
her flying over the edge.

He yelled a graphic and earthy phrase of thanks,
then threw his head back, his neck straining, his teeth
gritted, and he buried himself so deeply inside of her
that she blacked out for a moment even as her body
gripped him again and again. When she came down
from a place so high and free and hot, she could
barely catch a breath.

He whispered her name before he started again,
thrusting faster than ever. Suddenly he pulled out of

her, shifted his lower body back, dropped his hips between her splayed thighs, and groaned deep and dark, his body releasing something wet and warm near her knees.

They lay there, bodies molded by sweat and exhaustion, heartbeats rapid and together. She was acutely aware of the feel of him, the hair on his chest and belly crinkled against her skin, the soft hairs beneath her flat palms as she ran them slowly over the small of his back. His weight, his breath on her neck, his hand still beneath her bottom.

Long minutes later, he moved up her body again and dragged his mouth along her neck and shoulder, tasting her. He lifted his head and gave her a cocky look. "You still think sex isn't fair and equal?"

"I'm not certain."

"What the hell do you mean you're not certain?"

She tried to look perfectly serious when she said, "I have to think about it."

His eyes narrowed, and she laughed then. But before she could think about anything, he shifted back on his knees, slid his hands under her, and flung her legs over his shoulders. "Here, sweetheart," he said against her, "think about this."

❧ 30 ❧

Margaret sat in the sand, her back against Hank's chest, and they watched the moon go down on a brooding purple night sky. The trade wind brushed her face. She hugged her knees to her chest, dug her toes in sand cooled by the night.

It was odd how she seemed to feel each thing so keenly. The touch of the wind, the coolness of the sand, the warmth of Hank's body and his breath near her ear and neck. It was as if her skin and her senses had come alive in the last few hours. As if she were a new person. She thought about what had passed between them and wondered if perhaps she was a different Margaret Smith. She smiled. Maybe she was Smitty.

She sighed like the wind, because it felt good just sitting there, as if she and Hank had their own private world. There was a rich sense of peace and kinship about them, something that made it seem as if for that one moment in time no one else existed but the two of them.

Long minutes passed in silence that was like a comfortable old friend, different from the long, tense silences that had been between them before—when they fought so hard to deny what was happening.

She waited awhile, watched the sky turn darker as the silky moon disappeared on the horizon. Then she tilted her head back against his bare shoulder. "Talk to me."

"About what?"

"I don't know," she said, trying to sound casual. "Tell me about your life."

He laughed that cynical laugh he had. "We don't have that long, sweetheart."

"Then just tell me about the important things."

He shifted, and she could feel him look down at her. "Like what?"

"Like where you learned to dance."

He laughed. "I had lessons."

He was teasing her. She shook her head, then waited. When he didn't say anything else, she grabbed a handful of sand and let it spill through her fingers. "Tell me about baseball."

His arms tightened around her, then fell away for a moment. She hadn't fooled him.

He shifted around her until he was sitting beside her, his legs drawn up and his arms resting on them.

He didn't look at her. "Baseball's a game. You play with a bat, a glove, and a ball."

She reached out and touched his arm. "Don't. Please. I saw you in the jungle. Hitting those nuts over the trees. Theodore told me you wouldn't teach him how to play. Why? What happened?"

He picked up a small rock made smooth by the constant motion of the sea. He tossed it lightly as if it were a ball. She knew now that she'd seen him do this before, never knowing it was not just a habit, but a clue to part of his past.

He turned. "How much do you want to know?"

"Enough to understand."

He waited, then said, "Sometimes, sweetheart, I'm not certain I understand."

"Please, Hank."

He stared at the rock, rubbing it with his thumb. "I left Pittsburgh when I was fifteen. It was leave or go to jail." He looked not at her, but at the sea. "I'd been caught stealing on the streets. The cop that caught me was tired of throwing my butt in jail and told me to get the hell outta town or he'd lock me up and see that I never got out.

"So I left and worked my way to Philadelphia. I lived under a railroad trestle for a few months with some others in a makeshift vagrant shanty, stealing food to get by, sleeping under scraps of tin."

"At fifteen?"

"Yeah." He gave a wry laugh and looked at her. "What were you doing at fifteen?"

"Going to school, playing Parcheesi with friends, just doing what most fifteen-year-old girls in San Francisco did."

He was looking at her as if she were batty. "Parcheesi?"

"Yes, well, better than playing poker."

"I didn't play poker at fifteen."

"You didn't?" She cocked her head and stared back at him.

"Nope. Didn't learn how to mark a deck of cards until I was sixteen."

She groaned. "Finish your story."

"I'd been living on the street for close to a year, when one day I went to a baseball field. I'd heard there was food to scavenge. The Athletics were playing Boston, and the park was filled. Street vendors flocked to the park to sell sausages and beer. But better than the food, there were pockets to pick. So I started hanging out at the ballpark, taking what I could.

"Then I picked the wrong pocket—the team owner, Billy Hobart—and got caught. Billy ran me down." Hank shook his head. "I never could run worth a damn, even as a kid."

Margaret smiled at him, but she knew they both were only smiling at his wry comment, the way people laugh at a carnival clown who gets a bucket of water thrown in his face. The way something can be funny, but painfully sad at the same time.

"He dragged me back by the neck and made me work, worked my butt off, cleaning the field, repairing the benches and fences in that ballpark. Hell, he even had me cleaning the privies."

"You didn't try to run away?"

"Only once. I got about as far as left field. The whole team cornered me. From then on he had a guard stand by me with a billy club in one hand and a .45 in the other."

He paused, staring out at the sea again before he looked down at the sand for a second. "I called that sonufabitch every name I could, but I worked. Before long he had me taking meals with the team and gave me a bunk in the corner of the player room. It took a few months, but by then I didn't want to leave. It was as if I had become part of the team, although I still gave Billy a passel of crap.

"The next season they had me hitting the ball once in a while and subbing in at practice. He pissed me off so badly one day at bat that when the pitch came I didn't see the baseball. All I saw was red. I hit that ball out of the park. Billy walked out to Whoop-la Hunter—"

"Whoop-la?"

"Yeah. Ballplayers have nicknames, Foghorn Wilson, Cannonball Morris, Grasshopper Jim Whitney."

"You're serious?"

"Yeah."

She shook her head. "Must be a male thing."

He gave a snort.

"Well it must be," she said. "They don't refer to Betsy Ross as Stitches or call Jane Austen Inky Fingers."

"What about Bloody Mary?"

Margaret raised her chin. "No doubt she was given that name by some man."

He gave her one of those male looks—where they try to act as if their patience is being tested.

She gave a short wave of her hand. "Go on."

"I forgot where I was."

"Whoop-la Hunter."

"Yeah, that's right. Anyway, he was on the mound. Billy told him to mix up the pitches. Anything Whoop-la threw at me that day, I hit. Two years later I was on the team, playing all over. Places like Cincinnati, Chicago, Cleveland, Atlanta, and Boston. After the pennant in '78 we even played exhibition games in England and France for a few months. That was why I learned to dance. They hired a dancing instructor for the whole team before we left the States. Once in Europe, we'd play ball games during the day and go to fancy dances at night." He stopped talking.

She waited. Finally she nudged his arm. "So what happened?"

"Billy died of a heart attack just before the end of the season in '83. There was a three-way tie for the pennant, to be played off in road games between Boston, Philadelphia, and Chicago." He tossed the rock aside and just stared down at the sand, his wrists resting on his bent knees. "Gamblers got involved and offered big payoffs to players willing to throw games." He stopped abruptly.

"And?"

He shrugged. "We lost. There was a big scandal, and players were blacklisted." He looked up again. "I was one of them."

"I don't believe you would have thrown a game."

"Hell, Smitty, I stole my first wallet when I was six."

"I don't care what you did before. I don't believe you would have thrown a ball game."

He was silent. "You called me a crook yourself."

"I was wrong."

"Jesus, the devil must be ice-skating."

"Changing the subject won't work."

"Yeah, it never does with you."

"I only have one question."

"Yeah, yeah, and you're right, I didn't throw any games. They blacklisted five of us. Two were guilty, and the other three were considered troublemakers by the new owner. And I dished out a lot of crap."

"That wasn't the question I wanted answered."

"It wasn't?"

She shook her head.

"What then?"

She smiled. "I want to know your nickname."

He laughed then, and she could sense the tension wash away from him. "You're crazy, you know that?" He shook his head, and she saw that he was less tense. He turned to her. "You and Billy Hobart would have had a lot in common. He was just like you. Stubborn, persistent, too damn smart for his . . . or your own good."

"I'm waiting."

He looked away, then rubbed his chin for a second and mumbled something just as a wave crashed on the shoreline.

"I didn't hear you."

"Hardhead."

She looked at him for a second. "Hardhead Hank?"

"Yeah. Hardhead Hank Wyatt."

She burst out laughing.

It was almost dawn when they slipped back inside the hut. There was no light except for a pinkish glimmer of sunrise in the eastern sky. They checked each child—all sound asleep, as was Muddy, his bottle lying on a mat next to him.

Margaret nudged Hank and pointed. Muddy was wearing his shoes.

They moved back into the darkness of the hut, and his arms slid around her. He kissed her with quiet passion and held her face in his rough hands as if it were made of china. She slid her arms around him and just let him hold her until their kiss was done, and they stood there, not wanting to leave the other but knowing they had to.

She didn't know how long they stood there. Being in his arms was everything safe and warm and loving. She had the fleeting thought that perhaps she didn't want to let go because she was afraid if she did, then she'd realize it was all a dream, that none of those beautiful things had happened

Finally he whispered they needed a little sleep. And she nodded but didn't let go. He swung her up into his arms and carried her to the hammock, laying her inside. She wondered if he knew that her heart beat a little faster whenever he swung her into his arms like that.

He stood over her for a moment, looking at her as if he expected her to disappear and he needed to look at her to keep her there.

She wondered if their thoughts were that close. Did a man feel what a woman did? Did he have those same doubts, those same thrills?

He brushed her cheek with his hand, then turned and walked across the hut. And she watched his broad back until he was only a shadow moving in a dim corner. She heard the rope on his hammock creak. Then there was nothing but the distant sounds of the shore.

They both lay in their hammocks, eyes closed, neither asleep because in truth they were too aware of the other, the scent, touch, and taste still lingering. The memory of the fire in his eyes. The misty look of passion in hers.

On this Christmas night, when across the world so many celebrated with gifts and love, Hank Wyatt and Margaret Smith each received a gift, something to cherish. In each other they found more than love and more than passion. They found a lost part of themselves. And they found it in the oddest place, a place that until a few weeks before they would have never thought to look.

It was the perfect day for a baseball game. The sky was clear. The breeze was light. And the men were playing against the women.

Ah, life couldn't get much better.

Hank gave Annabelle a pat on the head. He'd made a makeshift crib with trunks and she was happily playing in the sand with her new toys. He walked back to the mound and looked at Smitty and grinned. She was bent down so she could talk to Lydia. The sun was behind them, and Smitty's dress was that thin cotton thing that he could see right through when the light was right. The light was just right.

She moved behind Lydia and blocked his view. He tossed the ball in one hand. "All right now! Enough gabbing! Batter up!"

Hank looked at Theodore. The kid was doing just as he'd taught him, squatting on the balls of his feet and shifting his weight from one foot to the other, ready to move when the ball was hit.

He had the kid playing catcher. Muddy handled the outfield, and Hank was pitching and covering the only base. With such small numbers they played one base and home.

Strikes only counted if they swung and missed. Balls, well, the last he'd heard the National League couldn't decide if seven, eight, or nine balls constituted a walk, so he decided not to count 'em.

The ladies were up first.

"Batter up!"

Smitty and Lydia both stopped talking and turned to look at him.

"That means you have to hit the ball."

Smitty plopped her hands on her hips. "And here I thought we were supposed to eat it. Didn't you?" She looked around with feigned innocence, and Lydia giggled.

"That could be arranged, sweetheart." He tossed the ball, then held up a hand. "Wait! I forgot. You'd probably burn it."

"You're such a wit."

"I try, Smitty. Now *someone* come up to bat."

"Go on, Lydia. You know men, no patience whatsoever. Just hit the ball, dear, really hard. You can do it."

Lydia stepped up to bat. Theodore said something to her, and she let the bat drop and just gaped at him. "Did you hear what he just said?"

Hank grinned and gave the kid a thumbs-up sign. Nothing was more important in ball than learning the insults. They were attempts to break the other player's concentration. "Let's play ball!"

"But he just said I had ears like an elephant and I smelled like a pig!"

Hank cackled and gave the kid a wink.

Smitty pinned him with a look of warning. "A fine thing to teach children, Hank."

"Hey!" Hank gave an innocent shrug. "You wanted to learn how to play baseball. Insults are part of the game."

"Just ignore them, Lydia. They are only words, dear."

Hank threw a nice underhanded pitch. No sidearm to a little girl. Even he wasn't that cruel.

She swung and missed.

"That's okay, dear."

Theodore said something again, and Lydia stepped back from the plate. "My feet are not clodhoppers, you brat!" The kid just grinned. Hank didn't even look at Smitty. He knew what he'd see.

Lydia stepped up to the plate. He pitched, and she slammed the ball high in the air.

She ran toward the base, and they all turned and watched the ball sail right into Muddy's hands—he was flying at the time.

"You're out!" Hank yelled.

Muddy flew back to the mound, handed Hank the ball, and flew back to the outfield on a trail of purple smoke.

"Now wait just a minute." Smitty stormed toward him. "That is not fair. Muddy shouldn't be able to fly."

Hank shrugged. "It's men against women. If you ladies can't fly, well, that's not our problem. The rules were set. Men against women. No holding back. So that means flying, too. Now be a good sport and take your shot at the ball, sweetheart. You're not gonna win this argument."

Smitty gave Lydia a hug and a word of encouragement, then picked up the bat and strode toward the plate like a woman ready for battle. She stopped first and bent down and shook her finger at the kid. "One word out of you, young man, and I'll make you scrub the burned pots. Understood?"

The kid wrinkled his nose, nodded, and silently assumed the catcher's position.

"Now, Smitty, is that fair?"

"Be quiet and pitch the ball, Hank."

He sidearmed a pitch to her, and she whacked a grounder right at him.

She was on the base before Hank could take a step. He whistled and shook his head. That woman could run faster than anyone he'd ever seen.

She smiled sweetly and gave him a little wave meant to rub his nose in it. He watched her twitch merrily around the base for a minute. She turned back to him, spread her arms out, and sang, "Tah-dah!"

He just watched her, then turned and pitched to Lydia.

She swung and missed. Two times.

He tossed the ball lightly in one hand, then casually walked over to Smitty. He stood real close to her so no one could see between them and leaned down and said, "You run real good, sweetheart. You know that?"

She grinned real cocky and planted her hands on her hips. "Yep."

Very quietly he whispered thickly, "You jiggle in all the right places."

She didn't say a word.

"All those places I kissed last night."

She took a deep breath.

"Hmmm. You know where I mean?"

She just looked at him a little uncomfortably.

"Here . . ." He grazed the ball over her breast, and she stiffened. "And here . . ." He moved his lips close to her ear and touched her neck with the ball, then moved to her other ear. "Here." He lowered his arm and rolled the ball over the small of her back and onto her butt. "And especially here, where you're soft and white and feel so good in my hands."

Her mouth dropped open just enough.

"And you know what else?"

She gave a small shake of her head.

"Your foot is off the base, sweetheart. And you're out."

❧ 31 ❧

The ladies lost twenty-seven to three, even when they'd included Rebuttal as part of their team. She had trotted to the outfield where she gnawed on some monkey grass. It drove Hank nuts enough that he kept trying to give Margaret a hard time. She just smiled.

About fifteen minutes later, Rebuttal knocked Hank off the base. Twice. Just when he was crouched down and ready to run. Conveniently, Margaret had been right there with the ball, waiting.

The ladies took turns pinch-hitting for Rebuttal. But it didn't matter in the end. Although Margaret could run like the wind, no one could hit like Hank. To everyone's amazement, he hit the ball over the coconut trees every time he was at bat.

But now the game was done. They walked down to the beach so the children could cool off with a swim. Annabelle was perched on Margaret's hip and Theodore and Lydia raced through the sand to see who could hit the water first. Muddy flew overhead with a group of seagulls, mimicking their turns and making the children laugh and point. He'd promised Margaret he'd watch for sharks.

And Hank, well, he just shook his head and kept walking as if there wasn't a purple genie flying overhead.

Margaret turned to Hank. "I've never seen anyone hit a baseball like you did."

He laughed. "I had to learn to hit the ball hard. I never could run worth a damn."

"But every time?"

He shrugged, then looked somewhere ahead of

them. "My third year I led the National Association with a batting average of .492."

"Is that a lot?"

He laughed. "You are good for my ego, sweetheart. Yeah, it's good. I don't think anyone's beat it yet. But maybe now . . . in the last six years. Before I left the States it had still held."

Theodore came skidding to a stop in front of them. "Can I go out to the sandbar? Can I? I swim real good now."

Margaret paled, remembering that it was only yesterday when she'd shot the shark. "No!" she said more sharply than she intended. "It's too dangerous. And you could be hurt. You can't go out there. All kinds of terrible things could happen."

"You mean like the shark?" Theodore asked without a bit of trepidation.

"Yes," Margaret said more sharply than she should have.

"But the shark is dead. You shot it. Why can't I go? Why?"

Hank placed his hand on Theodore's shoulder. "You wanna know why, kid?"

"Yeah."

"Because you have red hair."

Theodore blinked up at him, frowned thoughtfully, then pulled a shank of his red-orange hair into his eyes so he could see it.

Hank gave him a perfectly serious look. "What color is it, kid?"

"Red."

"That's right."

"And you can't swim out to the sandbar if you have red hair?"

Hank shook his head.

Theodore stared at the sea, then looked up at his hair, his brow furrowing while he was thinking so intently. After a minute, he sighed, then said, "Okay."

He scuffed his feet through the sand for a foot or two and then he ran back into the shallow tides.

Margaret couldn't believe it. She leaned over and quietly said, "But that doesn't make sense."

"Hell, if there's one thing I've learned about kids, Smitty, it's that they have their own way of thinking. It doesn't have to make sense to us. Just to them."

Lydia came up to them. She and Margaret took Annabelle to the water and played with her for a few minutes. Hank stood at the edge of the beach, just staring into the distance.

After a short while, Margaret turned and gave the baby to Lydia so they could play in the sand. Hank was still standing in the same spot, his back stiff and his gaze lost in the past.

She needed to do something to bring him back here. To the present.

She started to trot toward him, then she ran faster and right at him.

"Hey, Hank!"

He turned.

"Any last words?" And she shoved him right into the next wave.

She laughed, and the kids laughed at seeing him sprawled on his backside in the water, the waves foaming over him.

But she stopped laughing when his eyes got the same look as the goat. Margaret took off running.

He shot up and ran after her, chasing her down the beach, laughing as she was. She kicked up sand behind her and shrieked when he made a dive for her feet. And missed.

She turned around and slowed down, running backward as she laughed at him.

He lay there, not moving.

"Hank?"

Nothing.

"Hank? Are you okay?"

He didn't even breathe.

She stopped, then slowly walked back.

"Hank?" She reached out a hand.

He tackled her at the knees.

She went down like a potato sack. "That's not fair!"

He pinned her to him and grinned down at her. "I know."

"Let me up."

"Okay." He got up and offered her his hand.

She put her hand in his.

He gripped it hard and laughed. "I can't believe you actually fell for that one." And before she could do anything but gasp, he slid his arm under her knees and picked her up. "You're not running again, sweetheart."

"Put me down!"

"No."

"You cheated!"

"Yeah."

"That's not fair."

"No, it's not. But it worked."

He walked toward the water as she tried to squirm free. She called him names and laughed at the same time. She made threats and promised he'd be sorry if he threw her in the water again.

Then she wrapped her arms around his neck and gave him a long look. She leaned close to his mouth and whispered, "Kiss me."

He did. A smack on the lips. "Good one, Smitty. I'd have tried that too in your place." Laughing, he swung back.

"Hank!" she hollered. "Don't you dare!"

And he threw her into the next wave.

Muddy bent over the lens of the camera and adjusted the tripod. "Everyone get ready!"

He watched them through the lens, then straightened and rubbed a mark off the mahogany camera case. He bent back and looked through the lens, siting the rock near a lush hibiscus bush that had the clear sky and vast Pacific Ocean as a background.

Lydia and Theodore were elbowing each other. Annabelle was running in circles around Margaret, who was bent over. Hank was staring at her backside.

Muddy opened the instructions and read them again, then affixed the plates. He put the focus cloth in place. "I'm ready!"

Lydia pulled Rebuttal into the group, and they all shuffled around for a few minutes. Margaret stopped to retie Hank's white tie and to adjust her ball gown. Theodore wore the baseball cap backward, and he held the bat, ball, and glove. Lydia wore all her shell necklaces and the combs Hank had made her. Annabelle sat in Margaret's lap, her fingers stuck in her mouth.

Margaret sat on a rock, Annabelle in her lap and Lydia and Rebuttal on her left. Theodore was on her right. Hank stood behind her, one hand resting possessively on her shoulder and the finger of his other hand pulling at the collar of the dress shirt.

Muddy smiled. "One . . . Two . . . Ready?"

They all nodded.

"Three!"

And Muddy took his first photograph—a family portrait.

Hank sat on the beach with Smitty, watching the sunset. Annabelle was asleep in Smitty's lap. Lydia and Theodore were fishing off the rocks nearby. The genie? Hell, he would bait their lines and fly out over the surf and drop the lines in the water. From Theodore's squeals, Hank knew they'd caught enough fish for a big meal even after Smitty burned the first few batches.

She was sitting with her legs drawn up, drawing absently in the wet sand. He just watched her, something that seemed to take up a lot of his time lately.

The breeze was light and warm, and it ruffled the hair that had fallen around her face. Her face was as close to perfection as he could imagine. Watching her, with the baby asleep in her lap, did something to him. She looked down at Annabelle and stroked her head lightly while she slept.

Hank walked over and stood above them.

"If you could be anywhere," she said, "where would you be?"

He sat down. "Why?"

She shrugged. "I was just thinking."

He laughed. "Yeah, I figured you were."

She smiled. "I know. You think I think too much." She blinked, then shook her head and laughed. "I think you think I think too much."

They both laughed.

Still smiling, she said, "Sounds like too much thinking all the way around, doesn't it?"

He didn't say anything. He didn't want to think. He just wanted to sit here. He just wanted to be.

She looked at him. "No answer?"

He shook his head. "I expect you know where you want to be."

She shrugged again. "I don't know. I had always thought I'd want to be exactly where I was. I was happy in San Francisco. Content. I had a home and my family—my dad and my uncles. I had my work."

"So tell me, Smitty, how does a woman become a lawyer?"

She looked at him. "The same way we'll eventually get the right to vote. By making men understand that we are their equals. By hard work and by teaching pigheaded men that they can be wrong."

He laughed. "You must be one helluvan attorney, sweetheart."

"My dad says I am. He was a brilliant lawyer before he went on to the bench. He's a California Supreme Court judge."

Hank groaned.

She laughed. "You'd like him. He loved to match his mind against others and win. He taught me his skills. When I was growing up, we'd sit down to supper and he would start a discussion and throw out a point. We'd argue, and he made me defend my view against his questions. Just when he had me cornered, he'd laugh and say, "Now switch sides, my girl."

Hank whistled.

"Then I would defend the very point I had been trying to shoot down just minutes before. He taught me to think. And he loves me very much."

"You miss him?"

She looked at Hank. "I worry about him. I'm all he really has. I wonder what he's been told. He must think I'm dead. I'm not certain what that will do to him."

"Maybe he hopes."

She nodded.

"You still haven't told me about how a woman becomes an attorney."

She scowled at him. "Women can be anything they want."

"Not ball players."

"Give us time."

He laughed.

"I went to college. Ann Arbor was the first to offer law degrees to women. But you don't have to have a degree. You can apprentice. I did both. I'm with a family firm. My father and uncles are all senior partners."

Hank groaned again.

"I've always loved the law, loved the challenge it presents. Law is never the same. Its interpretations are always changing. Sometimes only in the smallest increments, but still, it's never constant." She grew quiet, pensive. She looked out at the sea, then dug her toes into the sand and stared at them. "But you know something? Sitting here, the law is the farthest thing from my mind."

"Why?"

"It seems as if what I was—that other life—was someone else's life, not mine. And when I look at this"—she nodded toward the sea, then scanned the beach—"I don't think I would ever want to be anywhere else."

They sat there, neither saying anything. They didn't need to. After a few minutes, maybe less, maybe longer, she turned to him.

"Tell me about prison."

"Sweetheart, that's one thing you don't want to know, and I'm not certain I can tell you."

"Why not?"

He'd known this was coming. He looked at her. "Does it matter?"

"If you think telling me is going to change how I feel about you, you're wrong, Hank."

"You didn't answer my question."

"Yes, it matters. It matters to me because you matter."

It took him a long time to find the words, a few minutes of silence for his mind to dredge it all up again. "I'd been living in the islands, moving from one to another, never staying too long on any one island. A few months here, a few there. I'd gone to Papeete for a week to pick up a boat I'd bought. The boat wasn't there, and Laroche, the man I'd bought it from, was conveniently unavailable. It took me three weeks to find the bastard. I found him and beat the crap out of him when he pretended not to know who I was. I spent a week drunk, among other things.

"I don't remember much, except that I woke up when the local gendarmerie was dragging me out of my bed and down the stairs. While I'd been drinking and screwing away the last of my money, someone else had put a bullet in Laroche's head. I had a mockery of a trial a day later, where they told me I was guilty after two people testified that we'd had a fight earlier that week. Hell, I didn't even have a gun, something my joke of an attorney didn't mention."

"What?"

He nodded. "Yeah, the trial was in French. I didn't know half of what was being said, and no one bothered to translate. They gave me the verdict in English. Life in prison. My attorney said I got off lucky. They wanted to hang me." He paused, then looked down. "Next thing I knew I was in Leper's Gate."

She was quiet for a long time. "How did you break out?"

He told her. Quietly and with detail. When he finished, Smitty was crying.

He put his arm around her. She leaned into him. He just held her, feeling like he had a hard grip on the first real thing in his life that wouldn't slip through his fingers.

The breeze softly carried the clean, fresh scent of her, washing over him like the sea washed the rocks and the shoreline, touching, holding, seeping in between the small cracks that time and weather and experience had made in granite and limestone.

He held onto the woman who for him was like the sea that surrounded all the land on earth, hemmed it in, cupped it gently, sometimes raged at it, but was always wearing away at it. Until where land and sea met there was peace. And paradise. For him, she was like the sea. And he knew that where she wasn't, there was nothing.

It was a strange feeling to look at a woman and not see her for what he could get from her. Instead he looked at her and saw her twenty years from now, sitting there as she was now, beside him.

She turned suddenly as if he had spoken his thoughts. The sun glowed a golden pink on her face—the face that cried for him, the same face that made him forget he wasn't supposed to let himself care about anything or anyone.

She smiled a slow smile at him. An elemental understanding of who and where they were. Now, at this moment.

He reached out and drew a finger along her jaw as slowly as she had smiled. And somewhere, lost back in the vague recesses of his mind, he wondered if she knew the power she had.

He leaned toward her until he could taste her breath. He stayed there, not closing the distance between them. Because with Smitty, he wanted every moment to last. Then he said words he'd never said in forty years. "You know, sweetheart, loving you isn't going to be very easy."

"Loving me?"

He lifted her chin up with the knuckle on one hand, and he whispered against her lips, "Yeah. Loving you."

And she cried again.

The full moon rode across a cloudless and vast sky spangled with stars, more stars than anyone could ever imagine. Margaret and Hank silently walked along the beach hand in hand, their footprints melting in wet, spongy sand.

Another day had passed. Then another and another until the days blended into a week and more.

For Margaret, each day was somehow better than the last. Because of what was happening to her: emotions she'd never thought she could feel. She hadn't imagined such a thing was possible.

They'd talked about their childhoods, so different, yet equally lonely in some ways. He didn't tell all of what he had done in his lifetime. But some of it, the things they could laugh about rather than the ones that made her want to cry.

She stopped and looked up at the night sky because she was getting teary just walking with Hank. As naturally as if they been together for years, his arms slid around her and pulled her back against him. He locked his hands around her belly and rested his chin on her head.

She had the crazy thought that he was the only man she could think of who was tall enough to do that. They fit somehow, the two of them. They had so little in common on the outside but so much in common inside.

And he just held her. She let her head fall back on his shoulder, and she could feel his breath whisper against her ear, a sound as keen and constant to her as the rumble of the waves.

"I've never seen so many stars. Thousands of them. It's as if we were walking through the Milky Way."

"Hmmm" was all he said.

She smiled slowly. "You're not listening to me."

"I heard every word."

"Then repeat them."

His lips touched her ear. "You said that you had never seen so many stars."

"That's right."

He kissed her ear.

"What else?"

"If you want to see stars . . ." He took a deep breath that made his chest press warmly against her back. Then he whispered a string of earthy, elemental, and private things they could do together if they only had about five straight days completely alone.

Her mouth was dry and her knees a little wobbly when he finished.

"I promise you that after that you'd see a helluva lot more than just stars. You'd see clear through to heaven, Smitty."

She turned and kissed him with every ounce of love she had. Then she pulled back and ran her fingers over his mouth, that sensual mouth that could kiss her senseless and make love to her in ways she never would have imagined. "Are you bluffing?"

He laughed. "Hell, sweetheart, I just promised you heaven."

She shook her head. "You've already taken me there." She turned and slid her arms around his neck. "Take me there again. Past there. Show me the other side of heaven."

And he showed her heaven, a hundred different ways for long nights and days, until the breezes changed to winds and time went from days to a week and more.

❦ 32 ❦

Margaret carried Annabelle inside the hut. She had toddled over into Margaret's lap and fallen asleep after a busy afternoon of playing and helping the others bury Hank in the sand.

Margaret looked down at the baby sleeping in her arms. Her skin had the glow of a child who spent a good deal of time outdoors. Her hair was longer and more curly than it had been before. It had turned a lighter red from the sun. And she was heavier, talking more and running without falling.

They change so quickly, she thought.

Still holding the baby, she sat down on a barrel and looked outside at the beach. She couldn't see the others, but she could see the water and the sunshine and the trees and bushes and flowers of this paradise that was now her home.

She wondered what her father was doing. Was he in court? Was he in that rambling home? Was he in the study where he'd worked long hours teaching her how to research, how to prepare a case, how to win? And she a cried a little because she knew he didn't know she was alive. He would think he was completely alone now.

Through a mist of tears she looked down at Annabelle and understood something she never would have before. She understood some of the looks her father had given her over the years. She understood the fear that came with being a parent, the horrid fear of losing a child.

And Margaret cried, silently, until Annabelle shifted in her sleep, and her fist pressed against Margaret's rib. She studied the plump and tanned fingers on little hands that each day discovered something new. She made Margaret rediscover it, too. Something as simple as a feather, as complex as the intricate designs of a seashell. The flight of a bird, the smell of a flower. The awe with which a child saw the world.

Annabelle shifted again, then murmured, "Mama." Margaret swallowed to assuage the dryness in her mouth, and took a deep breath because tears were coming to her eyes. It was so silly in a way. So sentimental and so wonderful.

It didn't matter that she hadn't conceived Annabelle. It didn't matter that she had been someone else's child first. All that mattered was now and the future.

She looked down and stroked the baby's forehead again. "I'm here, sweet. Mama's here."

She hadn't known Hank was there until she looked up. He was standing in the doorway, watching her. She couldn't see his face. She didn't know if he'd heard her. But he came inside and stood beside her, then bent slightly and cupped the back of her head with a hand. It was a gesture she'd come to know, a natural and tender gesture from a man who looked as if he could never be tender.

She gazed up at him from eyes misty with emotion. He squatted down behind her and placed his hands on her shoulders. She felt uncomfortable, a little more open then she wanted to be in front of him. She stood, and his hands slid from her shoulders. "Let me put her to bed, okay?"

She crossed to the nearby corner and lay Annabelle down, then straightened, but she didn't look at him. She could feel his look, knew there was a question there. She could feel tension between them. It was coming from her. And yet she couldn't stop it. Her emotions were taut and had been for days now.

She glanced up at him. He was studying her.

She moved to the window and rested her hands on the moist, woven grass that was wrapped around the bamboo that formed the windowsill. She stared out at the sea and the sky, both flawless and blue, everything one could ever want. A paradise. "Do you think anyone will ever find us?"

"I don't know."

"What will happen if they do?"

She heard his feet as he crossed to stand behind her. "What are you worrying about, Smitty?"

"I'm not certain. Everything. Nothing. Us. Them."

"The children?"

"Yes. And the future. They have no one, and I won't let them be placed in an orphanage."

He took a deep breath, then said, "They have us. You're an attorney. What's the law?"

"Legally I can't do anything."

He was quiet. "Because you're a woman alone?"

She nodded.

"What about us? Together?"

"What are you saying, Hank?"

He was quiet for a tense minute. "We could get married."

She didn't know if she could have moved then, not after he'd said those words. Words she wanted more than anything but that frightened her. The words weren't the problem. Oh, God, she wished things were different.

He stepped behind her again.

She picked up the silver frame with the photograph that Muddy had taken and given her. She looked at it with a bleak feeling.

"If we're found, we'll go back to the States, get married, and adopt the kids. It seems pretty simple."

She turned and faced him. "It's not that simple."

He gave her a narrowed look. "Why not?"

"You have a past, Hank. A past that could destroy everything."

He laughed without humor. "Only here in the islands. Not in the States."

"You've been in prison. We can't adopt the children unless you clear your name. You said yourself you're innocent."

"Yeah, and you damn well know that I can't get a fair hearing here. What are the chances of them finding me innocent back home?"

She didn't say anything. They had no future without clearing his past.

He began to pace. "Hell, Smitty, that's a stupid excuse. If you don't want to marry me, then damn well say so!" He was shouting now and running his hand through his hair.

"I love you, Hank, but you can't keep running away."

"I'm not going back to prison. Listen closely, sweetheart. I won't let them lock me up again."

"I don't want you locked up again. But we can't have a life with this hanging over us. It would always be there. I couldn't live like that. We can't have the children. They need us. And someday you're going to have to learn to trust. Give the law a chance to work for you."

He closed the distance between them and grabbed her by the shoulders. "Look, we're arguing over something that's stupid. It might not ever matter. Who knows if a ship will ever come. We can go on like we are and worry about this if it ever happens."

She could hear the panic in his voice. "We're just

pretending on this island. It's not real. We're not a real family, Hank. What happens on this island isn't real."

"What I feel for you and those kids is real, Smitty."

"What I feel is real, too. But what we are together isn't. We're not a family. Those children aren't our children. They can't be because we're not legally their parents."

"Who cares if it's legal?"

"I do. And the law does. They can't be our children until the law says they are. I won't go against everything I believe in. And you have to understand that your past is not going to go away because you pretend it doesn't exist."

"Shit! I know that!"

"Stop shouting at me."

"I don't understand why you're bringing this up. Why are you worried about something that might never happen? We should live each day just like we have been."

"And never think about the future?" She could hear the sarcasm in her voice, but she couldn't help it.

He looked at her long and hard, and there was no doubt he was angry. "I told you before. You think too goddamn much." Then he turned and walked toward the door.

She called out his name, and he paused. "Remember what you said about never being able to run worth a damn?"

"Yeah?" His voice was bitter and rough.

"Well, you're wrong, Hank. You run away from things better than anyone I've ever known."

Then he was gone.

She stared at the empty door, then she buried her face in her hands and cried.

Theodore's fingers tightened around Muddy's hand as they stood in a dark corner of the hut watching Smitty sink to her knees and cry, her angry words and

Hank's still echoing in their ears and minds. Theodore looked up at Muddy with tears rolling down his freckled cheeks.

Muddy raised a finger to his lips. They moved quietly and left the hut together. The boy stopped and looked back, but Smitty was still crying, her back to them. His small shoulders began to shake, and Muddy led him down the beach to a quiet and secluded place where they could talk. Perhaps he could make the boy understand what had happened and why.

There was no moon that night—just a black, dark sky that looked and seemed endless above the secluded patch of beach where a boy and a genie stood. The others on the island were sound asleep. No one was talking much. No one smiled because harsh words and tension were all that was left of their paradise.

"Muddy?"

"Yes, master?"

"Will you take me flying just once more before you go?"

"Yes, Master Theodore." And the genie bent in a deep salaam, then straightened. He winked at the boy and held out his hand.

A moment later they were flying, the little boy's laughter singing through the night sky. They flew in circles and dove deep, almost touching the sea, only to soar upward like two hawks racing for a sparrow.

For two thousand years, the genie had his own dreams and wishes: to meet a believer, an innocent, and finally, even if it was for only a short while, he had found one.

And so they flew across the sea, the purple genie and the red-haired little boy who believed in things the rest of the world thought only a figment of the imagination. They flew over the land on a trail of childish laughter and smiles, creating magical memories that would live on in a little boy's heart.

They quietly landed in the sand in a place where no one could see them, and the small boy crooked his finger at the genie, who crouched down so the boy could whisper his last wish in his ear.

They said good-bye here, where no one else could heard the words they spoke. Then the genie bent once in a full salaam, giving the boy his respect and, perhaps this time, also giving this master a piece of his heart.

In a puff of purple smoke, the genie streamed back into the bottle. The boy brought the bottle to his eye one last time, paused for only the time it took a tear to fall, then he put the stopper back.

He took two steps until the soft waves lapped at his small ankles, and he gently placed the bottle in the water. He rubbed a hand across his eyes, then stuck his hands in his pockets and stood there as the bottle floated out into the sea, bobbing along as if it were flotsam—a bottle that was as old as time, a magical silver bottle that could make wishes come true . . . if one could only imagine.

❧ 33 ❧

"There's a ship! Look! A ship!" Lydia came running back to the hut.

Margaret grabbed the box of matches, picked up Annabelle, and followed Lydia out the door of the hut and down the beach.

There was a ship riding high on the horizon. She turned and scanned the beach looking for Hank. She could see his silhouette on the ridge, standing where he'd told her he had built a signal fire.

He hadn't come back to the hut the night before. She didn't know where he'd gone. She watched him intently, wondering if he would light the fire, or was he desperate enough to just let the ship pass?

It would be the perfect solution for him. The perfect way for him to keep running away.

She looked at Lydia, who had run down to the beach where Theodore sat watching the horizon. She opened her palm and looked at the match box. Then she turned and looked back at the ridge, at Hank.

A thin trail of dark smoke drifted up from where he stood.

He'd lit the fire.

She slid open the match box, her hand shaking. She took a deep breath and lit the other fire.

Margaret moved across the hut, gathering the things she thought they should take down to the beach. She stopped and looked out the window. She could see the ship getting larger as it moved closer to the island.

But there was no sign of Hank. She picked up the ball gown and looked at it for a long time, then she took a deep breath and packed it along with Hank's tails back into one of the trunks.

For the next few minutes she concentrated on packing, then she checked on the children. They were quiet. As quiet as she was. Lydia had packed a small crate with her doll and combs and necklaces, and she sat in a corner with Annabelle in her lap while she braided Rebuttal's uneven, ragged beard.

Theodore had hardly said a word. He was sitting next to a pile of his things and Hank's baseball equipment.

"Theodore?"

He turned around and looked at her.

"Where's Muddy's bottle?"

He averted his eyes.

"Did you pack it?"

He shook his head.

She watched him for a minute, then crossed over to where he sat. "Theodore?"

He looked down at the cap in his lap. "I don't have the bottle."

"Did you misplace it? We can help you find it—"

"I put it back in the sea."

She waited, then asked, "Why?"

He didn't say anything.

"Did you use the last wish?"

He nodded.

"For the ship?"

He didn't respond.

She waited, then said, "You don't want to tell me what you wished for?"

He shook his head.

She thought about talking to him. She thought through her argument. But she decided it didn't matter. "Theodore? Look at me."

He slowly raised his head.

"It's okay. It was your wish. Just gather your things and put them inside that open trunk, and we'll go down to the beach."

He was quiet for a second, then he asked, "What about Hank?"

Lydia's head shot up, and she could feel both of them staring at her.

"I don't know where he is."

"Can't we look for him?"

"He saw the ship, Theodore. I watched him light that other signal fire. He'll come." *If he wants to,* she thought.

Half an hour later they had dragged their belongings down to the beach and stood there waiting while one of the ship's lifeboat's rowed toward them. Margaret rested one hand on Theodore's shoulder and the other on Lydia, while the younger girl held Annabelle.

The closer the boat came, the stronger her sense of dread. She turned and looked up at the ridge. But there was no silhouette of a tall man. She scanned the beach, but he wasn't there. She stared for long minutes at the jungle. At the grove of palm trees.

He could stay on the island and never have to face his past. It was a way of running. Perhaps it would be his way.

By the time they were in the boat and the two sailors were loading their belongings, she knew he wasn't coming.

She looked at the children, wondering what she could tell them. Theodore and Lydia both were intently watching the beach.

"Is that everything, ma'am?" The crewman stood at the side of the boat, waiting to shove off.

Margaret looked up.

"Look!" Theodore shouted and began to jump up and down. "There he is! It's Hank! Hank!"

Margaret whipped her head around just as Hank walked out of the thick jungle, moving toward them with his hands in his pockets.

Hank leaned against the rail of the fishing trawler from British New Guinea and watched the island grow smaller and smaller until he could no longer make out the white slip of sand or the palm trees, only the dark outline of the small island where he had thought his life had begun again.

He heard a noise and turned.

Smitty stood in the passageway, her hands gripping the iron frame as she stared at the island, then she looked at him. She said nothing. They hadn't spoken since the day before.

They both stood there, and he saw in her eyes the same emotion he felt, that same sense of loss, and he closed his eyes for only the second he needed. When he opened them, she was gone.

He turned back and stared at the wake as the ship cut through the blue water, heading for Papua and Port Moresley, a British territory. A place of relative safety since it was under British control. He could go on to Australia or New Zealand and lose himself among a thousand other men with pasts.

It was easy now. Easy to run and hide.

He watched the water for a long time before he let himself think. Then he closed his eyes and took a deep breath.

Smitty was right. He always ran away as fast as he could.

And it was pretty clear to him now. He wasn't running from his past. And he hadn't been for all those years.

He ran from the future. Because it scared the hell out of him.

It was easier to run than to take a chance at something that might be real and lasting, before he became trapped or stuck in a place where he didn't belong.

As he stared at the water, he remembered that moment when he'd first broken out of prison, at the dockside when he realized that he didn't belong outside the prison walls any more than he belonged inside.

He stood there a long time, thinking. Smitty's favorite sport.

He didn't think a man got very many chances in life to change things. Smitty was probably his last chance. But hell, it didn't matter if she was or not. What mattered was whether he had the guts to not run this time. For her sake and for those kids.

Maybe he'd never felt as if he belonged anywhere because he'd never had Smitty. He'd never had the kids. He'd never given love to a woman or children.

Maybe it wasn't where a man was, but who was there with him that made him belong someplace. And he knew deep down inside of him, in that place he'd never liked to think existed, that he wanted to hold on to them, hold on tighter than he'd held on to anything in his life.

But damn, he was still scared. Because he was so afraid he would lose them in the end. It was almost as if some part of him could feel them slipping away, falling through his fingers like sand. And he had no idea how he could hold on tight enough so he didn't lose it all.

At the sound of her name, Margaret looked at the doorway of the small cabin. Hank stood there. Her heartache. He said her name again very quietly, and she felt the words pass right through her. She tried to stand a little taller, because she needed strength now when she wanted to give in, to run to him and say it would be okay to keep running away from everything. That in her heart she wanted to run with him.

He stepped into the light and stood there, looking awkwardly huge in the small cabin. "Where are the kids?"

"In there." She pointed at the adjoining door.

He looked at it, then turned back and just watched her as if it were the most important thing to him. She took a deep breath and wished and prayed that it were.

He shoved his hands in his pockets and looked away, scanned the room, his gaze not meeting hers. He stared at the floor for a long time, then looked up at her. "I'm not running this time."

She stood there unable to move because she wasn't certain she had heard him. All she could hear was the loud throbbing beat of her heart. She looked away for a second, confused and scared and emotional.

"Smitty."

She turned back.

"Did you hear me?"

She shook her head.

He gave a quiet and sardonic laugh. "Figures you'd make me say it twice."

"What?"

"I'm not running this time."

It took an instant for his words to register. She closed her eyes and exhaled, not even realizing until then that she had been holding her breath. She could feel emotion tightening her throat and filling her eyes. And a second later she was in Hank's arms.

They were married in Port Moresley at a small church that sat on a point where the sea crashed against cliffs and the wind blew a breath of warm wind over the land and through the massive crowns of banyan trees. The church was stark white with a high narrow steeple and green wooden storm shutters on its slim windows. A church that was as traditional as the wedding party was unconventional.

The bride was barefoot, with island flowers around her ankles and around one wrist. Orchids ringed her blond topknot. She wore a pink silk ball gown that rustled as she walked down the aisle with a baby dressed all in white hitched on her hip.

Beside her was a little boy in a brand-spanking-new suit with short pants and shiny brass buttons, and an expression of pure happiness. A young girl in a pink-and-white linen dress with a big bow and matching ribbons in her hair stood with them.

The groom wore evening clothes, white tie and tails, pearl studs, and a Chicago White Stockings baseball cap turned backward. They looked at ease, no wedding nerves, no guests, no one else at the wedding but this new little family.

The baby reached up and grabbed one of the flowers from the bride's hair and tried to stick it in her own hair, crying when she couldn't make it stay.

The groom bent and picked up the crushed flower

and tucked it into the toddler's white hair ribbon and told her she was gorgeous. Then he turned to the bride and said, "Almost as gorgeous as your mama."

Margaret stood beside Hank and the children and listened to the minister's words. Theodore was fidgeting next to her. Out of the corner of her eye Margaret saw Lydia pinch him, then heard her whisper for him to hold still. She smiled, then looked around her.

Had she ever thought of what her wedding would be like, this image would not have entered her mind. Margaret Smith, attorney-at-law, barefoot, a baby in her arms and children at her side while she married a tall, rugged ex-baseball player and convict.

But she looked at Hank as they said their vows, and she knew this was where she was meant to be.

The minister turned to Hank. "Do you have a ring to bless?"

She knew he didn't, but she didn't care about the trappings of marriage. If she had, she'd be wearing shoes.

Hank patted his coat pocket, then jammed a hand in his pants pocket. He grinned and held out his hand to the minister, whose eyes held shock.

Margaret looked at Hank's hand.

Sitting in his palm was the rose pearl. "Bless this. Soon enough it'll be her wedding ring."

She looked up at him, surprised that he was even somewhat prepared. And she made a vow to herself that from that day forward she would stop underestimating her husband.

He winked at her while the poor minister blessed the huge pink pearl and then handed it back to him. He took her hand in his and dropped the pearl in her palm and closed their hands over it.

He leaned over and whispered, "Are you crying?"

She nodded and looked at him through a blur of emotion. She saw him give a small shake of his head. But that didn't stop her. She cried when the minister pronounced them man and wife. She cried when Theodore jumped up and down and shouted, "Kiss her! Kiss her!"

She cried when her husband kissed her. She cried even harder when he swung her and the baby up into his arms and carried them out of the church with both children running and laughing at his side. It was a silly thing, this crying, because she had never been happier.

Hank stood on the veranda of their room in the Port Moresley Hotel. Cast in moonlight, the bay stretched out before him, and he could see where a few ships were anchored at the docks, their lanterns spilling light on the rippling black water. They were scheduled to leave in two days on an American liner that was coming into port the next day. In less than three weeks they would be in San Francisco. Three weeks.

He took a deep breath and leaned on the wooden railing, lost in thoughts of what-ifs. In the street below a few wagons and carriages moved past even though it was late, close to midnight.

"They're finally asleep."

He turned at the sound of Smitty's voice, and leaned his hip against the rail. She stood in the doorway, limned in soft light from the lamp inside their room. She had bathed earlier and was dressed in some frilly woman's robe she had bought at the dry goods store where they had gotten the kids' clothing.

He supposed he should comment on it. Hell, he was a husband now. But he didn't care what Smitty wore. In fact, he liked her best in nothing but that come-to-me smile of hers.

He straightened and closed the distance between them. "Let's go inside."

She turned, and he closed the French doors behind him. Then, just for good measure, he looked at the adjoining door. Theodore had come through that door at least five times.

"He's asleep. I made certain."

He shook his head. "That kid talked for about fifteen hours."

She laughed. "He's excited."

They were both quiet for a moment, then Hank looked at her. "I wonder what exactly that kid used the last wish for."

"I don't know. He refuses to tell anyone, even Lydia."

"He could have wished for the ship."

"I'd say from that satisfied smile on his face when we were at the church that he probably wished for what he wanted all along."

Hank looked at her. "What?"

"He wanted a dad."

Hank gave a wry laugh. "Well, now the kid's got one. What's he gonna do with me?"

"Probably talk your ear off for the next thirty years."

They laughed together for a moment, then Hank reached out and drew a finger slowly along her jaw. He slid his knuckle under her chin and tilted her face up so she was looking at him. "And how about you, sweetheart?" He grinned. "What are you gonna do with me?"

She slid her arms up around his neck and pressed her body against his. "Probably talk your ear off for the next thirty years."

He laughed hard and pulled her into his arms.

She looked up and gave him that smile. "And what are you going to do with me?"

He slid his hands down the buttons on her robe, flicking each one open. A touch here, a touch there, a heartbeat or two, and that smile was all she was wearing. He swung her up into his arms and carried her to the bed. "I'm going to love you, sweetheart."

❧ 34 ❧

Six weeks later, San Francisco, California

The mansion was tall and proud and stood high on the hillside above the bay like a reigning queen. Bright pink bougainvillea grew up the south side of the home. A paved carriageway ran beneath an arch of willow trees bent together by the strong Pacific winds. There were gardens in back, hedges of manzania hemmed gravel walkways and dormant rose bushes, while a lion-head fountain stood nearby. There, a goat wearing pink hair ribbons drank from the water that spilled into the tiled base.

Inside the house, the walls and staircase were made of rich California redwood polished until it shone deeper, darker, and more intricately grained than mahogany ever could. And echoing off those walls were the sounds of children's laughter.

A back door slammed, and there was the sound of gravel spitting up as a young boy's shoes ran over the pathway to a bench where Hank and Margaret sat talking.

Theodore skidded to a stop in front of them, his voice excited and out of breath. "Grandpa Harlan says you have to come inside!"

Hank's hand closed over hers.

She looked at him.

"Could this be about the extradition hearing?"

She laughed. "No. It's only been a week since we met with the courts. There couldn't possibly be any word this soon." She stood and held out her hand. They walked inside and went down the back hallway. Margaret tugged Hank along with her, following the sound of voices to her father's study.

They walked inside, and she stopped suddenly at the intensely serious look on her father's face. "What is it?"

He glanced down at a paper in his hand and took off his glasses, then set them down on his desk. His gaze moved past her to Hank, who suddenly released her hand.

Margaret whipped her head around, catching some look that had passed between her father and her husband. She walked over, and her father handed her the paper. She skimmed it, then looked up at the men in the room. "This is an order to take Hank to the state penitentiary." She turned to her dad. "This is some kind of mistake. At the hearing they released Hank into your custody. I thought it was all taken care of. What is going on?"

"This is Mr. Cornelius, Margaret, from the state attorney general's office."

A man in a black suit that was too long for him stepped forward. "The French government has asked the Justice Department, and they in turn directed the state, to deny custody and keep Mr. Wyatt incarcerated until this issue can be fully investigated."

"But he voluntarily turned himself in. We were told this wouldn't happen."

Mr. Cornelius spoke to her as if he wanted to pat her on the head so she could better understand. "Since the charges against him are for murder, and because he escaped—"

"He's not going to run away."

He smiled. "I'm certain you believe that, Mrs. Wyatt. You are his wife, but the governments involved believe otherwise."

"I'm also an attorney, Mr. Cornelius, and you can tell the French government and the Justice Department to go to hell."

"Margaret!"

"I promised Hank, Dad. This is just bureaucratic nonsense."

The entire time Hank just stood there, not saying a word. Her father went over to Hank and put his hand on his shoulder and said something. Hank blinked, the only sign that he'd heard anything.

One of the men stepped forward and took a pair of handcuffs from his coat pocket. "I need you to put your hands behind your back, Mr. Wyatt."

Margaret watched Hank take a deep breath and drop his hands behind him. He wasn't looking at her. He was staring somewhere over her head.

Margaret grabbed her father's arm. "Dad! I promised him. Please! Can't you do something?"

He took her arm and pulled her aside. "I'll try to do what I can, but you're making this harder on Hank. Stop it. For his sake. He has no choice and neither do we. He has to go with them."

"Hank." She said his name in a half plea and turned to him.

"Margaret." Her father leaned closer and whispered, "If you love him, don't do this. Leave the man some pride."

She pulled her arm out of her dad's and stood with her back pressed to the study doorjamb, her hands behind her, clutching the door handle. As they walked by, she looked at Hank and mouthed, "I love you."

He stopped for a second, nodded, then turned and walked from the room.

"That's my dad!" Theodore's voice echoed down the paneled hallway.

Her head shot up, and she saw Lydia and Theodore standing down the hallway, staring at them.

She saw Hank stumble when he saw the kids.

Theodore came running up to Hank. "What are you doing with my dad? Why is he in handcuffs?"

Margaret walked down the hallway and put her arm around Theodore and Lydia, who was standing there quietly. Margaret could feel the little girl's shoulders shaking and her gaze was on Hank's handcuffs as they led him past.

"Are they taking him to jail, Smitty?" Theodore asked. "Are they?"

"Only for a little while," she told him, hoping it was the truth.

Lydia pulled her hand out of Margaret's and ran to Hank. She hugged his waist tightly, pressed her cheek to him, and squeezed her eyes closed.

Hank stopped. The men with him looked helplessly at the little girl. Hank's gaze was on Lydia's head, and Margaret saw him swallow hard.

Her dad stepped forward and gently tugged on Lydia's arms. "Come with Grandpa now." And he gently pulled her away.

"Leedee?" Hank's voice sounded perfectly normal.

A brave front, Margaret knew, that cost him a lot to put up.

"Take care of that damn goat, okay?"

She nodded, tears streaming down her face as she stood with her grandfather.

And they took Hank out the door and down the front steps to the open doors of a black carriage with two mounted police escorts. They got inside.

Margaret stood, staring at Hank's profile. She reached out a hand to Lydia, then pulled both her and Theodore close to her side. She said quietly, "Your dad will be home soon. I promise. He'll be home soon."

They took Hank down a dank hallway with gray linoleum and dirty chipped walls. The deeper into the bowels of the prison they walked, the more tight the air seemed, as if a door or window hadn't been opened in a century or two.

The sounds were eerie and sharp. The clicking of typewriter keys from a nearby office. The strong scent of hair balm and onions as they passed by a man who sat in front of a wavy glass door. The rustle of papers, the click of the guard's bootheels on the floor. The jangle of the chain on the handcuffs, a higher-pitched sound than that made by ankle cuffs, but the same kind of ringing noise that mocked him.

There was the jangle of keys, the click of a locked door. A solid metal door slid open with a loud grating of the sliders, and Hank just stood there, staring at a wide bay of iron cells as if he'd stepped back into his worst nightmare.

The guard nudged him forward with a billy club. He walked slowly because he felt as if the walls were moving toward him, closing in. It was harder to breathe. It was harder to walk, to lift each foot closer.

And it was even harder not to yell and fight and try to run. Because every instinct inside of him said, "Run, run, do it! Do it! Sucker! You're a sucker. A chump!"

They stopped in front of an empty cell, and he heard the familiar rattling keys and the lock opening. He walked inside, staring at the cement brick walls, at the enameled tin pitcher and bowl that sat in a dark corner, at the bunk with one thin wool blanket folded neatly on the edge of a striped tick mattress and one flat feather pillow.

The cell door closed hard, clanging clear through him. He didn't flinch. He listened to the guard's heels clicking down the cell block, listened to the door squeak open, then close with a bang. Then he listened to the silence.

He didn't know how long he stood there. The only light was from a weak lamp outside the cell. He heard another prisoner cough, a hacking static sound.

Hank walked over to the wall, looked at the gray bricks, the solid bricks. He slammed his fist against them three . . . four . . . five times until his hand was bleeding. His breath came harsh and abrupt as if the air wasn't there.

He looked at his knuckles, stared at the blood. He drew back to hit the wall again but then stopped and stared at the swipes of blood on the concrete bricks— bloody brown against gray. Blank, void gray.

He leaned into the wall, his palm flat against it, his forehead resting on his arm.

His hand began to shake.

But no one saw it.

His shoulders shook, too.

But no one saw him standing there.

No one saw his face.

It was buried in his arm.

And no one knew he cried.

The door of the visitation room closed, blocking out the sounds of Theodore's chattering as the children left with their grandfather.

"Smitty."

Margaret looked at Hank sitting on the other side of a divider with a guard behind him.

"Don't bring them here again."

"Hank, please."

"I mean it, dammit! Don't bring them here. Children don't belong here."

"Neither do you." She gave him a direct look. "I'm sorry. I never wanted you to have to go through this again. I—" She stopped, because words seemed useless.

He touched her hand, and she threaded her fingers through his, needing to touch him. Something told her he needed this even more than she. He lifted her hand to his mouth for just a second and pressed it against his lips, his head bowed, his eyes closed.

She didn't say anything. She just waited.

He took a deep breath and set their hands back on the table. Then he looked at her without any emotion in his eyes. "Promise me, Smitty, that you won't bring the children here. Promise me."

She took a deep breath and nodded. "I've sent telegrams. So has Dad. So has everyone we know. We're just waiting. It can't be much longer."

He shook his head. "Don't."

She couldn't say anything to help him, to help her.

She knew it and he knew it. So they sat, just holding hands because that's all they could do.

She heard the monotonous whir of the ceiling fan above them. In the distance she could hear paper rustling and voices down the back hallways. Someone laughed somewhere far away, yet she could hear that laughter. It almost seemed mocking. She could smell the acrid scent of the resin they used to polish the wood that was in the room. Then she heard the sound of heels on the floor tiles.

"Time's up, Wyatt." The guard looked at her. "Mrs. Wyatt."

She started to rise, but she realized with something worse than despair that she needed help. So she didn't move.

Hank stood stiffly and without a word he walked to the door. The guard opened it. Hank turned back, just once, and looked at her.

There was a long and difficult pause, each one desperately trying to reach across the emptiness. But neither Hank nor Margaret knew how.

Hank was truly scared. For the first time in his life something mattered. Four special people. Instinct made him want to kick and fight and beat his way out of there, to grab his family and run like hell back to that island where they could be safe.

But he couldn't. And he wouldn't. Because Smitty believed that this godawful world was fair and equal and that good would triumph over evil and all that other horseshit he'd never believed in. But he'd been willing to try for her and for those kids. For a future with them.

He knew that he would live his whole life over, every shitty day. He'd beg. He'd crawl. He'd relive each second if he could make it through this.

He was not a man who lived his life believing much in God, but now he prayed. He made more promises and more deals with God than he'd ever made with anyone in forty years of living.

IMAGINE

Because he had nothing left to bargain with except his black soul. For one last chance at a future worth living, he'd do anything, give anything. He had no pride left. He had nothing, if he didn't have his family.

It was early when the telegram came. Almost too early even for Margaret. She heard a bicycle bell ringing, and she jumped out of bed and looked out her bedroom window. The messenger's bicycle was lying on its side by the front steps.

She threw on her robe, tying it as she ran out the bedroom door and down the stairs. She jerked open the front door just as the messenger had raised his hand to press the door chime.

"Telegram for . . ." The kid squinted at the envelope. "Harlan Smith and Margaret Huntington Smith Wy—"

She snatched the envelope from his hand, grabbed a gold coin from her purse on a nearby table, and shoved it at him. "Thanks."

She stood there staring at the telegram, her heart in her throat. She ripped it open, read it, then read it again.

She reached out and grabbed the edge of the open door, gripping it hard. She took a deep breath. One, then another. A second later she fell to her knees, bent over, and hugged her waist. She sobbed so hard she couldn't get her breath.

It went on for a long time, those tears, weeks and weeks' worth of tears. Then she pushed herself up and stood there, taking deep breaths as she tried to stop crying, tried to catch just one full, deep breath. She walked slowly to the staircase, looked up, and called for the children.

Hank heard the guard's footsteps. The key in the lock, the creaking of the cell door. He blinked in the darkness of the cell, disoriented, jarred from sleep that hadn't come easily.

"Get up," was all the guard said. "Follow me."

Hank stumbled to his feet. They felt as numb as he did. He walked down the small hallway to the outer cell. The guard unlocked the door and slid it open, then waited for him to pass through.

Another guard waited on the other side. The man just turned and walked a few feet. He opened a door to a room Hank hadn't seen before. He tensed. He looked at the guard holding the door. Neither said anything. Hank slowly went inside.

He saw his father-in-law across the room. The older man turned and just looked at Hank for a moment, then crossed the room and handed him a telegram.

Hank's hand shook as he reached for it.

This was it.

He took it and stared down at it, unable to focus for a second.

To: The California State Justice Department, San Francisco, California

From: Monsieur Guy De Partain, Laison de Justice, Papeete, Tahiti

Due to new information and a confession from Jean Laroche, brother of victim Henri Laroche, all charges against United States citizen Henry James Wyatt were dismissed on December 5, 1896, three days before he escaped from Leper's Gate Penal Colony, Dolphin Island. No further action is needed.

Hank read it again, then looked at Harlan. "This is true?"

"Yes."

"Before I escaped?" Hank stared at the telegram again, and the words were blurring. He swallowed hard and drove a hand through his hair and stood there, unable to move because he couldn't believe it.

"You're free, son." Harlan slid his hand over Hank's hunched shoulders.

Hank nodded, because his throat was too tight to speak.

"Your family's waiting." He pointed to another door. Hank moved toward it, half afraid the door would be locked.

But it wasn't. He jerked it open.

There was a long, dark hallway. He ran down it, then turned and ran down another hallway, running faster than a forty-year-old ex-ballplayer should have been able to run. Then he saw the open doorway filled with sunlight.

He ran faster than Smitty ever could, down the hall and out the door. Into the daylight. He stopped and blinked for a second, blinded by the light.

And he saw them. Just their silhouettes—a tall woman with a toddler on her hip, a young girl with cockeyed braids, and a small boy who wore a baseball cap backward.

And Hank Wyatt, the man who had run away from almost everything for forty years, ran like hell toward the one thing he believed in. His family.

Somewhere in the Pacific Ocean

The bottle was as old as time.

It floated on the sea, bobbing along as if it were flotsam instead of intricately carved silver. The ornate stopper caught flashes of bright sunlight, which, to the gulls overhead, made the shimmering bottle look like a plump silver herring, a prize for the plucking.

Many a sea bird swooped down only to quickly dart back like reflections into the sky when their bills hit not the soft flesh of glimmering fish scales, but instead hard metal . . . and jewels.

For there, on that old silver genie bottle, shimmering in the sunlight like a hero's medal of valor, were five perfect pearls.

Inside, Muddy lay back against his pillows and let

the current rock him along. His wishes were granted, his last duty done. But unlike before, he wasn't worried that anyone would find the bottle. Muddy wasn't wishing for an innocent of heart who believed in that which they had never seen or known. He had found his dreamers.

He smiled and looked around the cluttered interior of his bottle. It wasn't quite as cluttered anymore. This time, he'd given away more than he'd brought back.

He looked at his leather shoes and clicked the heels together. No bells on the toes. He laughed, then turned and reached for something more valuable to him than all the inventions he'd ever gathered or all the jewels on his bottle.

A photograph of a family sitting on the bright sunlit beach.

New Recreation Park, San Francisco, California, 1908

It was a bright fall day in the two-year-old ballpark. The earthquake had destroyed the old park and much of the city. But San Francisco recovered quickly, rebuilding on the sheer tenacity and spirit of her people, a large number of whom were in the stands, there to see their team, the San Francisco Seals, play Portland.

Hank Wyatt drove his hand through his hair and paced in front of the Seals' player box. He stopped, and looked at the baseball team he had owned and managed for the last ten years.

The team looked back at him. Every last one of them had their hats on backward. For luck.

They were down five to eight in the last game of the regular season. Whoever won the game would be the champion of the Pacific Coast League and would go on to play the winner of the Central League.

Hank looked at the lineup and swore.

His worst player, Tabasco Reynolds, walked up to bat. The kid hadn't had a hit in two years. It was two out. The bases were loaded. Hank couldn't watch this.

He turned his gaze up into the stands.

His son Ted—Theodore—was waving at him. Hank frowned, and Ted turned his cap around a couple of times and pointed at Hank. Hank looked up and saw the brim of his hat. A second later he flicked the hat around, and Ted gave him a thumbs-up.

He was a good kid who worked out with the team in the summer and had just started Stanford that fall. But to this day, he wouldn't tell them what that last wish was.

Hank's gaze shifted to his wife, the attorney. She hadn't changed much in twelve years. A few gray hairs, a couple of laugh lines. She was one of the city's most respected attorneys, but to him, she was still the best-looking woman he'd ever laid eyes on.

She'd softened in all the right places and was a little fuller in the hips after the birth of three kids. Which was all right by him. It just gave him a little more to grip late at night.

Smitty had worked hard the last year and a half, helping to right the wrongs in the aftermath of the earthquake. They had been lucky and hadn't lost their home. Too many others had. And Hank knew his wife would work until every last person got a fair shake.

His gaze went to his children all sitting in the family box. Lydia sat on the end, smiling and waving, all grown up. She'd graduated from Stanford last June. The cockeyed braids were gone, and when he teased her about them, she told him, "Doctors don't wear braids, Dad."

Annabelle was tossing peanuts in the air and catching them with her mouth just the way he'd taught her. She was a happy girl who always had a smile and hug for anyone, even if she still slipped in a few of Hank's swear words.

Johnny and Jake were brothers, kids from the street that they'd found sleeping in a trash bin behind Smitty's office one winter morning some eight years ago. And Cora was seven, an orphan from the moment she was born. A day later she had a family.

Billy, Dennis, and Lucy. Well, Smitty had given him those kids, and they were as smart as their mother and just as argumentative.

Hank grinned. He and Smitty had a helluva good time making them. Not a day went by that he didn't thank God and fate and even an annoying genie for what he had.

Nine kids—enough for his own ball team. And every last one of them had managed to remind him that he still didn't understand them.

The loud crack of the bat split the air. The crowd roared, and Hank turned.

He watched the ball fly over the fence with a sense of stunned relief. His gaze shot back to the stands, where Smitty was cheering, waving, and jiggling in all the right places.

He watched her for a moment because he still had to after all these years. Finally, he turned with a smile and stuck his hands in his pockets as he walked out to the field where the players were, where pennants were waving, and balls and caps were flying. But he stopped for just a moment and looked back at the crowd, his gaze resting on his family.

And Hank Wyatt knew he had everything.